DAY OF THE DOVE

DAY OF THE DOVE

A Novel by

Rainer Rey

TURNER

Turner Publishing Company
424 Church Street • Suite 2240 • Nashville, Tennessee 37219
445 Park Avenue • 9th Floor • New York, New York 10022

www.turnerpublishing.com

Day of the Dove

First Edition: May 1998

This is a work of fiction. All the characters and events portrayed in this book are either products of the author's imagination or are used fictitiously.

Cover design: Glen Edelstein
Book design: Kym Whitley

Library of Congress Control Number: 2015933484

ISBN: 978-1-62045-999-7 (paperback); 978-1-63026-752-0 (hardcover)

Printed in the United States of America
15 16 17 18 19 0 9 8 7 6 5 4 3 2 1

To my grandchildren . . .
that they may prosper in a peaceful world.

DAY OF THE DOVE

TARGET OF THE DOVE

"YOU SEE THAT, HERCULE?" Saratov gestured to the ancient walls. "Our most historic Russian city was overrun. Not by the Moors, not by the Huns, not by the Khan. No. By the stealth of democracy, ripping us away from Mother Russia. Look at the damage it has endured." Saratov gripped the hand-rail as he looked out over Kiev. "Think of it," Saratov said in awe. "The great pendulum of justice is about to swing back. In a matter of days, the United States will *perish*."

'Today, the real test of power is not the capacity
to make war, but the capacity to prevent it."
—ANNE O'HARE MCCORMICK

ACKNOWLEDGMENTS

My personal thanks to those individuals who helped *Day of the Dove* become a reality.

First, my appreciation to my agent, Diane Gedymin, for her undying faith in me—and our lasting friendship.

Second, to those patient and helpful professionals for their expertise and inspiration, who granted technical knowledge: particularly Douglas C. Cannon III, retired FBI . . . Donald E. Reardon, nuclear physicist . . . Colonel Ron Myers (USAF, Ret.) . . . Cliff & Cleo Forbes and John Hudson of US West . . . Victoria Parker, librarian . . . and "JJ" Johnston.

Finally, to my wife, Jan, whose support and steadfast belief in my writing remains my constant motivation for further work.

FOURTEEN DAYS AND COUNTING

1

THE DRONE OF THE INSECTS hung heavily in the hush of the jungle, as late September sun filtered through the rain-forest canopy.

Thane squatted in the shadows, holding his breath as he squinted through the eyepiece. He pushed gently on the zoom, watching a spindly-legged tree frog with turquoise eyes move robotically into the patch of light on a banana leaf.

As the action unfolded in miniature through the viewfinder, Thane imagined how the edit would fit. The lemon-colored amphibian would be the title shot for his video on Rhacophoridaea, the one hundred and eighty-four species of tree frogs found on three continents.

To Thane's right, Kuintala rose to his feet. "A foul smell coming downwind," he said.

"Mmm?" Thane murmured, frozen in position. His assistant knew better than to disturb him during a take.

"It's death." Kuintala stepped away into the brush.

Thane heard the fronds part somewhere to his right, but he was too concentrated on the camera move. The skinny frog had made another spectacular four-legged glide across the leaf and stared back at the camera. Perfect. He needed five more seconds.

"I don't like it." Kuintala returned. "Sweetness. Of death. Don't you smell that, Adams?" He always used Thane's last name.

Thane exhaled and dropped the Ikegami camera from his shoulder. Kuintala stood off to Thane's flank wearing a gray T-shirt and charcoal cargo shorts. The brown leather equipment bag slung over his shoulder contained a camera trail kit for shooting in the jungle's exotic environments. With one hand on his rifle sling, Kuintala held his other in the air as if he were feeling the odor. The Bantu native's nostrils flared below his high cheekbones as he faced the wind. Dappled by sunlight, he resembled a classic warrior, two hundred and twenty pounds—muscular and handsome.

"Your overactive nose could have ruined my shot." Thane straightened the collar of his beige short-sleeve shirt and slid off the tree stump. They were similar in stature—over six feet, though Thane was leaner, with surprisingly well-defined shoulders and forearms.

"Yes, but this may ruin your day." Kuintala's thick-tongued English accent rolled theatrically. "It's stronger now. North of us." He lifted his nose further into an increased breeze. Then he gazed incredulously at Thane. "Don't tell me you cannot smell that." Kuintala pointed. "Use your nose."

Thane had a strong, sculpted face offset by a pair of playful light blue eyes, but his straight narrow nose had smelled very little other than the steam rising from the dark forest floor, a deep musty odor that followed the afternoon rain. Worms and beetles had picked over the mulch so thoroughly it resembled shredded tobacco.

Thane shrugged and wiped perspiration from his forehead. "Sorry." He set the camera down on the battery pack and ran a moist hand through his wavy, sand-colored hair. "My sinuses are clogged." Thane squeezed the bridge of his nose with a tanned right hand. "What do you think? A buffalo? Something big?"

"More. Many."

"Okay. Just a minute." Thane pulled the white handkerchief from the rear pocket of his khaki shorts and blew vigorously, then turned to where Kuintala pointed and took a whiff.

"Oh." Thane cringed. "You're right. That's ripe." The odor was nauseating, pungent with sickness and decay.

"The village of Mwadaba sits up the valley. I fear that stench. Could be human." The concern on Kuintala's face told the story. Intermittent virus outbreaks in remote rainforest villages had been a recurring problem. "We best go look."

"How far?"

Kuintala craned his neck, apparently trying to see higher ground, locating himself. "A kilometer, maybe two."

Thane put the camera into the black velveteen cover, stuffed a spent battery and the camera into the hard vinyl case, then threw the gear over his shoulder. Kuintala had already moved into the brush, headed west.

"I thought you said north," Thane called, following.

"Let's get up on the foothills. Sun at our back." Kuintala pushed small branches aside with his unslung rifle. "We should be able to see into Mwadaba from above. If it's Ebola, we won't approach."

Lagging behind, Thane watched Kuintala move into the foliage. For a moment, he considered forgetting Mwadaba entirely. They had two days left on his shoot schedule and he still needed general footage of tree cover for the introductory portion of the International Geographic feature. This would complete his seventy-eighth production. He had supported himself as a freelance cameraman for eleven years, following three years of shooting news footage for a Baltimore television station. The city's daily carnage and civil strife had depressed him and he had resigned, choosing to become a freelancer. He had gradually built a good reputation for his production values and became known for his artistic touches, his keen directorial sense, his willingness to shoot literally anywhere, even at personal risk. He went from job to job, traveling constantly, seeking work that led him to open country, which he preferred to the city life. His lifestyle made him a loner. He developed few lasting friendships, but when he did, they were solid.

Such was the bond he had formed with Kuintala in the six weeks they had worked together. Thane admired his friend's respect for the land and its people. But whatever the stench in the jungle might mean, Thane had a shoot to finish and a deadline to meet.

Thane considered recalling his companion, making a turn back to their base camp, but his journalistic instinct took hold. He was haunted by curiosity. "Did you pack the macro zoom?" he asked, hustling along.

Kuintala confidently patted the leather pouch as he continued to stride through ground cover.

Minutes later the two men struggled up an incline of sticky brown clay. Thane caught up, and together he and Kuintala crested a ridge. Their shadows tripped along vegetation down in the gully as they worked through the brush on the hillside. Trees covered the forest floor below like huge stalks of broccoli.

The hills of Africa occasionally reminded Thane of his childhood. Near his Pennsylvania farm, nine-year-old Thane had hiked through thick groves of maple with his father and younger brother Jeff, while Dad pointed out the tracks of deer, the hidden nests of woodpecker and squirrel, the abundance of tiny creatures that lived in the woods. Thane's family was only a memory now, but his love for nature had become ingrained and he still relished it in his work.

Kuintala pointed to the northeast. "Mwadaba." Some two hundred feet ahead, a clearing opened in the canopy. They would be able to look down into the opening from the crest of the hill just as Kuintala had predicted.

Pushing through long grasses, Thane felt the sting of a mosquito on his neck. The insect's nasty habit of mixing its own saliva with the blood of its victims entered Thane's mind. Never could tell where the mosquito had just been. With his free hand, he slapped and crushed the tiny creature. He studied the smear in his hand. An inordinate amount of blood streaked his palm. Thane's blood? Perhaps a previous host's? Wiping the mess on his khaki pants, he hoisted the camera strap higher so that it would cut less deeply into his shoulder.

Thane's short delay had Kuintala out ahead some twenty feet. He carried his rifle across his chest, striding like a tall long-distance walker landing strongly on his heels. Kuintala would track down his own anxiety. Thane bet that Kuintala's rifle's safety was off.

As Kuintala arrived at the lip of a bluff, he halted as if he'd collided with an invisible obstruction. "Adams, it's here!"

Pulling the camera off his shoulder, Thane rushed to his side.

Kuintala pointed down into the clearing.

The hairs on Thane's neck bristled at what he saw. "Give me the macro." He would see better through the zoom.

Kuintala undid the rawhide straps of the camera bag and retrieved the 10 x 200 lens.

Thane twisted the regular lens off the camera as he looked down, trying to make senses of the spectacle below.

Bodies were sprawled on the ground as if they had dropped from the trees. Lots of them, surrounding eight or nine thatched-roof huts. No movement or sound from the small village. Kuintala screwed on the macro lens as Thane fired the camera. A tiny high-pitched hum signaled that the batteries were sufficiently strong. Thane hoisted the Ikegami to his shoulder, then pushed the auto focus and began to pan the village.

"Ebola?" Kuintala asked, apparently assuming Thane could tell.

" I don't know." Thane scanned the area. Under a scalding sun, native people of various ages lay in awkward positions near the huts, some on their stomachs, some on their sides like game pieces knocked off a chessboard. "There must be forty bodies. Probably more in the huts. It's strange the way they're scattered."

"What do you mean?"

"If they were sick, why didn't they—" Thane zoomed to a group of corpses assembled in what appeared to have been the central meeting place of the village, judging from the campfire configuration. The fallen victims were partially unclothed, but the women wore chest coverings made of a broadloom fabric. The chaotic scene reminded Thane of a gangland shooting, yet there was no blood, no sign of trauma. Ebola's effects would have left signs of bleeding.

In the village "square," three men, two women, and a child lay in a heap next to a smoldering spit. The body of a small goat hung over the ashes. The victims' expressions were difficult to read at this distance. "They look like they were struck down," Thane said, still sighting through the camera. Kuintala's hand on Thane's shoulder signaled his impatient concern.

"Here, see what you think." Thane wiped his sweat from the eyepiece while Kuintala propped his rifle against his knee. Then Thane hoisted the camera to his friend's right shoulder.

Kuintala had used the camera for amusement over the last few days and had become familiar with its operation. Thane reached in. "I'm going to record this while you take a look." He hit the camera's red button. Spools through the small window of the cassette compartment rotated steadily.

Kuintala moved the camera slowly across his field of vision. "I see," he said in his low voice, easing the zoom in and out. "They are all in the open. Why?"

"It's as if they'd been caught off guard. If they had been infected with a disease, feeling sick enough to die, wouldn't they have been inside?"

Kuintala pushed the camera at Thane with both hands. "You look again."

Thane pressed the eyepiece hard to his cheek, concentrating on the image in the viewfinder. He panned from the village square to a group of three huts.

"I'll be a son of a bitch," he said.

"What?"

"On the far right, over by a shed, that structure made of branches. There's a dead dog."

"An animal?" Kuintala asked incredulously. "I heard of monkeys dying from Ebola, but no dogs. You?"

Thane zoomed in. "No. No dogs or cattle. It's a primate disease after all." The medium-sized hound lay on its side. Though difficult to see at this distance, the fur of the scraggy mongrel appeared strangely matted.

"Do you notice something else, Adams?" Kuintala stared at Thane. "Zoom in and look again. Check the color of the people's skin." Thane pushed the black button and enlarged the image once more.

'That's strange," he said, looking closer. "They look dirty or something. What is that?"

"They're dusty."

Thane felt dread crawl under his collar as he noted the light gray residue that covered the skin of each corpse. "Odd," he said, moving his gaze back to the initial grouping in the square. "It's as if they'd been rolled in some kind of powder."

2

LIGHTNING FLASHED OVER THE DISTANT hills and a rumble of thunder cut through the whine of a nearby freeway.

Danielle Wilkes fought wind and pelting rain as she trotted through cars in the flooded parking lot.

Finding shelter under the breezy cedar portico, she strode toward the inn's entry. She grabbed the brass handles of the outer doors, but suction created by heat from a fireplace in the lobby held them firmly in place.

Danielle pulled hard, breaking the air lock, then she stepped through the inner doors to the foyer, leaving the blustery weather outside. The change in air pressure rushed past her face, buffeting her long red hair. She brushed her bangs back and tugged at her amber silk scarf, which was tufted around her slender neck, tucking it away in the pocket of her bronze-colored raincoat.

Danielle looked around.

At the registration desk, a pink-cheeked bellboy stared; an annoyance to which she'd become accustomed. The young man, who might have been pushing nineteen, gave her an investigative once-over, his gaze lingering on her breasts.

"Restaurant?" she asked, brushing raindrops from her sleeves.

"At the end of that wing." He pointed, smiling.

As Danielle made her way past, the beardless wonder pursued a conversation. "Anything I can . . . get?"

"Older," she said, trying not to smile as she locked her green eyes straight ahead.

She walked by the lobby's river-rock-fireplace, feeling its warmth, hoping that she would find similar comfort in the grill room. Danielle's charcoal mid-heels were soaked. She had checked her raincoat and straightened her deep blue pinstriped suit as she settled into the black leather booth.

Dark wood banisters divided the red carpeted room into four tiers, two below and two above, and Danielle had chosen the upper section, only a few comfortable feet away from another granite fireplace at the back of the dining room.

She glanced at her watch: ten forty-five. The lunch crowd wouldn't arrive for another hour - hopefully private enough for Damita.

Her sister's tearful phone call that morning had pulled Danielle unexpect-edly out of a staff meeting. Her art director and account executives had been left in a state of confusion. But after hearing Damita's panicked voice, Danielle had tossed the artist renderings back to her crew and left the Othello Foods label designs lying in limbo on the conference table.

The sisters had decided to meet halfway. Danielle's one-hour drive from Boston pretty much equaled Damita's trip from New London, Connecticut.

A pale gray-haired waitress wearing colonial garb and a pair of white can-vas shoes appeared through the carved swinging doors. She approached and poured a cup of coffee, setting the canister on the table. "Will there be two of you?" she asked politely.

"Yes, thanks. But you can take my service away, I won't be eating."

The waitress nodded and gathered up one setting of pewter flatware. As she stepped aside to leave, she revealed tall leaded windows that framed the inn's rear entrance. And out beyond the parked cars, a familiar figure in a three-quarter-length teal raincoat scampered across the puddles in the parking lot.

Danielle hadn't seen her sister in months and couldn't help but shake her head in amazement. A fashion plate had arrived at the restaurant. Damita wore teal high heels, a tight black skirt that hampered her progress, and European sunglasses under a floppy black hat. "That's my girl," Danielle whispered. A sure way to look inconspicuous on a rainy morning. Why so secretive? Why so emo-tional? Damita's voice had actually shaken.

Danielle flashed on their father's favorite photo of the two of them at Hal-loween, two carrot tops with red clown noses sitting on their parents' front porch in Columbus. God. That was twenty-two years ago. Danielle had just entered second grade, Damita kindergarten. Because her father, John, had wanted the first child to be a boy, Danielle had been named after her grandfather, Dan. "Damita" was a tribute to the Spanish blood in the family. Danielle and Damita's mother, Margaret, had admired a distant cousin by that name, a flamenco performer who had danced in Madrid in the early eighties.

Now Dad was gone and Mother, overtaken by Alzheimer's, had trouble recognizing either of her daughters.

Danielle took a sip of coffee. It warmed her throat and thawed away some of the apprehension.

Strange how two sisters could differ so greatly—both personally and professionally. Danielle had taken after her father, seeking a solid, more stable existence. Damita, on the other hand, mimicked her mother, a lovable yet hopeless dreamer. Damita fell in love more easily, spent every penny she made, and frolicked through each new day.

This contrast had first become evident when Danielle and Damita both attended Ohio State University. Even though they were considered equally attractive, Danielle had been the more conservative nose-to-the-grindstone academician, while Damita came to rebel against conventional career thinking. Whereas Danielle applied herself to studies, Damita became a cheerleader, which affected her grades.

Upon graduation, Danielle made the big move to New York and found her calling in advertising. But when Damita followed her to Manhattan, she seemed to rebel against Danielle's early successes. Damita chose a wild ride in the fashion photo industry, complete with its artistic veneer and party atmosphere. And though Danielle considered Damita's lifestyle unhealthy and unstable, she could not convince Damita to follow in her footsteps.

As a result, Damita's career vacillated while Danielle's moved steadily upward. Whereas Damita engaged in a frivolous romp, Danielle sought professional success. And, while Damita had many men, Danielle had very few—and only one that counted. Even fewer after the tragic conclusion to that relationship.

Damita shook the rain from her coat as she entered the restaurant. The hostess pointed, and after peeking over her sunglasses, Damita made her way back through the handful of people seated in the nearly vacant dining room. She approached Danielle's booth in a gliding walk both sisters had acquired in gymnastics. Although they had been too tall to excel in the sport, their mother had strongly advocated the limbering benefits of floor exercises.

Danielle slid out to meet her. "Hello, Dee."

"Danny," Damita said softly, opening both arms. As they embraced, Damita suppressed a sob.

"Hey, take it easy," Danielle said, holding her. "I'm right here."

"I'm sorry I haven't been in touch, Danny. Thanks for coming."

"Sit down." Danielle tried to guide her into the booth's pleated leather padding.

"No." Damita pushed away. "I'd rather face away from the door." With her coat still dripping, she took a chair instead.

"What's wrong with you?'

"I just want my back to the room," she stuttered.

Danielle marveled at Damita's paranoia. As Danielle slid into the booth, she studied her sister, assessing her mood.

Damita glanced nervously over her shoulder. She placed a small teal lizard-skin clutch purse on the table and tugged off her beige gloves, trying to recover her composure. She chose not to remove either the hat or the glasses. "Thanks again for breaking away," she said, finally. "I'm sorry I disrupted your work."

"Don't be ridiculous."

"I have been. Ridiculous to you, I mean." Damita sighed. "I should have called you right after the wedding. God, I haven't even invited you to our home."

"Well, after all. Your trip to Europe. The honeymoon. I knew you were settling in."

Damita winced and rubbed her arms as if her skin itched. "Honeymoon." She arched her back. "Not anymore." With a shaking hand, she pulled a Kleenex from her purse, lifting the glasses to blot the tears.

Danielle was horrified to see swelling around her right eye. Makeup couldn't disguise the bruise. "What's that?" Damita's lower lip quivered. She refused to answer and looked around, distracted by the gray-haired waitress who reappeared, leaned over, and peered at Damita. "Something for you?"

Danielle pointed to her coffee cup. "Coffee?"

Damita shook her head. "Martini."

Danielle was shocked. It wasn't even noon yet. She wondered if this was her sister's first drink of the day. "Olive or onion?" the waitress asked patiently.

Damita waved her off. "Just bring the gin, straight up." The older woman pursed her lips, apparently offended by the retort. She waddled off, shaking her head.

"Breakfast martinis, something new?" Danielle asked.

"There's plenty new for me."

"Remember, you've got to drive."

"Danny, just don't."

Danielle had forgotten—mothering was something Damita no longer tolerated. "Okay. Sorry." Yet here she was, seeking help. Danielle leaned forward. "Where did you get the bruise?"

Damita took a deep breath and bit her lip.

"Well?"

"Hassan."

Though she had never seen him in person, Danielle envisioned the snapshots of Damita's handsome Iranian husband, Hassan Salaar, the serious dark eyes, the shiny black hair and groomed mustache.

Damita collapsed her hands in grief and nodded without answering.

"Why would he hit you, for God's sake?"

"Because I went out."

"What?"

"Last night around eight, I just had to get out of the house. I took the car to the store for some snacks, but he came home while I was gone."

Anger replaced Danielle's confusion. "What are you telling me? He punched you for going to the store?"

"He's never been this rough. I thought it was a bad sign."

"A bad sign? It's criminal."

"He won't allow me to go anywhere unless I tell him. I disobeyed. It's come to that. He's unreasonable and eccentric."

What a change from Damita's idyllic postcards. "But you said he was—"

Damita broke into tears. "Wonderful. That's what I thought. He seemed so totally attentive and kind. And he has given me a lot. Look." She pulled back the sleeve of her raincoat, revealing a generously encrusted diamond-and-ruby bracelet.

"Nice. The red on your face matches the stones."

"I'm supposed to be there when he returns. Available to him."

"Even when he goes out himself?"

Damita nodded.

"Since when?"

"The last month or so. It's all changed since we got home."

Danielle took another sip of the coffee and couldn't help the sarcasm. "I suppose the honeymoon was perfect."

"It was. Until we moved into that house. I suddenly felt like a statuette in his ivory collection. I can't have opinions. Unless we go to a party or have people over for dinner, I don't talk. Sometimes, when I express myself, he looks at me with those almond-shaped eyes as if I were a naughty kid."

"Excuse me." The waitress leaned in and placed a small coaster on the table, then set the chilled glass in front of Damita. She nodded to Danielle. "More coffee, miss?"

The pasty-faced woman appeared to have too few patrons, and Danielle wanted to avoid having to buy Damita another midday martini. She tried to smile. "Tell you what . . . just bring me the check."

"Very well." The large bow on the back of the waitress's apron wobbled as she retreated to the kitchen.

Danielle looked out the window. The rain continued to beat on the pavement in the parking lot. "Do you love him? Just as important, does he love you?"

"He caresses me and talks softly when we're alone. He's gentle enough in bed, but I feel like a goddamned pet. The leash is invisible, but it's there." Damita put the gin to her lips and looked over her shoulder again. "I'm starting to forget what it feels like to be free."

"Do you realize how you sound? Scared to death."

"It's the servants. And his people. His Middle Eastern business associates, Cali, Armitradj, and Samir, with his weirdo whisper and his bad leg. They're always dropping by. Hassan takes them into the den, locks the doors. I'll be walking the grounds and suddenly they'll show up. It's creepy."

Danielle studied Damita's eyes. Was she on something again? "You said he's in the import-export business?"

"That's right."

"Importing what?"

"He's never wanted to share that with me." Damita went into her fidget routine again, her nerves obviously shot.

Danielle tried to contain her frustration. "But these are things you should have known before you married him, especially someone from a different culture. Didn't you realize there might be some different expectations from an Iranian husband?"

"I know, a couple of my friends did warn me. But Danny, he's lived here for years. He was just so fascinating and always treated me with the greatest respect."

"Sure. To impress you."

"No." Damita sniffled. "It was real. So polite, romantic. It blew me away. But now he's become almost schizophrenic, not the man who proposed—that kind, over-attentive millionaire."

"That's why you married him? Money?"

Damita bristled. "That. And you."

"Me? You never consulted me. Of course, during that whirlwind courtship who had time to think?"

Damita grabbed the glass. "That's not what I mean. I know it was stupid." More agitated, she chugged the last of the martini. "Sure, I thought I loved him, but I finally had something you didn't have. Your success, that house you love, always a step ahead of me." Damita's face twisted with bitterness. "I finally had my own thing. A millionaire."

"God." Danielle couldn't believe what she was hearing. "You don't mean, to spite me?"

Damita removed her sunglasses as if conceding to a face-to-face confrontation. Her blue eyes reddened with tears. "I guess that was part of it."

Moisture formed in Danielle's own eyes. Too irritated to respond, she could only stare at her sister, finally defending herself. "If you felt that way about me, why call?"

"I'm frightened, Danny. They keep . . ." She paused as the waitress appeared, laid the bill on the table and walked off.

Danielle waited until she was out of earshot. "They? You keep saying 'they.' Is this a conspiracy?"

"It is. I'm a prisoner." Damita's melodramatic tone reminded Danielle of her sister's prior bouts of paranoia when she'd dabbled with drugs. "Dee, this sounds a bit larger than life—you know what I mean? Why don't you come to Boston for a few days and we'll sort it out."

"They know where you live," Damita whispered. "They know everything. They'd find me."

"Then see a lawyer."

"Hassan has enough money to choke me in a courtroom." Damita had apparently talked herself into a corner.

Danielle tried to grasp her hand. "All right. But if all this is true, you better do something about it."

Damita pulled away. "If? You mean you doubt me? I was just trying to tell somebody in case something happens."

"Happens? Like what?"

Damita raised her eyebrows in disappointment. "You don't see it, do you?" She pointed to her bruise. "Do you think I fell down the stairs?" Her hand trembled as she readjusted her sunglasses, then she took her purse in both hands. "Forget it." She rose to her feet.

Danielle couldn't believe her erratic behavior. "You're leaving? Just like that?"

Damita grabbed the back of the chair. "Why not? I don't feel anything from you."

"Well I'm damned worried about you."

"Sure you are—at arm's length."

Danielle gestured to the chair, "Please sit down. Get a grip."

Damita seemed momentarily frozen by the comment, then thrust her head forward. "How clinical. How analytical. How very much like you. Thanks for the fucking advice." Damita turned and dashed toward the lobby.

Danielle snatched the check off the table and hurried to her side, walking at her elbow. "You want more advice? I think you need outside help. A counselor . . ." They had reached the cash register.

"Jesus Christ!" Damita blurted. The middle-aged woman behind the counter looked up, amazed. Damita had whirled and faced Danielle. "You haven't changed, Danny. You're still treating me like a naive kid. Why can't you understand?"

Fearing the quarrel would separate them further, Danielle spoke softly. "I want to understand. I'm sorry if I didn't react as you expected. But you never even introduced me to your husband. What did you want me to do?"

"Nothing, obviously," Damita said cynically. The clerk's brow furrowed in reproach.

"Dee . . ."

"Forget I called you."

Danielle reached out in conciliation. "I don't want things to be like this."

"You created this," Damita huffed, pointing north to an imagined horizon. "Just go back to your ivory tower. This was a mistake." Then she spun around and stormed down the hall, leaving Danielle standing at the register.

3

TUESDAY—5:52 P.M.
Congo

LIKE AN EXHIBIT IN A macabre museum, Mwadaba lay bathed in a red glow from the evening sun.

Among the straw-thatched huts, bodies of villagers were scattered in various still-life poses, surreal mannequins caught in a freeze-frame of death.

Thane and Kuintala stared down from the ridge above.

"Whatever it is, it's not Ebola," Thane had confirmed his feelings, based on his observation through the video lens. He had become well acquainted with the virus's symptoms prior to venturing into the back-country of Congo. The lack of blood around the mouth and the nose of the bodies convinced him.

"There are other diseases." Kuintala gazed out over the treetops.

"None that leave people thrown around like they'd been tossed by a tornado."

"Diseases of the mind," Kuintala corrected him.

Thane remembered legends of the rain forest: vindictive tree gods had released spirits of pestilence to destroy those who ravaged the land. "I think we ought to take a closer look."

Kuintala's face went dead, his way of objecting.

"All right," Thane said. "I'll go. You stay here."

The inference that a man of Kuintala's tribal history might be a coward was apparently unbearable, even more than fear of the unknown. Without a word Kuintala set the video case, the equipment bag, and the rifle on the ground, then pulled off his T-shirt. He folded it over once and tied it around his head, using the sleeves to fasten the garment around his neck. The shirt covered his nose and mouth, giving him the appearance of a poorly disguised bandit.

Kuintala pointed. "You do the same."

Thane hesitated. In all the weeks they'd been together, he hadn't removed his shirt in Kuintala's presence. Doing it now would reveal the ragged scar on his back. He anticipated the inevitable questions, knowing that the explanation would bring back suppressed memories of flames, smoke, and screaming.

Kuintala gestured toward the horizon. "The wind is still from the north. We'll approach from there." He looked over, apparently waiting for Thane to do something with his shirt.

As Thane's hands rose to his buttons, Kuintala picked up his rifle and headed off, traversing the hill toward the northern side of the village.

Thane tied the garment around his head and breathed the smell of his own perspiration through the khaki cotton. He picked up the trail with the sun on his back.

After some two hundred feet, Kuintala paused at the edge of the gorge.

Thane joined him. "What's up?"

"I am checking to make sure the wind hasn't shifted."

Thane looked out over the sea of trees beyond the village. "I feel air, but I don't see branches moving."

Kuintala's face tilted up toward the north. "It is fine. We are upwind. I smell nothing."

"Good." Thane brushed past him. "Let's get on with it." He took a few steps down the incline through the ground cover.

"Adams," Kuintala said, moving along behind.

Thane stopped and turned.

Kuintala nodded. "That mark on your back. What evil bit you?"

"I was caught in a burning house," he said. "Escaped with my life, but I lost my family and left part of my soul behind."

"Some of your skin as well."

"The pound of flesh they talk about."

"I'm sorry to ask."

"I've gotten used to it," Thane said. He hadn't. "I was eighteen, in case you're curious." He regretted the edge in his voice.

Kuintala reacted; he looked humbled and gestured ahead. "My curiosity is only on the evil that is down there."

Thane nodded. "Mine, too." He hoisted the camera strap to his shoulder and began to sidestep down the steep slope toward the northern perimeter of Mwadaba.

Leaving the elevation of the ridge, they passed through tall grasses on the hillside.

Thane stopped, shifted the camera to his other shoulder, and Kuintala slipped by, taking the lead. Eerie silence closed in around them as they dropped into the shade of the forest.

Turning south, they cautiously approached the village. A few huts at the edge of the clearing came into sight through trunks of thick trees. Then, the realization struck.

"Kuintala," Thane said, "hold still." The rustling of the grasses under their feet ceased as they came to a halt.

They stood in a vacuum of sound. True silence. The constant hum of insects, the perpetual overtone of the African underbrush, had disappeared.

"Do you hear that?" Thane asked, looking off through sun-gilded bushes.

"Nothing." Kuintala spoke through his shirt.

"Exactly. Not a damn thing. No birds, no bugs."

The realization seemed to paralyze Kuintala. "First the smell. Now, the sound of death," he said, eyes wide.

Thane understood his friend's concern. "We'll take a quick look and get out." Thane edged past Kuintala and advanced toward two nearby huts that were now plainly visible. Creeping along, he found himself tiptoeing for no reason. You are spooked, he thought, sneaking up on dead people.

As they stepped from long grass onto the hardened dirt of the village compound, three adult bodies came into view. A middle-aged man and woman entangled in a posthumous embrace lay by the door of a hut. Another lone woman, her legs awkwardly twisted, lay off to the side.

Kuintala came up behind and startled Thane by placing a hand on his shoulder. "The skin, Adams."

"I see it." Thane hoisted the camera on his shoulder and began to shoot. Looking through the lens, he pushed the black zoom button, working in for close-ups of the bodies.

"Is it sand?" Kuintala asked.

Thane focused on the leg of the woman. "No," he said, moving the shot back to the initial grouping in the square. "It's ash gray. There seems to be some damage, too. Puffy. Swelling." As he panned the woman's body, it became evident that every inch of skin had been affected; her flesh was covered with a fine residue. He focused on the woman's chest, neck, and face.

"Son of a bitch." A chill rippled up Thane's spine. "Her eyes."

"They look closed."

"Not in close-up." Thane stared through the lens. "The whites aren't white anymore. It's hard to tell from here, but they've either turned black or they're gone."

DAY THIRTEEN

4

IN THE DISTANCE, ON THE eastern horizon, a white plume of foam trimmed the bow of a large freighter as it plowed through the wind-whipped Black Sea. The tugs had broken off and returned to the harbor, leaving the great ship to head southward toward the Bosporus Strait.

Bon voyage, Milcho Zishov thought as he stared at the freighter. The red-and-black giant would be sailing through the Dardanelles by tomorrow.

Seated beneath the green umbrella on his private patio at the seaside resort, Zishov's eyes ached as he glanced into the morning sun. The ocean's bright reflection punished him for drinking too much vodka the night before.

Breakfast and a two-hour Roman bath hadn't dulled the stinging aftermath of the binge, and his hotel room was still a mess. Behind him, in colorful shades of blue, lace curtains fluttered through the gray French doors, and inside, a heavily stitched goose-down quilt lay on the maroon carpet next to his still-unmade bed.

Zishov ran a wide hand through his charcoal-black hair. He grunted and tightened the belt of his beige bathrobe around his soft girth, averting his gaze from the ship, focusing on the purple-and-red bandanna worn by the old woman seated across from him.

Attired in a peasant dress and a light brown shawl, she had already begun her ritual, fondling the ornate saucer and cup Zishov had used for his tea.

He had summoned her early because he had a train to catch in the afternoon. And he sincerely wanted her to complete her work, just as she had every other time he engaged in a large business venture.

Gruschka, the acknowledged mystic of the harbor, swished the last droplets of the brown liquid from Zishov's demitasse into a saucer. Setting the small floral-patterned plate aside, she massaged the cup with both hands, rolling it back and forth, ostensibly to allow the tea leaves to settle.

Now the old crone stared into the cup intently, her smooth olive skin stretched over her bony face as she immersed herself in the mysteries before her. Her concentrated expression fascinated Zishov, who had no under-standing for her art but believed in it nevertheless. If Gruschka predicted happy passage, an exporter like Zishov could relax for the duration of the voyage. If she foresaw difficulties, steps could be taken, extra insurance purchased, clients warned of delays.

It was all silly superstition, of course, but in a country where over half the citizens believed in werewolves and other occult traditions, a reliable old gypsy's prophecies were regarded with respect.

Gruschka had become the sage of seamen, correctly predicting three shipwrecks in the last decade. Her notoriety had attracted an assortment of businessmen in the vicinity who called on her fortune telling, maritime or otherwise.

Zishov looked across the table, patiently awaiting the reading of the leaves. Gruschka seemed displeased with the tea's configuration, rotating the cup again and again.

"Well," Zishov said, impatiently. "Do you like what you see?"

"The images are not yet formed," she responded, staring into the cup, then glancing down at the money on the table. "You will disturb the ether with your questions." She shifted in her chair, casting a cabalistic glare from under her dark bushy eyebrows. He had seen that look before. The light blue and brown irises that ringed her pupils gave her eyes a disconcerting transparency.

"Perhaps the ether requires more fuel," Zishov said, reaching into his bathrobe pocket, stacking several more lev on the already generous pile of bills.

"My contentment affects the clarity of the vision." Zishov grunted again and pushed the money stack across the table. "Are you content now?"

"My spirit is serene," she smiled, "which bodes well for the message." Gruschka began to hum, gently turning the cup in her wrinkled hands. Her eyes half closed as her facial muscles relaxed around her angular cheekbones. She had drifted into a trance. Gruschka took several deep breaths as the rune stone amulets on her chest rose and fell.

Zishov leaned forward, anticipating her report, which might begin at any moment. He stared at her in silence as ocean waves lapped the beach below the patio.

"Ah," she said finally, furrowing her brow, "you are to make a great sum of money with this shipment." She opened her eyes. "More than usual."

Zishov nodded. "That's true."

'The cargo is bound for . . . an island."

"Very good. That is also true."

"And the goods are beautiful, artistic somehow."

"Excellent, Gruschka, you continue to amaze."

"And they will arrive safely."

"I am relieved to hear it."

"Yes," Gruschka said, pensively. "Relieved. You have worried about this cargo." She hesitated. "Because there are many people who..." Gruschka's eyes widened as she stared into the cup. Her chin jutted out in surprise, surprise turning to horror. She dropped the cup onto the table as if it were hot. "God," she stammered, clasping her trembling hands together. "This shipment should never have been sent."

"What is it?" Zishov asked, concerned for the old woman's health. She looked as if she would faint.

"I don't know exactly, but there is a great malady in this." She pushed the cup off the table. The demitasse fell and smashed on the stone tiles at her feet. "Great evil for you and for many others." Gruschka stood and backed away.

"You're crazy. What are you saying?" Zishov tightened his bathrobe and jumped to his feet. There had been some unusual negotiations involved in the transaction, but he had considered the client's request for secrecy acceptable. Moving around the table, he attempted to take her by the arm. "Are you frightened by a stupid crateful of Ukrainian statuettes?"

Gruschka pulled away, as if horrified by his touch, and her anxious gaze drifted out to sea.

Zishov followed her glance toward the freighter plowing south toward the horizon. "Yes. That's the ship. My cargo is on board."

"It goes to Cyprus," Gruschka said, bringing the back of her hand to her mouth. "But there have been others. This is not the first." She gathered her skirts, leaving the money on the table. He was astounded to see her turn toward the open patio door.

"The first?" Zishov asked, completely confused. "Yes, it is for me. But how do you know this?"

Clenching her hands, Gruschka paused at the transom, still staring tearfully at the ship.

"I hear the cries of the dead."

5

STILL DISTRACTED BY HER QUARREL with Damita the previous day, Danielle pushed through the large glass double doors of her advertising agency's lobby. Carrying her raincoat, she was impeccably dressed in a chocolate-colored business suit, her hair neatly bound in a French twist.

On a plum velvet wall ahead, under track lights, gilded letters gleamed. They read: HAMPTON, COOLIDGE, DENNISON & WILKES.

Joella, an attractive African-American receptionist in a crisp white blouse, seemed preoccupied with a call.

In response to Danielle's "good morning," Joella covered the phone with her hand. "Ms. Wilkes!" She rose from her chair and lifted a finger to catch Danielle's attention, but was forced back into the conversation. "No. No, sir. Mr. Hampton hasn't called. He's still in Los Angeles."

The party on the other end of the line apparently droned on, so Danielle resumed her walk, but Joella's pretty eyes widened further and she waved once more. "Danielle."

Danielle retreated a few steps and, resigned to the delay, patiently rested her forearm against the beige marble counter. Whatever the disturbance, she had learned to take the unexpected in stride. The advertising profession doled out daily surprises.

Joella's eyes rolled in exasperation as she continued to deal with the caller, leaving Danielle to contemplate her name on the wall.

At thirty-two years of age she had become the sole female partner in the ad agency. The previous year she had spear-headed the account team that acquired Arturo Fashions, Brigantine Maritime, and Othello Foods, accounts totaling sixty-four million dollars in annual billing. David Hampton, the agency's CEO, had quickly offered her the partnership on the heels of her energetic effort, concerned that Danielle had the power to waltz those accounts back to New York, where she had cut her teeth as an account executive.

Joella looked up and waved her hand desperately. "No, she is here. Ms. Wilkes just walked in."

"Who is it?" Danielle whispered.

"Dennison," Joella said, covering the mouthpiece. "Calling from his car."

Danielle envisioned Cliff lounging in his Jaguar.

She grimaced and shook her head. "Later."

Whatever Cliff Dennison wanted, it could wait. He was one of her least favorite people. First, he'd resisted Danielle's partnership in the firm and then had had the audacity to try and seduce her.

Dennison's family's millions allowed him to rub elbows with the heads of large corporations, and his country-club demeanor helped him rise in the ad industry. Unfortunately, he also became a permanent fixture when he bankrolled Hampton and Coolidge three years before after a lawsuit damaged the company's assets. Dennison was here to stay, possessing forty percent of the stock, a dominant share of the ego, and a meager measure of the talent. His playboy antics were the common currency: he had hit on every attractive woman in the firm, including Joella, who had again been pulled into the telephone conversation.

"I'll make it clear. Yes, sir." She pointed at the house phone on the marble counter and shrugged at Danielle. "He says you better talk to him. And Mr. Finelli is here, waiting in your office."

"What?" Danielle's mind shifted gears. The meeting with Finelli, Othello's new marketing director, was to have been canceled. Danielle distinctly remembered having told her secretary to postpone the meeting since she needed more time before her next presentation.

Joella's nervousness bothered Danielle and she reluctantly picked up the phone. "Hello, Cliff."

"I had a call late last night," Dennison began coldly. "Frank Finelli of Othello Foods."

"Why was he calling you?"

"Because you weren't available. Where the hell were you yesterday?"

Danielle bristled at Dennison's tone. "An emergency. Family business."

"Your name on our shingle means we're your family too," he said, acidly. "You've got a problem. Finelli tells me this is the second time you've delayed the presentation of his graphics."

"We've been handcuffed by his predilection for cartoon labels. We've had a hard time honing a new concept, and I just couldn't sign off on the art department's renderings yesterday. But we're close." Danielle regretted having to justify the decision. Why should she have to defend herself when she had won the Othello account for the agency in the first place? "What's the problem here, Cliff? I asked Janet to call Finelli and postpone the presentation."

"That didn't cut it for him. He's due at a grocer convention tomorrow and insisted on seeing your packaging ideas at nine o'clock this morning as originally planned."

Danielle checked her watch. It was eight forty-five. "He's early. Joella says he's here."

"I'm not surprised. He was pissed."

"Why didn't you alert me? You could have called me at home."

"I never asked you to baby-sit my accounts, Danielle. You can't expect me to chase you around when one of yours goes begging."

"Couldn't you at least have warned Janet?"

"I left her a voice mail this morning."

Perfect, Danielle thought, Janet doesn't come in until eight-thirty. "Thanks for all your help, Cliff," she said bitterly. "I owe you."

"From where I sit, you always have."

Danielle smacked the phone on the receiver. She was about to utter unflattering comments about Dennison, but held back in Joella's presence. "How long has Mr. Finelli been here?" she asked.

"Just a few minutes." Joella winced apologetically. "I tried you in your car."

"I was probably waiting for the elevator." Danielle gathered her thoughts. She would need her art director immediately. "Ring Kevin. Have him meet me in the west conference room."

Danielle left Joella and strode down the hallway through the executive suites.

HCD&W management occupied the thirty-fifth floor of the Commons Building. Media buying and bookkeeping took up most of the thirty-second floor. The thirty-third floor contained both art departments: one for commercial print applications and the other for multimedia production, CG and motion graphics. The thirty-fourth floor housed Internet programming plus the broadcast production division, audio/video producers, production managers, casting, etc.

Having apparently been alerted by Joella, Janet Tillman waited in the hall dressed in a high-collared sweater and a calf-length skirt. A slight middle-aged woman with a bad hip, she limped toward Danielle carrying a coffee cup. "Mr. Finelli," she said, breathlessly. "He's—"

"I heard." Danielle took the cup and Janet took her raincoat. "He seems rather irritable this morning."

Danielle smiled at Janet's polite understatement. "You mean he's ready to bite my head off."

"At the shoulders."

"Joella already called Kevin. Alert Michelle Michaels to have her newspaper schedules ready in case we get that far." Danielle rushed past Janet and approached the large oak door to her office.

"Oh, one other thing." Janet clutched the coat. "Your sister Damita phoned on your private line a few minutes ago. She sounded very upset. She wants you to call."

"God," Danielle whispered. "A five-alarm morning."

"Immediately," Janet added.

Danielle raised her hands in disgust. "I can't . . ." Grasping the brushed brass handle, she opened the door and launched herself into the office.

She was confronted by Finelli's broad back. Above the meaty furrows of his neck, black ringlets of curly hair tufted over his collar. He stared out at the city, purposely ignoring her entrance.

"Frank," Danielle said cheerfully, closing the door, "I'm so glad you're here."

6

HUMIDITY HOVERED LIKE A MISTY shroud in the trees as the rain forest settled into late-afternoon lethargy while its creatures were wisely tucked away from the heat.

The only sound in the noiseless landscape was the occasional whack of Kuintala's machete, clearing a vine as he and Thane trudged down the rust-colored footpath.

Their grueling march had lasted several hours and during the silent trek Thane's heartbeat had begun to ring in his ears. Like a machine his body had fallen into a laborious rhythm, and his steady breathing into a measured cadence as he tried to maintain Kuintala's blistering pace.

Droplets of sweat streaked Thane's neck, further drenching the khaki shirt he had used as a face mask at Mwadaba. The straps of his backpack burned his shoulders. Of course, the pack did contain the jungle hammocks he and Kuintala had slept in the night before, but something didn't make sense. Thane was bothered by his own sense of foreboding. He was haunted by images of villagers writhing in their final agony. He also felt inordinately sluggish. Maybe the dried rations he'd eaten the day before were contaminated. Whatever the reason, a troublesome fatigue had settled in his bones and he hungered for a square meal. He and Kuintala hadn't enjoyed fresh game in forty-eight hours, not since a small gazelle two nights earlier.

As the hike continued, Thane began to suspect that something unknown was festering inside him. Understandably, his paranoia had been compounded by the foul odor of the village, the stench of death. But as he walked, memories of the corpses affected his reason and blurred his perceptions. The blazing sunlight turned fierce and unfriendly. The ground itself appeared menacing. Every blade of long grass that brushed his legs seem to threaten to cut him.

To steady himself, Thane decided to look ahead at Kuintala's rippling back, but the frenetic pace of Kuintala's strides revealed his own apprehension.

Kuintala had also been visibly shaken by the Mwadaba experience, expressing an almost manic need to report it. He was right, of course; the horrific discovery required action even if it interrupted their otherwise successful video shoot. They had discussed options and decided that Thane would need two more days under the forest canopy to get his final shots, but only after Congo authorities were informed of the disaster. Then, if nothing else prevented it, they would return to their location to shoot as soon as tomorrow.

As he watched Kuintala move, Thane couldn't help admiring his partner's superb shape. Kuintala had grown up in the African wild, his muscles honed by the uneven land. And even though Thane had been a superior swimmer in college, a good physical specimen, he had trouble keeping up. Kuintala was laden with video equipment, yet nearly ran down the trail. Every so often Kuintala would glance over his shoulder, as if checking for phantoms in the forest.

They had hiked through the Katanga Mountain foothills since morning and Thane's thighs began to complain. He'd gotten some challenging shots of amphibians in the last few days that required strenuous tree climbing and now his body was paying for it.

"Hey," Thane breathed heavily, "how about a break?"

"Only two miles," Kuintala said without looking back. They were headed for Kolo's Kamp, the strip-mining outpost they had occasionally used as a base camp; the first site with an accessible shortwave radio. Kolo, the camp head foreman, would also allow them to use a tent and provide fresh food.

Kuintala had challenged Thane's endurance for his own amusement in the past, but now, Thane sensed that he was driven by anxiety. "Let's take a two-minute breather."

"Can't you make it over that next rise?" Kuintala scolded.

"We're not being chased by anything."

After a few strides, Kuintala almost whispered. "I feel we are. Something clutches my insides. A strangeness walks with us."

The response sent a chill up Thane's back. If it was imagination, it was telepathic. "What are you telling me? What strangeness?"

"I feel weak. Sick maybe."

"Maybe" was the operative word. Kuintala obviously felt the indescribable irritability that Thane felt.

Thane fought his own doubt. "Don't be concerned about disease. That village wasn't infected. Those people were struck down."

"Ebola strikes down. Marburg strikes down. Many viruses in Congo destroy fast."

Thane hoisted his backpack higher on his shoulders. "Yes, I know, but you saw the bodies. Nothing like that's been reported anywhere else."

"Rainforest fever comes like swamp water. Rises then drains away. I have seen slime become hard clay in a week." Kuintala often expressed his respect for the environment. He had spoken before of human inadequacies, human beings wilted by the powerful enigmas of the rain forest. Though unconvinced of the supernatural implications, Thane concurred that nature's complexity might never be fully understood.

"We're both just tired." Thane rubbed a handkerchief across the back of his neck. "Let's see how we feel after we rest."

Kuintala chose not to reply, but switched the rifle to the opposite shoulder and moved the camera equipment bag to the other side, evidence of his weariness.

Perhaps the weight of the equipment in the bag could be lessened for their return, Thane thought. Some of the tripods could be left at the mining camp during the two days of shooting yet to come. The bag also contained digital tapes with forty-two days of work, his only income for the year. He couldn't wait to get back to Kinshasa and watch the footage on a full-sized monitor. So far he had only been able to view his shots through the viewfinder. Hopefully, everything would look sharp and clean and he'd be able to fly to Cairo and on to New York, where he would assist in the final edit. His portion of the International Geographic special was to air in two months. He had patiently awaited that moment. His fifty-thousand-dollar advance was nearly spent. The other half would sustain him while he sought another project.

A distant rumble of heavy machinery through the trees indicated they were close to their objective. The strip-mining camp lay dead ahead.

"Kuintala," Thane shouted. "The way you feel . . . don't say anything to the men. Considering what we've seen, we don't want to scare them needlessly. I'm sure it's nothing."

"Okay, okay," Kuintala replied. "I hear the camp. It makes me feel better already."

"Good man." Their jungle imaginings might dissipate with the sounds of civilization.

Kuintala left the trail and Thane followed, crossing the underbrush using a shortcut through a row of trees. They broke through to a large clearing dotted with several olive-drab open-air tents.

Because it was late in the day most of the machinery had shut down. Some two hundred feet away, several men sat talking. They were gathered on the grass in folding chairs around a crude wooden table under a dusty khaki canvas canopy.

Thane looked toward the rise beyond the encampment as they approached. What had once been a rolling green mountain was now flattened into a terraced auburn scar. Lush country that had hosted thousands of animals and birds had been ripped up by bulldozers, back-hauls and heavy trucks. Traces of their assault remained cut into the side of the hill. African land had been raped for its copper and cobalt.

Four well-muscled seated men turned in recognition as Thane and Kuintala advanced. Kolo, the graying camp master, took a sip from his canteen and waved them over. "Hello, hello, hello," he said in a broken accent. His fierce face was punctuated with a large mole on his left cheek, and as his wet smiling lips parted, he showed a large gap in his front teeth.

The other men couldn't speak English. Thane recognized them from their prior return to the camp three weeks before. They gawked over their shoulders as Kolo got to his feet. He came forward offering to take Kuintala's baggage. "You early," Kolo said. "Good pictures?"

"Good pictures." Thane attempted a smile. "But not enough."

"Then why you come so soon?" Kolo asked, as he helped Kuintala set his burden on the ground next to the tent stakes.

"We found many dead people," Kuintala said. "The village of Mwadaba."

Kolo instinctively retreated a step. "Dead? You went there?"

"Yes. Close enough to see there were no survivors."

Kolo turned to the others and said something unintelligible. Two of the four men nervously got to their feet, the third gripped the table edge.

Kuintala vehemently shook his head and responded in their language. Whatever he said made Kolo's shoulders relax. The men at the table let out sighs of relief.

"I told them it was not Ebola," Kuintala said, turning to Thane.

"No, no." Thane waved his hands. "It was not the virus."

"What then?" Kolo asked, suspiciously.

"We don't know." Thane set his backpack on the ground. "Something deadly and very quick. We need to use your shortwave to call the assayer's office at Likasi. They can call the government officials in Kisangani to send a medical team."

"Sure, sure," Kolo said, now more relaxed. "Radio over there, in equipment tent." He pointed at the shelter with its flaps down and began to walk in that direction. "Come Adams, you call."

"Kuintala will," Thane said. "He speaks the dialect."

"Good. Come." Kolo again said something to the four miners, who spoke among themselves and watched with apparent interest as Kuintala led the way.

Thane felt the need to lighten things up. "Kolo, I'm parched." He smiled at the foreman as they walked the thirty feet to the tent. "Hotter than a hyena's heinie. You have something cool to drink?"

"You know nothing cool here, Adams," Kolo said. "I have warm English beer in same tent. This one." He pointed. "All right?"

"That might be more than all right," Thane said.

Kolo's heavy brows bunched in confusion. "Good. Only . . . what is 'heinie'?"

Kuintala translated and Kolo's eyes bulged as he broke into raucous laughter. He shouted something to the other men, who echoed Kolo's mirth, slapping the table. "I like the word, heinie," Kolo said, then repeated it again to himself.

Kuintala pulled on the flap, forming a doorway. Thane and the still-giggling Kolo entered the tent.

Inside in the dim light, Thane caught sight of the shortwave transmitter set alongside maps and a lantern on a small card table. Tool crates and several canvas bags containing mining gear sat on the ground nearby.

Kuintala stepped over and flipped the switch on the radio. "Channel nineteen, you think?"

"Try it," Thane said. "Then mess with the squelch until you hear the honing tone."

"Push the microphone button when you speak," Kolo added.

"That beer, Kolo? Kuintala, you want one?"

"No. Water," Kuintala said absentmindedly, fussing with the channel knob.

"Beer over there, behind bags." Kolo's stubby finger pointed the way. "I hide it." He smiled, revealing the split in his teeth again.

Thane wove his way to the corner of the tent and peered into the darkness, spotting a cardboard case with the words STOUT'S ALE stenciled on the side. Moving one of the crates, he leaned over the canvas bags to reach the open flap of the beer box.

A clicking at his knees distracted him. The image of a rattlesnake entered his mind and he startled. Then he stared down at his feet and chuckled to himself. Nothing there but an open tote bag filled with ore samples, a compass, and a Geiger counter, a small metal box with a glass gauge that had obviously responded to the ore in the sacks. Rattlesnakes in Africa? You are spooked, Thane thought. The erratic ticking continued as he reached for the beer. "Kolo, listen," he said, looking over his shoulder. "Your Geiger counter's still on." He grabbed the neck of one of the bottles and joined Kolo, who was busily assisting Kuintala with the squelch.

Thane twisted the top off the ale and took a swig.

"What?" Kolo asked.

"I said your Geiger . . ." Thane glanced in the direction of the equipment.

"I hear nothing." Kolo shrugged.

"Mmmm. Well, it was clicking. What you got in there, uranium?"

"No. Not even cobalt. Only copper samples."

Kuintala pushed the button on the microphone. "Calling Likasi, come in." The airwaves hissed. No reply. "Likasi, come in."

Thane took another sip of the beer and strolled back in the direction of the bag. Two feet from the canvas the ticking slowly began again. "See," Thane said, "it's on. I . . . holy shit!"

Kuintala looked up, distracted.

Kolo turned. "What is it, Adams?"

Thane set the ale on a crate and leaned down to pick up the device. "There's something . . ." The ticking increased. Thane picked up the Geiger counter with his right hand. The sensor on the end of the lead wire dangled in midair. Thane grasped the sensor with his left hand and the ticking kicked up wildly. Kolo came over and Thane spun round, handing him the device at arm's length. "Listen," Thane said.

Click. Click-click. Click-click-click-click-click.

Kolo stared at Thane's hand. "Adams," he said softly, his eyes wide.

"Here, you hold this." Thane thrust the apparatus toward Kolo's chest.

Kuintala had stopped his broadcast and stared at both of them as Kolo reluctantly took the counter.

As Thane released it, the ticking noise almost ceased.

"Point it at me."

Kolo took the sensor and stuck it in Thane's face. The clicks began again and the meter on the side of the box moved.

"Now point it at Kuintala," Thane said grimly.

Hesitantly, Kolo complied. He held the sensor in Kuintala's direction. The clicks began again with a frequency nearly equal to Thane's reading.

"Jesus," Thane said, his throat thick with the realization. "It's both of us." The images of the dead returned, their bodies covered with an ash like residue.

Looking back and forth from Kolo's face to Kuintala's, Thane could only think of one more word to utter, but Kuintala beat him to it.

"Mwadaba," Kuintala said, his face blank with awe.

7

AFTER THE DRIZZLE, THE CLOUDS had parted. The steaming rooftops of Boston's office buildings glinted in the morning light. Slivers of sunshine beamed into the conference room through the tall bronzed windows.

Frank Finelli sat at the end of a long oak table surrounded by the mahogany-paneled walls. His manicured nails tapped the waxed surface in an irritated staccato. He was unhappy when Danielle had ushered him to the meeting room and his mood hadn't improved.

At the other end of the table near the media center complete with its TV monitors and slide screens, blond, curly-haired Kevin Deetz stood motionless in shirtsleeves. The art director's underarms were wet with tension as he clutched the edge of the display easel.

Kevin's designs had flunked the test.

Finelli had insulted him and Danielle felt responsible for the young man's discomfort.

"Danielle, I'm not sure you take me seriously," Finelli said in a half-whisper, seething with barely suppressed anger. "First you put me *off*, then you put me *on*." He glared at Kevin. "Now you push this kid's illustrations on me. I'm not buying it."

"Kevin is the art director, not the illustrator."

"Whatever."

"First of all, Frank, the purpose of delaying this meeting was to present something worthwhile."

"This junk?" Finelli pointed at the art cards.

Danielle shot a look at Kevin's moist face. "This *junk* is a result of careful research and two weeks of board time." She regretted having Kevin in the meeting, but at this stage it was unavoidable. Danielle would have a difficult time translating the finer points of Finelli's artistic critique. The young man had to hear the stinging analysis firsthand to properly execute changes.

Finelli scowled and shifted his massive weight in the beige suede chair. "I wanted packaging with a wholesome cartoon style. You know Vince Corbonne is a *family* man. Othello Foods is a *family* business." Finelli's face twisted in a mock appeal as his chubby hands met in a professional prayer. "I don't want things fancy. Just convey a *family* feeling about *OUR family* of products. I want *traditional.* Is that too much to ask?"

"But a traditional—"

"I told you Norman Rockwell. I asked for Disney." Finelli slammed the table with the flat of his hand. "You give me computer-generated glitz."

Danielle let the comment ring in the room without reply. The diamond tie-pin on Finelli's broad chest heaved as he sighed and regained his composure. "Let me explain this to you . . . You remember the old Hunt's tomato can? Remember the face of the tomato on that label? He wore a top hat and a monocle. Big round cheeks. Shiny face. You remember? I realize that was before your time . . ."

Kevin raised a hand, hesitantly. "I remember that from our commercial archives."

"Okay, genius." Finelli refocused his intensity on the art director. "Then why didn't you give it to me?" He pointed. "Because of her?"

Kevin looked to Danielle for help.

Momentarily speechless and seriously doubting Finelli's aptitude for logic, Danielle found herself wishing Karen Favro were still her contact at Othello. Karen and she had shared an excellent rapport, which initially helped Danielle land the account. Finelli seemed to have forgotten that Danielle's advent the year before had led to an immediate eight-percent rise in sales. Sales fluctuations in the food business frequently came in single digits, and Corbonne, the company's CEO, seemed very happy. But then, Karen's pregnancy and voluntary retirement changed everything. A month ago, Othello had hired Finelli away from D & R Spaghetti. A cousin of Corbonne, Finelli was contentious by nature. He had bragged about his autonomy and seemed to harbor animosity for innovative ideas and contemporary lifestyles. Finelli's current whims had taken Danielle by surprise, and faced with this first real problem, Danielle chose to skirt his emotional outburst by appealing to the marketing director's reason.

"Frank, let's remember that I recommended photography, while you insisted on illustrations for your new labels. Out of respect for your wishes, our research department hosted three different focus groups in New York testing illustrative styles. We held the same tests in Chicago, Denver, and San Francisco. Results were identical across the board. Testing proved that up-to-date, forward-looking renderings of vegetable characters would attract buyers most efficiently."

"Your focus groups didn't use the art samples I would have used."

"Apparently not, judging from your reaction today. But your deadlines demanded that we test quickly—which we did—with generic samples to establish a creative direction."

"I suggest you test again, with a cartoon style that I approve."

"Well of course we can, but the delay caused by retesting makes your October packaging deadline unattainable, particularly if you want new product on the shelves by January."

Finelli's dark brown eyes narrowed. "You're fighting me, Danielle."

"I have your best interests at heart."

"Really? You're supposed to be the bright new star at the agency. But your account team has our conservative account confused with your other more progressive clients. You're treating us like a trendy impulse item. We're not a fad-crazed fashion line like Arturo, nor are we a glitzy high-tech powerboat manufacturer like Brigadoon."

"Brigantine."

"Whatever. We sell food. Staples of life. Vegetables, tomato sauce, canned peas. Your agency seems intent on making us look synthetic."

"It's not a question of artificiality, it's a question of appeal."

Finelli's face reddened. "No. It's a question of your ego versus mine."

Against her principles, Danielle considered changing her position on the subject, but was grateful for a sudden diversion—a knock at the door. Dressed in a black suit, Michelle Michaels entered, a sheaf of papers in hand.

Kevin stepped aside, apparently relieved that he might be off the hot seat. Danielle understood. A new topic of conversation might break the deadlock.

Danielle stood as the trim brunette edged toward the table. "You remember Michelle Michaels, our print media director."

With his eyes down, Finelli greeted the brunette's appearance with a wave of his hand. "You can excuse yourself Ms. Michaels. I'm not talking media until we have the art nailed down."

Shocked by this intransigence, Danielle couldn't disguise her disappointment. "I planned to address media as well as creative."

"Then change your plan." Finelli toyed with one of his onyx cuff links.

Confused, Michelle hesitated, looking at the door. Danielle leaned over the table. "It's important you approve schedules now, Mr. Finelli. If you don't, we won't be able—"

At that moment the telephone speaker in the media center beeped twice. "Ms. Wilkes, please pick up," Janet's voice said.

"I'm in a meeting, Janet," Danielle said, completely surprised by Janet's interruption. Danielle redirected her attention to Finelli. "Without your approval, we can't hold select newspaper space for September."

"Approving a schedule, "Finelli raised his eyes "implies that you're going to place the media."

"Of course, why not?"

Finelli straightened the knot of his floral tie and glared across the table. "I think the status of our relationship is in serious doubt, that's why not."

The phone beeped again. "Danielle . . ."

"Janet, I am not to be interrupted again." Hardening, Danielle met Finelli's gaze. "Are you threatening to take your business elsewhere?"

"Based on today's performance, I intend to recommend a complete agency review to Mr. Corbonne."

Danielle now suspected Finelli's motives. His animosity appeared too calculated, possibly predetermined. Perhaps his call to Dennison and his objections to the artwork were a fabrication. Perhaps he sought excuses to move the business to another agency for his own personal gain, financial or otherwise. She needed a sincere one-on-one to determine his intentions. Danielle turned to her associates. "Kevin, Michelle, that will be all for today. Thanks."

"Are we done?" Finelli asked, poised to rise.

"I hope not." Danielle edged to the chair and sat back down. "Please give me a few more minutes."

Finelli's chest heaved impatiently with a deep sigh. He averted his eyes, staring down at the wood grain of the oak conference table and resumed tapping his manicured nails.

As Michelle left the room, Kevin gathered the art cards from the easel. Watching their retreat, Danielle began to formulate her do-or-die speech, as the conference room door closed behind Kevin.

Danielle leaned forward in her chair. "The last twelve months prove that Othello Foods benefits from our advertising strategies. Nielsen numbers show positive velocities on most of your canned foods. Now, if I've personally done something to offend, something serious enough for you to consider changing agencies—"

She was interrupted by the conference room door being opened. Danielle couldn't believe it.

Janet leaned in. "Danielle—"

"Janet! I asked—"

"Your sister's on line three. It's an emergency."

"What? What kind of an emergency?"

"She says she must talk to you regardless." Janet hovered at the door, waiting for a response.

Danielle's composure collapsed momentarily. "Oh, God. Frank, I apologize." Finelli rolled his eyes at the ceiling. As Janet ducked back through the door, Danielle glanced over at the phone in the media center, then realized she couldn't gracefully handle Damita's needs with Finelli in the room. "Just . . . just excuse me for one minute. I'll be right back." Danielle hoped for an answer, but Finelli stared out the window in disgust. She took his lack of response as affirmation and left him seated at the table. The closest phone was just down the hall in one of the Xerox rooms, which was thankfully not in use. Danielle closed the door, and cautioning herself not to rail at her sister for the interruption, she lifted the receiver off the white wall unit and pressed line three. "Dee?"

"Danny, I'm sorry," Damita whispered.

Danielle heard traffic noises in the background. "I am, too. I overreacted. Now please—"

"I hope you believed me." Damita's voice shook. "I'm really in trouble."

This was worse than yesterday. "Dee, calm down. What is it?"

"Somehow Hassan found out about our meeting. He threatened me. Told me I was restricted to the house. When I disagreed, he . . ." Damita began to sob.

"He beat me." Damita's panic seemed all too genuine. "Dee, whatever's going on there, I want you to get the hell out. Where are you?"

"I walked to a phone booth at a convenience store half a mile from the house."

"Leave now. Come to Boston and stay."

"He's taken my car keys. Besides, he'd just follow me."

"We'll get a restraining order."

"It's not that simple. I was in the garden last evening. I stopped in the arbor to look at the sunset. Armitradj and Cali came walking down the path. They hadn't seen me. They were on the other side of the rosebushes, and I overheard Armitradj talk about a man who was going to be killed. They laughed about it."

"What man?"

"I couldn't understand the name. Something foreign. But don't you see what kind of people these are? I'm losing it. I'm scared. Not just for me, but also for you, if you get involved."

"That's ridiculous. If you won't leave, I'm coming to pick you up."

"Don't come tonight. Hassan is entertaining."

Her objection sounded absurd. "He beats you up and you help him host a party?"

"I told you. I'm a prisoner. I can't cause trouble." Damita's voice became frantic. "People who laugh about murder—"

"Settle down. All right, I'll be there tomorrow. What's the best time?"

"Hassan's going to New York for the day."

"What about his friends?"

"I don't know. They usually go along. We could try for late morning. But you can't be seen. I could meet you out back by the servants' entrance."

"How do I get there?" Danielle grabbed a pencil off the counter and wrote on a blank Xerox sheet.

"As you hit New London off I-95, turn south on 641, that's Exit 84. That becomes Highway 1."

"Wait." Danielle scribbled the directions. "Okay, go ahead."

"After Highway 1, turn right at Highway 156, right again at Rope Ferry Road, and then take a left at Almbaum Road. Almbaum dead-ends. We're the last large house surrounded by a black wrought-iron fence. To be safe, park up the street and come around to the servants' gate. Push 0-99-4 on the keypad. That code works for the whole house. Come through and wait at the servants' entrance, the back door. I'll meet you at eleven sharp. We can talk outside in the garden."

"All right," Danielle said calmly. "Now, Dee, just hang in there. I've got a great attorney. Whatever's going on here, we'll lick this thing."

"Thanks, Danny."

"I've been thinking about what you said at Toffler's Inn. I'm sorry that we were ever at odds. I never meant to hurt you by being one step ahead."

"It only hurt me when you didn't look back."

A wave of doubt swept over Danielle as she recalled the times ambition had dominated her life. She suddenly realized that even though Damita had been foolish, she also might have needed help in order to cope. Images of her sister as a precious button-nosed kid caused Danielle to choke up. How had they ever drawn so far apart? She forced herself to speak.

"Dee, I promise. We'll be shoulder to shoulder from now on."

"I love you, Danny."

"I'm going to show you how much I love you."

Danielle hung up, numbed by the fear in Damita's voice. Then she suddenly remembered.

Finelli.

"Holy God," she said out loud, yanking the copying room door open. She ran to the conference room. The door was wide open and there was no one inside. Perhaps Finelli had decided to use the men's room. She hustled down the hallway past the executive offices and burst into the reception area.

Joella looked up from her console.

"Finelli?" Danielle asked.

"He's gone, Danielle. I tried to stop him. You should have seen his face. He said to tell you he's not coming back."

8

ON A DISTANT TERRACE OF the strip-mined hill, the rumble of heavy equipment had finally faded away, leaving the rain forest to its evening calm.

The gloom in the camp's equipment tent was broken by an undulating ribbon of golden sunset that danced across the dusty floor, as a breeze kicked the khaki door flap back and forth.

Kuintala and Thane sat on mining crates in a dark corner, listening intently to a communication from Likasi, where clerks at the assayer's office had located Dr. Sawati, a geologist.

The articulate doctor asked questions in perfect Oxford English over the drone of the shortwave transmission. "So you saw no signs of an explosion? Over."

Thane pushed the button on the base of the ancient microphone that sat on the card table. "None. But we didn't hang around very long. Over."

"How long? Over."

"Not more than five or ten minutes. Over."

"That may have been your saving grace," Sawati said through the hiss of the shortwave. "Just hold one moment please, let me check my charts."

During the lull Thane looked over at Kuintala. "What would you say? Ten minutes at most?"

"It seemed longer. Perhaps fear lengthens time."

Over the crackle of the shortwave, Sawati returned. "From Kolo's description of the Geiger counter readings and your assessment of your stay at the village, I would estimate that you were exposed to roughly two hundred rads of radiation. The question becomes did you receive that exposure from an immediate source, or a secondary one from the ground itself or the surrounding area? Did you see anything that looked to be the source—rubble, a blast crater, or some other disturbance? Over."

"No. Nothing like that," Thane said, visualizing the scene. 'The huts were intact. Over."

"We will have to check to see if there have been reports of radioactive materials being stolen. Perhaps the villagers were in possession of hazardous material without knowing it. Whatever the case, it's indeed fortunate you didn't remain longer, or the level of contamination would have been far more extreme. Over."

Thane again pushed the talk button. "Are we likely to experience any aftereffects? And do we represent a danger to the men here in camp? Over."

"They would have to be very close to you for the next few hours, and even then it's only remotely possible they might feel some mild discomfort. The most sensitive individuals could feel some incidental nausea. But no, I do not think so. And as far as your aftereffects . . . since you were exposed some twenty-four hours ago and now feel only mildly ill, I think you are probably through the worst of it. Exposure to four hundred to five hundred rad levels for longer periods leads to repeated spells of vomiting for at least a day. But even cases of that nature recover within a week. Again, the short duration saved you."

A telephone rang in the background, and Sawati paused, spoke to someone in the room, then returned to the microphone. "That's the call from Kisangani. Do not break contact. I will be just a moment."

Thane looked up at Kolo, who stood just outside the tent flap in the sun. Beyond, some twenty yards away, four other foremen had been joined by workers who restlessly milled about. "Did you hear what he said, Kolo? We're not a danger to you or your men."

Kolo's split teeth showed once more. "I hear, Adams. But perhaps you and Kuintala should sleep in your own tent tonight."

"What?" Kuintala said boldly over his shoulder to Kolo. "You think I had wanted to sleep next to a rough-skinned rhino like you in the first place?"

"There is no offense in my words," Kolo said apologetically.

"You probably snore like a warthog." The edge in Kuintala's voice surprised Thane, but it was followed by a nod and a surreptitious wink.

The crackle of the radio ended the exchange.

"Hello, Sawati here. Dr. James Norman, an English doctor who works with the World Health Organization, will leave Kisangani in the morning with an assistant. They will travel by Land Rover and reach you by nightfall. I will follow and join them. I'm very interested in seeing Mwadaba. Over."

"Perhaps you should call Norman back and inform him I took video of the victims in the village when I was there. I could make copies—he could send one on to the WHO," Thane said. "It might be useful. Over."

"Video." Sawati paused a moment. "Have you viewed the video? Over."

"No. Why do you ask? Over."

"There is a significant possibility the radiation you received would also have damaged the tape. You should check. Over."

Thane's heart leapt into his throat. "Are you suggesting my tape is ruined? Over." In the tense moments following the Geiger counter readings and the hasty call to Sawati, the thought of potential damage to his equipment had not occurred to him.

The doctor replied in a halting apology. "I'm sorry, but I would fear the worst. My experience tells me your tape may have an image present, but most likely any picture would be streaked with particle residue from the radiation. Over."

Thane couldn't answer. He dropped his head into his hands. "Oh God."

Kuintala reached over and pushed the speaker button. "One moment."

Thane looked up at his companion. "You realize what he's saying?"

"Perhaps the video boxes . . ."

"They're not lined with lead, Kuintala. If one tape is fucked, they all are." Thane suddenly felt sick again. But this time it wasn't the radiation poisoning. A great weight settled in his chest. He knew that a professional disaster of this magnitude could affect his career. "Three months of work—absolute shit." He slapped his knee. "*Goddammit!*" Standing at the flap of the tent, Kolo witnessed the despair. "Is there something I can do?"

Kuintala reached across and gripped Thane's shoulder. "We will check them, Thane. Every one. We will hook up the battery pack and watch the video through the eyepiece." Thane marveled at the degree of empathy in his friend's eyes. Kuintala was capable of cool ferocity but also of warm compassion.

"Yes. That's exactly what we'll do." He squinted up into the sunny doorway at the camp master. "Kolo, my leather case and my camera bag are still out on your table. Could you have someone bring them? I'd do it, but I don't want to spook your men until you have time to explain our physical condition."

As Kolo left them, Thane looked over at Kuintala. "If those tapes are damaged, my deal with *International Geographic* is blown. You understand?"

Kuintala nodded solemnly. "I would help you again."

Thane felt another wave of affection for the man and patted him on the arm. "Thanks, but I know Dave Colt quite well, and he's not going to give me an extension." The *International Geographic* project manager had his own deadlines to meet. "I'd just have six days to do three months' work."

"You could call Colt and ask."

"You don't understand. The tree frog segment is also part of a subscription series that's sold to viewers. My portion can't delay the production of the mailing sequence. They would replace it with something else." Thane sighed, looking at the floor. "I was warned. In one week I'll be in breach of contract. They prepaid me for half of this project. If I have nothing to submit in return, I owe them money."

9

INTIMIDATED BY PLANE TRAVEL WITH its reservation systems and computer records, Milcho Zishov preferred the anonymity of the train. He had also looked forward to the serenity of a picturesque ride through Romania's beautiful Carpathian Mountains. The majesty of the countryside didn't disappoint. The tranquility of peaceful villages tucked among the deep green-and-gold peaks, the castles perched on crags over the valleys, were as breathtaking as he'd remembered.

Yet not even the beauty of the scenery could dispel the persistent burden of Gruschka's words.

The fortune-teller's manic reaction to what should have been a routine meeting on the shores of the Black Sea left Zishov beset by questions, questions he dared not ask Andrei Saratov, the successful commercial broker who'd arranged the export of the now-ominous cargo.

His relationship with Saratov had been quite cordial. The Ukrainian seemed normal enough, no different from hundreds of other businessmen who shipped material out of the former Soviet Union. Aside from requesting confidentiality and demanding a rigid procedure on how the transaction would be conducted, Saratov seemed straight-forward.

But then came Gruschka's hysterical outburst.

Now Zishov had his doubts. Could the gypsy woman have sensed a true calamity? Cries of the dead? What could that mean? Was Saratov responsible for some malady? Perhaps he was connected with the Russian Mafiya? Who wasn't these days? Zishov felt awkward making too many inquiries. Excessive curiosity was not only considered impolite, it could get him killed.

Arriving on schedule at the train station in Budapest, Zishov continued to mull over the mystery while he rode in the back of a cab dressed in his finely tailored pin-striped suit. As he passed through the cobblestone streets of Budapest with its early-twentieth-century metal lampposts and tightly packed buildings, he recalled his meeting with Saratov.

Only three weeks earlier the Ukrainian exporter had contacted him on his cellular phone in Varna, inviting him to visit Kiev to negotiate a highly profitable transaction.

After a one-hour plane ride, Zishov was greeted at the airport by a nattily dressed, heavy-browed man with gray hair and transparent blue eyes. This was a man of importance from the way he carried himself and the apparent expense of his cream-colored suit. The exceedingly pleasant Saratov showed Zishov estimable courtesy, and had reserved a first-class hotel room. After assisting with his check-in, Saratov treated Zishov to an expensive lunch at a gourmet restaurant. While they ate, he dabbled in social pleasantries and completely avoided talk of business. Finally Saratov had taken Zishov to a warehouse to show him the goods to be shipped.

When they arrived at the new building with its aluminum siding and fresh concrete floors, Saratov led Zishov to a back room where the six wooden crates were being packed. Only there did he divulge the terms of the agreement. Saratov made it clear he intended to save money for his client, a potter who had created fine ceramic ware. Saratov explained that shipping decorative art direct from Odessa to Cyprus would be extremely expensive. Tariffs on goods shipped from the Ukrainian seaport to Mediterranean countries could be exorbitant. But if the cargo were diverted through Bulgaria, and then shipped by Zishov to a Russian merchant named Pepkin in Cyprus, Saratov would save fourteen percent in fees, half of which he would gladly share with Zishov in addition to an extremely generous bonus for his time.

Routing goods indirectly to avoid discriminatory fees and levied taxes was not unusual, and Zishov accepted the explanation, though he remained mildly suspicious.

Saratov seemed to sense his hesitancy and encouraged him to examine the shipment as it was being crated.

As Zishov stood by, Saratov reached into a wooden crate and retrieved one of the small packets, peeling the paper back to reveal a charming statuette . . . a pigeon, Zishov had commented, pleasantly surprised as he handled the smooth hand-painted likeness.

No, Saratov replied, actually it was a dove. The potter had created several hundred of the ceramic figurines. Zishov admired the sculpture of the bird, delicately portrayed in a peaceful pose with its head under its wing. Each filament of feather, each tuft of down on the delicate fowl, was intricately etched in the finest detail.

Zishov had then taken a risk. He wanted to be assured there was nothing suspicious inside the figurines, since he would have possession of the goods for a day or two in transit. Drugs frequently found their way to other countries stuffed into otherwise innocent articles, and drug penalties in Bulgaria were severe. Zishov quickly added that he trusted Saratov of course, but what if his client, the potter, had meddled with the statues without Saratov's knowledge?

Saratov's blue eyes flared with indignation, but he responded by asking Zishov to reach inside the crate and select one of the birds at random. Somewhat taken aback, Zishov complied, whereupon Saratov hurled the package to the cement floor. Kneeling down and opening the paper, Saratov pointed to the bird.

It was clear from the shattered pieces that the figure was solid throughout. With humble apologies, Zishov agreed to the deal then and there, voicing regret over the broken statuette.

Saratov replied that the mold for the ceramic bird could make many others, and added that the destruction of one statue was well worth assuring Zishov of his credibility.

On their walk back out to his clean but simple office, Saratov stated he was in no mood to have Ukrainian authorities aware of his honest, yet unpatriotic business practices. He therefore insisted there be no further communication between them until the shipment safely left port.

That said, Saratov gave Zishov his final instructions: once the shipment was safely on board the freighter, Zishov was to receive payment in Budapest at the Magyar Empire Hotel, where Saratov would await his arrival.

Zishov was to check in, go to his room, and, to avoid any chance of the hotel lines being tapped, call Saratov on his cell phone.

They shook hands and Zishov departed, comfortable with the transaction. It was only Gruschka's strange behavior several days later that made him uncomfortable.

By the time his cab pulled into the luxurious circular drive of the Magyar Empire Hotel, Zishov had succeeded in convincing himself that Gruschka's behavior was a result of senility. He climbed from the rear seat of his taxi, deciding that he wouldn't call upon her again. Her ritual was sheer superstition anyway.

With that decided, Zishov entered the lobby of one of Europe's finest hotels. The Magyar Empire had retained much of its Byzantine charm, though the air smelled mildly of cleaning solution. Elaborate crystal chandeliers hung from the gilded high-domed ceiling that graced the foyer. Thickly woven tapestries adorned the walls of the ostentatious lobby, depicting slim-necked horses in training. Hungarian fascination with equestrian excellence hadn't changed in two centuries.

Zishov checked in at the black granite front desk, where he received his key. Then an aging bellman in a nineteenth-century red uniform showed him to a stained-glass elevator in a brass cage that ascended to the fifth floor. When they reached the room, the old fellow put the luggage on the feather bed and asked if Zishov needed extra towels.

Smiling, Zishov declined. He tipped the hunched man and ushered him to the door, then looked around the lavishly appointed room with its quilts, tasseled lampshades, and stuffed chairs.

Revitalized by the opulence, Zishov opened his suitcase and pulled his cellular phone from under a spare blue suit. He settled his clothes back into the bag and stepped to the window, phone in hand.

His larger-sized flip phone was still popular in Europe even after lightweight narrow body versions became popular in the West, and Zishov was reminded that not all businessmen in Bulgaria had a cell phone at all—for him, a matter of pride.

Zishov pushed the white linen curtain aside and looked out over the city. The hotel was situated in the new Pest section; the old-world Buda area lay off to his left across the river. The famous blue Danube was gray under a cloudy sky.

Zishov was pleased he could see the buildings of the old EXPO World's Fair on the banks of the river. He would make a point to go see the exhibition after meeting with Saratov.

He fumbled for the number in his vest pocket, the small piece of yellow paper with its pencil scratchings. There it was, with the number . . . 974-2281.

Zishov pushed the power button. The phone beeped cheerfully and displayed a blinking red dot on the LED. He had a signal.

He held the phone chest high and dialed 9, 7, 4, 2, 2, 8 . . .

As his finger depressed the key for the last number, Zishov lost sight of his hand, which had inexplicably blossomed into a bloody red mist.

Instantly headless, his singed body was blasted back into the room, where it landed on the smoking bed.

Zishov's pride and joy, his cellular phone, had exploded.

10

ENGROSSED IN HER THOUGHTS, DANIELLE sat on the stairs listening to soft jazz as she sanded the rounded surface of a staircase baluster.

Her arms were already covered with a fine multicolored dust from the many shades of paint she had removed from the balustrade.

Working on her projects helped dispel the tensions of the day, and though she could have spent time painting the wainscoting in the dining room, or laid out the parquet design for her entry floor, she had chosen to sand instead, needing the physical exertion.

Danielle would frequently meet her best friend Melanie Kamin for a cocktail after work, but today she had come straight home, because Melanie, a buyer for a large publishing chain, had left for a literary convention in Europe.

After an unusually hectic commute, Danielle was relieved to arrive at the two-story Victorian house that she'd purchased just six months ago. The structure, originally built in 1893 and remodeled in 1932, was located in what was considered a "transitional" neighborhood. Depressed and dangerous during the eighties, Conklin Avenue had burgeoned with life in the last few years. New construction dotted the street that wound up the hill overlooking the distant Boston skyline.

Of all the restored houses in the vicinity, Danielle felt hers was the most dazzling, largely because it was a colorful Queen Anne, and the first of many homes Danielle hoped to restore over the course of her life.

As she pulled up to the curb in the fading rays of the evening sun, Danielle had paused on the front walk to admire her cheery peach-colored house. Its wide white eaves and multiple gables were festively highlighted by a burnt-sienna-and-melon trim. The porch was accented by a curved swan's neck pediment over a beautiful oak stained-glass quarter-paneled front door.

Once inside, Danielle hung her raincoat on the cypress coat rack in the spacious yet unfinished entry, and climbed the stairs to her bedroom. She kicked off her heels, removed her chocolate-colored business suit, and peeled off her nylons and bra.

She shook the French twist from her red hair and rummaged through her walnut burl dresser until she found her favorite frayed blue jeans. She stepped into the faded Diesel jeans and then sat down on the white wicker footlocker that served as a laundry basket.

As she tied the laces on her paint-spotted deck shoes, she caught sight of her hassled expression in the full-length antique mirror.

She forced herself to smile, to let go. She took a deep breath, and let her arms drop to her sides. Then taking a position in front of the mirror with her feet apart, she rotated at the waist, loosening the kinks in her lower back. Tilting her head from side to side, she eased the muscles in her neck as she watched herself stretch. Her excellent posture continued to accentuate her youthful shape. She was tall yet delicately boned and had been blessed with a slender neck, smooth shoulders, well-shaped breasts, a narrow waist, and long legs. Almost identical to Damita in stature and even an inch taller, she could easily have become the fashion model that Damita had wanted to be. And though Danielle had used her intelligence rather than her figure to achieve success, she was keenly aware of her professional appearance; something she'd sharpened over time, a weapon in the combat they called advertising.

No combat here, she thought, as she peered out into her bedroom with its large four-poster bed, the matching rosewood provincial dresser, and the Bradbury & Bradbury floor-to-ceiling wallpaper. She had decorated the room herself, adding delicate touches: a hand-painted commode set on the bureau and bronze French light fixtures on the wall on either side of the bed.

Danielle found her favorite shirt hung on a hook on the back of the door, a ragged Cambridge University rugby sweatshirt Clayton had given her on a rainy weekend. The battered jersey was torn under both arms and spotted with paint. The splotches on the sleeves documented all the different hues she had used while painting her second floor: aqua, green, fuchsia, and amber. Danielle loved the colors of the Queen Anne style, something she had not experienced until she'd been in Clayton's home on Long Island. His beautifully restored baby blue Revival Colonial had inspired her, and though Clayton was gone, she had taken great satisfaction in restoration herself, welcoming its echoes of a prior happiness.

Now suitably grubby and not hungry enough for a full dinner, Danielle had moved on to her unfinished downstairs kitchen for a glass of cold apple juice and a few bites of Jack cheese. She located her medium-grade sandpaper in the toolbox on the basement landing. Then, since her favorite radio station played uninterrupted soft jazz in the evening, she turned on the large antique radio that sat on the mantel of the blue-tiled fireplace. With the mood set and her toolbox in hand, she stepped into the hall, ready for work.

The Italian hanging stairs descended dramatically from the top floor to the entry. Once finished they would again be magnificent, the highlight of the house. The black walnut balusters had been imported from Germany, according to the home's original blueprints acquired from the Boston Historical Society. Each one could have easily been displayed as a separate work of art. They were skillfully doweled, shaped like long narrow chess pieces, each a tall bishop. And fortunately, though the balustrade had been painted many times over the decades, the banister's handrail itself had remained untouched, retaining a pleasant shaded patina. It was Danielle's plan to stain the walnut uprights but leave the rail natural. She intended to finish the stairs in a rich maroon riverboat carpet she had bought at an auction.

Restoration of each detail of the house had become an act of love. For Danielle, stress relief came through menial tasks. As she worked, she would systematically rehash the day's events, and now she pondered the implications of Finelli's rude and abrupt departure, and her subsequent phone call to Corbonne.

She had tried to reach the CEO of Othello immediately, but was unable to do so until after lunch. Corbonne's response to her concerns indicated that Finelli had reached him first—Corbonne remained friendly yet detached, asserting his support for his cousin. Politely and firmly, Corbonne stated that Finelli would make all marketing decisions from now on, including the need for an agency review.

Corbonne had concluded the conversation by expressing his gratitude for Danielle's efforts during the last year, but made it clear that Finelli's policies must be honored. If an incompatibility in management style surfaced, the agency would either adjust or be passed over.

She remembered Finelli's expression during the meeting—the vindictive gleam in his dark eyes. Had she threatened him somehow? Perhaps her status bothered him? She definitely made a better executive than he did. Some businessmen couldn't deal with that. He had cynically referred to her as the "bright new star at the agency."

"Your ego versus mine," he had said—words that drew a line in the sand. Of course, Damita's phone call had robbed her of the one-on-one she desperately needed at the time, giving Finelli the perfect excuse to leave.

As she finished the first baluster, she resolved to see Corbonne personally. By the time she finished the second, she had devised a plan to devote all her agency resources to a new presentation so she could retain the account.

She had almost finished a third when her arms grew tired. She checked her watch. Almost nine. She'd had enough therapy and enough rumination. Tomorrow was another day.

After using a small whisk broom to sweep up, she put the toolbox away in the kitchen. She munched on an apple, nibbled some more cheese and crackers, and grabbed a bottle of Merlot from the pantry. Drawn to the music in the living room, she found her favorite spot by the fireplace, a Louisiana-walnut-and-peeled-oak rocking chair.

The lights of Boston twinkled in the distance through her living room bay window as she sat back in the rocker sipping the wine.

She closed her eyes, losing herself in the drone of the sax as it oozed past the synth vibe to take the lead, accompanied by bass and piano. For a few precious moments she attained the desired serenity. The muscles in her legs relaxed as the darkness behind her eyes gently spun around. Black turned to blue, navy blue like the ocean . . . Images of sails on the Long Island Sound filled her mind. Pinpoints of white bobbing on an eternal sea. She had found love with Clayton out there. Life had glistened and sparkled. She struggled with the images, began to feel the sorrow again, but soon mercifully dozed off.

The radio station ended its broadcast at midnight, and the sudden silence jerked Danielle back to reality. She found herself slouched in the rocker with an empty wineglass balanced in her lap.

She sat up, her mouth dry with sleep. She contemplated having more wine, but decided against it. She would have to be mentally alert tomorrow, when she would see Corbonne after she collected Damita from her New London home.

She wasn't looking forward to her trip to Connecticut, to a house she had never seen, occupied by a man she had never met.

Danielle stretched and turned off the radio, scooped up the wineglass, and headed for the kitchen. En route, she paused to check the pictures in the hall.

In the dim light she could barely see the faded color photographs. One showed her mother and father two decades ago on a swing slung from the huge walnut tree in the front yard of their Ohio home. Next to it was a snapshot of Danielle and Damita gloating over their collie, Maxie. They were just in their teens. Danielle smiled. Damita still had freckles in those days. Back then it seemed so easy to have fun.

She stared pensively into Damita's bright blue eyes—eyes very much like her own, though hers had been described as kelly green. What a shame "Dee and Danny" weren't as alike in spirit as they'd been in their appearance.

The rift between the sisters had begun when Danielle was twenty-five and Damita twenty-three and they were sharing a flat in New York. Dynamos of energy and ambition, the two young women craved new experiences. A dreamer like her mother, Damita's fantasies consumed her. Her political science degree went to waste as she was drawn to the glitz and glamour of modeling. In contrast, Danielle, like her stubborn and determined father, had utilized her business administration degree to gain employment as a senior secretary.

Danielle's situation improved dramatically when she met Clayton Muir in a bar. It was Clayton, a product development genius for Cunningham & Walsh, who introduced her to advertising and gave her talent a rightful home at his agency. Her career blossomed. Flushed with her newfound success, Danielle consulted Clayton and offered Damita a position at the agency. Damita refused and pulled further away. She fell into a superficial arty crowd, hung around singles bars. Looking back, Danielle blamed herself for not reacting to Damita's withdrawal. Perhaps she should have been more aware of Damita's cycle of nightly parties and recreational drugs.

Admittedly, Damita had been elusive and Danielle had had enough to think about, namely, a new career and a budding love affair. With Clayton, Danielle had an addiction of her own—a whole new world had opened up. The young woman from the midwestern plains now spent her leisure time sailing with a man from New England, in Clayton's sleek sloop, the *Fascination*. She loved the feeling of freedom, scooting across the waves, sharing the excitement of the sea with the man she loved. The memories resembled the stuff movies were made of: the fury of white foam, the glorious wind in her hair, and warm embraces at the helm.

Unfortunately, the fascination and the rush of that adoration ceased in one horrifying moment a few miles from Newport, Rhode Island.

Returning from a sailing regatta alone in his car, Clayton was killed in a head-on collision when a drunk driver in a flatbed truck crossed the line on a two-lane beach road. While the other man escaped with minor cuts on his legs, Clayton's Porsche was ripped in half.

After Clayton's death, Danielle had had no one to turn to. With her mother succumbing to Alzheimer's and Damita only distantly sympathetic, Danielle had fought the depths of her despair by burying herself in work. Day after determined day, she gutted it out, constructing a fortress of success. When the opportunity at HCD Advertising came, she fled the memories at Cunningham & Walsh and blew into Boston for the big bucks. With her newfound power, Danielle was once again able to offer Damita a job, but Damita declined, already set on marrying Hassan Salaar.

Now things seemed to be finally changing. Danielle had healed somewhat and Damita was asking for assistance.

The first step was to get Damita away from the abuse—abuse that seemed real enough, judging from the bruises. But what about this other nonsense? Someone talking murder in the garden? Perhaps Damita imagined that. Maybe she'd had one too many martinis and conjured ghosts that weren't there.

Danielle straightened the photograph and patted Damita's likeness on the cheek with a forefinger. She made her way down the hall to the kitchen and put the wineglass in the sink.

It was time for bed. She turned off the lights just as the telephone on the counter rang.

Surprised anyone would disturb her at this hour, she answered brusquely, "This is Wilkes."

"Ms. *Danielle* Wilkes?" a man's voice asked on the other end.

"No solicitations, please." She almost hung up, but the voice responded quickly.

"This is an emergency."

Danielle tried to fathom the word, thinking of her partners' itineraries. Hampton would be home from LA. Where would Coolidge be? "Who is this?"

"This is Officer Reynolds, ma'am, New London Police Department. The Tarrington Nursing Home gave us your number."

Danielle still fought the fog. "Oh, God. Mother."

"No, no. *Missus* Wilkes is fine." The officer hesitated. "It's your sister. Her Mercedes was found partially submerged in Dimmick Creek near Goshen Cove. Seems the car went through the guardrail."

Danielle clutched her throat. "Oh Jesus, how is she?"

"We don't know. There's a team setting up to drag downstream."

Tears welled instantly. Images of flashing lights on the riverbank. Wreckage in the water. "What? You mean she wasn't—"

"No, ma'am, not in the car."

"Then you don't know if she's alive..."

"We don't. There's blood on the dashboard and the windshield was blown out. She must not have been wearing a seat belt."

Overwhelmed, Danielle tearfully tried to make sense of the conversation. "You're sure it was her car?"

"Registration says so."

"Anyone else with her?"

"No sign of it."

"What about her husband?"

"We've called the Salaar home, got an answering service. We have a black-and-white on its way there, now."

"I'm coming down."

"The car is just being towed away, ma'am, there won't be much to see. Why don't you call me in the morning? My name's Reynolds. You can reach me at the New London station house. Hopefully we'll have more answers by then."

"Answers," she said, numbly. A corpse he meant. Damita's remains pulled from dank water. "She must be alive." Danielle found herself envisioning her sister partially submerged, clinging to the brush on the riverbank. "You're going to keep looking, aren't you?"

"As long as there's a reasonable—"

"Don't stop. Did you hear me, goddammit? Don't you stop looking until I get there. I'm leaving now."

DAY TWELVE

11

BEYOND THE CAMP IN THE hills, diggers, and graders could be heard churning the earth.

Thane would have given anything to be out in the open air shooting video instead of sulking in the stagnant air of the equipment tent.

The heat of the sun radiated down through the canvas ceiling onto Thane's bare shoulders as Dr. James Norman, dressed in a khaki smock, moved his stethoscope up Thane's back.

"Breathe deeply," Norman said softly. "Good. And again." The doctor spoke in a genial, deep voice as his fingers tapped repeatedly below Thane's shoulder blades.

Thane liked the curly dark-haired Englishman immediately.

Norman's pleasant broad face and rather widely spaced blue eyes expressed a welcome empathy. Norman's young associate, on the other hand, seemed skeptical and arrogant. A sharp-tongued French medical-research volunteer named Paul Pardux, he was taking notes nearby.

Norman again moved the stethoscope to Thane's lower back. "One more breath. And one last time. Excellent."

Seated on two stacked crates, Thane tried not to think about his ruined video. He and Kuintala had checked all the tapes and each one showed signs of radioactive tracing. Thane estimated that only three minutes of clean foot-age remained out of over three hundred and twenty minutes of exposure. Even the brief viewable sections were ragged—well below broadcast quality.

Thane nodded to his partner, who sat cross-legged on the floor. Even more than Thane, Kuintala seemed devastated by the ruined work. After they had viewed the video, Thane had tried to quiet Kuintala's disappointment.

As Norman completed his examination, Thane forced a grin, making eye contact. In response, Kuintala mustered a half smile, then glanced up at Norman, awaiting the doctor's comments.

Norman's lips were pressed pensively together as he sidestepped the comer of the table and faced Thane. He seemed mildly disturbed. "While Kuintala sounds perfectly dry, Mr. Adams, you're congested in the bronchial tubes."

"Am I? Well, I'm getting over a sinus infection, maybe some of that sunk into the chest."

Norman nodded slowly, then his face relaxed in relief. "Ahhh, yes. That's possible. Good. Then it may mean nothing after all. Many viruses travel to the lower respiratory area in latter stages."

"Well, that aside, Doctor, do you see any radiation damage?"

"Only slight signs of irritation. Your pulse is a bit elevated and your skin appears slightly flushed, but other than that, no. Has your nausea left you? How do you feel tonight?"

"No nausea." Thane glanced over. "You feel better, Kuintala?"

His associate put a hand to his chest. "Stronger."

"Stronger? What? The nausea?" Pardux asked redundantly, standing in the background. He was a strange bird in a tight black T-shirt revealing burly arms with fleur-de-lis tattoos on both biceps. Kuintala's lack of response seemed to bother the Frenchman. "I asked if you are still nauseous."

"He's fine." Thane reached down for his shirt that he had folded on his lap and began to put it on.

Norman restrained him with a pat on the arm. "That scar on your back," he said sympathetically, "that's quite a bum." Thane nodded. "Have you considered reconstructive surgery?" Norman asked.

"I have." Thane stuffed his arms into the short-sleeved shirt.

"It might remove the damage completely."

"Maybe later."

"Why wait?"

"I guess I've decided to heal myself from the inside out."

Norman locked on Thane's eyes, contemplating the response. "Oh, I see."

"How did you burn yourself?" Pardux asked, tapping the pencil on the pad.

His black bangs were drenched with perspiration.

Thane began buttoning his shirt. "I don't think that's pertinent."

"You are involved in a WHO investigation," Pardux said curtly.

"So are you," Thane replied. "Did I ask how you got your tattoos?"

Norman sensed the rising tension. "The radiation. Do either of you have a theory about it?" he asked, looking from Kuintala to Thane.

Thane shrugged. "No. Do you?"

Norman hesitated, looked over at Pardux, almost embarrassed. "A few. Although they're quite unorthodox. We've been so attuned to virology in the past, it's odd to speculate about something so different. This Mwadaba business raises somewhat unfamiliar issues."

"Which are?" Thane asked.

"Massive contamination that isn't biologically endemic. You see, here in Congo we've been almost exclusively assaulted by natural plagues that arise from the rain forest. I came in during the Kikwit epidemic—a cleanup man, you might say." Norman bent down and tucked the stethoscope into the black bag that sat on the dirt floor.

Thane swung his legs around and faced him. "Nasty business."

"Requiring constant vigilance."

"So you don't believe something natural killed Mwadaba's people?" Thane asked.

"Well, there have been cases of natural radiation poisoning among miners on occasion, but no, in Mwadaba, I think it's man-made." Norman gave his associate a nod. "Pardux is convinced the residents of the village may have found a dangerous toy."

"A toy?" Kuintala spoke up, visibly incensed by the word's levity.

"Not in the true sense of the word," Norman replied. "We mean something the villagers may have found that captivated them . . . an errant radioactive device dropped from a plane."

"Like a nuclear bomb," Pardux said casually.

Thane considered the suggestion far-fetched. "There was no sign of anything like that."

"In a hut perhaps?" Pardux added.

"As I recall, most nuclear devices carried by aircraft weigh a ton or more." Thane directed the comment to Norman. "Not easily moved."

"Dead elephants weigh more than that." Pardux's black eyes blinked dismissively, as he scribbled something on his note pad. "Tribes manage to move them. A bomb might be considered a fascinating keepsake."

Thane glanced at Kuintala, who sat with his eyes downcast, having tuned out. Thane found Pardux's suppositions ludicrous. "Are you seriously suggesting that a thermonuclear device fell and cracked open somehow?"

"Perhaps the villagers opened the device."

"Before speculating, wouldn't it be logical to check if a bomb's been reported missing?"

"With whom? The United States?" Pardux asked dryly. "I doubt they would admit it."

"Oh, and I suppose France would?" Thane shrugged. "Come to think of it, France might. They've been bold enough about their illegal nuclear testing over the years."

"France isn't the issue here. I think the radiation is an American problem."

"And why?"

"Who else but your country still flies nuclear equipment through the stratosphere without respect for the sovereignty of the nations below?"

"God," Thane said in disbelief, "we don't even have a sound diagnosis and you're trying to create an international incident."

"That's because I work for an international organization." Pardux smirked. "I am not required to bow at the knee of les Etats-Unis."

"Oh, I get it. A Yankee hater." Thane smiled helplessly at Norman. "A political activist in the heart of the jungle." Norman turned patiently to Pardux. "Mr. Pardux, perhaps we could restrict our discussion to medical issues."

Kuintala had apparently had his fill. He turned toward the tent flap and looked back. "Adams, I'm hungry. Let's eat."

"We're not finished here," Pardux said, reddening.

Thane began edging toward Kuintala. "Good," he said to Pardux, "you and Norman have a rousing discussion about some wayward B-1 that used Mwadaba as ground zero."

Dr. Norman stepped forward, restraining him apologetically with a hand on the elbow. "Mr. Adams, we may be out of our element, but bear with us, please."

"There's nothing more to say."

Norman's eyes rounded with concern. "There must be. We're required to radio back our initial impressions this evening. The WHO wishes to make sure there is no cause for undue panic."

"Well, panic might be a damn good idea," Thane said, pointing west through the tent wall. "Someone ought to get pretty excited about that pile of dead people out there." He glanced at Kuintala. "But we've had our share of that, and I've told you what I know."

"Allow me one more speculation," Norman pleaded.

In response, Pardux had moved a step toward the tent flap as if to block the exit.

Kuintala's eyes clouded with impatience, but Thane reluctantly complied. He folded his arms, leaned back against the card table, and watched Norman's desert boots raise small puffs of dust as he began to pace. "Let's put Pardux's argument aside for a moment," he said, rubbing his chin with his forefinger. "From what you saw, could the villagers have been poisoned?"

"Poisoned? You mean in the common sense of the word?"

"Not exactly. I'm talking about an accident that may have occurred due to people's naïveté." Norman's hands clasped as if in prayer. "I realize an autopsy will reveal much of this, but until proper lead-lined gear arrives, we're left to rely on your impressions. Now, from the presumed suddenness of the event, can you imagine that the entire tribe might have ingested . . . well, something like a plutonium cocktail?"

"All of them? Eaten something radioactive?" Thane found himself again doubting the doctor's judgment. "Would that cause the residue on the outer skin I described? The external swelling?"

"Epidermal necrosis may have been secondary to the initial internal damage. Conjecture, of course. But since we don't yet know the exact time of exposure, or how soon you arrived upon the scene, those external symptoms you saw could have developed over hours, even days."

Fatigued, Thane sought the capping statement. "Doctor, perhaps you'll determine these things tomorrow morning when you see Mwadaba yourself."

A voice from the rear interrupted. "And Judapi." Everyone turned toward the tent flap. A ruddy black man in his mid-forties in a remarkably clean white shirt had walked in and stood unsmiling, measuring each of them. Kolo, the sweating camp master, crowded in from behind, stating the obvious.

"Dr. Sawati is here."

"How do you do." Sawati nodded all around.

"What's this about Judapi?" Norman's eyes squinted as he stepped forward to accept Sawati's extended hand.

Sawati made the rounds, walking from man to man, shaking hands and searching their faces as he spoke. "Our speculation will have to include the village of Judapi, where similar mass deaths have occurred . . . bodies partially decomposed, some beyond recognition."

"Judapi. Where the hell's Judapi?" Thane asked.

"Judapi lies on the banks of the Chicapa River close to the Angolan border, some eighty miles northeast of Mwadaba. Prior to my leaving Likasi, a transmission arrived from Dilolo. Hunters just returning from the Judapi region had reported a situation not unlike Mwadaba. Damage appears more severe."

Kuintala spoke up. "And the hunters?"

"Both extremely ill from radiation poisoning."

Kuintala flinched at the pronouncement. "Bad? Worse than us?"

"One of them may die."

Visibly shaken by the news, Dr. Norman stared up the tent pole. "Good God. What could possibly have caused all this?"

No one answered Norman's question. With the sunset waning, a sea of crickets could be heard outside the tent as each man contemplated Sawati's announcement. Whatever had happened in Mwadaba was apparently on the move.

"Well, Mr. Pardux?" Thane glanced at the French researcher. "What do you think . . . two bombs? Two fascinating toys dropped from the skies eighty miles apart?"

12

DANIELLE LINGERED AT THE TOP OF the bank looking down into the black water twenty feet below. Dimmick Creek was more like a small lazy river. The unhurried current moved southward as reeds and tall grasses on either side were bathed in pulsing waves of red and blue light from the cop cars on the road.

Downstream some hundred yards, lights from the police boat panned the waters. As divers surfaced, an occasional splash echoed through the night. The continuing search concentrated on the immediate area of the accident since a body wouldn't have moved very far in the slow-moving stream.

After answering Danielle's questions, Officer Reynolds, a man in his late thirties with graying dark hair, brown eyes, and a perpetual five o'clock shadow, had returned to his car, sensing Danielle's need to be alone.

A metal guardrail, its bolts twisted at one end, had been ripped from a wooden post and now hung in space at a rakish angle, suspended over the bank. Tire marks on the embankment and gravel strewn on the roadway showed where a tow truck had pulled the vehicle out of the mud at the creek's edge.

But near the bent guardrail there was no sign of a vehicle having lost control—no skid marks, no gouges in the dirt. Reynolds had said that the car had probably left the highway at around forty-five miles an hour.

Adjusting the collar of her raincoat, Danielle looked back at the pavement where investigators had drawn chalk lines on the asphalt, showing the assumed angle of the careen. The Mercedes seemed to have traveled on the opposite side of the road for some distance. Judging from the angle at which it struck the guardrail, Reynolds guessed the driver was probably asleep at the wheel.

Reynolds had asked about Damita's habits. Had she been a heavy drinker?

Danielle asked the reason for the question. Reynolds quietly replied that a broken bottle of Absolut Vodka had been found in the front seat.

Nodding, Danielle admitted that it was possible, at least recently. Damita's morning martini at Toffler's Inn gave some credence to that. Yet the entire scenario made little sense. And where had Hassan been?

The gravel crunched and Reynolds removed his hat as he approached Danielle. She looked off and wiped away the tears. Damita's accident had stirred an overwhelming sense of remorse, particularly since their last meeting was a petty, pointless exchange. Danielle would have given anything for a chance to relive that moment.

"Ms. Wilkes," Reynolds said softly as if he were disturbing someone asleep. He held his hat in his hands, his hair curled and matted from the night's humidity. He blinked his long eyelashes as he looked out over the creek. "Don't you think you might . . . ?"

Danielle chose to ignore his hints that she should leave. "Was anyone home at the Salaar house?" she asked instead.

Reynolds nodded. 'The officers finally roused a servant woman named Astia. Apparently the house is like a fort, fenced and secured."

"And?"

"Astia says your sister's husband left for Greece."

"He left?"

"Earlier today. I guess he's an importer?"

'That's right. But you're sure he's gone? Did your men search the house?"

Reynolds seemed surprised at the suggestion. "Without due cause?"

"Due cause?" Danielle asked, angrily. "What if this is a homicide?"

"What?" Reynolds glared at her. "Maybe there's something you know that I don't, Ms. Wilkes, but at this point there's no suggestion of foul play here. There's some logic to the accident. Namely the blown-out windshield, the victim's blood on the dash and the bottle."

"Damita said that he beat her."

"Well, if there are any prior claims—"

"Is a black eye claim enough?" Danielle turned to face him. "I saw it." She tried to control her frustration. "Just tell me how you're making arrangements to contact him." Reynolds shrugged. "My precinct is sending a fax to Athens to an office the servant woman mentioned. He was expected to call there in the next day or two."

"The next day or two? What the hell am I supposed to do for the next day or two? Can't you—"

She was interrupted as an approaching police boat changed the pitch of its engines, training its four lights up the bank. Danielle shielded her eyes and made out several silhouettes in the flat-bottomed boat. "Reynolds!" someone yelled.

Reynolds waved. "Over here."

"Found something."

"Oh, God." Danielle stepped to the edge of the grass. She was about to descend the slippery mud bank, but Reynolds grabbed her by the arm, pulling her back up.

"Wait a second," Reynolds said, "please." He slid down the bank sideways, grabbing the tops of the reeds. The skiff's motor wound down. A diver in a black wet suit sat on the stem with his mask pushed up on his forehead. Two officers stood nearby, one running the lights and the other with his hand on a long tiller. Reynolds reached the water's edge and grabbed the craft as it nudged the bank. The man running the lights stepped to the bow and handed something to Reynolds, who examined it, then spoke softly as Danielle waited impatiently.

"What is it?" Danielle shouted.

"I'm coming," Reynolds replied, waving. He began to climb up the hill with the item tucked under his arm. Dew spotted his slacks as he reached the top, breathing hard. He straightened up and presented the article.

Danielle gasped, recognizing it immediately.

"Was this hers?" Reynolds asked.

His use of the past tense struck Danielle like a blow. She took the object and couldn't speak, barely able to nod.

Danielle lifted the clasp and opened the first flap, releasing some water that dribbled onto the gravel shoulder at her feet. Silt had smudged the clear plastic that held the driver's license.

As she wiped the mud away, Danielle stared at Damita's picture in the teal-colored lizard clutch purse that Damita had carried during their last meeting at Toffler's Inn only two days before.

DAY ELEVEN

13

"YANNI MANDRAKOS." THE VOICE ON the Olympic Airways public-address system was paging him. "Please call extension eleven."

Mandrakos sat with other maintenance personnel in the gray freshly painted forty-foot lunchroom of hangar three. He checked the white-faced wall clock. The black hands showed that he had twenty-two minutes left on his lunch hour, enough time to take the call. He took a last bite and rolled the rest of the grape leaves, rice, and lamb into a tight ball in the wax paper. The leftovers would make an excellent late-afternoon snack. He stuffed the food into a small paper sack and tucked it into his coveralls.

Whistling happily, Mandrakos stepped to the wall phone and dialed the intercom extension.

A woman's voice answered in Greek. "Main switchboard."

"Mandrakos here, you paged me?"

"You have a visitor at the east gate."

"Visitor? Who?"

"A relative. Do you want me to check with the guard?"

"No. I'll walk over. Thank you."

As Mandrakos hung up, he realized he had to relieve himself.

Visitors were rare. And no relative had ever come to his work place. Who would be passing through? Certainly not his mother. He had just seen her last Thursday. The only possibility would be his cousin Nikolo, who lived in

Khalkis. Or his nephew, Phillipos. Either one of them could have chosen to come to Athens to say hello.

He stopped by the rest room at the rear of the dining area, used the urinal, and then viewed his face in the mirror over the sinks. As he brushed a hand through his curly black hair, he wiped a bit of grease from the corner of his mouth. Then, it occurred to him. He stared into his own brown eyes. Perhaps this wasn't a visitor at all. Perhaps it was a messenger from Hercule, or Hercule himself. Perhaps Mandrakos would finally be asked to complete his small task, a limited but important part of the much larger mission he might never understand.

The realization made his stomach ball up.

Nervously, he went to his green locker at the far end of the men's room. His fingers felt numb as he fussed with the combination lock. Stop it, he thought. Stop acting like a civilian. You're a soldier in an army. You knew that. His mind spun in circles and he realized that for no reason at all, he had paused to stick the wax paper ball of lamb and rice onto the top shelf, a diversionary act, something to delay what might be the inevitable encounter.

If it is Hercule . . .

"So be it," Mandrakos said aloud. He had known this would come. His brother Stavros knew it as well. You've been compensated in advance, he thought. Mother's operation was paid for when you asked for help. You were given extra financing on occasion, when you requested it.

He closed the door, made his way out the side door of the hangar, and began to walk the hundred and fifty meters across the tarmac to the east gate. The smell of jet fumes wafted over from a taxiing DELTA 767. The American aircraft reminded him of his brother, and the commitment they had both made.

As members of an aggressive yet secretive underground Communist party in Greece, Mandrakos and his younger brother Stavros had attended meetings, loyally supporting their recruiting program. In fact, because they both worked as maintenance personnel for Olympic Airways, the brothers were considered highly valuable to the cause; after all, airports played an important role in international affairs.

He was proud that he and Stavros, the Mandrakos brothers, were known among members of the party as fighters, men of zeal, not highly educated, but solid, reliable workers. Four years ago, he and Stavros were approached by Hercule, an international agent of the Communist party. They heard the terms of a proposal and proudly accepted. Understanding the benefits to his mother and his family in general, Stavros had transferred to Olympic Airways in the United States without regret, and both the Mandrakos brothers knew that one day in the future, they would be called upon to serve. When that time came, they were told, there could be no more contact between Stavros and his family until the mission was finished.

As he approached the gate, Mandrakos squinted, trying to see past the guard shack. Through the chain-link fence, he noticed a shiny blue SAAB sitting on the opposite side of the street. Clearly, the visitor was no relative.

Vyssiz, the stocky security guard, saw him coming and stepped forward with a clipboard. "Mr. Mandrakos"—Vyssiz pointed—"your uncle asked that you join him in the car."

"Thank you," Mandrakos said, signing the clipboard. As he shuffled across the asphalt, the driver's-side window rolled down. A pudgy hand waved him to the passenger side. He went around the car and got in.

The tan leather interior of the vehicle was obscured by the six-foot bulky frame of the man at the wheel. "I apologize," Hercule said as he creaked the driver's seat with his weight. "I know this is unexpected."

"I am always ready to see you," Mandrakos said, then realized he was wringing his hands in his lap. He quickly set one on each knee.

"Things have accelerated. Not on our end." Hercule's cologne filled the car. He wore his usual blue suit and black fedora with a broad headband. "In the US, itineraries have changed. You don't really need to know." Through members of the party, Mandrakos had heard rumors about Hercule. Originally Algerian and a former KGB agent, the well-traveled man used no last name and was said to have no emotions.

"I came to see you today because the materials for transfer will arrive this afternoon on a flight from Nicosia, a black leather pouch checked through by one of my associates on Mediterranean flight 312." Hercule handed him a small green stub. "Although you won't need it, here is the claim check."

Mandrakos looked at the small tab in his hand. "How did you—?"

"It's a forgery. Early check-in allowed my operative to email my computer here in Athens, where we scanned and printed it. The claim check is a precaution in case you are bothered by curious security personnel."

"I should get this bag?"

"Yes. We prefer you take it off the conveyor before it reaches baggage claim. But if not, use the tab to retrieve it. Put the contents in your locker."

"For how long?"

"Your Olympic Airways flight 44 nonstop to New York departs this evening. An Airbus, if I'm not mistaken."

"As always."

Hercule shrugged. "Will you be one of the ground crew?"

"Janitorial duties."

"Well, do as we planned."

"In first class?"

"Yes. Only in first class."

"How many are there?"

"Thirty-nine," Hercule said, frowning. "You'll be pleased to know that outwardly, they look completely harmless, like plastic flash drives."

"And these small containers . . ."

"Hold photo files. They even have a small logo on the lids. Quite unassuming."

"Are they very important to the greater cause?" Mandrakos asked, out of pride and because he knew so little about their ultimate use.

"Without them, the dove of freedom cannot take flight." Though it sounded somewhat vague to Mandrakos, the phrase was adequately inspiring and bolstered his determination. "Has my brother Stavros been informed?" he asked, eagerly.

"Do not bother yourself."

"No, I know, no contact whatsoever, but you can understand my curiosity."

"Be assured, our American comrades have been in touch with Stavros this morning," Hercule said, studying his manicured nails. "The Internet is a marvelous thing. Stavros will retrieve the containers during his maintenance duties just as you will have placed them. He has already been given a drop point." Hercule put a hand on Mandrakos's knee. "I want you to know the party is very grateful for your efforts. You have helped us avoid needless scrutiny of luggage arriving in the US. I congratulate you." With that, the thick-cheeked Hercule leaned back with a satisfied look on his face, put his hands on the steering wheel, and stared at Mandrakos.

"Is that it?" Mandrakos asked, almost embarrassed. "Yes. If done correctly, it completes your obligation." "Good. I mean, I'm ready." Mandrakos nervously noticed the time on Hercule's Rolex. "I must get back." He grabbed the passenger door handle.

"By all means." Hercule smiled as Mandrakos began to slide out. But at the last moment, the big man put a hand on his arm. "Incidentally, I stopped by and said hello to your mother on my way here. I'm delighted she feels so well. I'm happy we continue to remain influential in her care." Mandrakos caught the glint in Hercule's gray eyes. "I am too, Hercule. Grateful to you and the party."

"Good fortune then, Yanni. Do well."

Mandrakos smiled as best he could, then tucked the luggage tab in his overalls as he crossed the street, feeling Hercule's gaze on his back. As the car pulled away, Mandrakos waved. He stepped up to the guard, took the clipboard and signed in.

"Your uncle drives a nice car," Vyssiz said.

"He is an influential man," Mandrakos said as he walked away.

As he recrossed the tarmac, his mind turned to the task at hand. Tonight, during the routine cleanup of flight forty-four, he would be able to unzip the seats and tuck the small zip drives into the underside panel of each cushion. He felt confident the cartridges would be small enough that passengers would never notice as they sat sipping their champagne.

13

THE INDIAN-SUMMER HEAT HUNG HEAVILY over New England.

Night rains had washed the coastline following a series of thunderstorms.

Because the air conditioner had malfunctioned, Danielle had opened the windows and lay naked under a bare sheet. She had dozed earlier for a few hours, but now sleep was impossible.

Occasional passing headlights illuminated the textured ceiling of the motel room, giving the craggy mortar the look of a flattened moonscape. As her restless mind tripped through memories of Damita, her eyes explored the plaster pockmarks above her head.

Fighting an intense loneliness, Danielle hungered for any new shred of evidence that might support the faintest possibility that Damita was alive.

The night had yielded no further feedback, no word from Damita's husband. The servants at the Salaar home had given an Athens phone number to the police—an unpronounceable business office where Hassan was to check in. But his departure remained mysterious. Damita would have mentioned his leaving, particularly since, anticipating Danielle's visit, she would have been relieved that he'd be away.

Though Danielle had struggled with exhaustion while driving back to Boston, something else compelled her to stop. Perhaps it was the lack of closure, the sense of incompleteness. Whatever instinct coerced her, she had opted to delay, lingering on the north side of New London, where she had registered at the motel around 1:15 A.M.

Now she had been awake for over an hour assessing the crisis. She realized that the lack of tangible proof in Damita's disappearance would probably plague her for life. The longer she waited, the wider the gap would be. Reynolds had been supportive, yet professionally distant, and she had to find someone else to talk to . . . someone who could shed further light on the mystery. Danielle felt odd bothering her friend Melanie Kamin in Europe on this strange matter, yet she had no other family except her mother, Margaret. Danielle dreaded visiting Mom to inform her about the accident. She envisioned driving the sixty miles to the Tarrington Nursing Home in northern Connecticut only to find her mother unable to understand what had happened.

The longer Danielle lay in that bed, the more incensed she became. The feelings of helplessness were driving her crazy. She had to do something, anything. In a fit of frustration she rolled and found herself face-to-face with the phone on the laminated nightstand. Her handbag sat beside it. That was it. She would call the Salaar home and speak to whoever answered, even if it were only one of the servants. She scooted up and turned on the light, fumbled in her purse until she found the number. She dialed nervously. The ringing pulsed in her ear. After six rings, the call was answered.

Danielle held her breath, then gasped in anguish.

It was Damita's voice. A recording. Hello you've reached the Salaar home . . . As the cheerful message played, Danielle found herself mouthing Damita's name, speaking to a damned machine. She smacked down the receiver, suppressing the urge to throw the phone across the room.

Reaching past the ceramic bedside lamp, she pulled the tartan plaid curtain aside and looked out the window. Beyond the flashing yellow neon lights of the Tulip Motel, black skies had turned a chalky gray on the horizon. It was nearly dawn. Another workday at HCD&W. Her staff would be waiting for her, expecting a prescribed course of action. She had to come up with a plan to recover Othello, somehow reassure Hampton and Coolidge that she was still in charge. All that . . . besides dealing with Damita's disappearance.

There was no time to waste. Danielle threw the sheet back. She would visit the Salaar home just as she and Damita had planned. At least then she might feel empowered, actively dealing with the mystery. No matter what, any answer, even an unpleasant response, would be better than none.

Showering quickly and dressing in her slacks and blouse, she skipped breakfast and beat the commuter traffic onto the freeways.

In the bleak rain-streaked morning, Danielle drove her BMW down Highway 95. From her car phone, she called Joella, who had come in by eight as usual. Danielle left a specific message for Kevin, Michelle, and Janet, explaining her intention to hold a meeting with them later that afternoon. That, she reasoned, would give her time to complete her visit to the Salaar house and still formulate an Othello strategy.

After the call she felt relieved. The rain had turned to drizzle and her office worries receded behind the calming rhythm of the windshield wipers. She could now mentally prepare herself for her visit to the Salaar house and the strange people she might meet. As Danielle drove on, Damita's voice echoed through the whine of the highway: not the cheery Damita on the message service, but the one who had called the ad agency in Boston, the panicked voice filled with fear. As Danielle remembered their conversation, one remark kept recurring, about the men in the garden. What were they called? Samir? No, he was the one with the whisper. Armitradj and Cali. Damita said they had laughed about the word murder.

Murder . . .

The timing of Damita's accident on the heels of her cry for help seemed much too coincidental. Danielle decided that, police apathy aside, she would launch her own investigation. It would begin this morning.

Following Damita's driving directions, Danielle left the highway, and after winding through back roads, she approached an affluent neighborhood, fully aware that only two miles to the south, Dimmick Creek flowed peacefully past the broken guardrail.

As her BMW entered the intersection of Almbaum Road, she reviewed her strategy: best to do what Damita had suggested, park her car near the convenience store. She avoided the coffee-and-donut crowd and pulled in at the far end of the parking lot, near a phone booth—almost certainly the one Damita had used a few days before.

The realization shook her, and she blotted her eyes with a Kleenex.

The rain had stopped and the sky was brightening as Danielle got out of the car. She began her walk up Almbaum Road.

It was a quiet neighborhood and there were no people in sight. She passed several attractive early-'fifties homes separated by manicured lawns. After roughly a quarter mile, she looked out from under a row of curbside elm trees. Across the street, beyond a large green belt, she spied a set of turrets. The Salaar home was just as Damita had described, unmistakable. Beyond a tall laurel hedge that lined a driveway sat a large English Tudor bedecked in stucco and stained glass. It was easily the most ostentatious property on the street and the only home surrounded by an eight-foot wrought-iron fence; the medieval-looking barrier ringed the house and its immediate garden area. According to Damita, Hassan had owned the mansion for three years.

She approached cautiously on the other side of the road.

As she drew nearer, Danielle suddenly heard voices at the rear of the Salaar home echoing between the main house and a second building out back that she could barely see, a guesthouse perhaps. Someone slammed a car door, shouting in a foreign language.

Feeling threatened, Danielle scurried across the street, over the parking strip, and found adequate cover behind the laurel hedge that sat to the left of the house and across the driveway.

After a momentary stillness, another door slammed. Parting some of the laurel branches, she now had a partial view of the rear complex of what seemed to be servants' quarters and a three-car garage.

A hunched older woman in traditional black Iranian robes was being ushered by two men into the backseat of a gray Mercedes limousine parked at the rear of the home. Could one of them be Hassan Salaar? Difficult to see through the leaves. The car's ignition cranked, and in a moment, the glistening vehicle purred through an automatic gate at the side of the house and turned toward the street. Droplets of dew from the laurel hedge sprinkled her shoulders as Danielle crouched low, pushing into the foliage to avoid being seen. The elegant automobile rolled down the pavement past her hiding place and bumped gently over the street gutter. Then, turning right, it sped off toward the convenience store where Danielle had parked.

With her heart pounding she watched the car disappear. The buzz of the engine faded away. She listened for any further disturbance near the house but there was none. Everything was dead quiet. Inching out from behind the hedge, she made her way across the walkway to the ornately hewn black gate with its heavy hinges and polished brass handle. She pushed the talk-back button on an electronic keypad nearby.

Several minutes passed. No answer.

Perhaps all the inhabitants had left in the car. Dare she use Damita's combination? She remembered it perfectly: 0994. That code works for the whole house. But if she were to use the code, it wouldn't be in plain sight here at the front gate.

She retraced her steps and, just before the hedge, turned right into the estate, creeping along the cement driveway, working her way up the side of the home between the fence and the hedge. As she neared the side gate where the limo had emerged, a sprawling back garden came into view with the arbor Damita had mentioned. Behind the gate, she could now clearly see a spacious turnaround for service vehicles in front of the garage, and directly be-hind the home a guest house or servants' quarters.

She reached the gate.

Her wristwatch read 8:36. She checked the mansion's windows. No move-ment. But though no one had answered the front door, lights were visible in sev-eral rooms. If anyone remained inside, they had been instructed not to answer.

There was only one way to find out, and she had the means to do it: to the left of the gate was another keypad on the side gate.

She leaned over and pressed the code: 0994.

Instantly, the large black wrought-iron gate creaked and swung inward. Danielle took one last look around, and walked through. The gate closed behind with a clang as she hurried up the back driveway toward the house.

As she rounded the nearest corner turret of the house, she located the ser-vants' entrance, tucked away in an alcove. A sign over a button read: DELIVER-IES—PLEASE RING. Another keypad waited on the wall next to the sign. Would the code work?

With a forefinger poised to enter the code, Danielle suddenly felt like a thief—a justified intruder, but a thief nevertheless. She eyed the sign. Best to ring first, make absolutely sure everyone had left. She pushed the small silver button and heard the trill of a bell within.

As she waited in the shadows on the small step, she surveyed the rear grounds. Beautifully sculpted shrubbery lined several paths that led down an incline to a pond Damita had previously described. Another laurel hedge crossed at right angles across the back of the garden. The arbor arched its trellis above several large rosebushes set under weeping willow trees.

The garden seemed blissfully peaceful; deceptively so. She glanced through the window of the kitchen. Still no one.

She rang again.

Hearing a chirping behind her, she turned. A flock of swallows cavorted among the weeping willow branches. Their cheery calls seemed inappropriate, their companionable flight a mockery of her mood this morning. After several acrobatic displays, as if driven away by Danielle's scrutiny, the swallows darted off into the distant trees, leaving her to the stillness of the grounds.

Danielle peered more closely through the crosshatched window. Recessed lighting above a large bronzed range hood shone down onto gas burners. Tile on the counter gleamed white. The kitchen was reassuringly immaculate. The clock on the wall read 8:42.

She contemplated her options. She could return to the car, but then what? Drive to Boston? Call the police from the car phone? What good would that do? The officers had been here only a few hours ago.

A chill ran up her back as she pushed 0994 on the keypad.

The door handle buzzed. She tried the round doorknob. It rotated easily. She pushed firmly, and the door swung open. Stepping inside, she closed the door and listened.

The only sound that greeted her was the soft hum of the large refrigerator. She took a few tentative steps past a Mediterranean-tiled breakfast nook and crossed the black-and-white-checkered floor across the length of the kitchen.

She leaned forward, glancing down a hallway.

"Hello," she called, her voice cutting through the silence. "Is anybody home?"

15

MILE AFTER MILE OF SUN-DRENCHED rain forest stretched in all directions from under the helicopter's belly.

At the controls, Jasper, the gray-haired chopper jockey, perspired heavily; the hollow of his neck, his lower back, and both armpits of his camouflage green T-shirt were drenched. Below his boyish gray bangs, the aviator's sunglasses were blotted with sweat as he maintained the HH-43 helicopter in a steady hover at four hundred feet off the southern perimeter of Judapi village.

"This work for you?" Jasper yelled over the *wop wop wop* of the blades.

Thane peered through the lens of the Ikegami camera. Dissatisfied, he turned to Dr. Sawati. "Can't we go any lower?"

Sawati's round face bunched with concern, as he looked at the read-out on the Geiger counter on his lap. "No. We've reached the limit. Take your pictures and let's go."

Thane spun around from the open hatch and shouted over the engine, "Give me the zoom."

In the aft seat, Kuintala reached into the bag. He stretched forward and handed him the lens.

His own hands moist with heat, Thane threaded the 10 x 200 and looked through the viewfinder. Acceptable. Not good, but acceptable. "Give me a couple of minutes." He glanced at Sawati, whose eyes were locked on the Geiger counter's LED. "Okay? Two minutes?"

"Yes, yes. But hurry. You should not be here at all with your prior exposure," Sawati said, nodding at the counter.

"We are getting trace radiation. Do it and go."

These digital reels wouldn't be broadcast quality either, Thane thought, but if he was lucky, there might be enough of an image for news coverage.

He pushed the record button, aware even as he shot, that a disgusting smell from the jungle floor had risen on a hot breeze.

At this altitude, the zoom gave Thane a few decent wide shots, nothing tight. Computer enhancement might get him close-ups, if things turned out at all.

Through the viewfinder, the reason for the stench became all too clear. The bodies on the ground were seared purple.

"Their skin. It's bubbly," Thane said. "Blistered."

"Sounds ugly," Jasper yelled. "If the huts were burned, you'd guess napalm." The middle-aged American pilot, who worked for the Katanga Mining Company, was obviously still mired in his military past.

"There's no sign of that," Thane shouted, still panning. "I don't see one stick out of place. Their homes are untouched."

"You should have seen it in Iraq, man," Jasper yelled over his shoulder. "F-16's took out half the valley tryin' to flank some rag heads when our guys got pinned down. Talk about an inferno."

Thane looked over. "One disaster at a time, do you mind?"

Jasper's eyebrows knitted above the shades. He shrugged back. "Cool."

They had flown over Mwadaba thirty minutes earlier. Nothing there had changed. But as Thane viewed the destruction at Judapi, brutal memories from his own past began to haunt him. He shook them off and concentrated on focusing the video.

Thane shot one more pan of the village from left to right, estimating sixty people in view. They were sprawled, scattered in disarray among the huts as if a strong wind had tossed them to the ground.

Thane switched off, looked at Jasper. "I got it. Let's go." Jasper nodded, cranked the stick, and peeled to the right. The chopper rolled gently across the jungle, heading east once more over the short two miles to camp.

Thane moved aft and settled in the seat next to Kuintala across from Sawati. "If this is the same thing that happened in Mwadaba, why is it so much stronger? Symptoms still sound like radiation to you?" he asked Sawati.

"I believe so. Although like Mwadaba there is no blast crater, no concussion from a bomb of any kind." He pointed out the window. "The people are still obviously terribly burned."

"From what?" Thane asked, tucking the Ikegami into its case.

"Radiation presumably." Sawati's face was shiny from the heat. "Without a closer look, one can only guess." Sawati put the Geiger counter down on the chopper deck. "Judapi does seem markedly different. In Mwadaba, something else was at work. That powdery residue you described. Perhaps the medical people can decipher it."

"How soon do they go in?"

"The fallout suits should arrive from Tel Aviv this afternoon."

"Israel?"

"The closest friendly source on the continent. It was that or Saudi Arabia."

Thane nodded and looked over at Kuintala, who sat, knees together, arms locked across his chest. His lanky body seemed compressed in a pose that suggested withdrawal, revulsion. Aware of Kuintala's love for the land and its people, Thane imagined the wounds that had opened in his friend's psyche.

"Here ya go, boys," Jasper shouted over his shoulder as he dropped into a bumpy descent.

Their makeshift camp appeared through the chopper's bay door. Below, Dr. Norman and his assistant Pardux stood in front of the tent, buffeted by the wind. The now-familiar card table held the radio, maps, field binoculars, and Kuintala's rifle. Norman waved frantically and headed for the helicopter, trailed by Pardux.

The chopper neared the ground, wobbled, bounced a few times, then settled into the grasses forty yards from the tent.

Carrying the equipment bag, Kuintala jumped through the door first, followed by Sawati, hauling the Geiger counter.

As Thane sat on the transom, about to exit, Norman grabbed Sawati by the arm and restrained him from leaving the landing site. He shouted something in Sawati's ear, then walked to the helicopter door. Leaning past Thane, he stuck his head inside and gestured to Jasper.

"Pilot!" Norman yelled. "Could you turn off your motor for a moment?"

Jasper swiveled in the pilot's seat. "I'll be back in an hour. I'm gonna refuel at Bangui. Then I'll take you all to Kinshasa."

"No. No. There's another."

"Another what?" Thane shouted.

Norman turned to him, his blue eyes squinting. "A third village."

Thane nearly dropped the camera. "God! You're kidding."

"Unfortunately not," Norman said. "A tiny place named Butombu, on the banks of the Lulua River. We just heard on the shortwave. One of the villagers, a woman, was off gathering vines. She returned to the village and saw the devastation, then floated downriver in a tiny boat to report the deaths of her family." Norman turned to Jasper. "You must take us there, now."

Jasper glanced at his gauges. "I'm flyin' on fumes. I've gotta make Bangui first to fuel up."

"All right. Bangui, then Butombu. We don't have time to break camp," Norman said as his dark hair wafted in the wind. "Make room, Adams."

Thane got up on his haunches, allowing Sawati to push forward into the chopper. Pardux stood a few steps back, waiting for Norman to get in.

As Sawati brushed past, Thane glanced over the waving grasses toward the tent. Kuintala had found himself a place on the ground nearby and sat crosslegged, staring off into the trees.

Norman and Pardux began to board.

Thane blocked their entrance. "I'm out of here."

"You're not going?" Norman shouted, as Thane jumped to the ground.

"No. I think we've seen enough. We'll pack up the gear while you're gone. When you get back, we'll all fly to Kinshasa."

Norman appeared perplexed. "We could be a couple of hours."

"No problem. We'll be here."

"As you wish. But don't let me forget, I'll need your name and US address for our files in case it's something infectious. Precautionary." As Thane nodded, Norman turned and hoisted himself into the chopper.

Pardux brushed Thane's shoulder as he passed, taunting him with a smile. "Your black friend looks sick," he said, nodding toward Kuintala. "I suppose you're feeling nauseous, too?"

Face-to-face with the Frenchman, Thane smiled. "Not anymore, now that you're leaving."

Pardux squared his shoulders toward Thane. "What did you say?"

"I said *bon voyage*."

Overhearing, Norman leaned out to restrain his assistant with a hand on his arm. "Pardux! Get in. Adams, go along now."

Pardux scowled and hauled himself into the helicopter.

Thane ignored him and waved to Norman. "We'll see you back here." Slinging the camera on his shoulder, he made his way out from under the swirling blades.

As soon as Thane was clear, the chopper lifted off.

Jasper gave Thane an enthusiastic thumbs-up from the cockpit, gunning the engine. The olive-colored helicopter ascended, barely skirting the trees.

Seeing the aircraft in this jungle setting reminded Thane of all the battlefield news footage he had studied in college. The HH-43 had been the primary rescue vehicle in Vietnam, nicknamed the "Jolly Green Giant" by the troops. It was a relic, and it was no rescue vehicle now. There probably wasn't anyone to rescue.

From what Norman had said, there was no one left alive where they were going.

16

DANIELLE'S HEART COULD HAVE EASILY kept time with the pendulum as it swung. The grandfather clock's ticking seemed excessively loud in the hall of the otherwise silent house.

Amid the mild odor of lemon and teak she entered the corridor and left the kitchen behind, tiptoeing between the wood-paneled walls toward the front of the home.

The oil paintings that lined both sides of the hallway portrayed classic Middle Eastern scenes: desert ruins under moonlight, horses galloping in a dust storm, veiled women bathing in a tiled fountain. At another time, Danielle might have been fascinated with their overt sensuality. These beautiful originals were part of Damita's home, something she must have enjoyed. But Danielle was hardly in the mood to critique art. She moved on, creeping past each doorway—dining room, sitting room, cloakroom . . .

She paused at the den, which looked more like a throne room. Six-foot-tall brass candleholders framed a massive window seat that looked out on the grounds through lead-lined cross-hatched panes. A large mahogany desk and oversized pleated black leather chair dominated the center of the room. Danielle found it hard to believe that Damita could have fallen for this garishness.

Hassan's presence permeated this place, reminding Danielle that she had entered without an invitation. Her skin prickled with anxiety as she became suddenly unnerved. Then she calmed herself with the rationalization that if caught, she could rightfully claim to be a family member. After all, she was Hassan's sister-in-law.

She continued her search, crossing a thirty-foot expanse of jade-colored terrazzo tile—a sizable entry hall with its eight-foot, brass-hinged double door. Then she came to a palatial living room. Under a large brass-and-crystal chandelier, a plum-colored sectional flanked a huge black Steinway grand piano, complete with candelabra.

Danielle was saddened by the sight. She visualized Damita, dressed in designer eveningwear, entertaining guests in this opulent room. What a dream this must have been before Damita woke up to the brutality.

Danielle retreated into the entry hall. A sweeping staircase dropped down into the center of the foyer. Oversized finials in the shape of carved ivory elephant heads seemed to stare at her from the tops of twin banister posts. And up those stairs, somewhere on the second floor, she would find Damita's bedroom.

Danielle counted twenty-four steps as she ascended, and when she reached the top, she stopped to listen once more.

Still no sound.

Heading instinctively to her right, she passed several guest bedrooms, each decorated in individual color schemes, teals, pastels, powdery earth tones, all relatively tasteful. But as she reached the end of the hall, Danielle confronted a marked contrast.

Hassan's predilection for North African art dominated the master bedroom. A twelve-foot-high ceiling rose in a Byzantine dome. Gold-colored walls were hung with Ottoman tapestries, framing a massive four-poster bed. Each post was carved into ornate representations of the hunt; animals chased by saber-wielding robed men on horseback. Bison. Lion. A herd of zebra. Different scenes twined from top to bottom. The miniature displays seemed bloodthirsty, barbaric. This wasn't Damita's bedroom—it was Hassan's arena.

She walked by the large bed with its huge silver silk shams and with her attention still on the animal scenes, imagined the lovemaking on the spacious mattress. Brushing the vision away, she entered another doorway that opened into a plush, carpeted, twenty-by-six-foot walk-in closet. Inside, a gold valet, two footstools, and a long mahogany dresser stood against the far wall. This small haven provided a sense of comfort, more suitably reflecting Damita's tastes. Lovely figurines of various birds perched on the dresser, and at the far end, a beige cloth-framed photo of Danielle sat next to a Bavarian music box.

Danielle reached out, tilted the picture, and studied herself. Clayton had snapped this shot on Long Island Sound on the bow of his sloop. She looked younger and more naive, wearing a blue-and-white striped yachting blouse, her red hair flowing off her shoulders in the breeze. Clayton had taken the picture only two months before his head-on collision.

Danielle fingered the frame. Danielle's expression in the photograph spoke of unconditional love for the man behind the camera. She remembered the moment as if it were yesterday—her unbounded joy, which had been snatched from her in a single moment.

How different life would have been if a drunk driver hadn't crossed the centerline. Had Damita been drunk when she crashed through the guardrail?

Feeling light-headed, Danielle leaned against the dresser, suddenly realizing how fatigued she really was. The convergence of past memories and the present crisis overwhelmed her as tears began to flow freely.

Needing a distraction, she opened one of the drawers. The perfumed compartment contained Damita's undergarments. And in a second drawer, she found Damita's accessories: earrings, belts, and scarves. Her sister's small mementos might be all that she had left behind. When a life ceased, what a cruel vacuum remained. Damita's passing would be impossible to accept. She searched for something to wipe her wet face, a handkerchief, anything. Rummaging through the accessory drawer, she found a soft orange scarf. As she pulled it out, a white slip of paper fell from within the folds to the carpet.

She retrieved it and recognized a Saks Fifth Avenue receipt. Turning it over as she placed it on the dresser, she noticed a half-finished sentence in Damita's handwriting on the back. It read: Danny, the doves. They're taking me.

Obviously in a great hurry, Damita had scribbled the words. She'd apparently been interrupted, most likely last night, after the phone call, otherwise she would have mentioned something on the phone.

They're taking me . . . where? What the hell were the doves?

She tucked the note in her raincoat pocket and glanced over her shoulder.

It was time to get out. With thoughts racing, she retraced her steps. Was Damita forced to crash? Was she in the car at all?

Danielle hurried back down the hall. She was about to rush down the stairs when something made her pause. Directly ahead stood one last doorway . . . the only closed door on the second floor.

She edged forward. If she didn't check it out, she would wonder about it forever. She put her ear to the wood-paneled surface. No noise within. Gripping the door handle, she twisted as gently as she could, opening the door just a crack, far enough to peek inside. She sighed in relief as she pushed the door ajar to reveal a recreation room with velvet-lined walls. In the center, an ornately carved billiard table stood on an immense Persian rug. Several brightly colored tasseled cushions were stacked on the floor, and beyond, in front of an easel, five chairs seemed to form a miniature classroom. The easel faced the window.

Curiosity won out. Danielle walked softly across the carpet. As she approached the stand, she glanced out the window that overlooked the front yard. Still no one in sight.

She turned back to the easel.

Displayed on a ledge was a three-foot-square map of the North African continent—certainly in keeping with the other African items in the home. But then she studied the graphics more closely and noticed that the country of Congo had been circled in red.

Three names had been written in blue ink on the map's white border—strange hyphenated names, difficult to pronounce.

Danielle tried mouthing them phonetically.

They appeared to be a mixture of an African language and French.

From top to bottom they read:

Judapi-Pardux

Mwadaba-Claudon

Butombu-Flobert

17

THE REAR WINDOWS OF THE parked Citroen van had been coated with dark Plexiglas so pedestrians couldn't see the passengers inside.

Hercule's large frame fit into the cushy seat in the rear of the van, while Uri, Hercule's right-hand man and chief expediter in the eastern Mediterranean, sat forward with his back to the driver's seat, his knees drawn up to his chest. The TV receiver, monitor, and shortwave transmitter were placed comfortably between the two men.

Dressed in his usual blue three-piece suit and black hat, Hercule had finished the last sips of *anisette kafe*, sesame crackers, and olives. Placing the tray of food aside, he wiped his hands on a lace napkin. The son of a French-Algerian prostitute and a Russian immigrant, Hercule had risen from streets of poverty. He was a gutter rat at heart and he knew it. That was precisely why he relished his comfortable lifestyle. A valued assassin for the former KGB and now the underground Communist party, he was a feared international butcher. And in a few moments, with the help of Uri's toys, he was about to enjoy the spectacle of another kill.

"When did you say he does it?" Hercule reached forward, flipping the switch on the transmitter.

Through a set of large binoculars, Uri scanned the third-floor apartment in the stucco building. "Before six. At least that's been his pattern." Uri had been tracking the amiable Vladimir Pepkin for a week.

Hercule stared at the color TV monitor, expecting to see Pepkin enter the screen at any moment. Uri had mounted a lipstick-sized video camera inside a white wicker laundry basket to record activity in the apartment bathroom. From its point of view through an opening in the wicker weave lid, the lens showed a light-colored room with a white porcelain sink, a claw-foot tub with a shower curtain hung from a brass oval ring and a pull-chain toilet. Yellow towels hung on a wood rack next to the sink.

Uri's leather jacket creaked as he rocked back and forth. "He bathes after work every day."

"So where is he?" Hercule asked, wiping his mouth with the back of his hand. Saratov had given the word. Pepkin had completed his assignment and was now more of a risk than an asset. A shame, Saratov had said. Pepkin, a Russian capitalist, had moved his import-export business to Cyprus only a few months earlier in search of more commercial freedom, following many of his countrymen and women who felt that Russia's democracy was too fragile for total autonomy. Like Milcho Zishov, Pepkin's capitalist ambitions made him Saratov's victim. Pepkin had agreed to receive the shipment from Zishov and then reship the cargo to New York under his own name as if it had originated in Cyprus.

Hercule unbuttoned his vest, patted his stomach, leaned forward, and adjusted the contrast on the monitor's picture. "The video quality is really quite good, considering . . ."

"I wanted to mount it in the shower head, so we could look down into the tub," Uri said, "but the metal housing set the lens apart and the glass would have reflected too much light. This isn't bad, though, is it?" Uri was one of the finest "second-story men" in Europe; he could climb drainpipes, jimmy windows, pick locks, and circumvent alarm systems. When Saratov's underground power pulled Uri out of a Ukrainian prison, the party owned him for life.

"Wait, what's that?" Hercule's hand reached for the transmitter.

A body had appeared on the screen, crossing the frame.

"Oh, that's just his wife, Berea," Uri said.

The blowzy brunette pulled up a rose-colored floral print dress and sat down on the commode. The tiny microphone inside the lipstick camera picked up the faint trickle of urine in the bowl.

"Amazing sound," Hercule said, admiring the fidelity.

"Japanese." Uri referred to the electronics.

"Vladimir!" She reached for the toilet paper. "I'll draw your bath." She stood and pulled the chain on the ancient tank above.

"That's where the compressor sits," Uri said, pointing. "It's quite small . . . only twelve centimeters long. Fits nicely just between the tank and the ceiling."

Berea had begun to move out of the monitor's picture. "What?" she yelled. The microphone picked up a muffled reply from somewhere else in the apartment.

"Astounding," Hercule said, cocking his head. "We can hear that."

Berea's two thick calves and heavy shoes crossed the tan linoleum floor. She bent over the tub and flicked two white ceramic handles on the wall several times. Water began to gush into the tub through the chrome spout.

After she left the room, Hercule gestured toward the screen. "What if we can't see him? The steam."

"I coated it with alcohol and siloxanes," Uri said. "Condensation won't stick."

"Ah. As usual." Hercule marveled at Uri's consistent efficiency.

Moments later, Vladimir Pepkin, a balding, slightly overweight man in his fifties, made his entrance. He stepped up to the tub, onto the furry-looking blue bath mat, kicked off his black house slippers, and let a plain gray bathrobe fall to the floor. The camera's angle from the laundry basket gave particular emphasis to his derriere, which appeared sizable on the screen.

"I've had to look at that ass all week," Uri said, smiling again.

"I sympathize." Hercule sat forward, readying himself.

Pepkin had leaned over the tub and spun the handles to turn off the water. Then he raised a naked leg, about to step into the tub.

Hercule's hand moved to the small red button on the transmitter control, but Pepkin had hesitated and swung his foot back down on the floor. "What is he doing?"

Pepkin pivoted toward the toilet. "Oh God, now it's his turn," Uri said, as the figure on the screen sat down on the bowl. Both men were once more subjected to the sound of trickling urine. "I'll bet no one at his export business knows he pees sitting down."

"Least he doesn't do it in the tub."

On his feet again, Pepkin lumbered to the bath and stepped into the water. His eyes closed as he leaned back, both arms braced on the tub edge.

"Now?" Hercule asked matter-of-factly.

"Perfect," Uri said, moving closer to the monitor. Hercule pushed the button. The transmitter sent its signal to the small compressor and its miniature gas chamber that Uri had attached to the back of the toilet tank.

"About three seconds for the coils to heat," Uri said as he began a running commentary. "Now the prosic acid and toxic petrolatum will drip down onto the nichrome wiring. Naturally, there's nothing to see."

On-screen, Pepkin coughed and then flinched, catching Hercule's attention. "It's starting." Pepkin's hand gripped his throat. With the other arm thrashing, he tried to rise from the tub. Instead, he slid back down into the water, gurgling as his head partially submerged.

"What's the response in the body?" Hercule asked, fascinated.

Pepkin gasped repeatedly as his head shook back and forth, throwing small waves of water over the lip of the tub.

"The physiological effects are identical to heart attack. That's what the doctors will call it."

Pepkin's legs gave a final kick, splashing water onto the tile floor.

Berea's call from the other room was audible over the foreground noise. "Vladimir! Are you all right?"

Ripples on the bathwater subsided as Pepkin's head sank out of sight. Berea's voice sounded nearer now, somewhere in the hall.

DAY TEN

18

WEARING A NEW YORK YANKEES baseball cap, jeans, and a T-shirt, Yanni Mandrakos sat contentedly among the patrons of the Kastoria Kafe drinking dark Turkish coffee to prepare himself for the drive home. The caffeine would help clear his head after three glasses of *ouzo*. He felt relaxed as he celebrated his success.

Olympic Airways flight 44 had left on schedule, and during a routine cleanup, Mandrakos had successfully stashed thirty-nine small canisters in the first-class seats.

The bottom cushions of the seats were promoted as removable flotation devices in case of a water landing, and when unzipped, they easily had enough extra space to accommodate a cylinder two inches tall and one inch in diameter. To make sure, Mandrakos had tested several. No passenger would be able to discern anything unusual.

Silently toasting his mission, Mandrakos took a sip. The bite of the coffee at the back of his palate broke through the licorice sweetness of the ouzo, and he swished the pungent liquid between his teeth once before swallowing. Things couldn't be much better. Yesterday's recovery of Hercule's black leather bag from Nicosia had gone smoothly. In fact, better than expected. He had retrieved the goods from the conveyor belt immediately after it left the plane. That was less dangerous than risking exposure in baggage claim inside the main terminal. Had he been questioned, he would have explained that as an airport employee, he had chosen to intercept his bag early to avoid inconvenience. His security clearance gave him full run of the airport.

Mandrakos smiled at how he had pulled it off. For purposes of disguising the transfer, he had tucked an empty Olympic Airways duffel bag into his coveralls. Then, with the highly visible Olympic Airways logo emblazoned on his back, he had strolled by the docking port where the Mediterranean flight from Nicosia had landed. Frantic baggage handlers had driven up to the conveyor belt with their heavily loaded flatbed carriers, and Mandrakos had waited calmly nearby. After the first series of bags had been piled onto the belt and it rumbled toward baggage claim, the handlers had rushed back for another load.

While they hurried away, Mandrakos spotted the small black leather bag Hercule had described. As it came by, he checked the tab on the handle and quietly stuffed the bag into his duffel. Assured that the baggage handlers had been too preoccupied to notice his deft maneuver, he had simply walked away, crossing to the Olympic Airways maintenance center immediately next door.

His locker served as the bag's hiding place until this morning, when he was back on shift. Pockets of his baggy coveralls had served to conceal the canisters as he boarded the Olympic Airways 767 with his vacuum cleaner. And after he left the first-class cabin clean, rigged with its secret cargo, he stood by the hangar and from a distance watched the plane launch into the sunset.

Following instructions, his brother Stavros would by now have recovered the shipment during his own maintenance shift in New York and delivered the goods to his assigned checkpoint.

Done.

And done well. With the money Hercule had promised, life would be easier from now on.

Even his mother had no suspicions of his activities and considered Hercule a kindly family friend, nothing more. Mandrakos's debt to the party had been paid. And having fulfilled their contract, his brother Stavros, though comfortable in America, had the option to return to Greece if he so chose. Their reunion would be a great day for celebration. They hadn't spoken in months.

Mandrakos felt the weight of responsibility slide off his shoulders. He took a deep breath. The extra oxygen made him a bit light-headed, perhaps aided by the coffee, which, combined with the ouzo, had simultaneously bombarded his metabolism with stimulants and depressants.

After the last sip, he gave the waitress a glazed smile. He left a large bill on the table and wandered toward the door.

Outside, the late sunshine brightened his mood even further. He would go home, make a quick meal, and change clothes. Then at sunset he would bring a bottle of red wine to Helena, a robust but pleasantly passionate divorcee who lived upstairs. With any luck at all, after a few glasses she would satisfy his desires.

He lived only three miles from the Kastoria Kafe, in a suburban community in the western half of old Athens, a short distance over the hill on the other side of the Kifisos River.

Mandrakos strolled up the side street toward his small car, an old Fiat that sat some two hundred feet away.

In a park across the street, children played in a sand pit. Their mothers sat on the stone benches near the worn statues of nameless Greek patriots. Passersby milled about, tarrying in the unseasonably warm weather.

To his left, a heavy-set woman scrubbed the top front step of an apartment building. Water spilled down into the stone gutter. He nodded. She ignored him. From overhead on the third floor came a beautiful song sung by a young girl, perhaps rehearsing a lesson.

As he reached his Fiat, he opened the door and climbed into the driver's seat. A tight fit, but he didn't mind. The used vehicle was perfect for a man who drove very little except to work and back.

With knees cramped beneath the steering wheel, he fussed with the keys. The ouzo had slowed his senses, pleasurably disabling him. He didn't mind the slight delay while he found the keyhole for the ignition.

The key finally slid into the slot and he twisted it forward. The starter cranked.

For a fraction of a second, Mandrakos was aware of an aura of white light as heat and flame filled the interior of his vehicle.

He never truly felt the pain.

As his senses left him, the concussion of the C-4 explosion dulled his brain, his Fiat's windows blew out, and his body separated into three sizzling sections.

19

ON THE HILLS WITHIN THE city, pockets of yellow and deep orange had appeared as if overnight. New England's deciduous trees had been painted by fall's impatient brush.

In the hazy midday sun, traffic on a distant freeway moved like a well organized battalion of ants. Sitting in her rocking chair, Danielle watched the lethargic parade of vehicles through her bay window as she listened to strains of elevator music over the living room phone.

The police operator on the phone had been polite, returning several times to apologize, explaining that their lines were jammed on weekends.

But Danielle didn't care. She had called as a result of culminating pressures, the personal stresses and the business tensions that had been imposed by yesterday's meetings at the agency.

Late Friday afternoon, Danielle had visited David Hampton's office in order to reach some accord on how to deal with the Othello crisis in light of her own. And she had expected a modicum of consideration from her senior partner.

She was fond of Hampton, whom she considered more sensitive than the sexist Dennison and the pragmatic Coolidge, largely because Hampton had come up through the creative side of the business instead of the shark-infested account service area.

But as she began to explain the note she had found at Salaar's home and her suspicions of an abduction, Hampton's initial sympathy about Damita began to change.

To Danielle's surprise, the more she recounted, the more Hampton showed latent skepticism, implying that she might be overreacting. He reminded her that since Danielle had lost touch with Damita over the years, she might be misreading the facts. Hampton intimated that her suspicions about Hassan Salaar were farfetched. "I don't mean to sound cynical, Danielle, but a Middle Eastern husband and a mysterious disappearance? White slave girl sequestered by a sheik? It sounds so Arabian Nights."

She was so shocked by the comment that she had exploded.

Hampton attempted to calm her, yet at the same time made it clear that loss of the Othello business might well lead to cutbacks in Danielle's staff. His final words: Deal with your anxieties, then rescue the account. She left Hampton's office and returned to her own, dismayed by his lack of understanding.

Her recollections were disrupted as the operator came back on the line. "I'm sorry, ma'am," the woman's lazy voice droned, "today is Officer Reynolds's day off. He can't be reached."

Danielle immediately asked to speak to someone in charge, preferably Reynolds's superior. The operator put her back on hold and Danielle's thoughts once again drifted to the Hampton incident.

Thirty minutes after seeing Hampton, she had called her people together. They had filed in one at a time, sitting down across from her desk, their faces tense with apprehension. Danielle toyed with a letter opener as she surveyed Kevin, Michelle, and Janet.

"You've probably heard talk about Othello," she began, "and what's going on in my family."

"We're very sorry about your sister," Janet said quickly.

"Is there anything we can do?" Kevin asked.

Danielle liked her mild-mannered art director. "On a personal level, thank you, no." She paused, staring at the letter opener. "But on a professional note, we're going to fight for Othello. And if it should turn out that the deck is stacked against us because Finelli is sabotaging the account, then I'll do everything I can to make things right for you."

"You're saying there might be cuts in our account team?" Michelle asked softly.

"Not if I can help it. It's not over 'til the proverbial fat lady sings." The best thing she could do was keep idle hands busy, even make them productive. "And I plan to give the chubby bitch some laryngitis." She managed a smile, stood and began to pace the floor. "I'm seeing Corbonne next week." She focused on Kevin. "I realize some of your illustrators will have to work over the weekend, but I want a whole new set of boards. Give me ten or twelve samples of Othello's vegetable line in cartoon form, as traditional as possible. Rekindle a thirties style but give life to the eyes of the characters. The expressions on those ancient renderings are too flat. I want vibrant yet authentic hand-rendered drawings. Let's see Finelli reject those." She turned to her media director. "Michelle, first thing Monday morning, clamp down. Without making waves, have your media buyers call every chain, every rep firm. Renegotiate our rates. Use the entire agency's clout when you go to the table, not just the food division. We'll make this buy too attractive to pass up."

Finally, she turned to her secretary. "Janet. Gather as many stats as possible on Othello velocities versus the competition last year. I know our growth curve has them beat. Then talk to the research department and have them do comparatives with other major brands—sales figures on Del Monte, S&W, and others. They'll know the routine. I'll set my meeting with Corbonne for Tuesday or Wednesday. So I need everything Monday afternoon." She looked at each one of them, encouraged. They were excellent people and they had responded with determined expressions on their faces. "Good," she had said. "Let's go to work."

And they had. She knew Kevin was at the office now, even as the operator came back on the line. "I've checked for you, Ms. Wilkes. Officer Reynolds's shift commander is Sergeant Tolliver. He's on assignment and unable to take the call."

Danielle realized she was burning nervous energy, but she wanted action and she wanted it immediately. "Well, then I want to talk to his boss."

"Ma'am, I don't think you understand. We have certain chains of command—"

"Who is Tolliver's superior?"

"Captain Kelly, but normally we—"

"There's nothing normal about my sister's disappearance, operator, now will you please put me through?"

"1 don't think he's in today."

"Then I'll hold while you page him."

"Ma'am, I have strict instructions not to interrupt the captain on matters of—"

"Operator, you tell Captain Kelly I have a competency issue to discuss that could have legal ramifications. I will take it all the way to the governor's mansion starting first thing Monday morning if he can't give me five minutes on the phone. I'll hold while you ring."

"Ma'am, I really can't—"

"What is your name, operator?"

"Straley. Susan Straley."

"Susan, will you please find him."

"All right. I'll try." As she left the line, the operator's voice trailed off in the background, complaining to fellow workers on the switchboard.

Danielle decided she'd stay on the line all day if she had to. The call to Reynolds had followed her frustration in trying to trace Damita through various medical facilities. Danielle had been on the phone most of the morning, checking with hospitals in both Connecticut and Massachusetts for a patient matching Damita's description.

If Damita had been knocked unconscious, found later, admitted senseless to an emergency room without her purse, she might have been listed as a nameless patient. Most of the hospitals had been sympathetic and helpful, checking their admittance records, but with no luck.

The operator returned to the line. "All right, ma'am. I'll connect you now."

Less than a minute later a man's voice answered. "Hello, may I help you?"

Encouraged, Danielle jumped in. "Yes, Captain Kelly, I'm sorry to disturb—"

"The captain asked that I take your call, Ms. Wilkes. This is Sergeant Tolliver."

"Oh. So the chain of command is linked again."

"I'm sorry?"

"Never mind. Sergeant, I couldn't reach Officer Reynolds, so—"

"What's this about incompetence?"

"Competency, Sergeant. I didn't say incompetence. I'm calling to assure myself that my sister's case is being handled responsibly."

Tolliver sounded predictably defensive. "Well, we'd like to think that's how we work. Do you have a specific complaint?"

"I do. I think you're incorrectly classifying my sister's accident Wednesday evening as a fatality. And on that assumption, you're letting the investigation slide."

"Is this the accident at Dimmick Creek?"

"It is. My sister was not in the vehicle."

"I read the report, but I see no reason to argue with Officer Reynolds's conclusions. The facts are the facts. And I review facts, not assumptions. After a thorough search of the creek bed—"

"I'd like you to take another look."

"Are you suggesting that Officer Reynolds—"

"Sergeant Tolliver." Danielle's voice cracked as she attempted to sum up feelings that had been building for two days. "If your sister had been in that car, would you take a second look?" Tolliver didn't reply, so she continued. "I suggest you conduct a diligent review of all existing evidence. I also suggest you light a fire under Officer Reynolds and tell him that I am not beyond going to another law enforcement agency either public or private. You see, if my sister is alive and has been harmed due to your miscalculations or delays, I will seek retribution against your department and those individuals responsible to the fullest extent of the law. And incidentally, I don't consider that a threat. It's a fact, like those others that you insist on reviewing."

20

SATURDAY—7:30 P.M.
Kiev, Ukraine

ANDREI SARATOV SAT AT THE wooden kitchen table and tore the bread roll in quarters, stuffing the doughy, bite-sized pieces in his mouth. The sweetness of the fresh bread cut the aftertaste of the spicy borscht.

Across the table, Guga Volchenko sat under a frosted glass lamp that hung from a single brown cord. His huge eyelashes veiled his languid blue eyes as he looked down at his plate. He was engrossed in finishing his meal, as he wiped the last of the beef sauce from his bulbous upper lip with the back of his sleeve.

Strange, Saratov thought, that such genius resided in the body of an oaf. As he watched Volchenko, Saratov used his own oversized spoon to scoop the last of the potato chunks out of the ceramic bowl. The amber-colored soup tasted doubly delicious since the ceramic bowl from which he wiped the borscht had been fired in the same kiln that had seared Volchenko's doves to shiny hardness—the doves Zishov had called pigeons the day he came to the warehouse.

The borscht and Volchenko's use of his sleeve as a napkin reminded Saratov of his boyhood summers in the country, working as a field hand on a commune. Volchenko's plebeian earthiness and peasant-like simplicity brought Saratov back to his roots.

The two men hadn't spoken for a few minutes when Volchenko broke the silence. "Thank you for dinner, Saratov. Your cooking is marvelous." As if he had waited for just the right moment, Volchenko timidly took the envelope of money off the table and lifted it in the air. "And thank you for this. My wife will appreciate it, for new furniture. Our living room couch is coming apart." He tucked the envelope into his gnarled woolen jacket.

Behind Volchenko some twelve feet, through the crack in the pantry door, Saratov noticed the cloth of a hat and the glint of gray eyes peeking through. It was Hercule, who had silently returned by the back door and had chosen not to be recognized.

"Don't thank me, Guga." Saratov smiled as he chewed. "You are the one who deserves thanks, from me and the party." Volchenko's acceptance of payment sealed their bond even tighter.

"It's good to feel the power of the party at work." Volchenko rubbed his hands together. "These talks are reassuring."

"Don't worry, things are going well." Saratov laid his spoon in the bowl, eager to hear Hercule's report. He nodded Volchenko toward the door. "You just tend to your ceramic aviary. Let it flourish." He shifted his weight to rise.

Volchenko took the hint and grabbed his own hat, looking disappointed that the meeting was over. "I'll show myself out, please remain seated."

Saratov eased back into the chair and reached for another bread roll, satisfied that he still held sway over Volchenko's genius. "Next week, then."

"After you return from Athens," Volchenko said, pausing at the kitchen door as if he had forgotten something. "I take it the dominoes are still falling? You dispatched the importer in Nicosia?"

"Yes." Saratov looked up, bread in hand. "Like Zishov and Mandrakos, Pepkin's death will remain a mystery. The dominoes topple steadily without a trace. Pardux has only to finish his work in Africa."

Volchenko fidgeted at the door.

"Don't look so distraught," Saratov said.

Grasping the doorjamb with one stubby hand, Volchenko patted the envelope in his jacket with the other. "In a weak moment, I have wondered if . . . "

"What is it, Volvchenko? Speak your mind."

Volchenko's thick gray eyebrows furrowed in concern. "My usefulness to the party may soon be over. Do you think that I, too, might become a domino?"

Saratov glanced at the pantry, where Hercule was waiting. He threw his arms in the air with great flourish. "Oh, my friend, what a question." He kicked the chair back as he rose, stepped forward, taking Volchenko by the elbow, and led him into the gloom of the small living room. "You are one of the fathers of the new revolution. Like Guyenov in Moscow. Salaar in the United States.

Muhadeen in Iran. Nahbrid in Iraq. And look at the support from party members throughout the world. These others are tools, expendable mules who transport material. Their deaths are necessary to assure security."

As he walked, Volchenko gazed at the floor, wringing his hat in his hands. "I'm not a power broker or a politician like the rest of you. I'm a scientist."

They had reached the front door of Saratov's apartment and Saratov put an arm around him, patting the envelope inside his woolen jacket. "A valued scientist to be sure. And a rich one. It's only the beginning. Don't worry. Guyenov has plans to make you his minister of science, remember?" Volchenko's cow eyes blinked as he nodded.

Saratov patted him on the back. "Without you, how would we continue to control our enemies? Don't worry, comrade, you'll be at the seat of power with the rest of us. Never fear." Saratov reached for the brass handle to open the door.

Volchenko placed a hesitant hand on his arm. "My mind tortures me. The vastness of what we do . . ."

"I know. Of course. But human events often change with a huge roar. Remember that there are still people all over the world who yearn for freedom. The Iranians are right when they call it the Great Satan. That gluttonous machine harvests the rest of the world." Saratov squeezed Volchenko by the shoulder. "And look at Mother Russia, broken and bastardized. Oppressed by Western reforms. Victimized occasionally by sanctions. We'll break the bonds of the computer elite who strangle us. Isn't it marvelous that we are using their Internet as our communications tool? We must overthrow these technocrats—you understood that necessity from the beginning." Saratov held him by the shoulders and studied his face.

Volchenko seemed to be weighing Saratov's words. A social idealist and a loyal communist, he thirsted for dogma. He had withheld his genius from democratic reformers in the Ukraine due to their chaotic misdirection, and clung to old acquaintances like Saratov who espoused the rebirth of a single ideology.

"And just think"—Saratov projected excitement into a final rhetorical volley—"we'll accomplish our goals without the loss of a single Russian life!"

"You're certain?" Volchenko's voice broke. "I have nightmares about . . . what if Russia, Belarus—"

"No, no," Saratov said. "We're visionaries, not butchers. Guyenov has his political machine oiled and ready. When the Duma in Moscow sees the dove's incredible destruction, it will become evident that no one, anywhere, is safe.

Power will return to us without a shot being fired." Saratov felt that one more analogy would seal it. "In a fashion, this purging is no different from what the United States did to Hiroshima—a merciful strike."

Volchenko's large eyes squinted. "Their President Truman agreed to that."

"He did."

Volchenko sighed. "It's still war."

Saratov shook his head. "But not on our soil."

Volchenko seemed sufficiently re-inspired. "Good enough." He grasped Saratov's hand and nodded repeatedly, the large whites of his eyes glinting with moisture. "Ultimately, it's for the best."

Saratov gave him two pats on the cheek. "Of course it is, Guga."

"Bless you for your strength, Saratov. Lenin would have embraced you."

"I embrace you." Saratov gave him a bear hug and finished by opening the apartment door, nudging Volchenko gently into the dimly lit hall. "Now go to your work. I will keep you informed."

Volchenko smiled and, with a half bow, wandered off.

As he watched him shuffle away, Saratov marveled at how the beautifully conceived conspiracy was dependent on this waddling genius.

In a stroke of desperate vision, key leaders of the KGB loyalists and the Islamic revolutionary groups had realized their unity of purpose; the two organizations most oppressed by the United States had coalesced, agreeing to cooperate based on a frightening device invented by this humble man.

Returning to the kitchen, Saratov found Hercule standing on the veranda in the twilight. Saratov's prime assassin had a bowl of borscht in his hands, trying not to spill on his blue three-piece suit. Although the two men had communicated by coded email, it was the first time in two weeks that they had seen each other.

"Well?" Saratov said. "Have Hassan's people received their shipments?"

"Hassan's Web site says they get everything tonight. In the meantime Hassan completes his meetings in Athens and waits for you." Hercule tipped the bowl toward him. "By the way, this is tasty."

Saratov ignored the compliment. "Any word from Pardux?"

Hercule munched, leaning on the wrought-iron balcony. "He's worried about this intrusion by the American. Adams apparently shot some video footage, which makes things more complicated. Pardux believes he's on his way back home. We've contacted Hassan's people and ordered our own US agents to find him, but I suggest I go to Congo to make sure things go smoothly."

"All right. Then leave immediately. Take Uri with you. Stay as long as you must to alleviate problems. I don't want to have to make excuses. Has Pardux completed his radiological analysis?"

"The death range was as expected, roughly six kilometers in radius. Excluding an excessive residue of hydrocarbons, everything will clean up nicely." Hercule gave Saratov a smile. "Not that it matters."

"It matters if it happens here," Saratov said sternly.

Hercule stopped chewing. "But you told Volchenko—"

"I told him what he needs to know. Once this starts, we may have to finish it." Saratov felt the importance of the moment. In only a matter of days, Hassan's men could be ready to disembowel an unsuspecting nation. What followed was unpredictable.

Deep in thought, Saratov looked out over the city. A gray haze hung over the buildings directly below. Lights were beginning to twinkle. He gazed east.

His apartment sat on a hill on the western side of Kiev, overlooking the Dnieper River. On the other side, the old section of the city endured, even through the countries recent unrest. In the late twilight Saravatov could make out the silhouettes of disheveled old castles and ghostly fortifications.

"You see that, Hercule?" Saratov gestured to the ancient walls. "Kiev, our most historic of Russian cities, was overrun. Not by the Moors, not by the Huns, not by the Khan. No. By the stealth of democracy, ripping us away from Mother Russia. Look at the damage it has endured." Hercule had stopped chewing out of respect for Saratov's discourse. Saratov gripped the handrail as he looked out over Kiev. "Think of it," Saratov said in awe. "The great pendulum of justice is about to swing back. In a matter of days, the United States will *perish*."

21

THE THREE-PLANE CONNECTION FROM KISANGANI to New York via Cairo and Frankfurt had been a tiring ordeal. Fatigue weighed heavily on Thane as the Lufthansa 747 made its final approach to Kennedy Airport.

Dressed in a pair of cargo pants and a cream-colored safari vest, he sat with his seat belt fastened and his eyes closed.

An ethereal buzz from two glasses of white wine filled his head. He felt almost weightless as the engines lowered in pitch and the plane banked gently to the south.

Thane's thoughts drifted to the freckle-faced woman that would not be at his flat to greet him when he got back to Brooklyn Heights. Lorrel Campbell had moved out three weeks before his departure for Africa.

A nature lover like himself, Lorrel had received her MA in forestry, working in Maine analyzing acid-rain damage to old-growth timber. She and Thane had met at an environmental conference where Thane had presented some of his wildlife videos. Lorrel was a bright wispy blonde with an attractive figure, strongly defined features, and an athletic radiance that gave her a ruddy glow even without makeup, which she wore sparingly.

She and Thane had found common interests as well as a strong physical attraction. After two months of casual dating, they became roommates. Convenience was as much the motive as anything else, since they were both often away on assignment.

They shared the rent and enjoyed passionate encounters when their sched-ules allowed. But as the months passed, their initial passion gradually faded into predictability. Although Lorrel's personality was pleasing in an unaffected sort of way, Thane found himself missing more acute mental stimulation.

All this came to a head when Thane realized that his growing indifference was one-sided. Lorrel hadn't lost her fascination for him at all, which became apparent when one evening at dinner she batted her white-tipped eyelashes and, to his surprise, suggested a more permanent relationship, as in marriage. He evaded the commitment as gently as he could, requesting time to consider. The rejection hit hard nevertheless and made her realize that their two-year experiment had failed.

Only days later, perhaps expecting him to object, she suggested that she move into her own apartment.

The experience left Thane disgruntled and pondering what it would take to find a woman who could be a wife, a lover, and a friend.

As memories of Lorrel faded, the descending plane encountered a wash-board of turbulence. Thane opened his eyes briefly as the flight attendant walked by. As he closed them again his thoughts turned to his last moments alone with Kuintala at the base camp outside Judapi, just before Jasper's chop-per returned to fly them to Kinshasa.

Having folded the tent and packed all the equipment, they had sat together under the shade of an Iroko tree while a variety of parrots had cavorted nearby. Thane was concerned with Kuintala's attitude—he had displayed a deepening sadness over the day's events.

Thane studied Kuintala carefully as he sat cross-legged in the heat, perspira-tion dotting his black forehead. Kuintala had been immersed in concentration, pulling on the thick grass between his legs. His hands were lithe, almost deli-cate, capable of weaving fronds, yet at the same time sinewy and strong. Staring at the ground, he had finally spoken.

"I will return to my home in Saurimo to my brothers and sisters," Kuintala had said softly. "My land is not far, just down the Chicapa River."

"You're worried about them?"

Kuintala brushed his chin with a blade of grass. "I fear for us all."

"Don't worry about Pardux's bomb theory. He's full of shit."

Kuintala looked up and the corners of his mouth had quivered in amuse-ment. It was the first time that day Thane had seen Kuintala smile. "Your face,

Adams," he had said. "Like a leopard around the Frenchman."

"I usually get along with everybody, but I don't like this guy. Didn't from the first moment. Something slimy about him."

Kuintala nodded. "He changes like a shadow."

"What do you mean?"

"There is another that moves him. If he is here with the WHO and works for health in the world, why is there sickness in his soul?"

Now Thane smiled. "Interesting point."

Kuintala gazed into the boughs of the tree above, stretched his shoulders, and, settling his dark gaze on Thane, asked where he had grown up. Outside Stewartstown, Pennsylvania, Thane had said, but he hadn't been there for years. Kuintala mulled the next question. "No brothers?"

Thane sighed. "Right. No family. All gone in one night."

Kuintala gestured to Thane's back. "When the evil bit you?"

Sensing he might not see his friend for some time, Thane decided to clarify. "The scar on my back is from a melting shower curtain that fell on me as I fought my way out of a burning bathroom."

Kuintala reacted to Thane's chagrin. "You were brave."

"I was scared to death. I had come home late, taken a bath. Fallen asleep in the water. When I woke up, the whole bottom floor of our home was smoke and flame. I tried to get into the hallway to reach my mother, younger brother, and kid sister, who were trapped upstairs. I was naked, straight out of the tub. They were screaming, but the smoke was so thick, I couldn't breathe, couldn't see." Thane's shame made it difficult to speak.

Kuintala reached out and put a hand on Thane's knee. "The scar inside you is larger than the one on your skin."

"I used a bath towel to kick out a frosted window over the tub. Thought if I got outside, I could find a ladder to save them. I ran to the barn and returned, but the entire second floor was engulfed. They were gone."

"Why do you feel guilty? You tried."

Thane swallowed hard. "It was one o'clock in the morning, on a Saturday night in winter. My dad had died just a month before. The farm was my responsibility. I blew it. Went out with some friends who had a yen for Kentucky bourbon. The fire chief said an electric heater in the living room shorted out; a heater I turned on when I got home. If I hadn't been so groggy, I could have saved them. Can you imagine me standing there nude in the snow with a ladder in my hands when the firemen arrived?"

"Dr. Norman asked about the scar."

"I know."

"But you refuse to lose it. I understand. My ancestors carried scars from great hunts, battles, things of meaning." Kuintala's eyes penetrated his. "But you were not at fault in this. The guilt is not worthy of a mark on your skin." Thane looked up and caught the fierce simplicity in Kuintala's eyes. "Thank you," he said to his friend.

Kuintala had resumed pulling on the grasses, picking up a handful, then letting them fall to the ground as the breeze caught them. "I would go home for a while, Thane. Home is a good place to begin a new journey."

Thane shrugged. "We'll see. Home right now is my apartment in Brooklyn Heights. With my debts, I'll probably have to sell the Pennsylvania land. Either that or get a ton of jobs. I'll call my manager to find work. And I've got an old college buddy, Bob Davis, who works at CNN. Maybe I can sell him the helicopter footage for his news network."

Kuintala had gotten to his feet, though Thane wished their conversation would continue. "Where are you going?"

"To get the video camera." Kuintala gestured toward the stacked gear. "Ebola was news. Mwadaba, Judapi, and Butombu must also be very important."

"I agree, but I've shot everything."

"You have pictures, but no story," Kuintala said, pointing toward a sunlit patch of ground. "I will point the camera at you over there and you will tell what has happened here." Then he began to amble off toward the equipment.

"Me? I'm no reporter."

With hands on hips, Kuintala had turned tolerantly to lecture him. "If you are to sell your video, you must become a reporter. You are here, where it has happened. You were the first to see the villages. You are a man who speaks wisdom." Then Kuintala's stern expression faded. His smooth face was broken by a grin. "Besides, the camera will like you, Adams. You have an exceedingly pleasant face."

Kuintala's smile in the dappled sunlight of the jungle was jolted away as the tires squealed and skidded on the runway. The 747 had touched down and settled into a bumpy roll. Thane opened his eyes and peered out the window. He was on American soil.

Moments later, he stepped from the jetway into the concourse, where he was immediately struck by the frantic flurry of activity at the gates. Looking around, Thane felt like an alien, dressed as he was, carrying his small black overnight bag.

The airports in Cairo and Frankfurt had been nearly as noisy, but a US crowd created a particular ambiance—an almost metallic inflection in the voices, an urgent brassy twang. This was America on the move, bent on getting where it was going.

And although Thane felt energized to be back in the US, his immediate reaction was to get away from the racket.

He passed the security checkpoint where outbound travelers waited for clearance, then took a right turn toward the main terminal's baggage claim, making headway against a steady flow of people coming in the opposite direction. He had progressed another sixty yards among the perfumed scent of the gift shops and the greasy odors of the lunch counters when he suddenly noticed two large men in gray suits flanking him on either side. The blond one in the raincoat to his right grabbed his arm.

"CIA, Mr. Adams. Just keep walking."

Thane tried to pull away. "Excuse me?"

A dark-haired man on his left clamped onto Thane's other arm. "He said keep walking. Let's take this real easy." Thane detested the strong-arm approach. "What the hell do you want?"

"Don't get excited, just cooperate. Let's move along quietly." They had him pinned between them as they escorted him through the oblivious crowd past a newsstand and toward a bank of key lockers next to a men's room.

Thane spun around as they reached the lockers. "You mind if I see some ID?"

"Please keep your voice down, sir. Everything's fine." The man pointed. "Step over here."

"The ID," Thane said, backing toward the wall. The guy with the quarter-inch crew cut blocked his access to the rest room.

"All right. Relax," the blond man said, smiling, flipping his billfold open to a plastic identification card that carried the seal of the United States. He pointed to a name at the bottom of the card. "I'm Bulatzik, and this is McNair."

He tucked the wallet away. "We have a car waiting outside. Now, give me your ticket folder, please."

"My . . ?"

"To claim your bags."

"I don't understand." Thane reached into his vest, fully aware that he had his wallet, passport, and his cellular phone tucked into pockets on the other side. He retrieved his airlines folder and stared at Bulatzik, whose blue eyes were deadpan, though he was still smiling. Thane reluctantly handed him the ticket and claim checks.

Bulatzik tore the tiny green tabs from the staples and returned the folder to Thane. "Thank you." He gestured. "Shall we go?" McNair had a hand on Thane's elbow.

Thane began to edge toward the passing crowd. "What's this about?"

"Your video," McNair said matter-of-factly. "It's a matter of national security."

"So I'm being detained?"

"No, you're not," Bulatzik said in a robotic cadence. "We just need to ask you some questions."

Thane glanced from one face to the other. These guys were little more than automatons trudging through their assignments. Thane thought of how Kuintala would have described them. Shadows, he would have said. Another pair of shadow walkers, moved by someone else. Thane's instincts told him this was all terribly wrong. They were only thirty yards from a carousel marked LUFTHANSA FLIGHT 1264 FRANKFURT. The conveyor belt began to rotate.

They stepped through the security gate, and Bulatzik gave Thane a nod, steering him toward the carousel. They found a vantage point among the rest of the passengers, standing directly in front of the conveyor-belt door, which began spewing bags onto the interlocking polished chrome plates that formed the carousel platform.

"How about if I ask you some questions?" Thane said, looking directly into Bulatzik's face. "How did you know about the footage?"

"We're an international organization," Bulatzik said stoically, staring at the luggage. "What do your bags look like?"

"Metal camera case. A large black duffel, and one more . . ." Thane turned to McNair, hoping to coax information out of these ape-men. "By the way, who reported this? Norman, the Englishman?"

"We were given instructions by our New York office. We don't personally know any of the individuals involved."

"You don't?" These guys didn't like conversation. Thane rallied with a strategy to disrupt. He looked around at the other passengers who were preoccupied with their bags. "But surely they briefed you on all the details." Thane raised his voice. "I mean you just don't go around picking people up without knowing the facts."

"We just follow orders," Bulatzik said, retrieving the camera case.

"But the number of people I had contact with is so limited. This doesn't make sense."

Bulatzik looked around nervously. "It doesn't have to." The bags were coming in bunches now and Thane's voice began to rise with urgency. "I have a right to know why my privacy has been invaded. That footage is my personal property."

"No one is invading anything," McNair said intensely, grabbing the black duffel.

"I want to know the connection. Did your information come from Congo? Was it Sawati? Norman? Jasper? Couldn't have been Kolo. He's got a camp to run. But how about that Frenchman—now there's a guy who's made for intrigue."

"Would you shut up, please?" McNair said.

"But why would the World Health Organization call you guys? They have their own investigation. They already interviewed me. And by the way, they're way off-base with their theories, especially that French guy."

Looking at the bystanders, Bulatzik had had enough. He turned to Thane and spoke in a harsh whisper. "If Pardux reported this, he must have had his reasons. We're following orders and I want you to shut up."

Thane stared at Bulatzik. Now he knew he'd been set up. Not once in his machine-gun prattle had he actually named Pardux or associated him with the WHO. That was something Bulatzik had done on his own. The big man was lying.

Thane made an instantaneous decision: not the kind made with rational forethought, the kind made when fight-or-flight adrenaline surges through the body.

"There's my leather case," he shouted, pointing at the carousel.

McNair, who was on Thane's right, made a move toward the passing luggage. In that moment, Thane threw an elbow into Bulatzik's chest. The big blond man grunted and reached out, grasping at Thane's sleeve, but he came away with nothing more than the black overnight bag.

While astounded bystanders gaped, Thane leaped onto the carousel, dancing around the tumbling luggage that emerged from the conveyor.

"Get the hell down here, Adams," Bulatzik barked, while McNair looked around nervously. Having arrived at the apex of the carousel, Thane balanced precariously on the lip. From this higher perch, he spotted a security guard some seventy yards away, walking casually in their direction.

No time to hesitate. "Security!" Thane shouted at the top of his voice, waving an arm. "Security, down here!" The black man in uniform began to run in his direction.

"You asshole," McNair growled as he tried to jump up onto the carousel, but losing his footing, he fell back. Bulatzik reached threateningly into his raincoat breast pocket, revealing the glint of a nickel-plated handgun.

Thane froze, but Bulatzik hesitated to pull the weapon, looking around.

Seizing the man's hesitation as his cue, Thane vaulted through the conveyor-belt doorway. He found himself in the dark, clambering on black rubber, a hundred-foot-long sloping beltway. He made his ascent, hip-hopping over bags, and as he neared the daylight at the top, he heard the high-pitched whine of jet engines. As he reached the crest, however, the belt mysteriously came to a halt, tossing Thane on his face.

He got to his feet, climbing over yet more suitcases. Then, as he broke into the open air of the upper loading platform, he was confronted by two armed men and a woman in blue security uniforms who dashed from a police car that had just screeched to a halt.

The lead man pointed his .45 and yelled, "Move and I'll drop you! Put your hands on your head."

Thane obeyed. "No problem. Two men were—"

"Shut up and raise 'em," the man yelled.

While both officers covered him with their weapons, the tough-looking woman came up behind and cuffed him one wrist at a time.

"Officer, didn't your security guard in baggage claim see the two men?"

"All he saw was you doing your gorilla act," the woman answered.

"I was trying to get away—"

"Well, you didn't." The woman pushed him toward the car.

"They stole my bags," Thane responded as he was shoved toward the backseat.

"You can explain it to the captain," she said as he sat down.

As the car door slammed, Thane looked out at a passing 757 taxiing toward the runway. Somewhere in the airport, now probably carrying his luggage, Bulatzik and McNair would have disappeared into the crowd.

22

IN THE MISTY GLOOM, THE armor-plated blue Chevrolet Suburban sat motionless on the frontage road near the railroad tracks just off Columbia Street. Beyond the chain-link fence, Manhattan's lights twinkled across the Hudson River.

From the rear seat of the vehicle, Samir had a full view of the warehouses that lined the pier, including number 15, a gray metal-sided structure Hassan Salaar occasionally used for storage.

Armitradj, a long-haired, angular man of medium height dressed in a black turtleneck and gray slacks, rocked back-and-forth at the wheel in the front seat. He was Samir's half brother, of Iranian and Indian blood, whose mother still lived in New Delhi.

The two men had been in the truck forty-five minutes, and Armitradj restlessly patted the small black billy club in the palm of his hand. "Some of our men question me," he said in a thick accent. "They ask, 'What of the Russians?' This Saratov and this Guyenov, those Bolsheviks. Could Guyenov be another Stalin?"

"What?" With his gloved hands, Samir tucked his beige camel-hair overcoat around his knees. He was a muscular man with high cheekbones, a thin nose, and a protruding forehead. His deep-set gray eyes and short hair gave him the look of a boxer.

"An egomaniac. Like Stalin."

"Leave the politics to Hassan," Samir whispered. His usual hoarseness was caused by crushed vocal chords, a legacy from his time in prison like his missing right leg. Samir wore flamboyant clothing and jewelry to compensate for his physical shortcomings, handicaps no one mentioned for fear of their lives.

"The men talk about the communists."

Samir couldn't shout. "They are to serve Allah and the jihad, not the communists." He checked his watch, an expensive French timepiece with a jade face.

"Forgive me." Armitradj shrugged. He was the only one, aside from Hassan, who dared converse with Samir as an equal, a privilege he held because they shared a father. "But I have concerns. Like this man Adams."

"Cali's men will find him."

"Before the police find us? Imagine living in the hell of an American prison."

"I need not imagine. I know what prison is like." Samir flashed back to his political confinement. When he'd been a child, the Shah's men had held him in a mountain hellhole near Daran. After torture, Samir's right knee had been crushed under the weight of a boulder, then amputated. He shook the horrors away. "Why are you suddenly full of this talk?" he asked angrily.

"Sometimes I wonder about Hassan."

"He is our leader. No need to wonder."

Armitradj stopped tapping the steering wheel. "But this other business." Armitradj seemed hesitant to say the name. "Damita."

"Must you speak of this again?"

Armitradj tugged his cheek in exasperation. "I mean no disrespect. But why, in this crucial time?"

Samir smirked. "Hair of fire, a milky bosom."

"Still, that his desire would interfere . . ."

Samir's whisper rose to a rasp. "He intends to take her home."

Armitradj snickered. "To Iran? You think she would wear the chador?"

"She is his bride."

"And his undoing." Armitradj folded his arms and looked out at the river. "The nuisance refuses to eat because of her bruised face. She looks unhealthy."

Used to Armitradj's impetuosity, Samir chose not to reply and focused on the pale lime glow created by the warehouse floodlights.

Armitradj had bothered Samir enough. He knew just when to stop. As brutal as Armitradj and Cali could be, Samir had the cool blood of a lizard. The men told a story about Samir and Armitradj: They were having dinner together at a

Greenwich Village restaurant. An impudent waiter had derided them because he'd had difficulty understanding Samir's whisper. The waiter had used racial slurs several times. Finally Samir had fixed his gaze on the man, causing Armitradj to try and dissuade him. But when the meal was over, Samir followed the rude fool to the employee rest room and slit his throat. Samir left the corpse sitting on the toilet in a stall, limped back to the table, and paid the check, leading Armitradj out of the restaurant without another word. It was known among the men that Armitradj and Cali were excellent soldiers, both trained by the elite Iranian Secret Service, a punitive body of government operatives formed in 1990 under Rafsanjani. They killed out of loyalty. But Samir was different. Samir killed on impulse as if he were swatting a mosquito.

"Car lights," Armitradj said, squinting into the darkness. A vehicle rolled up the road. "You think it's a patrol car?"

"Nonsense." Samir retrieved the leather briefcase from the floor. "It's Mandrakos in a VW Passat. Get out and signal."

Armitradj hopped down on the pavement, putting the billy club in his pants pocket. With briefcase in hand, favoring his right leg, Samir followed.

Armitradj entered the glow of the headlights and signaled to turn them off. The Passat obeyed, rolling to a stop near the warehouse. The driver swung the car door open and got out.

Armitradj waved. "Stavros Mandrakos?"

"Which one of you is the Catcher?" Mandrakos asked in an awkwardly obliging tone of voice, using the Internet code name.

Samir hobbled forward, whispering as loud as he could, "I am."

Mandrakos rushed to them and it occurred to Samir to reach down for his knife, until he realized the Greek's excitability and his simple desire: to shake hands.

"I just want to thank you." Mandrakos pumped Samir's hand.

"Thank me." Samir was genuinely taken aback.

"For my mother. The party's generosity. For the revolution."

"Oh, yes," Samir said, as Armitradj flanked the man. "How is she?" An inane question considering that Hercule had strangled Mrs. Mandrakos that afternoon and Yanni had been fried in his Fiat.

Mandrakos smiled. "Sir, you're testing me. You know I've had no contact since the mission began."

"Good for you." Samir smiled as he patted the briefcase. "This is your money. Now where's the satchel?"

Mandrakos looked over his shoulder. "In the car."

Samir began to limp toward the Passat, but Mandrakos bowed slightly and with a gesture toward Samir's gimpy leg, said, "Oh, please allow me, I didn't realize . . ."

Samir froze. "Excuse me?"

"Your leg."

"I have a left one and a right one. To which do you refer?"

Mandrakos crumbled into servility. "Forgive me. My mistake."

"Please, no apologies." Samir set the briefcase of money down on the cement and hobbled three steps toward the edgy Mandrakos. "Don't be shy. You see," he said, "one of my legs is plastic. A bit clumsy, but quite practical. Take a look." As Mandrakos bent down, Samir pushed his coat aside, revealing the cloth of his fake inner right thigh. "I keep things inside."

Mandrakos was completely at a loss. "Inside?"

"Yes. I don't show this to others." He opened the small cloth-covered hatch on the thigh of his pant leg. "Unless I intend to kill them." With that, Samir grasped the ten-inch dagger from the hidden compartment and rammed it through the soft tissue under the Greek's chin.

Stepping aside with a quick twist of the scalpel-like blade, Samir filleted Mandrakos's neck, slicing through the esophagus and larynx, and ended with an artistic flick through the carotid artery.

Mandrakos dropped to the ground with a gurgle. He squirmed as life left him, then finally came to rest.

"What are you waiting for?" Samir pointed at the warehouse. "Get rid of him."

Armitradj approached the body, looking down at the spreading pool of blood that had formed around Mandrakos's neck and chest.

Samir stepped across the body. "But first, bring me the satchel." Samir wiped the blade on Mandrakos's chest, hid the knife away, and closed the compartment in his leg.

A speechless Armitradj scampered to the backseat of the Passat, brought the leather bag, unzipped it, and handed one of the small canisters to Samir.

Samir snapped the cap off the exact replica of a plastic film cartridge. The contents looked innocent enough. He took the satchel and began to hobble toward the Suburban. "I'll wait in the car."

Starting for the warehouse to get a barrel, Armitradj picked up the neglected briefcase and held it in the air. "Perhaps you should take the money."

Samir stopped and looked back. "You still don't get it, do you?" He broke into a grinding, wheezy laugh. "Keep the money if you like. Or throw it away. In a week's time, that currency will not matter anymore."

23

SATURDAY—10:17 P.M.
Montauk, Long Island

LARGE LUSH CHESTNUT TREES LINED the narrow street, shading the parked cars from moonlight. Thane guided his white rented Dodge Charger down the avenue looking for 1348 Atlantic Lane, the new home of Grant Goodeve, his friend and business manager.

His visit would be premature since Grant didn't expect him until the next morning, but the close call at Thane's apartment in Brooklyn Heights less than an hour ago prompted Thane to change his schedule. After leaving Brooklyn Heights he had used his car phone repeatedly to try to reach Grant. But Grant's line had remained busy, not unusual considering Grant did business at all hours.

After twenty minutes of dialing, Thane had decided to simply drive out to Long Island and warn his manager of that night's further complications.

On the way home from the airport, it had occurred to him that there wouldn't be any food in the house, since Lorrel had moved out. Consequently, he had decided to stop for groceries at Harold's, a friendly neighborhood deli. Working his way down the store's narrow aisles, he had happened upon his upstairs neighbor in apartment 4B, the effervescent and talkative Morton Sussman.

Retired from the garment business, the pleasant but nosy sixty-nine-year-old Mr. Sussman focused his energies on keeping track of everyone and everything in the building. He was the first to know if Mrs. Kravitz in 2C had a new corn plaster or whether the plaster in the hallway needed repair.

Thane had habitually tried to avoid Sussman's long discourses on the condition of the plumbing, but there Sussman was, his ruddy face lit by white neon, leaning against the glass meat counter. With a rigid forefinger stabbing the air, the balding Sussman was complaining to the bespectacled Harold about the freshness of the salami. Noticing Thane, Sussman turned a quizzical eye. So there you are, Mr. Adams. You are back from Africa. But what happened? Why are you in trouble? Do you know that Mrs. Gardner nearly had a coronary when those Gestapo-looking guys interrupted her dinner? Can you imagine our government paying scary people like that? People? Thane had asked, anticipating the answer. Yes, big people, bruisers, Sussman had replied, especially the big blond guy in that coat. Besides guns, they had ID, Mr. Adams, and Mrs. G. had to reluctantly give them a passkey to your place.

Thane had heard enough. He didn't even wait to buy bologna, realizing in an instant that the name tags on his luggage had led Bulatzik and McNair to his home.

As Thane continued to look for Goodeve's house numbers, he was relieved that at least his stolen luggage had substantiated his abduction story. Without the theft, the airport authorities might not have let him go. And the minute they did, Thane's first call had been to Grant.

Hearing Thane's account, Grant had suggested that Thane come by in the morning to pick up a disk copy of the Judapi footage.

Even during his encounter with Bulatzik and McNair, Thane had known his footage was secure. He had wisely decided to send the digital original to Grant via dropbox a day prior to his departure from Kisangani. Security had been one motive, but speed had been the other. And while Thane was in transit, he put Grant to work. His manager took immediate steps to contact Dave Colt at International Geographic. Unfortunately, Colt had rejected the offer of the video's contents as a partial settlement of Thane's contract. So, acting on a second option, counting on an old friendship, Grant had called Bob Davis at CNN, Thane's swim-team buddy at Penn State. Davis had reacted favorably and Grant had forwarded a file of the Judapi footage down to CNN in Atlanta, negotiating a deal for ten thousand dollars, which, as he put it, was at least enough to keep Thane eating for the month.

Judging from Davis's reaction, the video would air immediately, probably sometime the next day.

Thane imagined Bulatzik and McNair in some shoddy room, rummaging through Thane's gear trying to find the video, then looking up to see it on television.

He also imagined them searching for him again.

Whoever these ape-men were, they'd known enough about him to pick him out of a crowd. And now they'd been inside his apartment. Thane prayed they hadn't trashed the place.

One-three-four-eight. Thane was shaken out of his thoughts as the numbers glinted in his headlights.

Through an open gate, he spotted Grant's house, a small two-story colonial with white sculpted eaves. The living room lights cast a warm glow onto the front lawn.

Thane decided to pull the car to the curb. He opened his cellular phone, trying Grant's number one last time, wanting to announce himself in case his single friend had female company. Still busy.

Thane drove up the driveway, mulling the same questions that had haunted him all evening.

Could Bulatzik and McNair actually be CIA?

Was Pardux directly responsible for having them show up?

Would the airing of the footage on CNN be the end of their harassment? Or the beginning?

He hated the thought of being hunted, of not knowing why. Perhaps he could find a way to turn the tables. He grew angrier remembering McNair's last wild grab at the baggage carousel, and the look in Bulatzik's eyes as he began to pull his gun from his raincoat. Perhaps Grant had ideas on how to proceed.

After reaching Grant's front porch, Thane stopped the car. He got out and looked around.

A warm Indian-summer breeze blew in off the Atlantic Ocean that lay less than a mile away to the south. The sky was streaked with high clouds, and a half-moon lit the driveway, a narrow strip of black asphalt lined with juniper bushes. The world seemed so peaceful. A stark contrast to Thane's restlessness.

As he climbed the porch steps, Thane continued to mull questions. If Bulatzik and McNair were government agents, why were they connected with Pardux? Bulatzik's comment had indicted the Frenchman. But were the others involved? Sawati? Dr. Norman? And was Kuintala in jeopardy? Thane vowed to find out, wishing he had an immediate way to contact Kuintala, who had no phone in Saurimo.

Thane had stepped through the white pillars and crossed the front porch. He rang the bell. Chimes sounded within. Several minutes passed. Grant didn't answer. A confirmed bachelor. Grant lived alone.

Thane tried knocking, then turned the door handle. It was locked. Someone should respond. He grew suspicious and tried to peek inside through the front door window, but he couldn't see through the purple and maroon stained glass.

He left the porch and decided to circle the house. Though the rooms were lit, Thane saw no movement inside as he walked around the manicured lawn.

He reached the backyard, where the white lattice and vine-covered trellis vaulted a bleached brick patio. Stepping over a miniature white-picket fence that bordered the flowerbed, Thane approached the curtained French doors.

Another light shone from within, but it was impossible to see any detail through the sheers.

Thane tried one of the doors.

It opened.

The moment he poked his head into what he assumed was Grant's den he was on alert. The telephone, its receiver off, lay askew on the rolltop desk in the comer. Drawers in a walnut hutch had been ransacked. Books from shelves that lined the rear wall had been dumped on the floor. The small tan suede love seat was littered with paper. One of two brass lamps had fallen on its side on the end table.

Thane stepped inside.

A sound system played a song somewhere in the next room. As he tiptoed across the den, moving toward the open doorway that led to a hall, he was tempted to call Grant's name but thought better of it. Instead, he crept off the carpet onto the hallway's oak floor, approaching a closed whitewashed door on his right.

Suddenly, he felt something sticky under his soft-soled shoes. He looked down. The grained floorboards were covered by a dark, maroon-colored stain. Thane immediately recognized it for what it was.

He pushed and the door swung open, revealing a pool of blood, deep red against a white linoleum floor. Thane's gaze followed the puddle to the center of the room where Goodeve lay on his back.

Under a shock of curly brown hair, Grant's pale blood-drained face looked almost peaceful. His cardigan sweater lay open beneath him, spread on the floor like gray angel wings. His Pendleton shirt was hiked up around his bare chest and his unzipped pants were pulled down just below his hips, exposing a shredded pair of briefs that had been cut or torn away.

Blood still oozed from the ragged hole where his genitals should have been. The poor bastard. Someone had mutilated him.

He had probably been dead for less than an hour.

DAY NINE

24

SAMIR SAT IN THE BREAKFAST nook gazing out the window at the dark grounds of the estate. He pushed the cup and saucer aside, having finished the chamomile tea he sipped to soothe his sensitive throat. His bejeweled fingers toyed with multicolored stones in the inlaid Mediterranean table.

Stavros Mandrakos's satchel rested at his side on an upholstered leather bench.

The servants had been dismissed in preparation for the final abandonment of the home, and the Salaar household was quiet except for the ticking of the grandfather clock in the hall.

Hassan was not expected to return until tomorrow.

Samir relished this moment of solitude. Earlier, he had loosened the leather straps that held his artificial right leg in place, hoisted the sleeve of his pant leg, and taken a few minutes to massage what was left of his upper thigh, kneading the sore tissue at the tip of the stump, a five-inch extension of his leg that protruded from his hip. Like fourteen other pairs, his pants were specially fitted in two sections, one with a normal pant leg for his left leg, and another stovepipe piece that fit the artificial leg, each with a trapdoor flap to accommodate the hidden compartment in his plastic thigh. After easing his discomfort, he had refastened the leather straps and clasps that had been cleverly fitted in Velcro-lined folds camouflaged within the fabric.

He leaned forward and put his face in his hands, eyes closed, focusing on details, formulating the report he would give to Hassan upon his return.

Cali's side of the operation had not gone well. It was Cali who acted as liaison with a sizable group of ex-KGB agents, Russian operatives who had been stranded by the end of the cold war. There were eleven in all—whom Saratov and Guyenov had recruited through their worldwide network—loyalists eager to participate in the revolution, men from all walks of life, including some who had been double agents and law-enforcement personnel. Since Hassan's Islamic Revolutionary Front acted with autonomy in the United States, Saratov had arranged for these ex-agents to act as a support group, well suited for security work and the kind of cleanup the Thane Adams incident demanded.

Cali had been trained by the Iranian Secret Service and, being an agent himself, was not only a field operative but an experienced and vengeful killer.

An hour ago, Cali had called and reported that he had recovered a digital disk from Grant Goodeve's home. After checking it on Goodeve's DVR, he believed it was the one Adams had taken in Congo. Samir hoped it was the only one in existence, which it might be, since Bulatzik and McNair reported finding nothing in Adams's luggage. Bulatzik and McNair had been disappointed by Adams's failure to return to his apartment. And all Cali could coax out of a dying Goodeve was Adams's last known location somewhere near the airport.

Still, Goodeve divulged to Cali that Adams was expected at Goodeve's home in the morning. So Cali had reconnoitered with Bulatzik and McNair for one last look around Kennedy, and if unsuccessful, they were to come back to stake out Goodeve's house before dawn in anticipation of Adams's arrival.

Cali mentioned Goodeve's murder. Death by castration—the punishment of an infidel—an act that Samir neither endorsed nor decried, but one that Cali vindictively enjoyed. What would the difference be, Cali had asked, as long as he was dead? With Mandrakos, that made two kills in one night. There would be more.

As Samir's eyes grew heavy, he nodded, almost asleep, but startled again as the kitchen door opened.

Astia, Hassan's elderly house manager and personal servant, had entered wearing a long robe and a blue shawl to cover her gray hair.

"Why are you here, woman?" Samir asked, in his coarse whisper, rubbing his eyes.

"I saw lights." She closed the door.

Samir was careful to address her politely. She demanded courtesy.

Hassan had brought her from Iran and treated her like his surrogate mother. "You should be sleeping."

She shuffled toward the table. "I have seen a strange thing."

"Strange?"

"Something bothersome on the machines." She pointed to the hallway, referring to the home monitoring system that recorded signals from four hidden television cameras.

Since he was in charge of Hassan's safety, Samir took the suggestion as an affront. "We had no alarms."

"True. But as you know, I had gone to the city to say good-bye to some friends, and when I returned, I went to the master's room." She smiled proudly. "One of the dresser drawers in the bedroom closet had been left open"—she showed him with a gnarled left hand—"only so much."

"What of it? The master probably packed a few things." She shook her head. "No, I am the one who packs for him. Remember, these rooms are like my own. I keep them perfect for his comfort." She waddled toward the hall, talking as she went. "But you men were busy with other matters of importance."

Disturbed by her inferences, Samir followed, hobbling past the grandfather clock, the large oil paintings, and the dining room. Astia led the way into a wood-paneled sitting room to an oak-framed louvered closet.

"I found the drawer odd." She opened the door. "So I came and looked at video, as we are able to do."

Samir stood behind her as she rummaged among the shelves in the dim light. Above her head, a wooden case held five DVR machines stacked in a series. The second from the top hummed softly, recording the signal of a split-screen composite from all four cameras, which were hidden in air vents in the kitchen, the hall, the entry, and the upstairs, and shown together in four small split-screen images on a single monitor on the top shelf.

Astia located a black disk cover and turned to Samir. "This is the one. Observe." She slid the disk into the top machine and pushed a button as the monitor switched to playback.

The screen flickered as the CD aligned and played, and Samir watched the less-than-perfect black-and-white screen as a woman walked into the downstairs hall. From the high camera angle, he recognized her. "Damita," he croaked assuredly. "This disk is a week old."

"It is not," Astia said. "It is yesterday. And that is not Damita. It is her sister, Danielle. I have seen her in the photographs upstairs."

Samir squinted. "We've been cursed with another redhead." On the monitor, Danielle left the hallway and crossed into the terrazzo-tiled entry. "But how could she enter with no alarm?"

"That is your problem." Astia stared at him. "So what do you think?"

In miniature, Danielle crept across the screen and exited the frame, disappearing into the living room.

The pretty bitch had violated the sanctity of his mentor's home. Samir scratched his chin. "I think . . . you are watching a dead woman."

25

THE SUNSHINE FLOODED THE COUNTRYSIDE, which blossomed white like an overexposed photograph.

Giggling, Danielle ran through the daisy field.

Damita followed close behind, wearing a garland of loosely knit flowers she had made herself in the tree house their father built.

The two girls exploded out from under the shade of the green apple trees and danced across the grasses.

The celebration of the meadow had begun. Butterflies floated above the poppies, bees darted in zigzags, the ground hummed with crickets as the two redheaded children romped over the rise, running toward the crest of the hill.

From down in the hollow, the irresistible aroma of apple pie wafted up the knoll . . . Mother was baking. Out in the backyard, the chatter of Dad's hedge trimmer could be heard as he groomed the patio for the Fourth of July party.

Tumbling to the ground, Danielle rolled and came to rest on her side. She looked back at Damita, whose freckled cheeks flushed with the heat of the day as she came charging toward Danielle, hurling her daisy garland into the air. With a great gasp, she launched herself onto Danielle and wriggled about, laughing. Danielle felt the wonderful warmth of her sister's gingham dress, and the tiny ribs within pulsing as she tried to clutch Danielle's sides and tickle her to death. Their gingham dresses would be grass-stained, but ultimately, in the comfort of dinner, that sin would be forgiven. Childhood glee would subdue parental discipline on a sun-drenched day like this.

Danielle pushed on her sister's chest, wrestling her away, but the little urchin clung hard and climbed on top. Danielle was once more forced under Damita's chipmunk smile as the two grappled with each other. Danielle looked into the brilliant sky-blue eyes of her sister. She was only seven.

It was within this halo of joy that Danielle fought back the bitter reality. Things had only been this heavenly once. The smother of the pillow on her face intruded into the image, and Danielle's face twitched in recognition as she floated over the threshold of the dream. Even in her nether state she knew that euphoria, no matter how engulfing, must by nature dematerialize. Paradise would dissolve away. And so it did now with gray-and-white shreds tearing at the color images, finally leaving only blackness that became the dark of her bedroom.

Everything was dark. Blacker still when she confronted the possibility that Damita might be dead. She might never see her again.

Danielle buried her face in the pillow and began to cry.

The release was healthy and somehow she knew it, letting all the tension go at once. She visualized the bent guardrail, the depth of the murky water, Officer Reynolds's helpless expression. Had her call to the New London Police done any good? Her frustration poured out and she bled herself of grief, hoping that if she could get it out, she might be able to force the hurt away and go on without breaking down again.

After a few moments she wiped the tears and pushed the dampened pillow away.

She lay staring upwards, trying to orient herself. Some wine had lulled her to sleep in her bedroom. She felt terribly alone on her large four-poster bed. From the lights in the stairwell, and a background drone downstairs in the den, she could tell the television set was still on.

Still dressed in her slacks and blouse she sat up, finding equilibrium hard to capture. In her stocking feet, she walked out of the bedroom across the landing and down the stairs to the kitchen.

A glass of chilled ice water from the refrigerator tasted refreshing, though she spilled some on the counter and realized how tired she was.

Slowly, she made her way back through the hall into her den, located across the entry from her living room. On the far wall, a large TV dominated the built-in oak bookcase that was filled with professional marketing manuals and advertising case studies. She reached up to turn off the set and noticed a handsome tanned man in a khaki shirt talking on the screen. Not that she cared, but his name appeared at the bottom of the image and his sun-bleached sandy-colored wavy hair blew in a tropical breeze as he pointed off-camera. He was saying something about mass death in the jungle. She paused, staring. The picture changed to aerial scenes of corpses lying near huts in a village. Then the camera cut back to the tanned man with a map of Congo graphically superimposed next to his shoulder. As he spoke, the map showed three red dots in the southern quadrant of the country.

"So, at this time, there are only three known sites of this strange poisoning: the villages of Judapi, Mwadaba, and Butombu."

The man disappeared as the picture faded, and an anchorwoman on a news set concluded, "World Health Organization officials have recovered one body from each village. The remains are now being shipped to Kinshasa for lab tests." A graphic reading DOLLARS AND SENSE then materialized on the screen. "We'll be back with today's stock market report and other financial news."

Still sleepy, Danielle picked up the remote, hit the power button, and the TV picture went black. Setting the remote down on the teak-trimmed coffee table, she stood staring out the den window at the lights of Boston.

Judapi. A map. Congo.

Judapi, Mwada . . . what was it? At the Salaar house. Next to Congo on the map. But there were more names. More than three.

She grappled with the remote and turned on the TV again, hungering for a replay. Unfortunately, the screen was now filled with a Dow Jones graph.

Dazed by the impact of the story, she realized that there must be a connection. The maps. Something about Congo, somehow a link between those names. But how to find it? She looked up at the TV. Channel 22, CNN. She plopped down in the upholstered armchair and grabbed the den phone. Dialing information, she asked the operator for the number of CNN in Atlanta.

"Subscription information?" the operator asked.

"No. Corporate offices." Danielle dialed and got a recording. The CNN administrative office was closed for the day. The voice mail gave her a menu of useless options, but then she heard the one she wanted: News Desk. She punched the number.

She clung to the phone and struggled with the message that she reached on the line. "Push seven for more details on today's breaking stories."

Maybe? No, the hell with it.

"If you have a breaking news story . . ."

Sure why not? She pushed nine.

A female voice came on the fine, a human voice. "Hotline."

"Hello," Danielle said. "I'm trying to find someone."

"Do you or don't you have a story?" the voice asked impatiently.

"I don't know yet. It's vital I identify the man on your CNN broadcast just a few minutes ago. Adam or something. The story about Congo. I have to talk to him. Where can I reach—"

"Congo? Just hold a moment."

Silence. Danielle rubbed her brow and tried to remember the other names . . . there were six.

The woman returned. "Sorry. He's not a staff reporter. I'm not sure I can give out that information."

"He was on your news, for God's sake. Please."

"You might check with our production department, they'll be open in a few hours—"

"1 don't have time. This is an emergency."

Danielle's tone of voice must have swayed her. "Hold one moment. Let me try production."

Silence. Danielle wasn't sure what it all meant. But with nothing else to go on, she knew that Hassan, Damita, and the man on the screen were associated somehow, and the words on the map were the key.

"Hello, caller? I have clearance to give you the name. It's Thane Adams. But we have no authority on any further information."

"But how do I reach him?"

"Best I can do is tell you that he was working for *International Geographic*, that's all we know."

"*International Geographic*? Where?"

"Their New York branch office."

"Do you have that number?"

"No. Not offhand. Besides, they're undoubtedly closed at this hour."

Danielle suddenly realized how disoriented she must be. "God, what time is it anyway?"

"What? Well, it's . . . 3:43 in the morning eastern time. Good night and good luck."

26

A PALL OF FUMES HUNG over the runways. The whine of jet engines carried across the tarmac as aircraft taxied among hazy hangars on the horizon.

Dressed in a gray suit and rather unimaginative brown oxfords, a perspiring Saratov cursed the heat as he followed the endless metal fence along the airport's east perimeter.

As he approached the parking lot he spied a lone man.

With arms stretched above his head and his long graceful hands gripping the chain-link wire, the man seemed to pull on the barrier as if he were enclosed in an imaginary cell. Understandable, Saratov thought, since Hassan Rais Salaar and Samir Abadan had, as young teens, both been prisoners of the Shah's government.

Saratov's old KGB network had developed an extensive dossier on Salaar. His father, Achmad Salaar, had been a prominent businessman and landowner, descended from a family of tribal leaders, which accounted for the family name: "Chieftain of many tribes." Achmad had been a man of breeding, educated in England, and raised his son to be multilingual. But the more young Hassan learned about Western culture, the more he found it corrupt, and when his father died in the mid-1980s, at the age of fourteen, Hassan Salaar became a follower of the Ayatollah Khomeini, working in the underground against the Shah. It was then that he met his right-hand man Samir. Both boys were imprisoned and endured torture at the hands of the dreaded Savak, the Shah's secret police. Hassan Salaar was released in January of 1989 and during the Rafsanjani regime, he thrived as a successful merchant but never married until recently.

Saratov remembered accounts of Hassan Salaar's immense wealth, his intense religious beliefs, and one telling statistic: his mother had been among the two hundred ninety people aboard the Iranian Aerobus airliner mistakenly shot down by the American navy ship Vincennes over the Persian Gulf on July 3, 1988. The incident had altered Hassan's life, fueled his hatred, and forged his political ambition. He had become a vengeful and resourceful man, crystallizing his loyalty to Islamic principles and vowing to wage war on the United States. As a primary agent for the Islamic Revolution in the United States, Hassan had flirted with extremists like Saratov before. It was Hassan's innovation to use Internet servers in Egypt, Greece, and Germany for secure intercontinental communications among conspirators. The rotating use of several Web sites in different countries made it nearly impossible for government agencies to track messages, particularly when they were written in nebulous jargon.

Unusually tall for an Iranian, Hassan Salaar had the bearing of a man of culture, education, and formality. Even on this hot morning, he wore a black suit.

As Saratov approached and waved a greeting, Hassan pushed away from the fence and stood stiffly at attention. The two men had met twelve times in the last three years. It was an uneasy bond, maintained only by their desperate alliance in a battle against a common enemy. This was to be their last meeting. Once their victory was complete, the conspiracy between Russian communists and the Islamic Confederacy would yield to diplomacy between communist leaders like Guyenov and the statesmen of Iran, Iraq, and Libya. Although, as Saratov knew, their paths might cross again in the role of emissaries for their own people.

Saratov respected Hassan. Their meetings had been polite, if not friendly. But today the Iranian's darkly handsome face appeared sullen as he stepped forward. Saratov extended a hand and addressed him in their common language— English, ironically. "It's good to see you again."

Hassan ignored the cordiality. "Are the African test results conclusive?"

Saratov nodded. "The variations are negligible."

"What do you mean by negligible?"

"Death is the result in all cases. The degree of physical damage sustained by the victims appears to be random."

"So the desired result is guaranteed?"

Saratov did his best not to look too smug. "Of course. No need to be concerned."

Hassan's deep black eyes flashed in the sunlight. "I was more impatient than concerned."

Since Hassan appeared particularly ill at ease, Saratov was anxious to change the subject. "How are things in New Jersey?"

Hassan clasped his hands and rubbed them together. "We received the satchel if that's what you mean."

"So Stavros Mandrakos . . ."

"Sleeps in the Hudson River."

"And the dove figurines?"

"Pepkin's airfreight shipment arrived in New York. And the crate your man Hercule smuggled through Athens has arrived in Halifax and is well on its way from Nova Scotia."

"Your heavy water supply?"

"Secure. It was easily delivered through Quebec into the US. Without your resources, we wouldn't have a mission. But I must tell you, your men, Bulatzik and . . ."

"McNair."

Saratov had been informed of their problems. "Yes. They actually had that American, then lost him."

"I understand. But do not let these matters of security distract you. Utilize our eleven men. You have their complete cooperation and their equipment—excellent surveillance gear."

"Thank you," Hassan said coldly. "But in this Adams matter, I insist that my man Cali takes care of things. You agree that as a liaison with your people he remains—"

"In command, absolutely. I've contacted Bulatzik to confirm that. I assure you." Saratov was embarrassed that two of his ex-KGB agents didn't perform better. Wondering how to justify the error, he was grateful that, at that moment, a KLM 747 approached at full speed, roaring overhead on takeoff. Neither man attempted to compete with the decibel level. Instead, they began to stroll along the fence. Their rendezvous here had not been coincidental. Well aware of modern surveillance devices, they had deliberately picked a noisy open location.

As the smell of the 747's fumes descended and the engines' blare subsided, Hassan gestured to the hangars where Yanni Mandrakos once worked.

"Well, at least here in Europe the circle has closed—the Greek brothers, their mother..."

"Zishov and Pepkin," Saratov added.

"Excellent. In these cases old KGB methods proved effective," Hassan said, making amends. "My compliments to your man Hercule."

"Thank you. And we erased our tracks, just in case." Saratov paused, realizing that he was about to imply that things might go wrong in the United States after all.

"We won't have any problems."

Saratov threw his hands in the air, trying to dispel any negative impression. "Of course not. One worries about the FBI, the Secret Service. But I'm sure you've taken measures."

"We have," Hassan said, his eyes closing in a peevish squint as he looked out over the tarmac at a 737 taxiing toward a hangar. "My final concern is the climate in Moscow. Any further news from your underground KGB leadership?"

Saratov realized anything he told Hassan would be conveyed to extremists in Tehran, so he spoke carefully. "Frankly, Mafiya pressures on the reformists are so severe, we aren't sure that doves on US soil will impress our enemies in the parliament. We may have to resort to revolution, as we feared."

"But will Guyenov move immediately toward a truce?"

"His coup should avert blind retaliation by the Europeans, particularly if Russia goes fully communist, and if your operation is so well veiled it discourages indictment against a particular country."

Hassan pulled a small cigar from his breast pocket and proceeded to try and light it in the buffeting breeze. The smell of the smoke reminded Saratov of the smoke-filled room at Guyenov's home when he had brought the loyalists together recently in Moscow.

That night, Guyenov's excitement had been contagious. It was no longer important that the USSR had lost the cold war, the war of ICBMs and nuclear submarines. Among the communist faithful Guyenov had recruited a scientist named Volchenko, whose most recent discovery had intimated a new strategy—like the Russian Revolution, future wars could once again be won in the streets.

As the plan developed, it seemed feasible that another Russian Revolution might logically follow the chaos in America, particularly if the communists held the upper hand in weaponry. From the communist perspective, their Islamic alliance was ideal. In case of failure, an Islamic terrorist operation was the perfect way to divert blame. In case of success, a Russian/Islamic agreement would seal a lasting peace. The Europeans would do little, since oil still ruled the planet.

Hassan clasped his hands together. "We are anxious to begin. Do I have your assurances about Congo? No further difficulty? No traces?"

Saratov shook his head. "The dove literally vaporizes, except, of course, the batteries. Those pieces must be found. Pardux has begun the search and should contact me in two days. In the meantime, tell your people in Tehran nothing has changed. Guyenov looks forward to an Arab alliance, you know that."

"What we know is that the world's balance of power will shift in your direction as if the very axis of the earth had tilted toward Moscow. Obviously, once the US is crippled, Russia will be next in line as the only superpower. Muhadeen, Nahbrid, and Lybia's man Kabril have expressed their wish for a f inal pledge."

"Of course. We guarantee it. From Guyenov himself if you like. I will have his pledge delivered."

"Just put it on the Web. As for the rest, Cali will take care of Adams. But make sure your Frenchman finishes in Congo."

"Pardux says that though Adams was there by chance, his television report put Pardux and his assistants in an awkward position. He became part of the investigation instead of being able to clean up. Don't worry. Pardux is Hercule's cousin, well trained."

"But slow . . ."

"Please." He had never seen the Iranian so irritable. "Is there something else troubling you?"

Hassan studied Saratov's face, apparently bothered by the question. "Why do you ask?"

"Because we are at the threshold of this mission, and I want no misunderstandings, not even the suspicion that things are amiss between us."

Hassan's dark eyes riveted on Saratov's. "I give you that impression?"

Saratov became suddenly uneasy. "Forget what I said. We are both challenged by this business. It may be just my own anxiety."

To Saratov's surprise, Hassan's eyes softened. A look of understanding flooded the Iranian's face. "I apologize. I've had a few domestic problems that weigh on my mind. Nothing stands in our way. The fire I feel in my heart will soon fall upon our enemies."

27

SHAFTS OF MORNING LIGHT FELL over the rolling hills.

The great sprawling grasslands were washed by nature's watercolors as the sun transformed murky fields of gray to glistening meadows of gold.

Thane drove on a two-lane ribbon of highway, hoping his dulled senses would come back to life. He stretched his tired muscles, trying to shake himself back to reality. Slowly, the chill of the previous night's violence seemed to melt away in the warmth of the sun.

Devastated by the sight of Goodeve's mutilation, Thane had jumped into his car and mindlessly driven into the night. He wasn't sure how to deal with the sheer savagery of the crime. The more he thought about Grant's murder, the more Thane realized the immensity of its implications. For the foreseeable future, there was no way he could go back to his apartment. Thank God Lorrel was out of his life. At least she was out of danger.

Visions of his empty flat plagued him. He wondered what might have happened to his African collection, his valuable animal photo library. What if Bulatzik and McNair had ransacked his den and trashed his mementos?

He had had the strongest urge to drive straight to Kennedy and hop a flight back to Africa, but he was without a camera and carried very little money. Besides, with maniacs like Bulatzik and McNair running around the terminal, Thane decided it would be best to try a departure at a later time, from another airport.

As his mind reeled with details, he discovered he'd driven through New York City and was now heading for New Jersey. Beyond lay Pennsylvania.

Perhaps it was the need for money. Perhaps it was the need for closure. Whatever the reason, Thane began to rationalize his decision to go to Stewartstown, take one last look at the burned-out Adams homesite, and make a commitment to sell it. Being good grazing land, the property might bring upwards of two hundred thousand dollars . . . money he would need. He could call Henry Jameson, the attorney in town who had managed the family estate, maybe even get a loan using the land as collateral. It would be a way to clear his mind and his affairs, plus escape from the chaos in the process.

Kuintala had been prophetic. Thane was headed home.

Even as he had settled on his plan, the nagging question still remained: Who had caused that chaos? There was little doubt that Grant had died because of Thane and because he had been in possession of the Congo footage.

Someone wanted that video badly enough to murder for it.

The bitter irony was that Goodeve had been slain for nothing. Thane's feature had aired anyway, several times, as he discovered well past midnight driving through New Jersey. Carefully disguising his nervousness, he had made a cell call to his college friend, Bob Davis, in Atlanta. Thane hadn't spoken to Bob in three months. Though Bob had grumbled about being awakened, he'd admitted that he was happy to hear from Thane, and yes, the CNN executive added, he had used Thane's name on the screen, why not?

Thane expressed his gratitude, saying he wanted to use the story as a showcase. He asked if the story had gotten much reaction. Bob told him that there had been some public response during its three airings, mainly from people concerned with Ebola. Thereafter, it had been hard to judge because Bob's boss had yanked the story. Something about an official request from the Feds. A national security issue. Feds, who? Thane had asked. CIA? Bob knew nothing further. Can you check? I'd be curious, Thane said, without sounding too manic about it. Realizing he had imposed enough, Thane apologized for the late call and then asked a favor—immediate payment, by overnight mail to the Stewartstown post office.

Davis promised to send a money order for four thousand dollars the next morning. In case of a shipping glitch, Thane gave him his cell phone number and, thanking him warmly, hung up.

Minutes later, still plagued by guilt, Thane geared himself and made a call to a Long Island police precinct, anonymously reporting Goodeve's murder.

After that he'd shut the phone down. Alone with his thoughts, he had driven from New Jersey to the outskirts of Philadelphia and stopped for something to eat at a truck stop. Satisfied with the meal, he'd remained parked at the restaurant and taken a two-hour nap in the car. When he awoke around 3:30, he headed west into the night on Interstate 76.

Once out in Pennsylvania's Amish country, he turned south to bypass York, planning to cross the Susquehanna River on Highway 372.

Now, south of Lancaster, with the morning sun higher in the sky, the farm country glistened with the new day and Thane found himself rejuvenated, relishing the land like an old friend. Though familiar, the countryside also seemed somehow new again. It was hard to believe he'd been away fifteen years.

As the morning dew evaporated and the earth's dry heat began to rise into the vehicle, Thane opened the windows and a breeze blew through the car. It seemed to gather strength, becoming a wind that combed the great expanse of yellow grass, weaving streaked patterns of brown and gold across acres of barley and rye.

Ahead, on a hill dotted with small farms and a windmill, Thane spotted a small horse-drawn cart. Amish. As he passed, he checked the driver in the rearview mirror, a man dressed in the traditional black hat and black slacks, wearing a white shirt and suspenders. A beautiful sight. How tranquil this journey might have been under different circumstances.

He checked his watch. It was 8:45.

He had another difficult call to make. Dave Colt should have been at work for an hour by now. Under the guise of touching base, Thane would assess Colt's feelings, ask about future prospects for International Geographic without mentioning Goodeve. With Goodeve gone, Thane would have to confront Colt anyway to renegotiate Thane's blown assignment.

He pulled the Dodge into a rest stop shaded by a grove of birch trees and powered up the phone, coaching himself to sound positive as he dialed the number.

Colt, a cocky, successful senior executive in charge of his own specialized division of the company, answered his private line. The conversation began rather formally, but after a few inane comments about how busy he was, Colt came right to the point. "Are you calling because I rejected Grant's offer about your video?"

"No. Frankly, I wanted to talk to you one-on-one. I don't think what happened was my fault, but I feel responsible."

"How you feel isn't the issue, is it, Thane? Fact is, without the tree frog footage, you owe us cash."

"No question. I just wanted to see if there were any other assignments, preferably overseas. I'd take a discounted rate, free if necessary, to start paying you back."

"I don't think you understand." Colt had a nasty habit of talking down to anyone who wasn't his superior. "You put my tit in a ringer. I have to send letters of apology to our subscribers, print a new subscription list, and change the copy on three different print ads, all explaining why the rainforest video series is short by one episode."

"Look, I understand—"

"Let me finish. The loss isn't just the money we advanced you. We've run up forty-four thousand dollars in hard costs, to say nothing of wasted staff time." An awkward pause followed. Thane waited, resigned to endure the browbeating he had expected. Finally, Colt continued. "Now we're disappointed things happened the way they did but you know how we work. We're booked months ahead." Colt rambled on, emphasizing that damaging video on a remote shoot was a blunder of horrendous proportion.

Thane interrupted him. "Look. Just tell me what you consider adequate compensation."

"My people regard your work as first-class," Colt began admiringly, then fell into his dry stoic tone. "But unlike them, I have a bottom line to justify . . . "

Thane couldn't tolerate further posturing. "Name your terms."

"All right. The terms are . . . pay us."

"I don't have it yet."

"Fine. As much as you can then. The rest in ninety days."

"Ninety days? The entire fifty thousand?"

"You asked for terms. I don't think we could contractually assess you for more." Colt sounded as if he regretted not being able to. "Why not sell your camera? You could pay us and have money left over."

"My camera?" His lack of compassion astounded Thane. In any event his camera was somewhere in the possession of his would-be abductors, but that was the last thing he wanted to admit to this asshole. Thane watched a hawk circle lazily over a silo in the distance. "Dave, I know I can't ask you for help, but I'm asking you for work."

"I told you. Nada. I'm not saying I won't pass stuff on. In fact, you've already had a couple of calls."

"I have? From whom?"

Colt hesitated. "If you get work through me I want a commission."

"Understood. Tell me."

"A woman . . . early this morning. She had seen the CNN piece, sounded a bit edgy, said it was personal and wanted to talk to you. I didn't know how to reach you, so I gave her Goodeve's number and suggested she also call Bob Davis."

"1 don't want people bothering Davis."

"Christ, you sound jumpy. What's the problem?"

"You said there was another call."

"Yeah, some guy with an accent. I had two calls on hold at the time. Couldn't make out what he was saying, so I hung up on him."

"Accent, from Africa maybe?" Thane was elated at the prospect of again getting work in Congo, and knew that his name had been circulated in Kinshasa and Kisangani.

"I don't know. I could barely hear him the way he whispered."

28

UNDER A HUMID CLOUD-FILLED SEPTEMBER sky, Hassan's black limousine pulled away from the curb at Kennedy Airport.

As Cali drove through the air pollution haze, Hassan twisted the tiny knobs of the radio in an overhead velvet panel and the limousine filled with Mozart. It was his way of relaxing. He closed his eyes, but after a few moments, without looking up, he asked, "How is she?"

"No better," Samir whispered, sitting across from him. "She rebels with each breath."

Hassan sighed. "One does not buy a thoroughbred without spirit." He leaned his head back against the dark blue velveteen headrest. "She is mine and she knows it. Has she asked for me?"

"Constantly." A lie, but Samir's only acceptable reply.

"And her nose?" Hassan's blow to his wife's face the night of her abduction had turned out to be fortuitous, allowing Samir to leave blood samples in the Mercedes along with the vodka.

"The swelling has receded. You will be pleased."

"Soothe her. Tell her I will join her soon."

"You're not coming tonight?"

"I must remain the grieving husband in New London for a few days. It will placate the police and give you time to get ready."

Then Hassan appeared to be sleeping as they entered the Van Wyck Expressway heading north.

As the car rolled on, Samir gazed out at an industrial park.

"What else?" Hassan asked, his eyes still closed.

Samir wanted to delay disclosing bad news and leaned forward. "Excuse me. Did Saratov show you?"

Hassan looked down through his thick eyelashes as Samir handed him one of the small fake film cartridges.

"No. I haven't seen them." Hassan took the lid off and pulled a small silver chamber out of the holder, balancing it in the palm of his hand. "Incredible, this battery-powered laser technology."

The emerald stone on Samir's hand flashed as he gestured toward the front seat. "And Cali says our molds are seamless. The Russians created tolerances that are less than a mil at the joint."

Handing the silver cartridge back to Samir, Hassan called forward to Cali. "Will the molds make the shells air-tight?"

At the wheel, Cali's gaunt face brightened as he looked in the rearview mirror. "I am certain of it, no particles will escape."

Hassan leaned back again, letting his eyes close. "Yes. But you're a part-time demolitions man, not a scientist."

Samir interjected with a harsh whisper, surprised at the criticism. "Hassan, he has worked very hard—"

"The final proof comes when we detonate," Hassan said quietly. "How will we test for seepage from these doves?"

"Why would we?" Cali asked. "If the Russians—"

Hassan's dark eyes flashed. "The Russians, who bungle assignments like this Adams fiasco? You think I want to risk any trace of radioactivity? This operation will succeed on our merits, and not from secondhand reports from Russian agents in Africa."

Samir assumed a position of humility with his hands tucked between his knees. "Are there unexpected problems in Congo?"

Hassan gazed out the window. "Beyond the video? No. But the villages made the news, and it brought greater scrutiny."

"It was unfortunate the American was there."

Hassan's dark eyes radiated displeasure. "With a camera, no less. It changed Pardux's agenda. He's disposing of evidence. They can't have someone find these battery remnants in the jungle, not at this stage. It might reveal the origin of the chemistry."

"Why not just bury them?"

"They're radioactive. Easily found with the right equipment, even a spy satellite. Pardux makes arrangements to hide them, and the complications may also force him to kill his associates, Claudon and Flobert. When I say 'also,' I assume the American is dead."

Samir regretted that the conversation would take a negative turn. "We're trying to find him," he whispered.

Hassan leaned forward. 'Trying? Cali! What is this?"

Samir was amazed. Hassan had actually shouted at Cali.

"His business manager expected him." Cali craned his neck from the front seat. "But Adams did not arrive at the home this morning."

"Then what are we doing?"

This was the moment Samir had dreaded. He began carefully. "We've assigned the surveillance duties to Bulatzik's associates."

"As Saratov expects."

"Yes. But Adams is not the only individual of concern. Something has arisen with . . . Damita's sister."

"What? Danielle? Has she made inquiries?"

"Much more than that."

"What do you mean?"

"Our monitoring system recorded her entry into your home."

Samir had never seen such a shocked look on Hassan's face. "That's impossible. Where were you?"

"Away with Armitradj and Astia in the city getting supplies. She may have seen the meeting room." Samir hesitated. "And the map."

A deep crimson sank into Hassan's cheeks. He rummaged in his coat for a cigar. Seeing his distress, Samir spoke even more slowly. "We might have to consider eliminating her."

Hassan's eyes threw daggers as he lit a match. "My wife's sister?"

Samir bore up under the reproach. "She's now a dangerous relative," he whispered. "I asked one of Bulatzik's men to watch her house last night. She left town early this morning."

"For where?"

"Philadelphia. What shall we do?"

"Tell Bulatzik to track her down, capture her prudently, and bring her up north. If she gets hurt I understand, but under no circumstances is she to be killed. And I want no suspicions raised that endanger our mission. Do it quick, do it quietly." Irritated, Hassan puffed on the cigar, filling the rear compartment with smoke. "Damn it! Why couldn't she stay out of it?"

29

AS THANE DREW CLOSER TO home, the farms and the fields became increasingly familiar. Like a flashback in a motion picture, sights and sounds along Highway 24 pulled him back to another time, a prior reality.

Apprehension began to surface as he rounded a long curve that bent and twisted over the rise known as Morgan's Bluff.

Tucked into the valley below, Stewartstown appeared with its old bell tower, Colonial Bank, and Bailey's Hardware Store.

Thane rolled down the hillside, dropping through small bedroom communities, tiny neighborhoods dotted with picket-fenced homes and maple-tree-lined streets. As he leveled off, he merged with traffic on Dewey Avenue, the main drag that led through the business sector.

Except for a few new buildings, nothing had really changed. Even the old diner was still there, where he'd spent many an aimless Saturday night in the back booth with friends watching the clock on the wall tick past twelve. What had they been waiting for? To grow up? For destiny to reveal its plan? When destiny finally arrived, it had punished Thane with pain and self-recrimination. His gut tightened as he remembered the hell he'd endured as a young man of eighteen.

Farther down the road in a white wooden church with a tall slender steeple, Sunday services were under way. As Thane drove by the First Congregational House of Worship, he heard a hymn being sung inside. He had been confirmed there. His mother had insisted on it. The gospel choir's strains sounded cheery and welcoming. How odd it was that the music's warmth conjured visions of peace in the rain forest. And how was it, Thane wondered, that God, whom he'd left behind in Stewartstown, had revisited him in the splendor and awe of Africa's immense grandeur?

Turning east on Highway 6, he began the ascent up a long stretch of asphalt known as Crow Valley Road, named for flocks of black birds that inhabited the area. After a mile-and-a-half incline, he topped the hill known as Jergin's Highlands, still crowned by a large elm.

That hulking tree used to be his boyhood marker when he rode his bike from town, because from this point on, Crow Valley Road sloped downward for the long coast home. As he drove past, its crooked branches reminded him of all the times he'd climbed into the tree's gnarled coolness to stare down at "his" valley.

And now, as expected, with the sun blazing across its ten-mile expanse, Thane's valley came into view with the same dazzle he'd remembered.

At the base of the sloping road, Cotton Creek glinted in the sun like a ribbon of mercury. Beyond a row of poplar trees, where the creek flowed under the covered wooden bridge, his driveway waited.

Off in the distance, farms and livestock dotted the hills, but as Thane drove, the focus of his vision remained on the driveway ahead. Passing mileposts seemed to mark the years melting away as he descended into the valley. Finally, the terrain flattened out and he drove past the poplars, clattered across the planks under the coolness of the bridge, and came to a large boulder that rested at the side of the road. The rock was the natural demarcation of the property line. He was now on Adams land.

The white initials T.A. he'd painted on the boulder at age twelve had turned gray. The split-rail fence his father had fashioned lay broken on the ground. The hollowed-out roadside ditch was dry now; Thane recalled one rainy fall day when, as a freckle-faced seven-year-old he had dressed in a yellow slicker and galoshes and sent toy boats racing down the gutter toward the culvert.

Across the pasture, among the long brown grasses, a rusted bucket, an old tractor tire, and a collapsed chicken pen indicated the general state of the farm's disrepair.

The old cedar house marker on a post that once read ADAMS lay on the ground. His father had carved it himself. Thane knocked it down the day of Dad's funeral.

As he drove into the farm with his car's tires crunching on the weed-spiked gravel, Thane's throat began to tighten. Two hundred yards ahead, the old red barn showed gray wood through flaking paint. The remains of the house sat off to the left, now just black spars of wood, a pit of ash. Beyond, on a cotton-wood-covered knoll, the granite monument with his family's four names still glinted white.

He stopped the car and stepped out, setting his safari shoes on dirt he never wanted to see again. The land smelled as sweet as it always had, but as he stood and looked around, just as he'd feared, the memories overwhelmed him.

A few feet away, next to the charred house, a river-rock walkway led to the garden where his mother had grown sunflowers. He could almost see her now, wearing dresses so bright they attracted butterflies. She would have been there between the furrows, hoeing the soil with rows of broccoli, carrots, and radishes. Now the tilled ground was so overgrown the furrows had vanished.

Beyond the broken brick steps to the house, Thane visualized a pillared red porch that no longer existed. His sister Angie's blond curls once fluffed in the sunlight as she toddled in a walker near where the kitchen window had been.

Out back, by the tool shed, he could almost hear the sound of Dad's tractor being tuned up. And beyond the barn, the coolness from a large grove of trees still carried the scent of late summer. He had spent many days in that grove, frolicking with his brother Jeff on acres of green belt that seemed to have no end.

He looked off to the west. Above the poplar trees that lined Cotton Creek, a large flock of crows circled over the parched farm. As they swirled, the birds' silhouettes seemed incredibly black against the sun. Black like the charcoal floorboards of the farmhouse.

He looked down. The ash had mulched with the dirt. The charred ruins of the house seemed so dark they absorbed the surrounding daylight.

His eyes played tricks as he flashed back. Everything around him went white as snow and he was suddenly there a decade and a half ago, looking up at the house as fire raced across the roof.

Above the roar of the inferno, he heard his mother's voice calling his name from the second floor. Ignoring the pain that seared his shoulder, he ran back and forth in the snow, looking for a place to lean the ladder, but the windows were filled with flames. Then as he watched in horror, the remaining red paint on the exterior walls of the house blistered orange and black all at once, and the entire structure burst into a huge fireball.

Thane stumbled backward, staggered by the recollection. With both hands covering his face, he collapsed against the fender of the black Dodge. He wept, remembering the self-condemnation he had endured kneeling naked in the snow in front of the flaming farmhouse. That night, crushed by his misfortune, he hated himself and the world that was left to him. Now, as the tears flowed down his cheeks, he sought forgiveness from God, sensing it might be easier to acquire absolution from the Almighty than from himself.

On his knees, very slowly, he let the burden go, let the years of grief peel away. He wiped his face and looked up. A halo of light rimmed the wispy clouds overhead, and he sensed that the God he had found in Africa had now sought him out in Pennsylvania.

In a moment of complete atonement, he said a short prayer, a short hello to the family he had lost to eternity's care.

Listening to his own breathing, he remained in that kneeling position for several minutes, letting the healing wash over him. He wasn't sure how much time had passed when the feelings of welcome relief were interrupted by an unfamiliar sound for the countryside. His numbed mind could hardly place it. Yet there it was again. On the front seat of his car, his cellular phone was ringing.

Thane rubbed the brightness of the sun and moisture from his eyes. He got to his feet and stumbled toward the open car door. Struggling to regain his composure, he guardedly answered the phone. "Hello?"

The woman's voice on the other end sounded full of expectation. "Mr. Adams, thank God you're in range. Where are you?"

"I'm . . . who's this?"

"My name is Danielle Wilkes. Bob Davis told me where to find you. I must see you. Are you in Stewartstown?"

"Just south. What do you want?"

"I've taken the Glen Rock exit off I-83 and I'm headed east."

"What the hell is this about?"

"I saw you on TV. I need to talk to you about those African villages. Please, I flew down this morning from Boston. This is very important."

Thane was completely unprepared for some crazy reporter. "Look, I'm not staying long, as a matter of fact—" He was interrupted by a thud on the other end of the line.

"Oh God!" Danielle suddenly sounded panicked.

"What's the matter?"

"Somebody rammed my rear bumper." Another thud. "Christ, they did it again! I think they're trying to run me off the road."

"What are you saying?"

"You've got to help me. They're—what should I do?"

"Speed up, I guess. Stay ahead of them."

"All right."

Thane heard road noise on the other end. "Are you there?"

"I'm trying. But they're right on my tail."

"What highway are you on?"

"Eight something."

"Eight fifty-one?"

"Yes, I think so. Oh Jesus."

Thane had jumped into the driver's seat. Hitting the ignition, he shoved the car in reverse. Kicking the driveway's gravel onto the asphalt road, he spun the Dodge around and headed north. "What's happening?"

"They're trying to pull up next to me and I'm doing ninety."

Thane hit the gas hard and accelerated up Crow Valley Road. "Don't let them. Daniels? Are you there? What are you driving?"

"It's Wilkes. Danielle Wilkes. A red Chevy . . ."

"Stay on your heading for Stewartstown, I'm coming your way. I'll try to raise the county sheriff."

"Where?"

"York, I think."

"Yes, call. No! That's too far away. Don't hang up now."

"I can't call if you're on the line."

"Stay with me. God, I hope I can hold this turn. I'm doing almost a hundred."

"Put the phone down and drive." Thane was doing ninety-five himself as he crested Jergin's Highlands.

"No, please stay. If something happens, I need you on the line."

"All right, where are they now?"

"Just off my left rear fender. Oh shit!"

"What?"

"He almost hit an oncoming truck."

"Who? Describe the car."

"It's a black Mercedes. No passengers."

"Try and keep him behind you. I'm coming."

Thane took the frontage road past Stewartstown, passing two other cars as he went. He turned west, headed for Glen Rock, and asked Danielle to once again describe her position. Fortunately, these country roads had very little traffic. It wouldn't take long . . .

On a long flat stretch six miles east of Stewartstown he spotted two cars running almost parallel.

"I see you," Thane shouted as he slowed quickly, pulling onto the shoulder. "Is that you in black?"

"Yes. Just keep coming. I'm turning around."

"What are you doing?"

"You'll see. Come up on my rear and we'll see if this guy has a taste for two against one."

"God."

Thane had accelerated again in pace with Danielle's approach. He was doing eighty as she closed on him. "Just stay in your lane. You got that?"

"As if I could move. He's tight on my left."

"He won't be for long." As both cars grew large in his rearview mirror and Danielle pulled up behind, Thane changed into the oncoming lane directly in front of the black Mercedes. Thane let his foot off the gas, and the Mercedes was forced to do the same. Danielle shot by on Thane's right, nearly sideswiping his passenger door. The Mercedes fell in behind her to avoid hitting Thane's rear end and again gave chase. Thane hit the accelerator and drew parallel with the Mercedes and its driver, a thick-necked, dark-haired man in his mid-forties who seemed shocked at the sight of Thane. Then the husky driver shouted angrily through his open window, pointed a handgun, and fired. The round ripped a ragged hole through the passenger window and passed just behind Thane's head, puncturing the tinted glass to his left.

Thane knew there was only one thing to do to save himself and protect the woman in the car ahead. This guy liked to play bumper cars, and Thane would oblige. Cranking his steering wheel hard to the right, he collided with the Mercedes, crunching the front fender. The driver glanced over, wild-eyed, as the Mercedes and the Dodge veered onto the gravel shoulder. Thane regained control of his car, tapping the brakes, dangerously close to losing it himself. But the Dodge's momentum had done the job. The Mercedes was caught in the soft shoulder's grip. It leaned hard to the right and the tires lost traction as the vehicle slammed into the ditch.

Thane looked back. The black automobile pitched over and rolled sideways into a cornfield. He shouldn't have looked at all. His own car was still partially off the road and he couldn't help hitting a drainage culvert.

As his right wheel slammed into the hole at fifty miles an hour, he heard a wrenching sound as the impact broke the tie-bar, bent the axle, and caused the tire to come away in shreds. The right front fender of his vehicle slumped and sparks flew off the naked hub of the right front wheel. Then the rear end of the Dodge swung dizzily to the left, throwing the car into a three-hundred-and-sixty-degree spin. Another crazy jerk to the right and the Dodge fishtailed into the oncoming lane and came to rest on the opposite shoulder with its rear end facing east.

Thankful to be alive, Thane shook his head. Regaining his bearings, he glanced back at the cornfield. No movement from the wide furrow of stalks that had been plowed by the Mercedes, just a plume of white steam rising slowly into a blue sky.

Up the road several hundred yards, he saw Danielle backing toward him. Grabbing his small overnight kit and his cellular phone, Thane opened the driver's door and climbed out.

He stood by the side of the road waiting as the red Chevy Impala came to a stop next to him. Wearing sunglasses and an emerald green blouse, Danielle leaned out the window. Her red hair caught his eye, flaming like the car in the sun. "Oh, thank you," she said. "That was incredible. Do you think he's dead?"

Thane gazed back down the highway. "I don't know."

"Shouldn't we check?" She removed her sunglasses.

"He took a potshot at me. I don't feel like becoming a target again."

She glanced at the black Dodge that sat crippled on the shoulder, then looked up at him with her large, incredibly expressive green eyes. "I'm sorry about your car."

Thane was struck by her radiance and found himself mumbling, "It's not mine, just a rental."

"So is this." Pushing the car door open, she hoisted herself over the center console into the passenger seat in her black slacks. "Why don't you drive?"

The invitation struck him as oddly casual, as if it had been offered by a pretty girl at a drive-in restaurant. Thane couldn't tell whether he was intoxicated by the chase or by this unexpected encounter with a spirited redhead. Somewhat perplexed, he wandered over and leaned on the door.

"Look, I'm not sure I—" He was interrupted as a gunshot rang out. "Holy shit!"

A puff of white blossomed amid the cornstalks where the black car had crashed, and a moment later another bullet whizzed past Thane's ear. Thane tossed his small bag in the backseat and jumped into the Chevy, hitting the accelerator as yet another round flew by.

A glance in the rearview mirror revealed a man silhouetted in the sun, stumbling up onto the shoulder of the road, firing his handgun. His bullets flew harmlessly by and the Chevy was out of range almost immediately as Thane brought the speed of the car up to seventy.

Thane couldn't help sounding a bit judgmental as he asked the obvious question. "Why is he trying to kill you?"

"Oh, he might have been chasing me," Danielle said, looking over her shoulder. "But I think he was shooting at *you*."

30

AS HE ABSENTMINDEDLY FINGERED THE bananas, Hercule drew a crooked smile from the merchant woman in the colorful dress, who lumbered forward spouting phrases in Swahili. She was nearly as wide as Hercule, and he had to move back to avoid bumping bellies.

"No. I don't want to buy," Hercule said in broken English.

"I do." Uri stepped forward and handed the woman a two-hundred-and-fifty-makuta coin. She shook her head vehemently. "Not enough?" Uri asked, opening his hand. With thick black fingers, the woman cherry-picked through the coins and came away with an additional one-hundred-makuta piece that she apparently considered sufficient. She tucked the money in the folds of her dress and handed Uri a banana.

"I'm surprised you don't want one," Uri said with his mouth full, looking disturbingly simian.

"My stomach is a bit upset." Hercule patted his middle. He suspected that the food on the flight from Cairo to Kisangani had been tainted. Now, he found the heat and the smell of the people's market nauseating. The natives seemed to ignore the flies that blanketed the fruit and vegetable stands, mere wooden crates filled with cassava, peanuts, sweet potatoes, and rice. Cattle paraded through the dusty street led by handlers, part of the day's goods.

"Maybe he thought we'd meet at the station," Uri said, looking more apelike than ever, stuffing banana into his thin face.

"No. This was his preference. Pardux always enjoys hiding in plain sight."

"Do you think he'll ask us?"

"What? To handle the other two? That's up to him. He's still in command. Saratov just wants us here for support. That's Saratov for you. Because Pardux is French and I'm part Russian, I'm his comfort zone, much like you are mine." Hercule pulled his khaki shirt that was sticky with perspiration away from his chest. Though he wore his hat, the heat had forced him to forgo his three-piece suit, and he disliked the tent like shirt and white shorts he had purchased in Kinshasa.

Having watched them patiently from behind her fruit stand, the merchant woman lost patience and came forward with a melon in hand.

"No. No thank you." Hercule shook his head and retreated again, but the woman reached out and patted his stomach, smiling toothlessly. Hercule hated being touched and brushed her away. She scolded him with a series of staccato Swahili clicks and chatters.

"If we have to wait here, you better buy," Uri said.

"I wish I could kill her where she stands."

Uri intervened, handing the woman more coins, just as a Land Rover pulled to a stop at the edge of the market. Pardux, Flobert, and Claudon emerged from the vehicle and the three men strolled into the marketplace. Thankful that the wait was over, Hercule grabbed Uri by his shirtsleeve and began walking.

The five men converged directly in front of the livestock pens, which were brimming with the sounds and smells of pigs, a handful of sheep, several goats and a variety of poultry.

Over the cackle of the chickens in the stacked wooden cages, Pardux greeted Hercule, grasping his hand.

"Sa va?" He gestured to the two men with him. "J'aimerais te presenter mes copains Flobert et Claudon." The two dark-haired Frenchmen were both wiry like Pardux. All three were dressed in tank tops and shorts.

"Mon plaisir." Hercule gestured to Uri. "C'est mon ami Uri."

The men shook hands all around.

"What would make you come to this hellhole?" Flobert asked in French. His thick dark eyebrows shaded his blue eyes.

"Mainly to assure our leadership in Moscow that things are as they should be," Hercule said, smiling graciously, also answering him in French. "You've done an excellent job, but as you well know, this unfortunate video is causing problems." Speaking over the squawks of the fowl, Hercule looked slightly bemused. "This is your idea of a confidential rendezvous?"

Pardux looked around. "It's just five Europeans visiting points of interest in Kolwezi. I like it. No one can hear what we're saying. What did you expect?"

"Something away. In the jungle."

"You'll get your fill of the jungle. Do you have luggage?"

"A few clothes, though little I can wear in this heat. Uri brought a few of his toys, that's all. We checked them at the railway station, not knowing what you intend." Though aware of Pardux's body odor, Hercule edged closer to him. "What's your timetable?"

Pardux nodded to Flobert and Claudon. "Norman knows we're planning to return to the villages. I told him we would check for intermittent half-life readings, which, by the way, are very low. It boggles the minds of the physicists Norman has called." Pardux leaned closer. "What the three of us absolutely must accomplish is the recovery of the shrapnel from the batteries, thanks to the damned American."

"Why didn't you kill him and destroy the video?"

"There were too many people about. And, of course, I had Norman looking over my shoulder every minute. I checked the Internet this morning. Adams continues to evade Bulatzik."

"So what do you want us to do?" Hercule asked, knowing full well that Pardux planned to eliminate his two partners as soon as possible.

"You and Uri relax at the Leopold Hotel. There's decent vodka at the bar and the food is acceptable. It's two blocks over on Lubudi Street." Pardux tucked a piece of paper into Hercule's breast pocket. "That's your room confirmation. It's all you'll need."

Hercule began to reach for the receipt, but Pardux stopped him. "Trust me. I've taken care of everything."

"I see. Thank you."

"These two are the lucky ones," Pardux said, smiling at Flobert and Claudon. "They leave tomorrow, assuming we finish our work."

"Ahh," Hercule smiled at both the men. "Well then, I wish to convey Comrade Saratov's compliments. He will make the appropriate deposits in your Swiss accounts. The French Communist party's contribution to this effort won't be forgotten."

After a short exchange in which Hercule asserted that he hoped he would soon see Flobert and Claudon once the revolution reached France, Pardux led his companions back to their Land Rover.

As Hercule and Uri began their trek to the railroad station, walking past a row of suburban homes built on stilts, Hercule pulled the note from his breast pocket.

"Well," Uri asked, "what was that all about?"

Hercule turned the paper over and read the handwritten message Pardux had penciled on the confirmation. "He's drawn us a map," Hercule said, smiling. "He's asked that we meet him at the end of a rail line twenty-six miles to the north tomorrow afternoon."

31

A TRACTOR TILLING ON A distant hill sent a puff of gray into a clear September sky as Danielle and Thane rode through the wheat fields toward Stewartstown.

The landscape seemed unsuitably cheery, considering that only moments ago an assassin's bullets had flown over their heads.

They were headed east and the sun bore down directly on the hood of the red Chevy, throwing a glare into the car, which encouraged Danielle to put on her sunglasses—softer on the eyes and more convenient for studying Thane.

From the first moment she had seen him on the road, she had been struck by his honest good looks and strong build. He was incredibly trim and moved with an easy elasticity. Of course, it wasn't often in Boston that she'd run into a man wearing nothing but a safari vest and cargo pants. She couldn't help noticing the deep tan on his sleeveless arms, which rippled with muscle as he gripped the steering wheel.

"I had a strange feeling when he pulled that gun," Thane said, keeping the car at seventy.

What an understatement, she thought. "So did I."

"That's not what 1 mean." Thane fixed his pale blue eyes on her. "Not because he fired it. Before that. In the car, the look on his face. He seemed to recognize me."

"Maybe he watches CNN." Seeing him up close, Danielle remembered Thane from the television broadcast, but noted that he hadn't shaved recently.

She surprised herself by wondering what the short stubble would feel like on her skin. Distracted by the notion, she folded her black blazer that had been lying on the front seat and tossed it back next to her suitcase. "CNN. That's where I saw you and that's why I'm here, to explain how we're tied to the same situation."

"Oh, you mean besides being in a demolition derby together." His eyes sparkled with a boyish exuberance when he smiled. "What a unique way to introduce yourself."

She was calmed by his casual assurance. "You know what they say about a first impression."

"I assume a dent in my fender wasn't what you had in mind."

What she did have in mind amazed her. She averted her gaze to the distant wheat fields, finding herself mesmerized by his presence. This guy wore his potency on his sleeve, and perhaps because he wore no sleeves at all, she was drawn to the potential of those strong arms.

Thane . . . a name as fiercely independent as this man seemed to be. Quite different from a Clayton Muir, with his navy blazers and polo shirts.

As she turned to study him, she caught a flash of something metallic out the back window and swiveled to look. No car was in sight.

"Something wrong?" Thane checked the rearview mirror. "You expecting more company?"

She recalled the incident in Boston. "Well even at the airport, I sensed—"

"That you were being followed?"

"Yes. The flight was full and because I was in a hurry, I bought my ticket at the last minute. I heard a man behind me ask the ticket agent about my destination."

"What'd he look like?"

"Scruffy. Jeans and a leather jacket."

"Big blond guy?"

"No. Medium build. I didn't get a good look rushing down the ramp. I just got on as they closed the gate."

"So he didn't make it?" She shook her head, and Thane jabbed a thumb over his shoulder. "But somehow your maniac friend back there found you. Who else knew you were coming?"

"I told my secretary I was flying to Pennsylvania but no one else." Then she remembered. "Oh, Bob Davis. He was the one who told me you'd be down here."

"And what exactly did you say to him?"

A hay truck approached from the opposite direction and lumbered past, followed by a rush of dust and wisps of yellow grass churning in the wind.

"Nothing. I said I'd seen you on TV and it was personal."

"Personal?" He gripped the steering wheel tighter. She noticed he wasn't wearing a wedding band. "What's personal? Africa?"

"Well, yes. Here's the thing . . ." She shifted in her seat, preparing herself. "Does the name Hassan Salaar mean anything to you?"

"Salaar? No."

Somewhat disappointed, she continued. "Okay, but what about the villages? I saw the names at his home. I can't pronounce them . . . Mwada . . ."

"Mwadaba, Judapi, and Butombu?" He sat up a bit straighter.

'That's right. I saw them written down."

"So?"

"That was before your broadcast."

Thane's tanned brow furrowed as his interest intensified. "Run that by me again."

"The day before you were on the air, I found a map of Congo at Hassan's home in Connecticut with the names of the villages written on it."

He shook his head. "You must be mistaken about the timing. This Salaar had to have seen them on the news."

She wasn't going to let this pass, particularly since her sister's life might depend on it. "I'm not mistaken," she said forcefully.

"Still, three names on a—"

"There were six." She glared at him.

"Six?" He seemed momentarily stunned. "You're suggesting there were more villages? Exactly how were they written?"

"Next to the map in two columns." She showed him with her hands. "The names that you talked about were on the left. Judapi, Mwadaba, and Bu . . ."

"Butombu."

"Yes. And the other three were written just across from them on the right."

His blue eyes narrowed. "Okay, go on."

"I can't remember them all, but the top one was something like Pardon— like 'excuse me' in French."

"Mmmm. French?" He frowned.

Placing a slender forefinger to her chin, she tried to recall the word. "Well, no. It ended in X. Parallax, Paradox, or something."

"Oh Jesus." He looked shocked.

"What is it?"

"Pardux," he said abruptly. "Could that have been it?" He looked over. "P-A-R-D-U-X?"

"I think so. Is that another village?"

Thane grimaced, ignoring the question. "This Hassan guy . . . any connections to the World Health Organization?"

"I don't think so. He's an importer."

Thane pushed his sandy-colored hair back. "Pardux is a man, not a village." His jaw tightened as he fixed his eyes on the horizon. "What were the other two names?"

"I don't remember. I had a hard enough time with Pardux, I was so nervous."

"About what?"

"Well, basically, I had broken into the house because my sister Damita, who recently married Hassan, has disappeared."

"You were looking for—"

"Anything. It's complicated. The police are assuming she's dead, but I didn't believe it. She was in this car crash in a river. No body. Just a note left for me in that home, two rooms away from where those African names were written." Her voice broke. "She's all I have left."

Without speaking, he looked at her and his expression changed. The fierce independence faded, replaced by sadness. "No other family?"

"Just my mother, but she has Alzheimer's."

"So why did you come to me?" he asked softly.

"I had to do something. The police are sitting on their hands. I thought you might help, maybe remember something. Those African names in that home may be terribly important."

They passed a sign: STEWARTSTOWN, 5 MILES.

Danielle had to make a decision. "Would you come with me?"

"Excuse me?"

"To Boston. To see the FBI?"

"I've already met the CIA."

"When?"

Thane waved a hand. "Forget it. Just some guys who hassled me at the airport. I need to see a lawyer about some land I want to sell, and I'm expecting Davis's funds in Stewartstown tomorrow. Then I'm out of here."

"Where are you going?"

"Africa."

"Oh, I didn't realize."

Reading the disappointment on her face, he started backpedaling. "Look. I'll see to it that you get straightened out. The first thing you want to do is switch cars. That guy back there obviously knows what you're driving. We can report my damaged vehicle and rent you another. Okay?"

"I don't think it's that simple." Bracing a hand on the dashboard, she leaned in his direction. "I think you're involved in my problem whether you like it or not."

Thane looked down at her manicured nails for a moment and then stared ahead as if he didn't want to hear any more.

Danielle pressed on. "Does the term 'doves' mean anything to you?"

"No."

"Those were the words in a note my sister left. Something frightened her. She had heard Hassan's associates discussing a murder—"

"What are you talking about? What associates?"

"Like Hassan—Middle Eastern men." She brushed her long red hair back, now confident that she had his attention. "I think she called one of them Cali, the other . . . Armitradj. The third one was named Samir. He's a weirdo with a bad leg and a whisper."

"What did you say?" Thane turned, his face flooding with disbelief. "A whisper? Someone at International Geographic said something about a guy with an accent who whispered"—he stared at her—"calling and asking for me."

"There, you see." She had touched a nerve. "Too many coincidences. Just another reason for you to stick around and find out what's going on." She moved closer on the bench seat. "Look, how much money is Davis sending you?"

"Four grand."

"Well, that'll still be there when you're ready to get it. I'll cover you until then. I'll buy a plane ticket to Boston this afternoon. I've already put a call in to the FBI. We can both tell them our stories. Anything to help find my sister. Come on, what do you have to lose?"

"Time and money."

"Look. I'll pay you well."

"For what?"

"I need someone to help find Damita. Just give me a few days." He seemed unmoved. "How about if I double what Davis is sending?"

Thane was stunned. "Eight grand for a few days?"

"You heard me." She waited.

He shot her a baffled glare, then looked at the highway and back to her again. She was relieved to see him fight a roguish grin.

"Are you crazy?" he asked.

She winked. "No, I'm liberated."

He broke into a smile and applied the brakes, slowing the car.

"What are you doing?" she asked hopefully, looking around. "Isn't that Stewartstown up ahead?"

Thane pulled off onto the shoulder and swung the wheel, putting the Chevy into a U-turn. "Yes, but my eight thousand and the York Airport is that way," he said, pointing. "And if this is your idea of women's lib, I can't wait to sample the rest."

32

IT WAS THE CHIN, SARATOV thought as he stared at Guyenov. Russian leaders had good strong chins; a foundation for robust faces that reflected the constancy of the land and its people. Guyenov had that look of having risen from the earth. Even his humble gray suit looked old, just shoddy enough to ward off even the slightest suggestion of prosperity.

Under the cover of night, his personal security guards stood watch outside the doors as Guyenov finished his speech to the twenty-six Communist party members he had assembled. Ironically, their secret meeting place was the basement of an abandoned Greek Orthodox church, and Guyenov's voice echoed through the bulky Byzantine pillars that supported the empty basilica above, soon to be torn down to make room for a factory.

Volchenko and Saratov had crossed the border from the Ukraine for this important meeting.

Like Saratov, the nineteen men and seven women in the room were members of the old KGB. All had worked together in Lubyanka headquarters in Moscow. But after Gorbachev's departure, due to their hawkish political views, they had become casualties of the reform government. Some four hundred officers were fired by Yeltsin's regime. They were outcasts, ostracized from the *Ministerstvo Bezopasnosti*, Russia's ministry of security, whose personnel called each other Chekisti, the name reminiscent of the Bolshevik secret police, the Cheka, the organization that preceded the KGB.

Guyenov had worked personally with each of the twenty-six including Eva Yatsukova, who represented thousands of disgrunded Russian women;

Alexander Popov, a retired general representing the many military officers who regretted the decline of Soviet power; Alexei Uprinian, who had helped Guyenov organize many of Russia's one hundred and thirty-five thousand KGB agents and secret police who resented the growth of Mafiya influence and the corruption of the regime; and Sascha Drubov, an activist from Sverdlovsk who headed a grassroots movement of underground communists who had met in private for years, scheming for a return to old ways.

These, like the others in the room, were key to the coup. Each was trusted and had been promised a position in Guyenov's future state, a position they deserved since they could influence opinion, have an impact on votes, and mobilize the masses.

All of them knew of the coming purge of the United States.

Tonight, Guyenov had brought them together to reinforce their solidarity before the crisis began. They would soon be asked to openly defy their government and support a people's movement to restore the Soviet Union.

As usual, Guyenov's oration was emotional—filled with sentimentality, a yearning for a time when Russia was respected by foreign powers, not just considered an economic liability.

In moments like these, Guyenov managed to generate a bit of moisture under each eye as he looked up at the gold hammer and sickle on the red flag that hung from the rafters.

"And so, my comrades, go back to your people and give them hope. Tell them that Putin's promise to give us 'a mighty assault on corruption, bribery, and general crime' has failed. But tell them that nevertheless, they will soon be rid of the parasites who infest our so-called reformed democracy." The last two words were heavy with scorn.

"This world event will reunite many communists who are without a country. Our brothers in Western Europe will be invited to return. Some key aging agents who were stranded in the US by Gorbachev will be asked to come back to us. Those who wish to join us will be welcome. And I am uplifted by reports that our brothers and sisters in Lithuania, Latvia, Estonia, and Belarus still look to a rising Russian sun. Our supporters in Kazakhstan, Kyrgyzstan, and other southern provinces still long for the Russian north wind when Middle Eastern heat billows from the south. And look what has happened in Ukraine—it is a sign of things to come.

"Tell everyone of the coming unity, the coming peace. The day has arrived.

Prevention of further wars is now"—he raised his arms, palms up—"in these hands"—he pointed around the hall—"and in yours . . . and in yours . . . "

Guyenov slowly paced the room, looking each person in the face. "I am confident no blood will be spilled on Russian soil. On the day fire ravages the United States, I will make my demands in the Duma and you"—he glared at them—-"will be in the field, guaranteeing that the coup succeeds. I doubt it will come to such extremes, but you must remain ready. If power is not passed to me, parliament will be destroyed. Thereafter, you would immediately receive instructions from Saratov to trigger a device at your targets."

Guyenov paused and looked up at the flag once more. "Some of you have asked what we will have left if the heavens fall. The answer is—the land itself, free of those who enslave us. Communists have never needed more than the land and the good people who live upon it." Guyenov's voice rose with intensity. "Here in Russia, we can do without capitalists. If the bureaucrats burn, so be it."

He looked back down at the gathering.

"Here is the lesson: Without dominant world power, Russia becomes putty. The West wields its knife, wedging us into cracks. But no longer." Guyenov pointed to Volchenko, who was seated beside Saratov. "The knife will be dulled by the might of the dove."

Mumbling and mild applause from the others greeted these stirring words. Volchenko looked about nervously, attempting a smile. Saratov was well aware of the scientist's apprehensions. Volchenko strongly disagreed with the distribution of the doves throughout his homeland, yet acquiesced when Guyenov made it clear their use would be a last measure of desperation.

Guyenov gestured to Saratov. "And Saratov. I make a tribute to our brilliant expediter, who masterminded the network to distribute the doves so efficiently."

Saratov nodded without smiling, and spoke up. "You should have all received your shipments by now." Several members of the audience nodded.

"And by tomorrow, your kilns should be hot," Guyenov added. He folded his hands, as if in prayer. The others waited as he immersed himself in contemplation, but the silence was suddenly disrupted by one of Guyenov's guards, who burst through the rear door.

"Sir, there's a night patrol of soldiers two blocks away." Guyenov pointed to the stairs. "All right, go upstairs quietly. There are four exits. Disperse. Thank you all for coming. Go in peace and prepare."

As the hall emptied, one of the guards retrieved the red flag. Saratov hurriedly shook hands with those leaving and waited by the podium with Volchenko. Alexander Popov, a bald, dominating man with an old-fashioned handlebar mustache and piercing brown eyes, had captured Guyenov's attention, leading him to the corner of the room.

Moments later, Guyenov's guards joined them, and Popov was forced to leave. Guyenov said his last farewells, then rejoined Saratov and Volchenko with his guards in tow.

"There's a basement exit." Guyenov pointed. "A tunnel to the rectory."

"Good. Lead the way," Saratov said. With flashlights in hand, the men entered the underground hallway. After some sixty feet they ascended an ancient set of wooden stairs into what had been the priest's humble living quarters, then exited the other side of the building into the open air.

Guyenov's guards led the way at a respectful distance. The street was virtually empty.

With Saratov at his side, Guyenov put an arm around the timid Volchenko, who carried his hat in his hands.

"How do you feel now, Guga?" Guyenov asked robustly, "about my call to arms, and our soldiers advancing to take their posts."

"I shudder to think—"

"I know," Guyenov said, patting his arm. "Don't worry. The devastation in the US will convince them. If not, a single dove in the parliament will solve it. Our provinces will remain untouched."

As they crossed an intersection under the street lamps, Guyenov looked over at Saratov. "Have you sent my shipment?"

Saratov nodded. "A crate will arrive at your warehouse in Moscow tomorrow."

Volchenko seemed disturbed. "If you've given all these people their quota, why have you asked me for more? What will you do—"

Guyenov shot Saratov a glance. "A crate of doves must be constructed and stored at a secret stronghold I have in Siberia. Remember, a large reserve arsenal is absolutely necessary. Once we initiate this action, we want to be sure we can finish it."

33

THANE HAD FALLEN INTO ONE of his restless, half-conscious slumbers that followed too many hours without sleep.

He was fully aware that he must be on a plane—the hum of the propellers droned at the edge of his consciousness. But that realization didn't prevent him from once again escaping to Africa in his fantasies.

He had begun to dream one of his favorite dreams: the lions on the beach.

He had seen the cats in person on a shoot south of Pangani, Tanzania, when he and his bearers had come across a rare lion pride frolicking in the late-afternoon sun. Their furry tails whipped like car antennas as they romped close to the crashing surf on a bleached sandy shore.

The scene had been spectacular: brightly colored seabirds swarmed overhead in a light sea haze while the sunlight glinted off the golden lions, who pawed at one another's hind quarters in a chase near pale blue water. But now, for the first time in his dream, his attention was drawn to one lion in particular, a large female that didn't frolic with the rest but looked on from the shade of a large tree.

Thane's mind zoomed in on the great head of the animal, so close he could hear her breathe. His consciousness seemed to blend with the lioness as the rumble in her broad chest filled his ears, and her pupils broadened with some strange understanding. Her green eyes were filled with a deep black sheen, strangely translucent, dimensionless.

Through those eyes, as if he were falling into them, Thane saw eternity. He suddenly sensed his own mortality. In an unpleasant flash, the dream disintegrated and he was running back and forth in the snow in front of his burning farmhouse. As flames engulfed the second floor, this time it was Kuintala who screamed from the window, wailing like a wounded animal. Thane struggled to get away from it all, pulling himself into another dimension. Rolling his head over, he landed a cheek on Danielle's shoulder.

"Excuse me," he said, embarrassed. He sat up and looked around the gray vinyl interior of the small plane.

The pilot and owner of the aircraft, a friendly-faced middle-aged man named Dobsen, glanced over his shoulder and noticed that Thane was awake. "Welcome back. We're about thirty minutes out."

Thane smiled and nodded, running a hand through his sandy hair.

Danielle nudged him. "That was quite a nap."

"I'm still catching up. Sorry."

"Don't be. You obviously needed it."

They were in the last two seats of a twin-engine six-seat Cessna 411 that Danielle had chartered in desperation after an abrupt change in plans.

Things had taken a strange turn as they approached the rental-car return at the York airport and Thane caught sight of a familiar profile.

A black-haired man had just risen from the bench outside the rental office and was heading for an outdoor restroom. Even from sixty yards away, the brush cut and the burly build were unmistakable. It was the man who called himself McNair. The driver of the crashed Mercedes had apparently gotten to a phone. He also, apparently, had friends.

Before McNair could spot their car, Thane had made a quick U-turn and headed to the private airfield next door. While they drove the half mile, Thane quickly explained his encounter with McNair at Kennedy. Danielle listened intently and agreed that the incident had established that all the men they'd encountered must be working for a single organization. CIA or not, Thane and Danielle had common enemies.

At the small airfield, Danielle made some quick phone calls, while Thane used her traveler's checks to negotiate a charter. Ten minutes later, they were in the air.

After the Cessna's takeoff, Danielle and Thane had talked in hushed tones that the pilot couldn't hear over the engine noise.

Thane was genuinely enjoying her company. How different she was from Lorrel, he thought. While he had appreciated his ex-girlfriend's virtues, Danielle was totally polished, mentally sharp, and intensely beautiful. Beyond that, she demonstrated something more: a fighting spirit, a strangely likable grit.

She had seemed to want to know all about him, and at Danielle's prompting, Thane told her of his past. Unsatisfied, she had continued to probe.

"What kind of a name is Thane? I've never heard that before." She had a gentle yet incisive way of asking a question, and she demanded frankness with eyes that could penetrate.

"I guess because Dad was a farmer—"

"You're kidding, so was mine," she said. "I'm sorry, please go on."

"Well, he would have named me Bill or Steve or something, but since my mother and father were both only children, I grew up without a lot of family— no aunts, uncles, or cousins. Anyway, Mom did a family tree and discovered that oddly enough my father's great-grandfather had been a Shakespearean actor in England. His name was Thane."

"What's it mean?"

"I'm not absolutely sure. It's supposed to be Gaelic for 'a landowner' . . . a knight who owned property."

"A knight?" Danielle's perfect mouth had formed a quick smile. "So . . . what was that car chase near Stewartstown? A joust?"

They laughed about their encounter on the highway. Then she asked what had made him leave Pennsylvania.

He tried to gather his thoughts. "Strange," he had said. "Until recently, I was convinced I was chasing my future. But you're right. Something made me leave. My family died."

"Family? Wife and kids?"

"No, my mother, brother, and sister. I was quite young."

"How awful. You want to tell me about it?"

"I really don't," he had said softly, looking her straight in the eye. "Maybe later. You've got enough on your mind." He didn't volunteer any more and changed the subject by asking about her own history.

She touched on her professional success and, perhaps because he was the first person she had found who would listen, she started explaining her current frustrations at the office. She nearly cried describing Damita's estrangement and her subsequent disappearance. When Thane asked about their childhood, she told him about her family—her father's death from a heart attack and her mother's dwindling life at the Tarrington Nursing Home. She admitted that she hadn't told her mother about Damita yet, feeling that until the facts were known, she saw no reason to risk upsetting her.

For an instant during the discussion, Thane saw her in a different light—she was someone like himself—a lost child grieving the memory of a whole family. Like all adults, she had developed a hardened veneer to protect her inner softness. He enjoyed watching her beautiful face, the depth of expression in her eyes. It had been a long time since he'd shared the honesty of inner vulnerability with someone, not since his mother died.

As he shook himself awake, Danielle turned to him, whispering so the pilot couldn't hear. "What were you dreaming? You were saying a word. Keen something."

"Keen? Oh." Thane grinned, somewhat embarrassed. "Kuintala. The friend who was with me at the villages."

"He's obviously on your mind."

"I haven't told you," Thane whispered. "He was there with me when I met Pardux."

"Are you worried about him?" Again, he was struck by the degree of emotion she could express with a glance. "Yes, but I respect him. He can handle himself."

"What's he like?" She smiled as she sensed Thane's affection for his friend.

"Over six feet, very muscular." Thane looked out at the passing clouds. They were slowly dropping in altitude, making their approach into Boston. "He's like . . . " He struggled for the right description. "You've seen a totem pole, an Indian representation? He's like that—part tree, part rock, part animal—all within the confines of a peaceful human soul."

She nodded and tilted her head pensively. "That's quite a poetic description. Is that how you see things?"

He mulled the idea before answering. "When I shoot video I 'compose' shots more than 'see' them. I guess it's that way with anything. The world is the world—how you read it makes you who you are."

She nodded. "And so you read Kuintala as—"

"Someone who absorbs everything. He told me that, as a young man, he learned to walk 'within the night.' The operative word is 'within.' He's like that in the jungle; he becomes a part of it."

"And you?"

"I wish I had his powers."

"And you wish you were still in the jungle."

"I do, often." He gazed at her. "Haven't you ever yearned to be totally free?"

She smiled wistfully. "I thought I was."

"Does success mean a lot to you? The money?"

"Success, yes. But money is a by-product of doing well. I despise greed, and I find it unfortunate that people make the pursuit of wealth a substitute for personal development. They think as long as they have the cash they should be admired."

Thane nodded. "I've met a few like that. They breed in the cities. Dreary, self-absorbed millionaires."

"The business keeps me going. It's always with me." She pointed to the cellular phone on her lap. "That's who I was calling at the airport. I had to assure my secretary that I plan to be there for meetings next week."

"You may not even be able to go home. How do you plan to get to your office without being tracked?"

"FBI protection, hopefully." She looked uneasy as she thought it over. "That was my other call—to my answering service. An agent from the Boston office had left a message. They're expecting me before six."

"Good. Maybe I can . . . " Thane paused, interrupted by the crackling of a radio message over the speaker in the cockpit. Dobsen tuned in the signal.

"Cessna Three Eight Bravo, this is Logan approach. Come in," the speaker said.

Dobsen replied, "Logan, this is Three Eight Bravo, go ahead."

As Danielle leaned forward to listen, Thane took a moment to study her profile—the even chin, the smooth cheekbones, and the straight, slightly pointed nose. He was distracted by another crackling transmission.

"Three Eight Bravo, be advised. Flight Service has requested your ETA at Logan."

Dobsen responded. "Roger, Logan . . . be advised we are VFR to Logan enjoying the ride."

"Copy, Three Eight Bravo, but say your position, Flight needs to know your ETA."

"Roger, Logan. Hold on." Dobsen looked back over his shoulder.

Thane moved forward into the second row of seats. "What's the problem?"

"No problem. It's just strange that they're asking. We're outside Logan's controlled airspace. Is there someone meeting you at the airport?"

"No, and we don't want an announced arrival. That's why we chartered."

Danielle joined Thane in the middle seats as the pilot turned and nodded. "Let me check this." He hit the talk button and spoke into the handset. "Logan, this is Three Eight Bravo. I'm still well out of range. Any idea why the request for my ETA?"

"Request originated in York, Three Eight Bravo. Can't say why."

Danielle gave Thane a troubled look. "Would someone at the York tower normally request that information?"

"Only reason it might happen," Dobsen said, "is, like I said, if someone's expecting you at Logan."

Thane whispered to Danielle, "We don't need this. It could be McNair and his CIA buddy trying to track us."

Danielle reached into her purse and pulled out three hundred-dollar bills. "Mr. Dobsen, would it be too much of an inconvenience to drop us off at a different airport?"

"The money's not necessary, Ms. Wilkes. You chartered the airplane. It will take you where you like." Dobsen again pressed the button and spoke into the handset. "Logan, I'm canceling my flight plan. We're going to do a little sightseeing up here. We'll be in touch." He turned in his seat and smiled at Danielle. "I'll just drop below radar coverage and we'll head for another destination."

"Is that kosher?" Danielle asked, still holding the bills.

"Perfectly." Dobsen unfolded a map on the seat and tapped it with a forefinger. "There's a nice little private airport outside Framingham, fifteen miles northwest of Boston. How would that be?"

34

THE MOBILE FBI FIELD OFFICE was housed in the Barton Building, an annexed section of the Government Center used by various federal branches for temporary office space. The hallways of the aging structure smelled musty, and the green tile floors were scuffed and needed wax. The entrance to the FBI office was purposely left shoddy, and the plain wood-framed frosted-glass door of the office bore no lettering.

Once inside, Danielle and Thane stepped into a bare lobby with plain walls and rented brown-metal furniture.

They were greeted by a straitlaced receptionist in a high-collared blouse, seated at a laminated desk.

Though the office was unimpressive, Danielle felt relieved to have arrived at their destination. Fortunately, the cab ride from Framingham's small airport had been uneventful, and even in these bleak surroundings she enjoyed a sense of security.

After a brief wait, an Asian-American woman, Jamie Gere, an energetic and friendly investigative assistant in her twenties, led them through a central hall-way with a number of small rooms on either side. Behind partially closed doors, muffled voices could be heard, along with the whir of a laser printer and the tapping of fingers on a computer keyboard.

At the end of the hall they were ushered into a tiny office.

Ms. Gere recorded extensive notes on a thick pad of paper as she questioned them. Then Danielle and Thane were escorted next door to a conference room.

There, in the bleak dimly lit room that looked out onto an alley with another building across the way, they were asked to wait for Agent Emory Carver.

When Carver finally arrived forty-five minutes later, he seemed harried. He reminded Danielle of a Marine sergeant forced into civilian duty, with rough edges worn down by Bureau discipline. His athletic frame was somewhat disguised in a blue business suit and his rugged face would have been considered almost attractive if it hadn't been marred by pockmarks.

Carver's darting, intelligent bright blue eyes peered out from silver-rimmed glasses as he clutched several pieces of computer paper. "I've looked over Gere's notes," he said as he joined them at the simple oak conference table. "Ms. Wilkes, you claim you have a kidnapping on your hands and that you've been chased and harassed."

"That's right."

"And yet, from what I see here, the New London Police have the fatality listed as a traffic accident."

"They have yet to find my sister's body. I've gone on record with them about my dissatisfaction with the way things were handled."

"That's all very well. But the FBI's involvement in cases like these is predicated by the law—namely proof of a kidnapping with some kind of interstate infraction."

Danielle reached into her pockets and pulled out the slip of paper. "Here's the note Damita wrote."

Carver studied the writing for a moment. "With all due respect, 'they're taking me' could have referred to a social event."

"Or an abduction," Danielle shot back.

"How many times have you heard of an abduction where the victim had the time or the presence of mind to write a note?" Carver asked, pushing his glasses up on his nose.

"But I was followed," Danielle responded impatiently. "And Mr. Adams was a witness to the attempt to run my car off the road in Pennsylvania."

"Well, a quick check did validate the fact that your rented Chevy had body damage when they recovered it. The car company was quite upset about the dents and that the vehicle wasn't properly returned."

"Just a minute," Thane said, "what about the wreck?"

"Which wreck, Mr. Adams? Damita's?"

"No. The black Mercedes we mentioned in our report to Agent Gere."

"Well, there again, we have inconsistencies. The Pennsylvania State Patrol records report no car of that description found either on or off Highway 851 near Stewartstown."

"What about my car?" Thane asked.

Carver shook his head. "Nothing. Though the car-rental company does show a Dodge Charger still rented in your name."

"They must have moved it. God. They didn't waste any time." Suddenly restless, Thane stood up and began to pace.

Carver shrugged. "They? Who is they, Mr. Adams? I can't work on assumptions."

"That's just it, we don't know." Danielle felt growing frustration. "Okay, forget about Pennsylvania. The reason Mr. Adams is here is the connection between his video and the map I saw at my sister's home."

"What connection, Ms. Wilkes? I noted the African business," Carver said, pulling a long earlobe. "The villages on Mr. Adam's video had been on the news and have become public knowledge. Meantime, I've checked with the CIA database. They show nothing notable regarding Congo. It may be too soon, or perhaps not worthy of their attention."

At the mention of the CIA, Thane came to a stop, gave Danielle a sidelong glance. "Hundreds of dead . . . not worthy?" he asked.

"Do you realize how many thousands of dead are reported annually in Africa, Mr. Adams? In dozens of countries. Do you think we investigate each of those? Your tax dollars at work? Famine. Disease. Civil wars. Ethnic purges. Certainly, organizations like the Red Cross, World Hunger Relief, and others become immediately involved. But unless these tragedies are strategically imperative, our government agencies don't take any action. And please keep in mind, our interests overseas are largely the domain of the CIA, not the FBI."

"Did you check on the men who met me at Kennedy—who represented themselves as CIA agents?" Thane asked.

Carver referred to a computer printout. "No such names on their register. Though that particular government agency is less than open about their personnel."

Danielle felt like she was swimming upstream. "But the names of those villages—right here in New London. Wouldn't that be a domestic issue?"

"With all due respect to the deceased, what appears to have been the domestic problem was Damita Wilkes's marriage. And if you're both suggesting that a homicide occurred, that remains a local police matter."

"I see." Danielle felt a growing depression. "Then the FBI won't help."

"I haven't said that." Carver looked directly into Danielle's eyes. "But the facts point to a traffic fatality: meaning the police report of a vehicle breaking through a guardrail, alcohol in evidence, blood on the dash, and a car in the river."

Danielle could feel her face redden as Carver continued.

He appeared to notice and turned to Thane. "And as far as your African villages are concerned, Mr. Adams, what are you suggesting, that the natives were bombed with some kind of weapon?"

"Maybe experimentation of some kind."

"By people who reside in New London, Connecticut?"

"No, that's not what I'm saying."

Thane's irritated body language made Danielle more uncomfortable. She glared at Carver and reached for her jacket. "You're deliberately trying to make it all sound ridiculous." She rose to her feet.

"Believe me, that's not my intent," Carver said, looking up. "But do you know how many daily bomb threats, terrorist tips, crackpot phone calls we get? This office still receives roughly five calls a month from people who can prove how JFK was killed, probably six to eight from folks who have aliens as neighbors, ten to fifteen regarding bogus bomb scares, and at least two that claim knowledge of alternative plots to 9-11."

"Mmmm. And what if even one of them is something meaningful?" Thane asked, pacing again.

"They are meaningful in the minds of the callers, but I'm trying to show you how selective we have to be to open a case."

"We appear to have fallen short of your criteria," Danielle said bitterly as she headed for the door.

"Carver," Thane said as he joined her. "You don't strike me as a man who'd make light of other people's problems. But I think you've got a damned casual attitude for someone who's supposed to help."

"Hold up, Mr. Adams." Carver threw an arm over his chair. "I haven't said I wouldn't act on this."

"What?"

"I've already placed a call to Officer Reynolds in New London. He's agreed to have the accident site reexamined and says he'll be happy to make room in his schedule to meet with me."

"I'll bet he was delighted," Danielle said, glancing at Thane, "particularly after my call to his boss."

"He didn't mention that, but I'm sure he understands that if the FBI becomes involved, it's not unusual for us to reassess the situation. Frankly, what I thought reasonable might be a visit to Mr. Salaar. I plan to drop by tomorrow morning with Reynolds as the investigating officer. A fact-finding mission, if you will. If circumstances warrant, I might recommend that we open a file, or if nothing comes of it, we'll have to let the matter drop."

Heartened by the opportunity to prove she was right, Danielle ventured back to her chair. "If that's your plan, I want to go along."

"Under the circumstances—"

"No, I insist. Mr. Adams as well."

Carver hesitated. "If I allow you to come, you'll do exactly what I tell you. Even if it means asking you to leave."

"That's fine. I just want to see his face," Danielle said sternly.

"Why are you doing this, after listing all the reasons why you shouldn't?" Thane asked.

"Call it my personal curiosity." Carver handed one of the computer print-outs to Thane. "While you were waiting, Bureau headquarters in Washington did a cross-check on the names and facts you gave Gere. You'll note that there was one rather interesting entry: the word 'radioactivity' and the word 'dove,' cross-checked. Here's what we found." He showed Thane the bottom of the page. "'Dove' was a relatively obscure term coined during the Nixon administration for a certain nuclear device. It was never manufactured, but it was discussed on occasion in Congress. It was called the 'dove' because it was considered a peace-keeping weapon. Its unique characteristic: while it could kill people, it wouldn't destroy property."

"Property," Thane said pensively. "The village huts weren't even touched. You're saying the US considered making that weapon?"

Carver patted the computer printout. "According to this information, the Pentagon took the official position that the weapon, essentially a hybrid of the 'neutron bomb,' was unfeasible. Impossible to build. A scientist named Ronald Colfax became the main proponent of the device, then, inexplicably, he reversed his position. Agreed it was unachievable."

"Pardux," Thane said, gazing out the window.

"What? Oh, one of your names."

"Someone who has answers. I think you'll find he's responsible for—"

"He's in Africa?" Carver shook his head, interrupting. "Remember . . . "

"Yes, I know. Not your area."

Hearing Carver's technical interpretation of the "dove" forced Danielle to recognize the kind of danger her sister was in. "Damita must have known."

"Ms. Wilkes, let me give you a piece of advice," Carver said. "I understand your need for conjecture, but try not to torture yourself with wild guesses about what all this means, until we have some basis for an investigation." Carver reached out to shake her hand. "You'll sleep better."

Danielle withdrew her hand, annoyed by his condescension. "Agent Carver, it's my intention to prove that there is a basis for an investigation."

"Then let's hope something comes of our visit tomorrow."

Danielle smiled politely, visualizing Hassan's home, silently vowing to find a way back upstairs. If she could just get her hands on that map, get to the room where the easel probably still stood. She remembered the layout of the house, the route she might have to take. If she asked to use the guest bathroom . . .

Carver turned to Thane and shook his hand. "Where will you be staying?"

"We've reserved rooms at a Hilton Garden Inn, south of town."

"Then I'll call for you there in the morning. We can drive down to New London together. I'm intrigued by what you described in Congo, Mr. Adams. In my early career, I was a member of a bomb squad."

"Mr. Carver," Danielle asked. "What about my note?"

"I'll hang on to it for now, Ms. Wilkes. But don't get your hopes up. All I can do is promise a visit to Mr. Salaar's home, nothing more, nothing less."

DAY EIGHT

35

MONDAY—3:05 p.m.
Kolwezi, Congo

HERCULE'S TENT-LIKE SHIRT AND HIS puffy white shorts were drenched with perspiration.

He had reached the ends of the earth or at least the end of the line. The line was the Katanga Railway, and at its end, on a jungle spur no one had used in years, sat an ancient freight car.

Covered with overgrowth, its door rusted half-open, the copper-colored conveyance had become a stationary hearse, the temporary resting place of Paul Claudon and Jean Flobert.

Preoccupied with the one-hundred-and-fifteen-degree heat, Hercule remained emotionally detached as he stared at the bodies. They'd been propped in the corner like two rag dolls, each having gained a third eye after being expertly shot through the forehead with a Ruger .22 by Pardux.

And like Pardux, they still wore their tank tops. Aside from what remained of their normal body odor, the heat had not yet caused them to stink, thank God, but they would start to decay soon enough. Flies had begun to swarm around the inside of the car, creating a constant hum.

Hercule checked his watch. Uri had been gone twenty minutes. "So how far is this cave?" he asked, patting the back of his neck with a moist handkerchief.

"It's where I said it was." Pardux toyed with two clear plastic sacks. "If Uri knew how to read a compass, he would be back by now."

"Ah! The compass could be inaccurate due to the radioactive battery parts."

"Oh. So now you're a scientist," Pardux said sarcastically.

"Well, am I right?"

Pardux swatted a fly from his forehead. "Yes, goddammit."

Hercule gloated. He was thrilled when he could one-up his cousin or Uri in matters of physics. "It must be hell walking two miles in a biohazard suit."

"One mile. He had to wear it on the way there, not on the way back. And you heard him. He didn't want to. He did it because you wouldn't fit into the suit." Pardux had separated the large clear plastic bags, laying one on each dead man's chest.

"No, he did it because he loves gadgetry," Hercule said, pondering why heat was more unpleasant for the obese. He nodded to the crate of dynamite in the corner of the car. "And because he couldn't wait to seal the cave with an explosion. Plus, the battery shrapnel fascinated him."

Pardux looked up, taunting his cousin. "He did the walking. You bury the bodies."

"What?"

"You're here, I'm going." Pardux pulled on Claudon's collar. The corpse's head flopped limply onto his chest, scattering the flies. Pardux placed the first plastic bag over his upper torso. "There's a shovel outside. I must return that suit. Dr. Norman seemed surprised about my wanting to keep it after we finished our airlift."

"So what did you tell him?"

"He thinks Flobert and Claudon have gone on to Europe for other assignments and that I'm still checking half-life deterioration."

"And he accepts that?"

"For now. But I have to get back to base camp or he'll wonder why I'm lingering in the forest."

"Linger long enough to bury these." Hercule gestured to the corpses.

"No, thank you." Pardux moved over and placed the second plastic sack over Flobert. "Norman wants me to accompany him to Kinshasa. He has a meeting with forensic experts this evening."

"And what do you think they'll conclude?"

"Nothing." Pardux smiled. "The average medic can't deal with conflicting facts."

Hercule noted that Pardux thought of himself as something beyond "average," even though he had been dismissed from medical school for performing an abortion on a female classmate. The tattoos and his cocaine addiction followed.

Pardux snickered. "How will a forensics man explain a corpse that shows every indication of having been in a nuclear accident yet exhibits no other signs of trauma?"

"What did they look like?" Hercule realized he had previously never thought to ask.

"Judapi's intense heat melted eyeballs from their sockets, blistered the skin. Mwadaba's shock was milder, so their skin simply shed a fine ash, body hair burned in less than a tenth of a second. The doctors have no idea why they were different."

"And why were they?"

"Proximity. The purpose of the test. We now know people within two kilometers look like the Judapi dead . . . from two to four kilometers, like the Butombu dead, and from four to six like Mwadaba."

"And no clues."

"None, except the battery shrapnel."

Hercule wiped his forehead. "And you decided the shrapnel had to be recovered because . . ."

"Because of this idiot Adams and his camera. God, I wish I'd killed him. Without him, we might have had days of extra time."

"And how did you find this debris?"

"First of all, I didn't." Pardux gestured toward Claudon and Flobert. "These two did . . . searching with a Geiger counter. Can you imagine sifting through the brush looking for scraps a few inches long? I was too busy playing medical volunteer for Norman. Locating the scraps wasn't difficult; a random search of the detonation sites, each some distance from the villages. Excessively high rad readings led to the pieces. Once Uri's sealed them in that cave, no one will spot the radiation."

The sound of rustling bushes outside the freight car caused Pardux to reach for his holstered .22. Hercule stepped back into the shadows as Pardux squatted, ready to fire, then lowered the weapon.

Uri appeared at the open door of the freight car, sweating profusely, a green biohazard suit slung over his shoulder.

"God, there were a million bats in that cave." He pulled a small electronic detonator out of his pocket. "On the first blast a few got out, but when the rest of that bundle went, you should have seen the blow. Nobody's getting in there. The bats might find a way out. With their echolocation sensors—"

"Hey. I really don't give a shit." Pardux holstered the weapon. "It won't matter anyway. Those bats will be dead in a few days." Uri had dropped the suit on the transom and Pardux knelt down to pick it up. "The radiation in that cave would kill an elephant."

"Or me." Uri hoisted himself into the car out of the intense sun. "I'm glad I wore that suit." He peered around the car, wiping the moisture from his arms. "This is hell," he said.

"No. *They're* in hell," Pardux said, pointing to the bodies. He knelt and jumped down to the ground, carrying the suit. "What about the dynamite?"

Hercule called after him. "Leave it. It's too dangerous to move in this heat."

Pardux disappeared and was back in a moment with a shovel. He tossed the spade to Hercule. "This will make you sweat like Uri. Bury them in the shade where centipedes and earthworms have softened the earth. When you're finished, wait for me at the Leopold. Tonight we'll drink vodka and I'll tell you how things went."

"Wait," Hercule said, as Pardux turned to leave. "One more thing . . . shouldn't we kill Norman?"

Pardux turned in the sunshine and shrugged. "I don't think so. He's confused. If it becomes necessary, I'll let you know."

"What did Norman tell the WHO?"

"With no external sign of a blast—no bomb, no meltdown in the area—he has absolutely no idea what to tell them. He can't even imagine the cause. Just as the Americans won't. They'll never know what hit them."

36

UNDER RELENTLESSLY CLOUDY SKIES, HASSAN Salar's house seemed even more forbidding than before. With its black wrought-iron fences and massive turrets the large English Tudor resembled a fortress. Even the dark wooden crossbars on the home's fascia formed X's on the white stucco, as if to say: Keep out.

Flanked by Thane and Danielle, Reynolds and Agent Carver waited at the front gate.

Last evening, she and Thane had rested at the hotel. Thane caught up on his sleep, and Danielle took the opportunity to call each of her staff members to see how things were progressing with the Othello damage control. She spoke with Kevin, Michelle, and Janet, grateful to hear that their morale was good and that presentation materials would be ready on time. She had assured each of them that she would follow up and get her appointment with Mr. Corbonne. That seemed a long shot now.

Carver pressed on the buzzer again. There had been no response for well over a minute.

Danielle glanced at Reynolds, who remained professionally deadpan. The policeman hadn't brought up her call to Sergeant Tolliver. As she looked up at the second-floor windows, Danielle pondered her plan of action and wondered if she should have told Thane about her scheme to get upstairs and find the Congo map. Her scheme would come to nothing unless someone answered the door.

Carver gazed up at the house, then looked back at Reynolds. "Maybe they've taken off."

Reynolds shook his head. "We were informed Mr. Salaar was in town."

Carver pushed the buzzer for the third time.

Thane glanced at Reynolds. "Your phone call must have alerted him."

"No, sir. At Agent Carver's request, when the servant asked who was calling, we simply told her it was an acquaintance."

Carver looked impatiently up Almbaum Road, then nodded to the police car at the curb. "Blip your siren a couple of times. Maybe that will rouse him."

As Reynolds stepped toward the vehicle, Carver nudged Danielle and patted his breast pocket. "I'd like to hold on to your sister's note, if you don't mind."

She nodded and watched Reynolds lean into the car, stretching for a button under the dash. The overhead blue and red lights flashed and the siren wailed briefly, then wound down.

"What if he refuses to see us?" Danielle asked.

"I didn't come down here to stand around." Carver reached inside his suit coat and, finding his cellular phone, glanced at the approaching Reynolds. "What's his phone number?"

Reynolds retrieved a small notebook from his patrolman's jacket, but Thane stopped him, pointing up at the house. "Wait. There's someone there."

The front door had opened.

A small woman dressed in a black chador stepped onto the front porch. After glaring at them, she glided down the stone steps and the shrub-lined front path to the gate; she placed a gnarled hand on the handle but didn't open it. Danielle was surprised to see the number of wrinkles on her face; from a distance she looked younger.

"This is a time of grief," the woman said in broken English. "Mr. Salaar is in mourning. Do you not respect that?"

"Our apologies." Agent Carver moved forward. "But we're here on official business."

"Yes, I've met Officer Reynolds." The woman's gaze came to rest on Danielle. "Oh. I didn't realize. Allah has sent you," she said, her eyes softening. "Are you not Damita's dear sister?"

"Yes," Danielle said, confused. "Who are you?"

"I am Astia, a servant of the house. Damita showed me your picture."

"I'm Agent Carver of the FBI. We'd like to see Mr. Salaar."

Giving Thane a dismissive glance, Astia again glanced at Danielle. "He would not deny you, I know that." Then turning to Carver she said, "But must it be now?"

"Please, just a few minutes of his time."

Astia folded her hands. "I go to announce you. If the master allows it, the gate will open." With that she turned and shuffled up the front path and disappeared inside. After a moment of silence, the lock buzzed and clicked, and the gate swung open.

Astia greeted them at the front door and ushered them across the large terrazzo stone foyer.

Carver and Reynolds led the way.

Girding herself to carry out her plan, Danielle checked the now-familiar surroundings. The huge illuminated chandelier that hung in the living room looked spectacular, and even the candles in the candelabra on the grand piano had been lighted.

"This is a hell of a place," Thane whispered.

Danielle pointed to a gold-framed eight-by-ten photograph of Damita that rested on a black velvet throw atop the piano. "That wasn't there before."

"Please have a seat." Astia indicated the plum-colored sectional sofa. Then she left the room.

Officer Reynolds sat down next to Carver as Danielle and Thane found a place at right angles to them.

"Where did you find the note?" Carver asked, indicating his pocket.

Danielle pointed at the ceiling. "Master bedroom, about there."

"And the map?"

"The other end of the house." Danielle pointed again. She withdrew her hand quickly as a tall handsome man in a black suit entered the room.

Danielle was struck by his appearance. Hassan Salaar was very attractive. His serious, yet serene expression was haunted by incredibly large dark eyes that dominated a smooth yet chiseled face accented by a narrow mustache. His nose was straight and hooked a little downward at the tip, giving him a classic Moorish countenance. His perfectly groomed slicked hair was so raven that it radiated tiny blue highlights. As everyone rose to their feet, Hassan fixed his gaze on Danielle and approached her first, extending a hand.

"My dear Danielle. Sorrow has robbed us of what should otherwise have been a moment of pleasure."

Danielle took his hand and found it incredibly warm. "Thank you, Hassan," she said, attempting to go along with the charade. "I don't know what to say."

"Of course not. There are no words." Hassan maintained contact with her for an awkwardly long time. "Your radiance puts your photographs to shame." Danielle pulled her hand away as Hassan turned to Reynolds. "I see your name on your uniform, sir, but perhaps you would introduce me. I am Hassan Salaar." Reynolds introduced the others. "Yes, Mr. Adams and Agent Carver, FBI."

"Mr. Adams." Hassan gave him a slight frown. "You're . . . "

"I'm a friend."

"Of?"

"Ms. Wilkes."

"Ah. Of course." Hassan turned to Carver, who started to show his ID. Hassan waved off the gesture. "That's not necessary. Please sit."

"It's procedure," Carver said as the others settled onto the couch and Hassan found his own place.

"I wasn't aware the FBI was involved."

"We're not—officially. But based on some new information, I'd like to ask a few questions."

"Information?"

"Yes. About your wife. Ms. Wilkes informs me that her sister shared some of her feelings—which may have a bearing on her death."

"Really? I was unaware that they had spoken. Damita had become such a recluse." Danielle tried to remain expressionless as Hassan glanced her way.

"I believe you were out of the country when she died?" Carver asked.

"No. But I was en route."

"But you were made aware of the police report."

"Naturally. I studied it very carefully."

"Then don't you find her behavior that evening to be somewhat out of character?"

Hassan's tone softened. "No. She sometimes drove around at night."

"Alone?" Carver asked.

Danielle tried to contain herself. Damita had been beaten up for even attempting to leave the house.

"More recently, yes. When she was troubled."

"About what?" Carver inquired.

"She was a victim of mood swings," Hassan said sadly. "She had fits of depression."

"Would that account for the vodka bottle in the car?" Carver asked.

"Unfortunately, her consumption had increased of late."

"So she drank excessively?"

"She was forbidden to do so, having become diabetic."

Danielle sat forward. "What did you say? Diabetes? Hassan, she never mentioned that to me."

Hassan shrugged. "It's a matter of record with our family doctor."

"And who is he?" Danielle asked matter-of-factly.

"Dr. Mahdi. You can check his records if you like." Danielle tried to disguise her distress.

"Mahdi? Is he an Iranian friend of yours?"

"He's practiced medicine in Connecticut for two decades."

Carver had both hands up, attempting to regain control. "All right, I don't see where that's pertinent. Mr. Salaar, I'm interested in addressing some concerns that Ms. Wilkes brought to our attention."

Hassan smiled warmly. "Anything Danielle requires, of course."

Carver looked at Danielle. "It seems that some of Damita's recent comments were somewhat upsetting."

"That I can believe, considering poor Damita's delusions."

Danielle couldn't take any more. "That black eye wasn't a delusion."

"Black eye?" Hassan asked, confused. "Oh, that time she drank too much. She fell in the shower."

"You're misrepresenting my sister's behavior," Danielle said in a controlled clinical voice.

"If that's what you believe, I apologize." Hassan dropped his head condescendingly, but then penetrated Danielle with a glare. "Your feelings about Damita might be unenlightened, Danielle, since you hadn't seen her for two years prior to our wedding."

Danielle was about to counter, but Carver jumped in. "Just prior to her death, your wife wrote a note that Danielle acquired." Carver patted his pocket. "Do the words 'the doves, they're taking me' mean anything to you?"

Hassan sat back on the couch and inhaled deeply, closing his eyes momentarily. He responded with one word. "No."

"You're sure?" Carver asked.

Hassan clasped both hands together. "As I said, Damita's mental state . . . she had a fixation about birds. I'd be happy to show you." Danielle was shocked when Hassan rose, walked to the entry, and pointed up the large stair-case. "Won't you follow me, please?"

Carver and Reynolds were the first to move. As they all ascended the stairs, Danielle hung back. Thane gave her a curious look as she picked up the rear and ushered him ahead.

At the top of the stairs, Hassan casually took a right turn, walking down the second floor hallway with Carver, Reynolds, and Thane immediately behind. Danielle trailed. She couldn't believe her good luck.

As Hassan entered the master bedroom, Danielle put a finger to her lips and gestured for Thane to continue on. He nodded and seemed to understand as she made a quick U-turn and scurried back to the room where she'd seen the map.

Tension buzzed in her ears and her hands shook as she tried the doorknob. The handle rotated easily.

Danielle opened the door and stepped inside, astounded at what she saw.

The window shades were drawn and the far wall was draped in black lace. The only light in the room emanated from several candles that burned on the windowsills and on tables arranged around the familiar easel, upon which rested a large oil painting of a redheaded woman.

"Damita," Danielle said, choking up. She tiptoed onto the large Persian rug and stood, transfixed, staring at the portrait. It was radiant.

"Incredible, isn't she?" Danielle startled as she turned to find Hassan standing a few feet behind her. "So like you in many ways." He changed his solemn tone as Thane and Carver appeared at the door. "Well, gentlemen, as long as you're here . . ." He gestured past Danielle. "This is my place of meditation. A shrine to my departed, if you will."

After Carver took a quick look inside, Hassan pushed impatiently past him. "Now, may I show you the birds?" Hassan stood by the door waiting for Danielle to exit. She caught a hint of his strong musk aftershave as she stepped into the hallway. Hassan closed the door and, taking the lead once more, headed toward the bedroom, where Reynolds waited.

As Carver and Hassan moved down the hall, Danielle hung back and whispered angrily to Thane, "That portrait wasn't there before."

"I couldn't stop him," Thane whispered. "He noticed you were gone and scooted out before we could say anything."

Hassan glanced back at the others as they entered the bedroom. "Right this way." He led them across the chamber, past the huge four-poster bed, and into the long closet. As Carver and Reynolds filed in, Hassan pointed to a large dresser and a grouping of bird figurines, several depicting pigeons or doves. As Danielle and Thane crowded into the closet, Hassan picked up a statuette. "You see," he said, stepping aside, "the poor thing loved birds. These in particular. She sometimes dreamed about flying with them."

Looking around at the dresser, the photograph of Danielle and the music box, Carver contemplated a moment and shook his head. "I think we've seen enough." He gave Thane and Danielle a baffled look and retreated to the bedroom.

Reynolds was next, leaving Thane to follow.

Danielle glanced back and found Hassan staring at her. She quickly turned to escape.

In that instant she had been alone with him, immersed in the seductive power behind his dark eyes.

37

A DEEP BLUE MANTLE OF stars blanketed what was left of a cloudy fuchsia sky. The cool of the evening settled over New England as the rented beige Chevy Tahoe hurtled across the countryside.

Danielle had insisted on driving, still somewhat frustrated with Carver's reactions to meeting Hassan that afternoon.

When Carver dropped them back at their hotel, Danielle had pushed for further explanations as to department policies, and the FBI agent had been quite candid. Carver again made clear that he would remain open to new information, but given the current facts and what appeared to be Hassan's lack of culpability, the FBI would presently forgo opening a case file. As to Danielle and Thane having been harassed, all Carver did was hand them each a fresh business card and suggest that they call if any further incidents occurred. As Carver pulled away from the Hilton lobby, his departure suggested an inevitable dead end.

The moment he left, Danielle voiced her frustration. With no new leads and little to look forward to, the investigation appeared to be a bust. Thane shared her disappointment and decided he should stay with her to show support. He accompanied her to her room while she made business calls. Some time passed before he realized the circumstances. He was alone with a beautiful woman, sitting on her bed, something he couldn't have planned any better.

His fantasy passed as Danielle hung up and seemed excited about having made a Wednesday appointment with a man named Corbonne, someone key to her professional future. Encouraged by that call, she seemed more determined than ever to pursue the case, stating that she was sure Damita's accident and Thane's experiences in Africa were linked.

They decided on a plan. While their search for Damita continued, Thane might also be able to initiate an investigation in Congo. After discussing options, they both left the hotel for an American Express office near the hotel. There, Thane called the Katanga Mining Company to speak with Jasper, the helicopter pilot, and convinced him to fly to Saurimo, Kuintala's home. Jasper was to tell Kuintala that he and Thane should make phone contact, using the helicopter shortwave as a receiver, sometime between nine and ten o'clock EST the following morning. It was Thane's plan to have Kuintala check on Pardux's movements and try to find out who he really was.

Thane and Danielle immediately sent a wire with Jasper's fee of one thousand dollars to Kolwezi. Then they stopped at a bank, where Danielle cashed a check and gave a reluctant Thane an additional thousand dollars in expense money. Since they were both tired, they had a short dinner and Thane retired to his room, where he fell asleep in front of the TV. Shortly thereafter, he was awakened by an urgent phone call from Danielle; she said she had just spoken to Reynolds on the phone.

Danielle's talk with Sergeant Tolliver at the police precinct had apparently prompted further efforts at the creek. During a renewed search fresh physical evidence had turned up. But before he submitted his data to the attorney general's office in the morning, Reynolds wanted Danielle to verify the find. He also wanted Carver to see it. Refusing to divulge more on the phone, he told Danielle he had spoken to Carver and made arrangements that they all meet at the creek immediately. Thane had agreed to come along, and together they had taken the half-hour drive across Massachusetts into Connecticut.

Danielle seemed to be mulling the potential evidence that lay ahead as she drove the Chevy SUV into the night.

Thane tried to assess her feelings. She hadn't spoken in some time and was showing signs of stress.

"Would you like to talk about it?" he asked.

"I just want to get there. You know how it is—your imagination takes over."

"New evidence? That's all he said?"

"Seems he'd been on the phone with Carver and they wanted me there around nine. I guess it's against procedure to discuss evidence on the phone."

Her leather jacket creaked. "He sounded matter-of-fact enough, but frankly, I fear the worst."

"You never know, it could be productive." She ignored his smile, and Thane turned toward the last wisp of a sunset's glow as it dissipated in the west.

"Whatever it is, I'll handle it," she said, her hands gripping the steering wheel. "God knows we need a break. No case. That's what Carver said when he left."

"Yet. He said 'no case yet.' Maybe Reynolds will change his mind."

They now entered the back roads leading to Long Island Sound. Danielle turned the car south on Highway 213. Darkness had fallen as they turned east down Niles Hill past Lloyd Road. Now they were out in open country.

A set of oncoming headlights on the two-lane road illuminated Danielle's green eyes as she looked over at Thane. "Dimmick Creek is up here about two miles. How do you feel?"

"Me? I'm on board with you all the way. Whatever it takes. I'm just amazed at Hassan. If he's at the heart of a conspiracy, he's awfully cool. Pretty damned secure." Thane hesitated. "And there is something weird bothering my gut," he said cautiously. "I've learned to trust that. Your gut can save your life when your brain's preoccupied." He visualized the dangers of the jungle at night. "In Africa, in the thick of the forest, I've had vibes like that. Circumstances where you're not sure, but the odds are you're in trouble— like you're being watched and you don't know it."

Her brows furrowed. "Oh, I think we know it."

"Yeah. But, we don't know why and we don't know by whom." Thane compared their current situation to following a bush trail. "It's like being stalked by leopards. You might not even realize they're watching. They study you until they know the route you're taking, then they select a tree up ahead and sit in it, waiting for you to pass underneath. If it gets to that point, you're dead." She flinched at the last word, and Thane bit his lip. "I don't mean to freak you out. But there's something strange about all this."

"No shit, Charley."

"No. I meant about Hassan and Carver. There's something . . . I can't put my finger on it."

"God. I'm almost out of my skin as it is."

"Sorry. Forget I said anything. I'm not the one who's normally right about that stuff anyway. My buddy Kuintala's the one with the second sight."

"Africa is so ingrained in your thoughts." It almost sounded like a criticism, but when she turned toward him in the glow of the speedometer, he read empathy in her eyes. "I know that's where you really want to be. But frankly, I'm grateful that you're right here."

"Africa will still be there later. Those villages, waiting for someone with answers. Right now the only thing on my mind is helping you."

"That means a lot," she said softly.

He found himself wanting to add something, but their exchange seemed oddly complete. As they rode on in silence, he looked forward to somehow recapturing the intimacy of that moment.

There were fewer homes and hardly any lights burning in the open country. Darkness had grown heavy as they crossed a steel bridge. A hundred yards after the trestle they rounded a bend and Danielle broke the silence by indicating that this was the turn where Damita's car had lost control.

Fifty yards farther, the Chevy's lights hit the police tape stretched along the side of the road where, as expected, a police car stood parked with its flashers blinking.

Danielle pulled in behind and killed the engine.

"Kind of quiet, isn't it?" Thane said, disconcerted by the gloom surrounding the car.

Danielle gave him an apprehensive glance. "You don't see any leopards, do you?"

Thane was glad she hadn't lost her spunk. He winked at her. "You don't see leopards unless they want you to. You stay in the car while I check." He reached inside the glove box. "Wonder if there's a flashlight." He located a cylindrical shape and hit the switch. The silver metal tube emitted a dim glow. "Not too bright. It'll have to do. Give me a second."

Thane got out and panned the light around. No one in sight. Everything beyond the perimeter of the patrol car's flashers was pitch black. The only sound he heard was creek water gently lapping against the banks below.

Leaving the passenger door slightly ajar, Thane stepped across the gravel shoulder to the guardrail. The damp smell of reeds and grasses rose from the river. "Officer Reynolds?" he called. "Reynolds!" he repeated.

Some seventy feet down the bank, the glint of a flashlight shone back in their direction. "Here," a voice shouted.

"He's there, Danielle. It's okay." In the murky half-light, Thane started to make out the figures of three men bent over at the water's edge some twenty feet beyond a willow tree. The stream was much wider than Thane had expected, some thirty to forty feet across at its widest point, a river more than a creek.

As Danielle joined him, Thane guided her past the patrol car to the edge of the road. One of the silhouettes below had headed up the bank in their direction. Reynolds stepped toward them, waving his light up the hill. Thane shook his own flashlight, which was rapidly losing power as the batteries began to fail.

"Is Carver with you?" Thane shouted.

"Yes. Come down."

Thane took Danielle's elbow and led her past the broken rail. She whispered, "This is where the car . . ."

"I see it." The ugly mangled end of the metal rail still hung off into space.

As Thane kept the faint flashlight's beam trained on the ground, they edged sideways down the soft footing of the embankment. Thane was grateful they both wore casual clothes, he in his safari vest, pants, and boots and Danielle in jeans and sneakers.

At the base of the hill, they stepped onto wet grass. Thane kept a hand on Danielle's sleeve as they worked through the long shoots, reeds, and cattails toward Reynolds, who had paused, anticipating their approach. His flashlight was trained in their direction.

Thane shook the car flashlight again, but it had faded completely by the time they reached Reynolds.

"What have you found?" Danielle could no longer contain herself.

"I think you should prepare yourself, Ms. Wilkes." Reynolds began to direct them toward the others. "This is not going to be pleasant."

"God. What is it?"

"There's a body in the water."

"Oh Jesus." Danielle clutched Thane's arm. "Damita?" Thane supported her on one side, Reynolds on the other as they crossed the uneven ground.

"Watch your step, you'll have to look over here." Reynolds shone his light on the rocks at the water's edge.

"It was my understanding that you dragged this area," Thane said, now a step behind Reynolds and Danielle. "How could a body surface two days later?" They had reached the tree.

"It didn't surface," Reynolds said as they reached the others. "In fact it isn't Damita."

Thane suddenly realized that his gut had been terribly right. In a quick move, Reynolds tossed his flashlight to one of the two men and grabbed Danielle, placing one hand over her mouth and putting his gun to her temple.

Another flashlight now glared directly into Thane's face.

Squinting, he tried to make out the shapes. A larger silhouette had limped two steps forward, pointing some kind of automatic weapon.

"The body in the water . . ." Reynolds said, grunting as he held a struggling Danielle.

"Is going to be you, Mr. Adams," the man with the automatic whispered as he continued his approach.

"Who the fuck are you?"

"I think it's fair you know the name of your executioner. My name is Samir."

Danielle uttered a scream, but Reynolds clamped down on her mouth.

"Reynolds!" Thane said through clenched teeth. "Some cop!"

"On your knees," the whispering man ordered, waving the gun at Thane. "Cali, tie him." The smaller of the two silhouettes revealed a coil of rope and stepped forward with his flashlight. Thane looked up into a pair of narrowly set brown eyes in a mousy Arabic-looking face.

Dead. That's what Thane was about to be. Danielle still had a gun to her temple. There was only one thing to do. "All right. Please don't shoot. I'll do whatever you want." Feigning what was expected, Thane began to squat, leaning slightly to his right. As he bent low, in a single movement and with all his strength, he hurled the defunct flashlight that he still held in his right hand.

Thane heard the impact as it hit Samir in the face.

Samir groaned, and reflexively fired the automatic rifle into the air. From his squatting position, just avoiding Cali's grasp, Thane propelled himself in an awkward racing dive out into the creek, instinctively sucking as much air into his lungs as he could.

As bullets rained around him, Thane plunged down into the water struggling for depth in the blackness of the creek.

Suddenly he felt a bite on his right thigh. One of the stray shots had tagged him, tearing across the side of his leg. He fought through the pain and scissor-kicked underwater as hard as he could.

A few more bullets plinked above as they broke the surface, streaking downward past Thane's face. He glanced back. Blurred lights flashed on the bank. Then he was down in the dark some ten feet under, feeling blindly along the plants, mulch, and slime.

The slow current pushed from his right, and he swam left diagonally downstream. The water grew colder as he reached the deepest point, a trough of gravel and silt.

He flashed back to his college swim meets and hoped that his wind would hold. Working through the muck, he suddenly confronted something jagged: a waterlogged tree trunk hung up on some rocks. He cursed, losing a few bubbles of air, as the tip of a branch scraped his cheek. Once over the tree trunk he began to ascend the other side of the creek bed.

Still underwater, he entered the shallows and was grateful to find himself surrounded by thick reeds. Finally he surfaced near the opposite bank, quietly taking in large gulps of air. Some one hundred fifty feet away on the other side, two flashlight beams waved erratically. Voices carried across the water.

"I think you hit him," the one called Cali said. Thane couldn't hear the response.

Farther up the hill, two huddled figures were climbing toward the road, barely visible in the flashers of the patrol car.

The car door opened, and in the glow of the interior lighting Thane made out Danielle's red hair. Thank God she was alive. She was being thrust into the rear of the vehicle by Reynolds. What was his game? A plant? A paid traitor?

If he could get out of the creek alive, Thane would repay that asshole. He'd find a way, even working with limited resources. He patted his safari vest to make sure he still had his wallet, passport, and phone. The cellular was probably ruined.

Then he froze. Beams were pointed in his direction. The men named Cali and Samir were headed down the opposite bank, their flashlights playing on the water.

Watching their every move with just his nose and eyes above the surface, Thane remained motionless in the reeds.

DAY SEVEN

38

DANIELLE'S DISORIENTATION WAS LIKE NOTHING she had ever experienced. It was as if in a split second her whole world suddenly disappeared.

After a short wait in the rear of the car with Reynolds, the whispering maniac named Samir had appeared with a small silver bottle in hand. Then the two men had forced her down.

After a desperate struggle against Samir and Reynolds in the backseat, Danielle suddenly felt enveloped by a black void. The handkerchief pressed against her face smelled of chloroform.

She found herself back in Ohio, among the butterflies and the sunshine. With eyes clouded by darkness, she smiled. Damita was calling her name. She knew it was Damita because no one else called her "Danny."

"I'm coming, Dee," Danielle called back as she climbed the hill toward the orchard.

"Danny, it's all right. I'm here."

"I see you." Her six-year-old sister sat under the great apple tree.

"Danny. You're dreaming. Wake up."

Danielle moaned as if in an echo chamber, her voice bouncing off the walls of her skull. Her forehead felt numb and her left shoulder ached.

As she reached up to touch her brow, she felt another hand clutch her own. Awareness returned and she smelled the dank air, sensed the deep cold. She strove to open her eyes, fighting the aftereffects of the chloroform.

In the dim half-light from a lantern on a wooden table, she saw auburn highlights of hair, much like her own. The hand, holding hers, also felt much like her own. Dee.

"It is you," she said groggily, trying to touch Damita's cheek to make sure it was real.

"I've been such a fool," Damita said softly.

"You're a live fool." Danielle reached out to embrace her. Damita bent down and they hugged each other as tears came to their eyes. Danielle relished the feel of her sister's shoulders, face, hair draped on her own: how precious, this physical presence that she thought had gone forever. "They said you were dead."

"I feel like I am. " Damita sat up.

Danielle noticed the Band-Aid on the bridge of her nose. "What happened?"

"I fought them. Hassan hit me. In my car, the night they took me."

"They set you up. Vodka on the seat, the Mercedes in the stream." Danielle suddenly remembered. "My God!" Damita reacted. "What is it?"

"The creek."

"Dimmick Creek?"

"Yes. I was there with Thane."

"Who?"

"The last time I saw him he jumped into the water to get away. They fired at him." Danielle suddenly remembered details. Reynolds with his gun to her head. Thane diving. Shots in the night. "They said they killed him."

"Don't cry, Danny."

"Am I crying?" She put a hand to her face. More tears drenched her cheeks. Danielle hadn't realized how upsetting the thought of Thane's death could be. "He . . . wanted to help me. I couldn't see much. The cop was holding me."

"Cop?"

"Yes. He was one of them. I couldn't believe it. No wonder. If I'd only remembered. When we went to your house, your servant, Astia, said hello to him. Somehow she knew him. It didn't strike me at the time. Why didn't I realize that?" She was rambling. Damita looked concerned.

"Why were you at the creek?"

"Reynolds, the policeman, called us. Thane and I showed up. Then suddenly guns flashed over and over again. They shot into the water."

"Did you see him get hit?"

"I think so. I saw blood in the water. I hope he's all right. I hope he got away. God, if he didn't—"

"What are you saying?"

"He may be the only one who knows what happened to me, or you."

"I wish you would stop, Danny." Damita wiped the tears that were silently gushing from the corners of Danielle's eyes.

Danielle fought to calm down. She looked around the room. They were surrounded by concrete. "Where the hell are we?"

"They won't tell me."

"They?"

"Samir and Cali have been checking on us from time to time."

"They treated me like an animal."

"That's how I get fed. A couple of trays a day."

"Where do those lead?" Danielle pointed to two wooden doors, shocked to see how badly her hand was shaking.

"That's a toilet. The other door is the one they use. When I woke up I was right here on this cot. They had given me a shot." Damita tapped her own shoulder. "Like yours." Danielle felt a sudden chill and noticed for the first time how warmly Damita was dressed. She was clothed from head to foot in a cushy maroon sweat suit. "Why is everything so damp?"

"I don't know. I haven't been out of here, and since I arrived unconscious, I can't tell which way I came in. Occasionally I hear the sound of machinery. They keep moving something. It's far away."

They listened as a rapping thud of metal on metal echoed somewhere outside the door.

"What is that?" Danielle asked.

"It happens a lot. And a chunking sound. Like a machine kicking in, lifting something."

"We're in a factory."

"Maybe."

Danielle rolled over on her side, wincing as she favored her sore shoulder. "Dee, we've got to find a way out of here. That note you left me . . ."

"You *found* it?" she asked excitedly. "God. I prayed so hard that you would." Damita scooted closer. "There's so much to talk about. Tell me about this Thane character."

39

RAIN PATTERED ON THE PHONE booth roof as Thane impatiently waited for CNN's Bob Davis to answer in Atlanta.

After last night's rainless skies, a weak low front had moved in from Long Island Sound during the afternoon and Connecticut was drenched in early fall drizzle. Cars passing the convenience store parking lot sprayed water up onto the sidewalk as their tires hissed along the wet pavement.

Thane glimpsed some of the drivers' faces, normal people leisurely going about their business, completely unaware of his predicament.

Whatever the motive, the thugs at Dimmick Creek were up to something huge. Thane realized that Danielle's kidnapping was just symptomatic of a larger conspiracy, big enough to reach from Africa to Connecticut, and something extensive enough to potentially affect many other people.

He shifted his weight; his right thigh throbbed under the bandage. Another debt to repay. Who were Samir, Cali, and Reynolds, the so-called cop? Whoever they were, they weren't fucking around.

Well, I'm not either, Thane thought, tightening his grip on the phone. As he continued to listen to the stale strains of on-hold music, raindrops gathered into rivulets on the windowpane. His thoughts fragmented into video clips and sound bites, flashes of Danielle on the riverbank, lights piercing the darkness, bullets splashing into running water.

His assailants had searched the creek bank for well over an hour. And even after they had driven off, Thane had remained waist deep in the reeds, allowing an extra fifteen minutes to make sure that they hadn't doubled back. The seventy-five minutes in the cold water had taken its toll. Hypothermia had caused a cramp in his left calf, though he massaged it vigorously to alleviate the tightness. Then it had taken a strenuous effort to swim to the opposite side of the stream. As he had dragged himself on shore his arms and legs had been incredibly stiff, and he had crawled across the mud like an arthritic amphibian, moaning from the exertion. Under the cover of the bank, he had lain on his back breathing hard, looking up into the starry sky and watching the cloud formations come in. As his eyes adjusted, the drifting clumps took shape, looking like slate gray haunches of huge animals lumbering across the heavens in a celestial herd. Danielle had said that Africa was ingrained in his thoughts. He had told her of his gut instincts—if only he'd trusted them. Maybe he wouldn't have walked Danielle into a trap.

Resting a moment, Thane had pushed up on one elbow, testing his strength. As the feeling returned to his legs, a dull pain throbbed across his right outer thigh and he saw his own blood flowing onto the mud. He reached down and fingered the rent in his pant leg where the bullet had cut across his flesh. As he touched the gash, he winced, and the pain quickly zapped him to greater lucidity. He began to focus on what he might do to search for Danielle. The questions had lined up in his mind: Was Reynolds really with the local police? Bulatzik with the CIA? Even Carver, was he really with the FBI? Nothing could be accepted at face value. For now, Thane had to find Danielle without police assistance.

After regaining his energy, Thane had hobbled through the back country, skirting the roads, avoiding the cops. He'd headed for the ocean, away from New London, making it to the town of Pleasure Beach at 3:00 A.M., where he was treated by a woman in the ER room at the medical center. He had given Dr. Amanda Justice a yarn about having torn his leg during a fall from a bicycle; fortunately the ripped flesh wound the bullet had made across his thigh seemed to go with that story, and he accounted for his wet clothes by explaining that he'd gone over the guardrail and fallen into a creek. Perhaps because of the way he was dressed, and perhaps because he told Dr. Justice he'd celebrated with one too many after returning home from overseas, she had swallowed the tale of his foolish ride.

After drying his clothes at the hospital, Thane had rented a small red Ford Probe in Pleasure Beach and driven to New London. His first stop was the Salaar home.

To make sure the place wasn't being watched, he had driven around the area several times. There appeared to be no surveillance from the police or Hassan's men, so Thane stopped at the entrance. The tall iron gate was locked like before. He had rung the buzzer, gotten no response, and considered breaking in, but was dissuaded by the security-alarm stickers on the house windows. Too risky.

He'd struck out. There was no one to question, nothing to do.

His next remaining option was to try to track down Hassan through his business connections.

A visit to the New London Chamber of Commerce had provided no hints. There were no import companies in Hassan's name. And calls on the pay phone outside the chamber office to Boston, New York, and the New Jersey Port Authorities yielded nothing further. Inquiries with customs officials at Kennedy, LaGuardia, and Logan Airports proved useless. No shipping records existed either in Hassan's name or any other name that might have been related.

Thane even tried calling the New London Police Department to ask for Reynolds, but he was told that Reynolds had not come in to work and was presumed ill. His home address was confidential and his phone number unlisted. Thane coaxed the desk sergeant to at least give him Reynolds's first name. Jack. Thane checked New London information. There were eleven phone numbers listed under the name Reynolds and no Jacks. Two Johns, and one J.

Thane called each of the numbers anyway. Again he came up dry.

Jack Reynolds had made himself invisible.

After burning eighteen dollars in change on the phone, Thane reluctantly called Bob Davis and reached him. He was immediately struck by Bob's distant tone. He was obviously disturbed by the Goodeve murder, which had by now made the news. Thane assured Bob that he had nothing to do with the Goodeve killing, but that he himself was being pursued by people who probably did, and needed help. Bob naturally suggested the cops. Without being specific, Thane told him that he suspected a conspiracy, that the call to the police would be too dangerous. The whole thing sounded dangerous, Bob said, and urged him to turn himself in.

Thane refused and reiterated his need for help.

Finally, Bob agreed to provide his computer database for a check on Hassan Salaar.

That had been one hour ago.

Having nowhere else to go, Thane had stayed in the phone booth and made more calls while he waited. First, he tried the Iranian consulate in Washington, DC. After several minutes on hold, burning another five dollars, the consulate informed him that his request to locate Hassan had been deemed inappropriate. Had he tried the local police? they asked.

Then Thane tried the Immigration and Naturalization Service in New York. They were pleasant enough, but could only suggest that Thane show up in person to apply for a file locator.

At three-thirty, thoroughly discouraged by his lack of progress, Thane reappraised his dilemma. Time was too precious. Not having a clue where Danielle was or where Hassan had gone, he might spend days, even weeks, trying to track down someone who quite obviously did not want to be found.

With his list of options shrinking, he decided to make one more call before checking back with Bob. He phoned the airlines and discovered that if need be, he could make a red-eye flight to Germany, connecting to Africa the next day. It would leave Boston at 11:00 P.M. Perhaps, as he and Danielle had discussed, the clues to Hassan were back in Congo. Perhaps, as he had mentioned to Carver, Pardux was the key.

With Thane's plans in the balance, an impatient Bob Davis finally came on the line.

"Thane, look. I know how important this must be to you, and I've really tried. We worked our banks as best we could, cross-referencing everything from import-export to cultural exchanges, diplomacy, and criminal records. Anything that might have hit the news since 1995. We're just not getting anything close."

"Nothing that even sounds like Hassan Salaar?"

"No. And there aren't that many Iranian nationals listed. Something should have clicked."

Thane couldn't disguise his disappointment. "Well, thanks for trying. It's all I could expect."

"Listen to me, Thane. I don't know what you're into, but considering my boss's censorship of the Congo story and what you've told me, it sounds like horrendously deep shit. I really think you ought to get legal advice, and I mean now." Bob was a straight-shooter, always had been, but how could he possibly understand? Thane knew he shouldn't ignore his good advice, yet once again his gut told him he'd be in even more trouble if he followed it.

There was too much at stake. He had to beg off as politely as he could.

"Thanks for everything, Bob. I'll remember all your help."

40

DEEP IN THOUGHT, DAMITA STARED into the lantern on the wooden crate that served as a nightstand. "I'm not exactly sure where the 'doves' came from." She paused, as if trying to formulate her thoughts. "But I know they're dangerous and they're going to use them. They talked about it the night they took me."

"At the house?"

"Yes. I had been asleep. It was after one in the morning when I decided to go downstairs and get some milk. Hassan wasn't in bed, but that wasn't surprising, since he often worked late in the den."

"Doing what?"

"God knows. Business plans. Imports, real estate."

"Go on."

"Well, I came down the hall and at the top of the stairs, noticed the light on in the second-floor study. The door was open a crack and I was about to go in to turn off the light when I heard voices. I tiptoed to the door and looked inside. Hassan was standing by an easel."

Danielle nodded. "I saw that; the day I found your note, I went into that room and saw the map of Congo."

"Right. Hassan was explaining the dove to Samir and three other men, something about how they burn people."

"Like the natives Thane saw in Africa."

"I guess. But what Hassan was saying scared me to death. I couldn't be exactly sure, but it sounded like he was talking about some of the doves being here in the United States. It sounded like he might use them." Damita's face showed disgust. "That's when I realized I wasn't just married to an abusive son of a bitch, I was involved with a terrorist. I was so shocked I couldn't move. Then I felt a hand on my arm and screamed. Cali had come up the stairs and pushed me into the room. Hassan went crazy. He started yelling, asking how long I had been at the door. I stood there in my nightgown, half-naked in front of Samir and the others, whom I had never met, feeling like I was about to die." Damita's eyes moistened. "Samir started to chatter in Iranian, and pointed a finger at me, giving Hassan furious looks. I could tell from Hassan's eyes that I was in terrible trouble." Danielle flashed back on Hassan's eyes, the sensuous power she'd seen in them. Obviously, Damita had been swept up by it.

On the opposite wall the two sisters' shadows danced in the light of the kerosene lantern.

Danielle reached out and clasped Damita's hand. "No matter what happens, Dee, I promise you, we will never be at odds with each other again. I'll always be there for you." Damita leaned down and gave Danielle a kiss on the cheek. "I'm so sorry I got you into this."

"Well, I'm here. We're together now. It must have been terrible facing those men alone."

"It was. I was so shocked I dropped to my knees. Right there in front of me, the men argued with Hassan about how I should be killed, as if I were an animal or something. Hassan yelled at them that he would be responsible. Then he screamed at me and told me that I was going to leave the house. I asked him why and where I was going, but he said to shut up, that I would be lucky to live at all. Then he told me to get dressed, and Cali, that little fucker, followed me to the master bedroom and kept peeking in the closet while I changed. I had about five seconds to scribble the note and leave it in my scarf drawer, praying that somehow you might find it."

"So the accident with the car—"

"All happened an hour later. The other three men left. Then we drove to Goshen Cove in the Mercedes. Samir at the wheel, Hassan and me in the backseat, and Cali in the Jaguar following behind. When we stopped at a light, I got out the back door and tried to get away. I ran into the woods but they caught me. Hassan threw me into the front seat and punched me in the face." She pointed to the Band-Aid. "Broke the skin. You wouldn't believe how my nose bled. Then Samir used a Styrofoam cup to catch my blood. When we stopped at Dimmick Creek he spattered it on the dashboard. Anyway, I watched from the Jag as they dented the windshield, put the vodka in the car, jammed the accelerator to the floor, and put the car in gear. The Mercedes traveled about a hundred feet and slammed into the guardrail." Damita took a deep breath. "Is this all making sense?"

"Completely."

"After a couple of minutes, I was blown away when a cop car pulled in behind the Jag. First I was elated. I thought I was saved. My mind raced about how to signal the officer. But Hassan got out and talked to the cop, pointing at the creek. That's when I realized how big this thing is. They have the cops on their side."

"Was it Reynolds?" Danielle asked.

"It must have been."

Danielle shook her head, visualizing the plan. "All neat and tidy. Reynolds was first on the scene, made sure everything looked right, then called in the accident. When I showed up, it was all very convincing. Naturally, I'd think you were dead. They never expected me to get into the house and see the map. Then Thane came on TV with the names of the towns in Africa."

Danielle flashed back on the sunny day in Pennsylvania, how she had tried to pronounce those mysterious names for Thane.

Now she wondered if she would ever see him again.

41

THE PHONE PATCH TOOK SOME DOING.

Jammed into a phone booth surrounded by the din of Frankfurt Airport, Thane was connected to the operator in Kisangani, who then had the call transferred ground to air over an Inmar Sat system to the shortwave in Jasper's helicopter.

The multiple connection depressed the volume of the call somewhat, but the clarity was good enough for Thane to hear Kuintala's distinctive accent, which was sweet music to his ears.

He updated Kuintala as briefly as possible.

"You can walk?" Kuintala asked.

"I'm limping pretty badly, but I get around. Fortunately, the wound was a graze, a tear that didn't even look like a bullet wound."

"So you did not call the FBI man?" Kuintala asked, over the sound of the helicopter rotors spinning in the background.

Thane finally got tired of the interference. "Can you ask Jasper to shut down the engine, I can barely hear you."

"Okay. Okay." Kuintala apparently muffled the receiver. Thane heard the scraping sound of cloth being rubbed over the radio's mike. Then Kuintala came back. "Jasper says he is worried about restarting to leave here. His choke is very cranky. I will speak loud. What of the FBI man?"

"After what happened, I didn't trust anyone," Thane said, watching passengers walk by in the airport corridor. "My feeling was—if there are phony CIA men on my ass, and corrupt cops, why should I assume that Carver is honest?"

Thane adjusted the bandage inside his right pant leg. The twelve stitches on the outer thigh itched painfully. "I've got to find out more about the villages and Pardux. I want you to meet me in Kolwezi."

"This is very important if you sent Jasper." As usual, Kuintala cut right to the chase.

"You're right. It's urgent. I believe there's much at risk."

"For many people?"

"For many countries. I'm sure that the deaths at Mwadaba and the others were just a test of some ungodly weapon and that Hassan and his people are behind it."

"And that is why the woman is in danger."

"Yes." Thane tried to ignore thoughts that Danielle might already be dead. "I don't believe they killed her. They could have done that there and then. They wanted her alive, I'm sure. She's a truly exceptional person, Kuintala." Thane flashed to his first sight of her, the glint of red hair in the Pennsylvania sunlight. "She's not someone you easily forget."

"And your leg has a hole in it."

"A flesh wound."

"You could have been killed, yet you speak more of this woman."

Thane visualized the knowing smile. "Stop the games. Can you meet me?"

"Okay. One moment." The same rustling of the microphone. "I will go now. With Jasper. Before his choke squeezes all the life from the engine. If we find Pardux, what then?"

The question gave Thane pause. There were no legal claims against the man. Nothing that would convince local authorities to hold him. "I . . . we have to do something. Force him to give us answers."

"I will help you."

"Good. Where will you be in Kolwezi? The Leopold?"

"The painkiller has taken your mind, Adams. I will be in the trees in my hammock."

"Of course you will. But go to the Leopold so I can reach you. I will call you again from Cairo. If you are not there, I will leave messages at the front desk. If you are detained for some reason, I will also call Katanga Mining. But listen, Kuintala. Bring your rifle and pick up another gun for me if you can. I believe Pardux is very dangerous. Do you understand?"

"Adams. Do not worry. And Adams . . ." A long pause. "I will bring your hammock, too."

DAY SIX

42

HERCULE WAS BORED. HE WAS reading the same newspaper for the second time—a worn copy of last week's *London Times* that he had stolen from a sleeping Englishman in the Leopold Hotel lobby.

His body occupied most of the double bed on which he reclined, his head against the antique white wood headboard and his legs spread. Room 16, a mere fourteen feet square, was far too small for a man of Hercule's size, and it was particularly confining when shared by two. But this was the last room available and at night Uri slept on the cot that now sat folded against the closet door.

Cloistered from the midday heat, the two men waited for Pardux to return.

Uri sprawled in the white wicker chair by the window, sipping on an orange soft drink, fingering the yellow message slip he had retrieved from the front desk half an hour before. With his small sweaty hands, he had fashioned the piece of paper into a tiny airplane.

The message itself was encouraging. Saratov had received an encrypted notice from Hassan that the man named Adams had been shot and apparently drowned in a Connecticut river. This was good news; Adams's death should assure a smooth conclusion to Pardux's operation. Then Hercule could return to the Ukraine, where he would wait out the last days.

Uri broke the long silence. "Why do they do that?"

Hercule sighed patronizingly, put the paper aside, then followed Uri's gaze up to the white fan. "What are you talking about?"

"The flies. You see how they fly perfectly straight and then take sharp right angles? They continuously form uneven rectangles in a clockwise direction. I wonder if they do that in a counterclockwise direction north of the equator."

A few flies did maneuver silently below the blades rotating lazily overhead. Uri was right. The small black specks tended to make erratic turns with geometric precision; another minute detail that had captured Uri's attention.

Finding himself actually contemplating the issue, Hercule suddenly felt ridiculous. "God." He shook his head. "Have we come to this? You're asking me about flies?"

"What else is there to talk about in this slime pit?" Uri put the bottle of orange drink on the windowsill, wiped his brow with his shirttail, then threw the small glider message slip accurately onto the tiny dresser that stood by the door. "And how about this," Uri said, shifting his weight. "As lowly as they are, in English flies have a name that tells you what they do . . . no other insect can say that. Flies fly. See what I mean?'

"Good Christ. Enough." Hercule's tank-top undershirt was soaked under both arms. "I'm calling Saratov. Let's go home." He reached for the bedpost and grabbed his tent like khaki shirt and his hat.

Uri looked up sharply. "What about Pardux?"

"We'll convince him. It's done. I'm going to the lobby." Hercule slipped into his sandals and headed for the door. There was only one public phone in the hotel, near the reception desk. "I'll be back."

Uri grunted acknowledgment, picked up the bottle, and peered through its narrow opening, undoubtedly contemplating its structural integrity. Hercule left him to his games and walked down the faded Turkish carpeting to the stairwell located at the other end of the building.

He had descended the whitewashed stairwell and rounded the comer of the landing when he spotted Pardux kneeling on the floor at the top of the next flight of stairs, peering through the banister, staring at something in the lobby as if he were stalking prey.

"What the hell—"

Without turning, Pardux raised a hand to indicate silence.

Hercule took the next stair on tiptoes, but Pardux was already creeping toward Hercule. They met in the middle.

"I spotted him outside and came in the back door," Pardux whispered. "I've been watching him for several minutes."

"Who?"

"Adams's assistant. He's sitting in the lobby."

"Who?"

"Kuintala. Assistant to Thane Adams, the video freak who reported the villages."

"Maybe it's a coincidence."

"No, it's trouble. It means Adams is coming."

"I seriously doubt that"—Hercule pushed past Pardux— "since Hassan's men killed him yesterday."

Pardux clutched his arm, his eyes squinting with intensity. "What makes you think so?"

"I was able to use the hotel computer, a message—"

"Then how do you explain that five minutes ago the desk clerk paged Kuintala with a call from Adams."

"That's impossible."

"From Cairo. I heard it. And, if Adams is in Cairo, then he's on his way here."

"Why are you so nervous?"

"They're here to find me. There's no other explanation. If I don't do something, they'll hunt me down. But they don't know about you and Uri." Pardux pushed Hercule against the wall. "You go pack."

Packing was something Hercule welcomed. "For home?"

"No. I want you to take the Land Rover back to the railhead. Wait for me there."

"For God's sake. I want to get out of here."

"You will, cousin. But we're not quite finished," Pardux said peevishly. "First a bit of murder, if that appeals to you."

"Then let's kill them both and be done with it."

"Fine. But we're not doing it in the lobby, are we? I'm going to lure them both into the jungle. Out there, we'll capture them, interrogate them, then bury them alongside Flobert and Claudon."

43

THE STRAIGHT VODKA STUNG THE back of Saratov's throat. He was grateful for it, and grateful as well for these quiet moments with Guyenov, who had asked that they get together one last time before the holocaust.

They sat in the darkest corner of the small bar at a wooden table, sharing a bottle of Chyvnyatol, an obscure yet delicious regional drink bottled in Kursk. A plate of pepper sausage and bread slices sat off to the side. A lone candle lit their faces.

"How is Volchenko now?" Guyenov asked, chewing on a meat slice.

"Worried, but then again, he always is."

"As long as his concerns don't cause him to open his mouth."

"To whom?"

"In my experience, under stress, the weak of spirit look to their peers. In his case, he might feel compelled to commiserate with fellow scientists."

"Nonsense. You know how loyal he is. Besides, he's finished with the work. I told him to go home to his wife and wait."

Guyenov nodded. "Call him tomorrow." He broke a bread slice in two and dipped one end into the vodka. "Make sure he sounds all right. Have you heard from Hercule?"

"Yes. He plans to stay in Congo for another day or two. Apparently, the American that Hassan supposedly dispatched—"

"What?"

"He's back, making a nuisance of himself."

"I don't like it. If he's that resourceful, he must be a government plant."

"Not according to Hassan. He sent us a lengthy message this morning—his reaction to Pardux's report that the American showed up in Africa. Hassan's people took the opportunity to vigorously question the woman Adams had been with."

"Vigorously? You mean torture?"

"It's his wife's sister, so who knows, he might have shown some reserve."

"Well?"

"She insists the whole thing with Adams is an accident. The fool stumbled into it. She did admit going to the FBI, but they have nothing. Absolutely nothing at all."

"And yet, Adams escaped once before. Make sure Pardux finds out what he knows before he kills him."

"That's what they have in mind."

"Good. There's no reason not to clean up loose ends." Guyenov stuffed another piece of sausage followed by moistened bread into his square mouth. "What else from Hassan?" he asked.

"Tonight they will test a dove. With proper results, we're five days away. Everything will be ready."

"Excellent." Guyenov smiled.

"Nothing to do but wait."

"That's not exactly true." Suddenly pensive, Guyenov took another slice from the plate. "I need your help."

"Name it."

"A situation has arisen. I want you to go to Moscow and meet with Alexander Popov."

Saratov recalled Popov's intensity at their last meeting. "Popov? Why?"

Guyenov shifted his feet under the table and looked down at the food. "I've been forced into a rather awkward position. A few weeks ago, my trusted security adviser, Rivkin, approached me. He made it known that among KGB military loyalists in Moscow, there is a strong feeling that they want to be more involved."

"But they are. Popov represents them. He was given three doves of his own."

"Yes, I understand. But he wants to have more."

"Isn't it a little late for that? We've seeded the country with our own people."

"Yes, of course. But Popov is powerful, as he demonstrated when he nearly launched his own coup during the Putin election. He has his own intelligence network both here and abroad. He's not to be ignored."

Saratov felt uneasy about this change. "So what is it you want me to do, exactly?"

"I want you to act as liaison between our effort and his."

"What do you mean, his?'

"That shipment that I told Volchenko about—the doves we were going to store in Siberia. They were actually for Popov and his people."

"You mean—"

"Popov controls twenty-three doves. Now do you understand the importance?"

"But that's as many as we—"

"Exactly. A balance of power."

Saratov stared into the candle, feeling somewhat betrayed. He had fancied himself the key player in the conspiracy. Suddenly, like in the old Soviet Union, the military held as great an arsenal as the politicians.

44

KUINTALA WAS OVERDUE.

He had been off in the highlands for well over an hour and the weather had changed. The colors of the jungle foliage shifted from pastel green to black as thick clouds moved overhead, occasionally revealing a half-moon.

A playful breeze had grown to a steady gale that pounded the back of Thane's neck, and he was bothered by the occasional rustle of the leaves and underbrush. The rush of wind kept the sounds indistinct, and it was difficult to gauge the distance of their origin.

Perched in the crotch of a tree some five feet above the ground and a few yards off the trail, Thane looked north in the direction in which Kuintala had disappeared. He used the two jungle hammocks as a cushion as he gripped the gnarled trunk.

Although Thane did not like the idea of them separating, Kuintala suggested that he alone would scout ahead to locate Pardux since Thane's bullet wound had become irritated during their hike.

Thane shifted his weight and winced. His machete had brushed lightly on his bandaged thigh. It was strapped to his belt next to the old .38 revolver Kuintala had commandeered from Jasper at the Katanga Mining Company. Dealing with a dull, yet constant pain, he would have preferred a day's rest, but Pardux's rapid retreat into the forest demanded that they follow immediately.

What had begun as a clear evening had turned overcast during their trek, and for sustained periods thick clouds robbed them of the stars and the moonlight, making it more difficult to see.

With the moon hidden away, there was nothing quite as dark as an African night . . . and nothing quite as oppressive as the moist jungle heat.

Thankfully, during Thane's vigil, a wet front had moved through with the wind, and passing rain had drenched Thane not once but several times. The damp ground below left the air thick with odors: the musty aroma of Iroko leaves, the pungent spice of the ferns, and the incense of rotten bark on the jungle floor.

The longer Kuintala was gone, the more the tension built, and pent-up adrenaline combined with moisture under Thane's khaki shirt had caused his skin to goosebump. To help alleviate the creepy feeling, Thane hugged himself, rubbing his triceps and running his hands over his forearms.

The "pricklies" reminded him of the intolerable delays prior to college swim meets, when his body would scream for physical exertion. The thought of swimming brought back the painful memory of his most recent racing dive into Dimmick Creek—the last time he saw Danielle. He was driven crazy not having a single clue as to where she might be, and he found himself praying she was unharmed. Still, he was convinced that his choice to come to Africa was correct. At this very moment he might have been sitting in some office, being questioned by police, or giving a deposition to a county prosecutor. It would have killed him to be so cut off from the action.

And tonight the action had become a hunt, not for an animal but a human being.

Kuintala loved to tell stories. One night by the campfire during their video shoot, Kuintala had described his hunts as a young man, how dangerous they had been, how at any given moment, the hunter could become the hunted. He told how as a teenager he had tracked a water buffalo for nearly two days. The beast led him to marsh country where, camouflaged in tall reeds, the animal had charged and nearly killed him. Such split-second reversals could be the difference between life and death.

Thane's thoughts were interrupted as the clouds parted and a half-moon bathed the land in a steady pale green. Now it was easier to see and he gazed in all directions to reorient himself.

As he looked north again, his nerves jangled. Through the thick trees he saw movement—a shifting shadow against the long grasses near the trail. He stared in that direction, tracking the play of light and shadow, but after a few seconds, the clouds moved again, partially covering the moon. It was impossible to tell whether the disturbance had been a man or an animal.

As a precaution, Thane unholstered his gun.

With the revolver resting on his knee, he breathed evenly, squinting out into the forest, trying to gauge the time it would have taken for the mystery presence to close the distance.

Suddenly, he realized that it had.

He heard the whoosh of something slashing the air. Then the blade of a machete struck a tree limb near his shoulder, severing the head of a smooth-skinned snake that had apparently been only a few inches from his neck.

With electricity shooting up his spine, Thane instinctively pointed his gun, then heard Kuintala's voice. "Adams." Bare-chested, Kuintala hoisted himself up into the tree with the body of the snake in his hand. "I'm sorry if I frightened you. It is a black mamba."

"Holy shit."

In the dim moonlight, Kuintala rotated the body of the beheaded snake in his left hand as shiny liquid oozed from the opening. "I have always considered those strange words," he said, staring at the mamba.

"What?"

"To defame God, by speaking of his excrement."

Glaring at the snake, Thane didn't share Kuintala's cool. "I damn near got bit and you're getting philosophical? I'm surprised I don't have my excrement in my pants."

Kuintala's white teeth appeared as he smiled.

"What's so funny?"

"There is a story." Thane marveled at Kuintala's conviviality while holding a killer reptile.

"Now?"

"A *short* story. Young Bantu men are sent into the jungle naked, wearing nothing but a dagger strung on a rawhide belt."

"I don't think—"

"Wait. They are told to crawl on hands and knees. When they meet a lion they are told to throw hunting excrement into the lion's eyes and stab him with the dagger." Kuintala waited expectantly.

"So?" Thane followed with the obvious question. "Where do they get this excrement?"

Kuintala smiled broadly. "The young men are told to simply reach back and they will find it. Tradition holds that when you meet a lion face-to-face on your hands and knees, hunting excrement will appear."

Chuckling, Kuintala tossed the black mamba to the ground and lifted his rifle by its rawhide tether.

Thane took a deep breath and slid his own gun back into its holster. "Okay. Are you done? We've had our bedtime anecdote. Now what's up?"

"I went parallel to the trail and found a railcar some two kilometers ahead."

"Railcar? As in train."

"Yes. I think they are inside."

"They? Someone with Pardux?"

"There is a Land Rover parked several hundred meters beyond the freight car on an old animal trail. Around the vehicle, the ground shows tracks of two men. From their shoes, they are European and one is very heavy."

Thane tried to make sense of it. "Hassan's map showed three names. Perhaps it's the other two. But why did the others drive when Pardux walked?"

"I am no longer sure. I don't think Pardux realized that I saw him on the hotel stairs. Yet he chose to run. Now he carelessly leaves us a trail like an elephant."

"You think he knows. Do we go in?"

"We must follow. But not in his way. Another, in case he has set traps. Walk in my footsteps when you can." With that, Kuintala jumped to the ground.

After dropping the hammocks to Kuintala, Thane eased himself down. Kuintala strung the bedding on his back and headed out. Limping slightly, Thane ventured from under the tree's canopy and caught up. "So what's our next move?"

"In hunting Pardux, we must remember that when a female lion walks past the wildebeest herd," Kuintala said as he strode through less dense brush near the trail, "the weakest prairie cow nervously moves away. But the cow does not know that in the tall grass on the other side of the clearing, another lioness waits with claws sharpened."

"Ah, so which lion am I?" Thane asked, hobbling behind.

Kuintala looked back and in the dim light of the overcast sky; Thane made out the hint of a smile. "Tonight you are the crippled prairie cow."

"I don't think I like your metaphors."

Kuintala had trained his eyes on the forest ahead. "Do not worry, Adams. You will like this one. I am a stampede."

45

IN THE DIM LANTERN LIGHT, perspiring profusely and dressed in a loose overshirt, Samir backed away from the red glow of the kiln. The heat from the metal oven radiated through the chamber, warming what would otherwise have been clammy stone walls. Two shirtless men stood off to one side, joking with Armitradj.

Samir did not share their merriment. Not only did he lack a sense of humor, he was burdened with responsibility. And he had opted not to remove his shirt since it concealed the leather straps to his prosthetic leg.

Lifting a lantern above his head, Samir squinted up at the digital dial of the kiln. The thermometer read twenty-two hundred seventy degrees. He turned to his men. "Armitradj," he whispered. "Go tell Cali we're ready."

Armitradj nodded, broke away from the others, and ran down the tunnel.

Last night's test with Cali's dove prototype had gone well enough. The goats and sheep Samir's men had tied to stakes one kilometer away from the detonation zone had perished, though their body damage was far greater than the test subjects in Butombu: their flesh had literally disintegrated. This was the expected energy release in an enclosed underground test site. In a sealed tunnel, the strength of the radiation increased as particles were refracted off rock and bombarded the animals.

An automated Geiger counter one and a half kilometers away read an astonishing ten thousand rads at the time of the burst, although this reading dissipated almost immediately. It was the nature of the device to generate immense, yet clean heat. Even so, four hours later the Geiger counter and the hapless animal test subjects could only be approached by men wearing lead-lined suits, since the surrounding earth, stone, and silicates were still emitting six hundred rads of radiation. In a matter of thirty-six hours, it would be less than one hundred.

One thing became clear: the dove Cali assembled according to Volchenko's instructions created a unique kind of hell. Even Hassan's men, whose careers had made them hardened to violence, were awed by the power.

Now that one successful dove had hatched, it was time to breed the rest. And so the kiln had been prepared to receive the cargo.

Samir looked down the tunnel as Cali approached, followed by Armitradj, who rolled a crate on one of the mining carts.

"Time to bake the birds," Cali said, smiling.

As the men set the crate down next to the small conveyor, Cali bent over and looked under the kiln, which had been constructed up and over a belt-driven turntable. On the turntable, a series of molds had been strapped into position. "After we've reached the point of liquidity," Cali said looking up at Armitradj, "I'll open the valve three times at five-second intervals. Then you rotate the table so that the next mold sits under the spigot, do you understand? Just like we did the first time."

"I have it," Armitradj said, moving over to the turntable's small electric motor.

"All right. Load the birds." Cali stepped aside as the other two men reached into the crate and began carefully placing Volchenko's dove statuettes onto the portable conveyor.

Cali hit a switch on the machine and the figurines, all with heads tucked identically beneath one wing, ascended the chute, disappearing into a hopper suspended on a metal frame over the kiln. Several hollow thuds echoed through the chamber as the statuettes dropped into the aluminum tub.

Donning a pair of goggles and wielding claw pliers, Cali then removed a peephole plug in the kiln. The fierce heat within threw a beam of light onto the opposite wall. The air was filled with the smell of hot brick.

"Stand back," Cali said as he yanked a handle over his head. The trapdoor on the kiln's lid slid to the side and the figurines fell out of the hopper into the fire.

A few small sparks spewed from the peephole as Cali peered inside. His face wet with perspiration, he removed the goggles and nodded repeatedly. "They're disintegrating. Only a few minutes now."

Imagining the meltdown, Samir couldn't help but feel satisfaction that Volchenko's compound had made the momentous journey through the Mediterranean to New York. The dove figurines were composed of a special lithium-deuteride-and-tritium mix, a plasticized substance that blended with Volchenko's silicates and his own space-age polymer he had discovered while working on heat shields for Russian satellite reentry. By firing the birds for the second time, the silicon compound would liquefy and separate from the earthen residue as it poured away.

"Well," Cali said, stepping over to Samir, sounding pleased. "Now we cure the shells for a day."

"I don't need another chemistry lesson." Samir rubbed his leg.

Cali reacted to his restlessness. "You're right. You don't need to stay."

Samir shrugged. "Perhaps I'll look in on our guests."

"How is the woman, Danielle, doing?"

"She will heal cleanly," Samir whispered. "Her cuts will knit without a mark. They were only meant to frighten. Sufficient blood without much damage. Hassan insisted I use the finest of razors in order not to scar her permanently."

"Did he?" Cali smirked. "You know what that means, don't you?"

Samir glanced at the other men who were within earshot and warned Cali, "Restrain yourself."

Responding to Samir's concern, Cali stepped closer and lowered his voice. "I think the older redhead is even more beautiful than the master's wife. I believe he plans to parade them *both* in Tehran."

46

SINCE NEITHER OF THEM WAS allowed to wear a watch, Danielle couldn't tell the time of day in the eternal darkness. She estimated the hour to be sometime after midnight.

The lantern had been turned down to its lowest setting, and Damita slept nearby.

Danielle's cuts had begun to itch. She resisted the urge to rub her forearms and tried to think of something else, but her mind turned to her hatred for that monster, Samir. His narrow ugly face had become the focus of her determination to escape.

If, as she and Damita had speculated, Hassan was now able to utilize the same fury that Thane had seen in the African villages, these "doves" could affect hundreds of thousands of innocent people. Was it possible that the United States would be his next target? She found herself praying. To God. For America. For God to save Damita and herself. For Thane. Somehow, he had to be alive. She pictured his playful blue eyes, the simple honesty of that smile. His courage on the road when he ran her attacker into the cornfield. His well-muscled arms. The strength of his physique. A man like him might survive the night at the creek. After all, his plunge into the water was a calculated move, not one of desperation. He knew what he was doing. He had to get away so that somehow he would come back. He had to be out there. God, let him be looking. Let him find a way to take us out of this hell, away from these freaks.

A tear ran down her cheek. As she turned her head, it fell onto the coarse canvas of the cot. She glanced at Damita, who was still fast asleep. Danielle had tried to be strong, not show her own horror at being tortured, but now, in the darkness, she finally allowed the self-pity to well inside. Being manhandled by Samir and his assistants was incredibly traumatic; she kept hearing the haunting whisper of Samir's voice, repeating again and again, "Who knows? Who knows about us?"

She had looked away from the blood, tried to avoid seeing his bony face, but Cali had held her arms and shaken her, grabbing her chin, forcing her to confront the animalistic glint in Samir's eyes as he inserted the blade just far enough, slicing down her skin toward her vein.

Although she fought against panic with all her will, after the second two-inch cut she had broken down and told Samir everything: Thane's suspicions about Pardux, Carver, and the FBI. But even when she had said it all, and made it clear there were no direct threats to Hassan, no real leads anyone could follow, Samir wouldn't stop. While Damita, who had been tied to her cot, screamed from the other side of the room, the whispering maniac continued to cut.

That's when Danielle became truly frightened; when it became clear that he was no longer doing the will of his boss but was simply having fun. At that moment she threw up. She had never been so humiliated, so brutalized, so dehumanized.

Now, as the memories came swarming back, she fought not to sob and wake her sister. Forcing herself to think about healing, she fell asleep.

Someone else was in the room. Someone standing over her in the darkness. She had dozed off, only to discover the tall figure hovering at the side of her cot. Dressed in black, the apparition startled her. She gasped and tried to sit up.

"Don't be alarmed," the figure said. It was Hassan Salaar.

Danielle glanced over at Damita, but she wasn't there.

"Where is she?"

"We wakened her and gave her something to eat."

"What time is it?"

Hassan tugged on his sleeve, revealing the white face of his watch, the only light-colored speck on an otherwise dark wardrobe. "It's five-thirty."

"You're up early."

"And you are confused. That's P.M."

The afternoon? Danielle had become completely disoriented. What had appeared to be the middle of the night had been midday. "I can't keep track of time in this hellhole. Where are we, anyway?"

"You will know soon enough." Hassan moved over to the lantern and twisted the small brass knob, illuminating the room. As he turned back, Danielle couldn't help but notice how groomed he looked: the sheen on his hair, the smooth face, the combed mustache. He was obviously quite comfortable in these surroundings. "I need to speak with you," he said, approaching her.

"Talk? After the way I've been treated?"

"Yes. You and I must understand each other." He gestured to the end of the bed. "Do you mind?"

"Would it matter if I did?"

He ignored the comment and sat, crossing his legs and folding one dark hand over the other with quiet dignity. Danielle noticed how each move appeared carefully executed. The black eyes held the intimidating threat of unpredictability, a masculine self-possession potentially both violent and erotic. Danielle understood why Damita had at one time been attracted to the man's mystery.

As if he knew what she was thinking, Hassan gave her a quixotic smile. "No more pain, I promise."

Danielle refused to answer and glared at him.

"First, you must know, Danielle, that had you not been associated with the man named Adams, you would not have endured this discomfort."

"You describe it as if it were a dental appointment," Danielle said. "You permitted that torture."

"Samir is a soldier. He did his duty. I couldn't allow anything to endanger this mission. Fortunately, from what you revealed, we know we have not been challenged." Hassan reached out toward Danielle's wrist. She withdrew her hand. "Let me see." Reluctantly, she allowed his touch. His hands were surprisingly soft. He turned her arm over delicately. "In a month there will be no mark at all."

"How comforting."

They were so close Danielle breathed in the fragrance of his pomade ... the sweet aroma of herbal musk. Hassan looked intently into her eyes. "Now listen. In three days we will leave this place."

"What are you talking about?"

"You remember Officer Reynolds, of course."

"Who could forget that treacherous asshole?"

Hassan allowed a slight smile. "He's much more than that. He is a skilled and highly effective KGB man."

"A Russian working for the police?"

"No. A KGB American who was stranded by detente. You would be amazed how many suffered the same fate. Hundreds. Reynolds, among others, has been working with us from the beginning, and even now is in Canada preparing for you and your sister's departure. Now, I could have you killed. But I would not do that to Damita. I respect family, and she will yet make me a good wife. And you—"

"I want you to let us both go."

Hassan gave her an openly condescending smile. When his eyes danced with authority he could look brutally handsome. "That's impossible. Besides, you will not want to live in this country when we are finished."

The edge to his voice chilled her. "What do you mean by that?"

"That's none of your affair."

"Finished. How? With these doves of yours?"

"That's what they are called." Hassan smiled again, toying with a concept in his mind. "I have a huge stockpile of conventional weapons that I collected over the years. But now they are unnecessary. The dove changed all that."

"You seem very proud of yourself."

"I am. I plan to be the first of Allah's defenders to really cripple this empire of yours."

"How?"

"I may tell you everything when 1 feel you are ready to understand."

"Understand what? Your viciousness?"

"Now, please. Hate need not be vicious. Hate has no superlatives. It is sufficient in its totality."

"But why hate at all?"

"Why? You ask me why?" He chuckled. "Such absurdity, that Americans are surprised they are hated. The average citizen of your country has no idea how oppressive its government has become. Yet as the decades pass, the US sits like ancient Rome, 'astride the world like a colossus.' The only problem being of course that other cultures, some as old as civilization itself, are being squashed by American needs. If you come to hate me for what I must do, remember that after decades of domination this may be our only way to stop the destruction of our land. After all, *we* were not in your part of the world, drilling for oil, corrupting your people with our greed."

"By we, I assume you mean Iran."

"I do. The country that will be your new home."

"Over my dead body."

He shrugged. "That is still an option. But, I think for Damita's sake, you will choose to live. Life could be very pleasant there. As you saw in my home, I am a man of breeding and imagination. I have gained immense respect and position in my country. You will be treated with dignity, and as a member of the family"—he reached out and put a hand on her knee—"with affection."

Danielle recoiled. "Don't touch me. You want to hear hate? You disgust me. And as far as your imagination is concerned, I think you're the tortured victim of your own inadequacies. Like those maniacs that follow you. I think you're nothing but a murderer."

A hint of anguish tempered the angry glint in Hassan's eyes. "Murder? I lost my mother over the Persian Gulf when an American warship shot down her civilian airliner."

Danielle was stunned. The admission left her momentarily speechless. Then she asked, "Does Damita know that?"

"No. The American navy said it was an accident," Salaar said bitterly. "There are no accidents. Not when the seeds of hate are sown. Your young men are taught to hate us and for good reason. We consider your culture a blight upon the earth. In the last campaign your American president spoke of a world without war. What he meant was within *your* borders. As long as there is no war in Illinois, there is no war. What a travesty. But war is about to arrive. And you will want to come with me to Iran, Danielle, after this country becomes a chaotic wasteland."

Danielle became further enraged by his arrogance. "They'll stop you."

"Really? And whom would *they* be? The FBI? Your friend, Mr. Adams?" Salaar stood and moved to the thick wooden door.

Danielle suddenly realized that Hassan would never have mentioned Thane unless there were a reason to include him. He must still be alive. "What do you know about Adams?" she asked, hopefully.

"Don't anticipate anything from him," Hassan said as he placed his hand on the iron handle. "I admit he proved to be very resourceful escaping that night. But he has chosen to run. According to our contacts, he has returned to Africa."

"Then he—"

"Has left you to your own fate."

DAY FIVE

47

DURING THEIR TREK, THANE HAD voiced everything with Kuintala: his deep concern for Danielle, the need to learn anything and everything from the tattooed Frenchman that would allow Thane to return to the US with facts and potential leads.

Pardux had to be taken alive—at least for long enough for him to tell what he knew.

That made things more difficult, but there was no other choice. From all appearances, Pardux had been chased away by Kuintala's presence in Kolwezi and had relocated to the railcar. It was troublesome that there were two other men with him, but since they had arrived by Land Rover, the meeting must have been prearranged. Who they were was unimportant. If they were with Pardux, they were probably part of the scheme.

While reconnoitering, Kuintala had circled the Land Rover and the railcar, satisfied that the fresh trail ended there.

As Kuintala described it, the Land Rover was over the hill from the ancient tracks, which sat in a ravine between two steep slopes dotted with trees. Though the freight car had two doors, it appeared that the door on the backside had been rusted shut. The front door remained half-open.

With any luck, the three men inside would be asleep at this time of night.

Kuintala suggested that he and Thane approach through the jungle instead of following the tracks, as Pardux had done. The railroad tracks ran north-south and were bare of tree cover, and because the half-moon was now making a sustained reappearance in a clearing sky, someone walking in the open could easily be seen.

The ideal alternative approach would be down the east slope of the ravine, since the moon would be in front of them in the west.

Thane and Kuintala agreed to the impracticality of a frontal assault on the railcar. Nor did they like the idea of a bold dash into the blackened interior, where Pardux might set an ambush; with Thane's limitations and his bad leg beginning to ache again, his movements in the jungle had become noisier than before.

Kuintala suggested that he flank the objective alone, coming in from the rear prior to Thane's approach from the opposite side. It was Kuintala's intent to quietly climb onto the railcar roof. That way, during Thane's advance, anyone exiting the car to escape or come Thane's way could be cut down by rifle fire from Kuintala's position.

Thane suggested that if Pardux and his party refused to come outside, they could be driven out by gunfire. The only problem was that a stray bullet might kill Pardux.

All options had been discussed by the time they arrived at the ravine's east side. Moonlight spread over the landscape, but a thick canopy of trees lining the railroad tracks obscured the view of the freight car.

Squatting in the shadow of bushes on the knoll, Kuintala motioned off to his right. "I will move diagonally along the ridge, then descend on the other side." He glanced up at the sky, tracking the moon, then pointed to Thane's watch. "Wait fifteen minutes for me to get into position, then you will become the prairie cow."

"Fair enough. I'll shout Pardux's name and demand that he come out."

"Yes. But stay hidden. The trees are only twenty feet away from the car. Remain in the shadows and wait with your gun. If Pardux comes alone, all the better. Secure him with your weapon. If he comes out with others, I will make my presence known. They will be in cross fire and will no doubt surrender. If they do not come out at all, fire a shot to make known that you are armed so they stay inside while I join you. Then we will flush them out together."

"With what?"

"Gunfire." Kuintala smiled. "Or hunting excrement." Thane was grateful for Kuintala's levity and for devising a strategy. Kuintala patted Thane on the knee. "I will take the hammocks. That way you are free to move. Be careful." With that, he heaved the two bedrolls on his back and, rifle in hand, walked off to the north, leaving Thane to his thoughts. Thane had faith in Kuintala's judgment, though he didn't look forward to playing bait, particularly with a bad leg.

Precisely fifteen minutes had passed when Thane made his way down the slope of the ravine. He moved as quietly as possible, trying not to disturb the underbrush. Even at this pace, he made a bit of noise that Kuintala would have considered a tumultuous din, though three Europeans probably wouldn't notice.

Thane descended from the uneven slope to the trees that lined the clearing. From there he had the railroad car in full view. It sat up against the buttress of the railhead, two tracks that ended in an old wooden barrier. The car appeared to be some fifty years old, a rectangular heap of rivets and metal plates resting on eight rusted wheels, nearly covered with brush. The moonlight distorted its color, which seemed to be a dark brown, possibly red. Climbing vines obscured the forward half of the car, nearly covering the K A T of the white-lettered *Katanga* and the R A I L of *Railway* below. The half-open forward door revealed nothing but a black hole, and there seemed to be no activity inside. There was no movement anywhere except for the long grass under the car that waved gently in a light breeze.

Keeping an eye on the door, Thane sneaked across the last few feet of the slope and found a good spot behind a robust tree in the shadows. He drew the .38, holding it chest-high, and craned his neck around the trunk. Checking the scene one last time, he was heartened to see a dark shape kneeling on the roof of the car, directly over the door. Kuintala had made it to his position.

Everything seemed ready.

Thane swallowed hard and took a deep breath. "Pardux!" he shouted, astounded at the volume of his voice in the still of the night.

No reply.

Thane shouted again. "This is Thane Adams. I know you're in there. If you want to live, come out with your hands over your head."

The silence that followed seemed to mock him. Absolutely nothing happened.

Thane decided to try again. "I know you've got others with you. Come out one at a time and you won't be hurt."

Still nothing.

Following Kuintala's advice, Thane leaned out and aimed the .38 past the freight car and squeezed off a shot.

The echo of the gunshot fell away in the night and Thane tried once more. "I'm armed. If you don't—"

Thane's words were interrupted by a horrendous roar.

In a split second, leaves and tree limbs all around Thane seemed to dance in anguish as the ground lit up.

He felt the singe from a flash of fire and the rush of a concussion that ripped him away from the tree and slammed him to the ground.

In that agonizing moment, Thane realized that the freight car had exploded.

48

DANIELLE LAY ON HER COT in a half slumber, aware of the minutes inching by. Random images plagued her—thoughts of where she should have been right now . . . visiting her mother with Damita . . . alone in her living room . . . she even indulged in a fantasy about having dinner with Thane.

At least Thane was alive. From what Hassan said, he must be.

Then, nagging questions about her business arose for the first time. What had happened when she didn't show up for her meeting with Corbonne? It had been scheduled for today, hadn't it? Or was today Thursday? She didn't know. All she knew was that she felt like hell and things with Corbonne had undoubtedly gone to hell. And where was Damita?

Finally, Danielle dozed off.

After a dreamless sleep, she awakened to the noise of the door bolt being unlatched. With a disconcerted look, Damita burst in, back-lit by an incandescent glow from the hallway.

Danielle rose on an elbow. "Dee, are you all right?"

Strangely, Damita's hair was wet. "I'm okay," she said tersely. "How are your arms?"

"Itchy. But the pain's gone away."

Damita slouched on the bed across the way, dabbing her hair with a towel.

Danielle sat up. "Where have you been? Tell me what you've learned."

Damita was suspiciously reticent and shrugged dejectedly. "Well, he has a luxurious bedroom suite."

"He? Hassan?"

"And I can tell you we're not in a factory." She knew more than she was saying.

"What?" Danielle swung her legs off the cot. "Could you see out any windows?"

"No. There aren't any."

"I don't understand."

"The walls are no different than the ones in this room. We're encased in concrete. We'll never get out of here. The whole place is like a vault."

"I wish you wouldn't talk like that," Danielle said. "We'll find a way." She paused at Damita's woeful expression. "Don't look so sad. Why is your hair wet?"

Damita tossed her head. "I took a bath."

"Good. You think I could? I feel so grubby."

"Grubby ain't the word for it."

Damita was holding back. Danielle reached out to her. "Come here and sit down. What is it?"

Damita moved to the cot as Danielle made room. She sat down, placing her hands in her lap.

Danielle gently laid a hand on her knee. "Tell me, Dee."

"A few minutes ago I came to realize what the rest of my life will be like. He forced me, Danny. He might as well have put a gun to my head. I lay there with my legs spread and he did it."

"What? He raped—"

"No. Not exactly. He didn't have to. All he had to do was remind me of you down here, and about Samir with that razor blade. While I was waiting in his suite, he told me he'd been down here with you and could have killed you without my even knowing."

Danielle realized her angry response to Hassan's overtures had caused this reprisal. "He's using me."

Damita's eyes flooded with anger. "That's right. Against me. He said that he would let you live, but only if I was exactly as before—the woman he married."

"That son of a bitch." Danielle spat the words. She put her arm around Damita. "Don't let that arrogant fucker get to you. We're getting out of here. That bastard's not going to have his way." She flashed on Hassan's advances toward her, realizing that Damita was right. Unless things changed, they were both going to become prisoners of their love for each other, and Hassan Salaar would continue to leverage their affection to have Damita, and, eventually, Danielle as well.

49

IT SEEMED AS IF THANE'S head would burst apart.

He pressed his hands to his ears, which were both ringing.

Lying on his side, he became aware of the smell of burning vegetation. Somewhere near his feet dry grasses had caught fire, and someone was trying to stamp out the flames.

When he rolled over, Thane realized that the back of his khaki shirt had been torn when he hit the ground, though his shorts and the leg bandage were still intact.

His eyes ached as he looked up through blurred vision at the small brush-fires. In the glow, he made out the silhouette of a man standing over him.

Thane's own .38 was trained at his face.

"If *I* want to live, is that what you said?" The French accent. It was Pardux. In his sleeveless tank top, he smelled like he'd been in the jungle for days.

"God." Thane put a hand to his mouth, which was bleeding profusely from a split lip. "What—"

"Dynamite," Pardux said. "We were sixty yards away, down the tracks."

One of the two men who'd been stamping out small fires came running. "Are his ears bleeding?"

"No. His mouth."

"If his ears—"

"Shut up, Uri. Put out the fire."

Running his tongue over his jagged lower lip, Thane sat up on an elbow and looked around. The man named Uri moved away and resumed his foot stomp. The branches of the tree where Thane had stood had been shredded and lay scattered about. All the surrounding trees were bare, with their leaves stripped. The immediate area within the ravine was lit by a large smoldering flame that burned on the floor of the railcar. The top half of the car had disappeared. "Kuintala," Thane said, desperately.

"Blown up," Pardux answered simply.

"No." Thane feared the worst. "He can't be."

Pardux turned toward the car. "Hercule! What did you find?"

Through the smoke, an obese man holding a flashlight and wearing a black hat and blousy shirt came waddling behind Uri. "There's no sign of the native fellow," he said in a Russian accent. "But I found this." Hercule held Kuintala's rifle in his thick hands. "There's blood on the stock and blood in the trees behind the railcar. Some debris in the branches. I see clumps of something. Probably body parts."

Kuintala. Thane's diaphragm heaved as if he'd been punched in the stomach. He could barely breathe. A sudden rage made him try to get to his feet, but a gun butt came down hard over his ear and he slumped back to the ground. "Forget it, Adams, or you'll be dead like your friend." Thane winced, trying to think beyond the blunt pain in his temple. He visualized what had happened. He was sure he'd seen Kuintala on top of the car just before it exploded.

Hercule moved in, training the flashlight on Thane. The fat man bent over and reached down, using a six-inch knife to tug on the khaki shirt. "Look at that scar on his back." Thane shoved his hand away, feeling like he was on display.

"He doesn't like to talk about that, do you, Adams?" Pardux brushed Thane's knee with his hiking boot. "But today he will talk about everything." Hercule hoisted his massive weight to an upright position, giving Pardux room to kneel down by Thane's face. "The blast took you by complete surprise, didn't it, American? One of Uri's electronic toys. We were waiting for you."

As Hercule's flashlight beam again disappeared into the smoke, Thane tried to right himself, pointing after the rotund silhouette. "Who's the Russian?"

With the .38 pointed at Thane's forehead, Pardux grabbed him by the collar. "He's only part Russian"—he shook him violently—"and don't ask questions. I do that."

Thane blinked. His lack of equilibrium hadn't been helped by the shaking.

"Why did you come back to Africa?" Pardux tightened his grip on Thane's collar. "You knew about me and Mwadaba?"

"Yes."

"Who else? The woman?"

Thane stared in amazement. "Danielle? Where is she?"

"I said I ask the questions." Pardux put the muzzle of the gun under Thane's chin. "Now tell me who else knows. Anyone else in Africa?"

"No. I hardly had time—"

Thane's face stung as Pardux slapped him on the cheek. "Who else in America then?" He slapped Thane again. "Tell me."

"A cop."

"Named Reynolds. And an FBI agent named Carver."

Thane glared at him. "How did you know that?"

Pardux slapped him for the third time. "My questions, remember? What do you know about the doves?"

Thane smirked. "You're asking me?"

"Smart-ass." Pardux hit him with a closed fist, spraying some of the blood off Thane's lip, knocking him back on his elbow.

Thane's head clouded from the blow. He wanted to maim this idiot, but began to realize he might never get the chance.

With Kuintala's rifle still in hand, Hercule came huffing through the smoke that had now filled the ravine. "What does he say?"

Pardux got to his feet, looking around. "Not enough. He needs encouragement."

Hercule pulled the knife from his pants pocket. "Why don't we gut him. He'll talk before he dies."

"That will take time." Pardux glanced back at Uri, who was still working on the small brushfires. "I don't like this. It's like a damned homing signal. Let's get out of here." Hercule moved forward. "I'll make short work of him." Pardux waved him off. "Listen, government patrols respond to forest fires. They may have already seen the smoke. We'll relocate. Then you can have your fun."

"I thought you wanted to bury him here with the others."

"That was before we created this inferno. You want to explain to Congo federals what we're doing here?" Pardux glanced down at Thane. "On your feet." Thane was slow to rise and Pardux landed a well-aimed kick at the bandage on his thigh. Thane let out a sharp groan as searing pain shot up his hip.

"Ah, still tender," Pardux said. "Perhaps reopening that wound will open your mouth. Get up."

Thane rose to his knees, then struggled to his feet. Pardux grabbed him by the shirt collar again, leveling the revolver at the back of his neck. He shouted at Uri, "Come on. We're leaving."

As Hercule led the way, Uri gave a final stomp and joined them.

"Did you see how the blast pattern fanned east?" Uri asked, getting in stride. "The open car door made the—"

"Uri, shut up," Pardux said, pushing Thane ahead. They marched across the ravine toward the railhead buttress with Hercule and Uri out in front and Pardux behind with Thane, the gun pressed to his neck.

As they passed what was left of the smoldering railcar, Thane got a heady whiff of burned powder. He tried to spot any sign of Kuintala. The brightness of the flaming floorboards in the freight-car bed made it difficult to pick out anything in the nearby darkness. But Thane could clearly see the damage to the car itself. The sides had been rent by the blast, severing rusty rivets, knocking the metal plates apart. The entire roof had been blown away and presumably lay on the ground on the other side in the brush.

Thane looked up into the trees for what Hercule had described as debris. But they were moving too fast and all he could make out were a few frayed branches.

Beyond the wreckage, the dim blush of a coming sunrise appeared in the east.

Goodbye, my friend, Thane thought, glancing back.

"Eyes ahead," Pardux said, tapping the cold muzzle of the gun to Thane's ear.

The four men walked in silence up the ravine's west side. Thane limped badly, but Pardux kept his left hand gripped firmly on his shirt collar with the gun pressed to the base of his neck. Pardux's rank body odor wafted from behind, giving Thane additional motivation to keep moving.

Dawn was due in an hour.

As Thane hobbled away from the fire's glow, it was easier to see their surroundings. With Hercule in the lead, they crested the west ridge and dropped down off the knoll, moving into thick trees under another canopy. They were walking along the animal trail Kuintala had described, apparently headed for the Land Rover. From the look of it, the narrow path had been there for decades, a route probably taken by deer and gazelle descending out of the highlands to the rivers below.

Hercule patted his pants pockets. "Who's got the keys?"

"I do," Pardux responded.

Uri pivoted and walked backward. "Where are we going? I'm hungry." He appeared cheerful after his successful explosion.

"We'll drive back along the Kuvai Canyon wall until we reach the Lubudi River," Pardux said past Thane's ear.

"You can eat there. We'll camp long enough to take care of Adams."

"A picnic . . . how nice," Thane said sarcastically, his mind racing with thoughts of escape. Once in the Land Rover, he might never get away. Hercule and Uri were a good eight feet ahead. Hercule carried the rifle unslung on his shoulder. Uri appeared unarmed. Pardux had his .38 in his right hand and carried a holstered .22 at his belt. If Thane could somehow get his hands on the .38, he might be able to take out the entire party. But how? Possibly a blow to Pardux's head and then a dash into the forest. A dash? He could hardly walk. Thane's eyes searched the surrounding underbrush. The men had funneled into single file as the trail narrowed through the trees. The Land Rover was some forty feet away. He might as well try something. Better to die here than go through torture. If he were to whirl around to his left, he might catch Pardux unaware, hit him on the side of the head . . .

Thane was rehearsing the move in his mind, ready to spin toward Pardux, when he heard Uri say, "Wait, what's that? Look out!" Then a sound like a giant horsewhip split the air.

A bent sapling some ten feet in length sprang free and came slashing across the trail, its base tethered to a large tree trunk.

The unsecured end, bristling with wooden spikes, struck Hercule square in the gut. Thane heard a popping sound as the fat man's belly punctured from the impact. He stumbled backward, rifle and all, causing Uri to go down.

Instinctively, Thane ducked and Pardux fired. The report of the weapon was deafening, but the bullet passed over Thane's head, and Thane took the opportunity to throw all his weight up and back, striking Pardux under the chin with his elbow.

The .38 fired once more as Thane clutched Pardux's gun hand with his own right. With a lock on Pardux's wrist, trying to keep the gun's nose away, he pivoted and drove with his legs, throwing Pardux on his back. Thane went down on top of him in the brush.

He heard a rifle go off, then the dull metallic thud of a machete.

"I've got this one," Kuintala shouted from somewhere behind. As elated as Thane was to hear his friend's voice, he was still more than preoccupied with the sinewy Pardux, who was trying desperately to regain control of the gun. Thane's superior size helped hold Pardux down, but while he had Pardux's right hand pinned above his head, Pardux successfully snaked his left hand between his waist and Thane's belly. He gripped the .22 in the holster at his belt and attempted to remove it. Realizing his intention, Thane reached down with his own left hand and jammed the weapon back into the leather.

Grunting, Pardux scrambled, trying to roll Thane over, tugging at the .22. The .38 went off again, blowing a bullet into the ferns, and Thane wondered why Kuintala wasn't coming to his aid. Pardux's legs squirmed as he tried to knee Thane in the thigh, and a partial blow to the wound broke Thane's concentration long enough for Pardux to yank the .22 nearly clear of the holster.

As Thane grappled for the gun, Pardux gave a forceful tug with his left hand. Somehow, Thane's finger was thrust through the trigger guard and the weapon fired.

Pardux screamed, his body going into a wild contortion.

Thane rolled off the thrashing Pardux, grasping both guns. As he got to his knees in the underbrush, he felt the moisture of Pardux's blood smeared on his pants. The Frenchman lay on his back, his blood-drenched shorts shredded. The bullet had apparently struck him in the groin.

Fearing that Pardux would die too quickly, Thane dropped his guns and grabbed him by the neck. "You son of a bitch. Tell me what's going on. Where's Danielle? Who's behind Hassan? Where is he? How do Reynolds and Carver fit into all this?"

Pardux writhed in agony, his face swollen with pain, his mouth frothing with saliva.

Thane shook him hard. "Tell me, goddammit!"

"The KGB has won." Pardux spat defiantly. "Just like those villages . . . your country will be in hell." With that, Pardux's eyes widened, his arms went limp, and he slumped back onto the ground, staring into the night.

"You asshole," Thane whispered, letting go of the man's neck.

Thane struggled to his feet. With a gun in each hand, he stumbled back toward Kuintala. He found his friend lying on his side, clutching a machete covered with gore.

Hercule, who appeared dead, lay on his back, bleeding from the abdomen. Uri lay beside him, a huge gash in the front of his neck, and the rifle lying nearby.

Kuintala reached up with a scorched hand. "I knew," he said, pointing at the trap. "No matter what. One way out."

"Jesus, look at you." Thane fell to his knees beside Kuintala's head.

Kuintala's face was caked with blood that appeared to have flowed from one ear and his nose. His hair was matted from the heat of the blast and he had taken Uri's bullet in the left shoulder.

Kuintala continued. "I set this trap when I scouted."

"Don't talk. Later."

Kuintala's head slumped. "Forgive me for not telling you."

Thane recalled Pardux's comment about the smoke attracting Congo federals. "We've got to get you out of here." He flashed on the Land Rover, looking back at Pardux's body.

"My left car," Kuintala said, shaking his head. "When the roof blew, I rode it like a platform. I was thrown into the trees."

"God. They said they saw body parts."

"That was the hammocks. But when I fell to the ground . . . " He pointed.

Thane noticed more blood covering Kuintala's bare legs. An ugly scrag of white bone protruded from his right shin.

50

SARATOV SIPPED BLACK COFFEE AS he sat in his living room, reading *War and Peace.* He had prepared himself a sumptuous meal as usual, and checked his computer every hour to see if the expected e-mail had arrived.

Saratov was mildly disturbed that Hercule hadn't logged on to the Web. If things went as Hercule had hoped in the jungle, he should have contacted Saratov through the Leopold Hotel's computer by now and be on his way back to the Ukraine with Uri and Pardux.

By nine, after finishing several chapters, Saratov's patience had worn thin and he decided to call Kisangani to speak to the only other person who might have news.

The Ukraine's phone system had improved in the last few years, and it only took a few minutes to make the connection. The operator had been able to forward the call to the residence of Dr. James Norman.

After explaining in English that he was a distant relative attempting to reach Paul Pardux, Saratov asked if Pardux had access to a phone.

"I'm sorry, Mister . . ."

Saratov quickly borrowed a name from Tolstoy. "Rostov."

"I'm afraid Mr. Pardux hasn't returned yet."

"And you don't know where he went?"

"He's been preparing statistics for a report I'm making to the WHO. I assume he's been off doing that. He can't be far because the Kolwezi police called about the Land Rover."

"Excuse me?"

"It seems the Land Rover Pardux was using was found on the street."

"Abandoned?"

"Nothing's truly abandoned down here, Mr. Rostov, merely deposited for later use."

"Isn't that somewhat disturbing?"

"Not really. Pardux is his own man. He comes and goes as he pleases."

Saratov formed the next question carefully. "But what would you do if he doesn't return?"

"If I don't hear from him by tomorrow, I'll call Paris and notify their WHO office."

"And the Congo police?"

"I told them to leave the vehicle where it's parked."

Silence followed. Saratov tried to formulate the next question without incriminating himself. "Incidentally, Pardux mentioned a CNN report about Congo? An American reporter . . ."

"Now, there's a fellow who might know. Name's Adams. He called me from Cairo yesterday. Interested in speaking with Paul as well. Said he wanted to interview him regarding his work in the field. Who knows, maybe Adams and Pardux met up with one another somewhere. Perhaps that's why Paul was detained."

After a polite thank-you, Saratov hung up.

He regretted that he couldn't give Guyenov a comprehensive report.

On the other hand, perhaps it was unnecessary. Even if Adams or Pardux, or both, turned up dead or missing, authorities in Congo would be much too slow in their investigation. The US and French consulates would take even more time when they got involved.

Yet what about Hercule and Uri? They were men of proven abilities. Was it possible something had happened to them?

TWO DAYS LATER
DAY THREE

51

STILL NUMB FROM HIS HELTER-SKELTER trip to Africa, Thane sat in the wooden chair, watching Gwendolyn Hardy struggle with her computer.

"Do you know anything about Dells?" The receptionist ran an age-spotted hand through her short gray hair.

"No, sorry," Thane said, shaken out of deep thought. "I'm a Mac man myself."

"Dr. Colfax has asked administration for new equipment, but we seem to be last on their list." She tried to boot up, punching the keys. "Look at that, it freezes every time I try to open Windows."

Sitting in this musty, peaceful haven, Thane felt very much the spectator of surreal events, as though it were another man who had just lived through the drama in Africa. Kuintala was barely alive, lying in a Likasi hospital. Weak but still lucid, Kuintala had had the presence of mind to lie to the native doctor, claiming that while hunting he and Thane had come upon old mining gear that, when placed too near the fire, had exploded. The concussion had triggered Kuintala's rifle to fire, catching him in the shoulder. Though Thane could not understand much of what was being said, the doctor showed more concern than skepticism and attended to Kuintala without question. Then he took care of Thane's facial cuts and leg.

Promising to return, Thane left Kuintala in Likasi. He drove the Land Rover to Kolwezi, where he scoured the seats, removing the mud and blood as best he could. Then he abandoned the vehicle.

He had been in Congo only thirty hours ago; since then he had flown to Egypt, on to Greece, to England, then to Montreal, crossing into the United States by rental car to avoid customs scrutiny. He'd also had no desire to experience another confrontation at Kennedy Airport. Thane wasn't sure whether Bulatzik and McNair's people were still in the hunt, or whether Agent Carver might now be seeking him out, but he couldn't risk detention.

Although exhausted and nearly out of money, Thane was certainly not ready to throw in the towel by turning himself in. Without new leads on Danielle, he had decided to focus on something he had noticed in Carver's office: a name on a computer printout.

The FBI database computer had cross-checked dove with radioactivity and come up with Dr. Colfax, the nuclear scientist who had been an early proponent of the device.

Perhaps Thane could speak with him and perhaps learn something about the origins of the dove to provide new clues. Thane knew time was short.

What had Pardux said? Something about the KGB winning, and the United States being in hell. The fact that Pardux also mentioned Carver and Reynolds in one breath bothered Thane. It might have been haphazard, but whether Carver was involved or not, Thane wouldn't risk calling him. Besides, if Carver were on the level, Thane reasoned, the FBI would be at work anyway. Thane would call when he found something significant, not before. And Carver wouldn't be the only one looking for him. Since Thane had alerted the Long Island Police to Goodeve's murder, those authorities would probably be seeking him as part of their investigation. There were now multiple risks of entrapment.

Just over the Canadian border, Thane had stopped in Plattsburgh, in upstate New York, to call Bob Davis once again, asking him to do another check on the CNN database for the name Colfax. Nervously, Davis informed him that the police had indeed made inquiries about Thane in connection with Grant Goodeve's death. Thane calmed Davis down, and he reluctantly agreed to help. With Thane on hold, Davis went to the computer banks and without great difficulty discovered that Dr. Ronald Colfax lived and worked relatively close by— in Connecticut, to be precise.

And so here Thane was, sitting in the reception area of Colfax's office on the campus of Yale University, an unannounced visitor, still aching from his encounter near Kolwezi.

Classes were not yet in session, but on this weekend prior to registration certain members of the faculty were working, among them Gwendolyn Hardy, who continued to wrestle with her Dell.

As the time crawled by, Thane grew impatient and decided to ask again if he could see the professor. He shifted forward in his chair and was about to speak when Hardy thumped the desk.

"Old warhorse," she complained, referring to the computer.

At that moment, as if on cue, the frosted-glass door opened and a man in a brown cardigan sweater peeked out into the room. It had to be Colfax.

"Gwen, do you have a transcript of my Williamsburg lecture? The reactor brief, the one about AEC work with the public sector?" He suddenly noticed Thane. "Hello." Then back to Hardy: "Nineteen hundred ninety-six, I believe, just before the Senate review." Colfax began to retreat into his office as Thane stood up.

"Dr. Colfax? Excuse me."

Colfax turned, obviously flustered. "I'm sorry?"

"Would you have a moment?"

He averted eye contact. "Do you have an appointment?"

"No. But—"

"Come back during the week. Ms. Hardy, acquaint him with my schedule." With that, Colfax closed the door.

Hardy shrugged. "I told you."

"This may sound melodramatic. But it really is a matter of life and death." He limped toward Colfax's door.

Ms. Hardy emitted a shallow gasp and, with oxfords clumping across the wooden floor, headed him off, blocking the door with her frail body. "No, you just can't."

Thane stepped back. "All right. Just tell him one thing for me. Please? If he says no, I'll leave."

Hardy squinted skeptically. "What thing?"

"Tell him the dove devastated some villages in Africa."

With furrowed brow, Hardy knocked twice, then with a glance over her shoulder, disappeared inside.

After a few moments, Colfax opened the door. Behind him at the oak desk, Hardy stood frozen in place with a phone to her ear.

"You're not a graduate student, are you?" Colfax asked, as Hardy glared through the doorway. "Some kind of crank?"

"No. I—"

"Ms. Hardy is about to call security. Is that what you want?"

"My video on CNN last week showed severe radiation damage in Congo. Hundreds dead, no blast. I was there. You want to talk about it?"

"That was you?" Colfax rubbed his bulbous nose, staring intently into Thane's eyes. "You look like hell. Why is your face cut up?"

"Oh. This?" Thane pointed to his cheek. "That's a tree branch. The rest is a scuffle in Congo. I just flew home. My name is Adams. I'm a cameraman."

"Well, you're either highly imaginative or . . ." Colfax swung the door open. He pointed toward the chair across from his desk. " . . . you've been introduced to some rather unique technology." He turned. "Hardy, see if our guest wants coffee."

THANE APPRECIATED THE OLD MAN'S understanding. Colfax sat quietly and listened while Thane explained his experiences in Congo. Surrounded by shelves crammed with physics books, Thane elaborated on the three mysterious villages, described his encounter with the perpetrators, and concluded with Danielle's suspicions regarding a conspiracy. Finally, he mentioned the note with the word dove found in the Salaar home.

Though Colfax seemed intrigued by the story, he remained skeptical, firmly stating that whatever Thane had encountered, it most certainly wasn't a "dove."

Thane's frustration prompted Colfax to explain. Asking Thane's permission, the professor lit his pipe, letting the aroma of a cherry-blend tobacco fill his office. Deep in thought, he swiped at the blue haze over his head, spreading it around the room.

"Some background on this mythical bomb," Colfax said, leaning back, exhaling another blue cloud, looking through his lead-lined windows at the campus. "Decades ago, during the Nixon administration, there was a good deal of discussion about a 'neutron bomb' in Congress." He shifted his gaze to Thane. "I, among others, went to testify. At the time there was much debate about the need for a battlefield weapon to counter Russian ground forces in Europe. Though Nixon himself endorsed the idea of such a device, Ronald Reagan later said he knew nothing about it." Colfax's eyes twinkled. "Perhaps it was the Alzheimer's." He cleared his throat. "Well, Nixon referred to this alleged device as a peacekeeping weapon. The 'peace' reference led to the term 'dove' in some private circles. Do you remember any of that?"

Thane hadn't yet been born until late in the Nixon years. "Sorry. No. I was probably teething at the time."

Colfax chuckled. "Silly of me. I keep doing that. At my age it all melts together. Well, anyway, that bit of history is somewhat amusing. The detractors of the 'dove' in Congress called the bomb an 'immoral weapon'—can you believe that anyone would make such a distinction? They considered it less ethical. You see, a neutron bomb theoretically would simply radiate and not explode. Anyway, after much discussion nothing ever came of it."

"Do you mean the project and research were completely dropped?"

"I mean that although a secret budget was allocated and rumors flew about that the Russians had developed an ultraclean neutron weapon, from what we know, no one anywhere actually managed to create it. And thank God, because if indeed such a controlled weapon existed, it would endanger the world with an entirely new nuclear strategy. In any case, it's not possible."

"And why not?"

"There are reasons. They existed then, and they exist now. Do you know how such a neutron weapon would potentially work?"

"I have no clue."

"All right. Here it is, in layman's terms." Colfax put the pipe in a stained tin ashtray and used his gnarled hands to help explain. "First of all, this would be a fusion device, not fission. Fusion is clean. Being clean, this neutron bomb would essentially be a nonconcussive device, as opposed to dirty, high concussion bombs like the atom and hydrogen bombs we all know."

"And why nonconcussive?"

"Because as opposed to destroying property with a shock wave, like most bombs, this—all right, let's call it 'the dove,'—would create immense energy as opposed to an explosion."

"And how would victims be affected?"

"That's conjecture," Colfax said, reinserting the pipe. "But much like what you described." He puffed twice. "Theoretically, they would blister and collapse immediately. The light or heat created would only last a fraction of a second, but with such intensity, the flash would blind and incapacitate all living things."

"But that's what I saw in Mwadaba, bodies with a powdery residue. In

Judapi, the skin had blistered like a grilled hot dog, with radiation readings to match."

"Now wait." Colfax bit down on his pipe stem. "I understand the temptation to jump to conclusions, but you're not only implying that the weapon exists but, from the limited area affected, that it's quite small."

"Isn't that a possibility?"

"Scientifically anything is possible . . . but let me explain what would be necessary. As I said, it would have to be a fusion apparatus, probably using both deuterium and tritium atoms—the same nuclear process that makes energy released by our sun. Now, to work, this procedure would need to occur in a fraction of a second, caused by cold fusion, a process dependent on platinum as a triggering device."

"So deuterium and tritium are the explosive?"

"Actually, that's a misnomer. Explosion by definition never occurs. Rather, energy is *generated*." Colfax leaned forward intently. "Here's the key. The triggering device would have to be fashioned from a platinum wire set in heavy water with deuterium and tritium. Electrical current from a battery, let's say, would run through the wire, vibrating the one hundred ninety-five electrons free from each platinum atom's nucleus. This electron vaporization would produce a very large compressive force on the deuterium and tritium atoms, sufficient to make some of them fuse, creating helium and producing a nuclear-fusion reaction."

"That doesn't sound terribly violent."

"Ah, but remember that in the cold fusion process, under laboratory conditions, fusion of deuterium and tritium atoms occurs at a temperature of about forty million degrees, releasing 17.6 million electron volts of energy. And this energy is released in the form of heat, namely, X-rays, alpha, beta, and gamma particles and neutrons bursting outward, in a blink of an eye, one huge flash of heat."

"Suppose that's what I saw?"

"All right. But the fact is . . ." Colfax retrieved his pipe and stabbed the air with it as he spoke. "You're suggesting that someone has succeeded in scaling down this laboratory process to miniature size for use as a military weapon."

"Yes, and what if they did?"

"I'm sorry, my friend, but this mythical dove just wouldn't fly."

"But if someone were able to do it, how would it happen?" Colfax pointed the pipe stem at Thane. "Well, the trigger itself would be the ingenious part. The platinum wire, miniature laser, and battery hookup. If that could be rigged—"

"The completed device. How would it look? Like a bomb?"

"It would likely be circular in design and have a highly reflective shell."

"Reflective? Like metal?"

"No. Neutrons are absorbed by metals. Metal isn't atomically reflective. It's absorbent. The shell would have to be some kind of light, homogeneous, non-neutron-absorbing material that contains a lot of hydrogen—a hydrocarbon-based material so neutrons would bounce back inside, crashing into themselves, creating intense energy. And the beauty of this fictional shell material, if made of a lithium-deuteride combination, would be that it itself would vaporize, leaving no evidence that the weapon ever existed. The ultimate residual radiation would read no more than one hundred rads . . . in other words, no final contamination."

"So no clues?"

"Well . . ." Colfax scratched his head. "No. Except possibly from the battery parts themselves, which would probably be quite standard and nondiffused."

"Isn't it strange, Doctor, that you can describe the dove in so much detail and yet insist on its impossibility."

"Well, like most things in science, imagining and doing are only separated by time. I admit to the eventual possibility. But it's highly unlikely that it exists now."

For Thane, it did. He had seen its destructive force. His thoughts had already jumped ahead. Colfax's mention of Alzheimer's reminded him of someone in a retirement home in Connecticut. "Strategically speaking, if the dove became a reality," he said, looking at his watch, "what then?"

Colfax's chair creaked as he sat back, folding his hands over his waist. "Well, strategically, you have a disaster. In the wrong hands such a weapon could be placed anywhere—even in a paper bag—and set off by anyone."

"How?"

"There would be a digital timer of some kind attached, like setting an alarm clock. Push a button and at a designated moment some days, hours, or even minutes later, after the soldier left the scene, a devastating flash of radiation would not only kill everything within range, but also permanently cripple all the electronics in the area . . . planes, cars, everything from computers to clock radios."

52

HASSAN SALAAR HELD FORTH IN what he called the "war room," a concrete-enclosed command center covered with maps and photographs of prospective target sites.

After leading the men in prayer, Hassan launched into one of his diatribes against the United States, recounting the decades of oppression and humiliation of Islamic peoples by the West. As his emotional momentum grew, Hassan whipped the three-dozen men in the room to a fever pitch.

If Samir could have, he would have shouted.

Hassan pointed to the map of the United States bristling with thirty three red dots, and punctuated his calls for vengeance by repeatedly stabbing a finger at Washington, DC.

In response, Cali and Armitradj led the others in cries of retribution. At one point, Hassan was forced to pause for several minutes while his men rose to their feet in a manic display of hatred.

This was to have been a planning meeting, but somehow as the hour of destruction drew nearer, it was impossible to suppress pent-up feelings as each man anticipated the ultimate retaliation.

Dressed in black from head to toe, Hassan strode back and forth in front of the map. His expressive dark eyes flashed with omnipotence as magic seemed to fill the room. It was as if those present were under the scrutiny of Allah himself.

"Remember, believers," Hassan said, looking out from under his dark eyebrows, "the infidel's seats of authority will crumble. There will be *no* court system to try this case. There will be no military effort to track us down. Madness will reign. The American citadel will be seared from within." Hassan pointed at the front row, which held the men who would hit the principal sites. "Those of you assigned to primary targets, Achmed, Habib, and you others, remember that a phone call to our command center is essential. It will indicate that you have succeeded in planting your doves." Hassan glanced at Samir. "Samir will monitor your calls, and as the field general, he will decide when to send a backup."

A nod from Hassan and Samir rose to his feet. The silent group anticipated his grating whisper. "I will be sitting by that phone," Samir said, pointing at the desk near the map. "If you do not make your call by midnight this Sunday, we will send a reserve weapon to cover the location unaccounted for, so that it is in place by Monday morning."

Hassan continued. "That's why it is so important to simply pick up the phone and call. Do not say your name, do not ask for anyone, just say the following words—'the dove descends'—and then add the location of your mission." He walked over and placed a hand on the head of one of the men. "In Achmed's case, he would say, 'The dove descends on the White House.' These code words will inform us that your dove is in place."

Hassan looked toward the back rows. "For the rest of you assigned to secondary targets such as the air bases, we obviously will not send anyone in response to a missed call." Hassan pointed to a series of photographs that lined the walls and waved toward one of his lieutenants. "Armitradj." Armitradj stood and gestured acknowledgment.

"I will meet with each of you one last time," Armitradj said, looking about. "Tomorrow morning, come to me at your assigned times, and we will discuss the specific placement at your target and your travel arrangements."

In the front row, Habib raised his hand. "What if we get to the target and our primary drop site has been disturbed?"

"It's the same for all of you." Armitradj walked over and pointed to a black-and-white photo of Pennsylvania Avenue, shot from the White House sidewalk across the street. The picture showed a bus stop, a park bench, and shrubbery beyond. "In Habib's case, for example, his primary drop site is behind these bushes. Should he arrive there and find something wrong, let's say the bushes have been trimmed back too far to conceal the duffel bag, his second option is to place the bag on top of the bus stop. His third placement choice is high in the crotch of this tree beyond the bench, here, as you see. Since you will be on this mission in the darkness of Sunday night, you should not have difficulty making these changes."

Hassan stepped forward. "Cali informs me that the shells are cured. The doves have been armed with triggers, sealed, and the timers will be synchronized to match your various time zones. Also, the detonators are set." He raised his arms and spread them wide. "Here in America they refer to a stock-market crash as Black Monday. Monday, at noon, eastern time, when all the doves explode simultaneously, this nation's markets will be depressed permanently." He counted off the factors on his right hand. "The US will be leaderless, without a government, economically crippled, without anyone to reorganize Wall Street's financial chaos, and powerless, without an upper echelon of military command. There will be no one to invoke a response. With the American intelligence community dead and survivors in flight, who would investigate? Who would be able to exact vengeance against such an unknown and unseen enemy?"

53

ELLA BREEN, THE ROBUST HEAD nurse, stared at the roses in Thane's right hand. In response to his question, the spunky brunette had given Thane a quick once-over. He was suddenly grateful that he'd taken the time to buy a presentable white shirt and some blue jeans.

Nurse Breen's violet eyes glinted behind her glasses. "If you're not a family member—"

"I've been asked to deliver these flowers to Mrs. Wilkes by her daughters." Thane gave Breen his most disarming smile and nodded politely to two other women working at the reception desk. "They wanted me to look in on her, that's all."

Laying the clipboard on the counter, Breen folded her arms, creasing her starched white tunic. "So how are Danielle, and . . . ?"

"Damita. Both very well, thanks."

She cocked her head. "But why didn't one of them—"

"A sudden trip to Europe. Business. The three of them, Damita, her new husband, and Danielle. They just asked that I drop by."

"I heard Damita got married." She scrutinized his leg, apparently having noticed Thane's limp when he entered. "And they sent you?"

"That's right." Thank God he'd taken a two-hour nap in a motel, showered, and shaved. At least he looked antiseptic enough for this place.

Nurse Breen frowned. "What happened to your face?"

"Oh." Thane scrambled. "Rugby. I scrimmage with the boys down at UConn."

"And you're a friend?"

This wasn't working. Bowing to the resistance, Thane decided that he would add to the pack of lies. "Well, actually, I'm more than that. Danielle and I are engaged." Nurse Breen's thick body relaxed as if air had been let out of a balloon. "Really? Oh, that's wonderful." Another once over. "I can see where the two of you . . . Danielle is such a joy." She actually smiled. "Come with me. I'll take you." She pivoted and pointed down the hall. "Now, you know Margaret's not doing very well. She may not understand."

"Of course." Thane patted the flowers. "I just want to give her these and have a little chat. At least I'll be able to tell Danielle that I saw her personally to see how she is."

"Some of her days are better than others. She's in the east wing."

Thane hobbled along beside Breen's bulky frame. As they made their way down the plain black linoleum floor, passing room after room, they occasionally encountered elderly patients who ventured into the hall. Some smiled. Others engaged Thane in conversation, but a few drab souls remained seated in their wheelchairs, heads down, chins on their chests. Thane was moved by the despondency. It had occurred to him as he drove up to the large brick building with white shutters that he had never in his life been inside a nursing home.

Nurse Breen cautioned him as they arrived at the open door of room 316. "Let me just peek in to announce you." She disappeared behind the white curtain.

Perhaps it was the fatigue. Perhaps it was the sad individuals he had just seen in the corridor. Perhaps it was the roses he clutched in his hands. But as he waited with the sun streaming through a window at the far end of the hall, Thane felt like an intruder. He debated whether to go through with the shameful charade. It might do more harm than good. He was tempted to just tiptoe away, but it was too late—Nurse Breen had pulled the curtain aside. "Come in, Mr. Adams."

Slightly embarrassed, Thane entered the room.

Beyond the bed, Margaret Wilkes sat humming to herself in a rocking chair by the window. She was a gaunt woman in her early seventies, dressed in a smock and a pale blue sweater. Her gray hair, still streaked with shades of auburn, stood out in wisps from her frail head. Her pale blue eyes lifted in a gaze that drifted aimlessly about the ceiling.

"Go talk to her," Breen said, warmly. "Give her the flowers."

Thane limped across the room, wondering how to begin. He glanced around for a chair, but there was no other furniture except the bed, and he found himself kneeling in front of Margaret, who continued to rock gently.

"Mrs. Wilkes," he said softly. "I want you to have these." He laid the roses in her lap.

Margaret flinched slightly. Her hum faded as the flowers rested on her delicate hands. Ever so slowly she dropped her chin, until, with a look of awe, her gaze came to rest on Thane.

"John," she said warmly as she ceased rocking. "You did come."

"Hello there," Thane said, captivated by her peaceful smile.

"You remember last Sunday how the arbor glistened in the sunset? We sat together in the porch swing." Margaret brought a fragile hand to her face. "When you touched me, you said my cheek was as soft as a petal." She brushed her fingers over her lips. "We were opening"—her fretful gaze drifted off to some faraway time—"like blossoms ourselves." She looked down at the roses. "Like these."

Thane glanced back at Nurse Breen, who stepped forward and leaned over, whispering, "John is her late husband."

"Of course," Thane said quickly.

"John." Margaret smiled tenderly. "Can we plant more roses by the arbor next year?" Her face had retained a delicate grace, a radiance reminiscent of the freshness that was now Danielle's. "You'll do that for me, won't you?"

Thane felt compelled to take Margaret's hand. "I would do anything for you."

Margaret squeezed his. "Do you think I'm pretty?"

"More lovely than I remembered."

She nodded, and then her expression went blank as she stared into space.

Nurse Breen laid a hand on Thane's shoulder. "Maybe . . ."

Thane looked up. "Just a few more minutes. Please."

Breen smiled. "Well, she does seem to be enjoying herself. I'll give you two a moment." With her crepe soles squeaking, she retreated and nodded to the wall phone. "Dial nineteen if you need assistance."

As Breen left, Margaret seemed to withdraw into herself again, resuming her humming and beginning to rock back and forth.

Thane eased himself up on his knees directly in her line of sight. She appeared to look through him.

"Margaret," he said, trying to regain her attention. "What about your ... our daughters, Danielle and Damita?"

A flicker of recognition. "My babies. Where have my babies gone?"

How ironic, Thane thought. "Do you know about Damita's husband? His name is Hassan Salaar. Did Damita tell you about him?"

"Damita isn't home from school yet."

"Did Damita talk about Hassan? What he does for a living? Did he take her to some interesting places?"

"Damita." She looked down at the flowers again, smiling knowingly.

"Yes. What does Damita say about her husband?"

"Damita."

"Yes?"

"John, Damita baked you the cutest Christmas cookies." She was hopelessly locked in the past. "Look in the jar over there on the counter." She pointed at the far wall, where a white water pitcher sat on an oak nightstand. "Go on. Look in the cookie jar."

"All right." Realizing it was hopeless, Thane got to his feet.

"Try one of the snowmen. She made the icing."

To accommodate her, Thane walked over next to the bed. A glance at the bulletin board showed pictures of Danielle and Damita at various ages. There was one of Danielle in a graduation gown, beaming.

"Do you like the cookies?" Margaret asked.

Thane picked up the water pitcher and went on with the charade. "Yes," he said with his back half-turned, "they're delicious." The ghosts on the bulletin board stared back. A man in a cornfield, apparently John Wilkes, wore a blue trucker's cap. A collie dog hugged by two little redheads. If Thane's mother had lived to old age, pictures of himself, Angie, and Jeff would have hung on a wall somewhere. Fate had robbed them all of memories, the richness of intertwined lives.

Thane glanced back at Margaret. At least he'd had the opportunity of seeing Danielle's mother. She was still beautiful and must have been incredible in younger years, just as her daughters were now. But this was a dead end. It was time to leave.

Thane replaced the pitcher and, looking down, happened to notice that the small drawer of the wooden stand was partially open. He pulled it open further, finding a black-bound Bible, reading glasses, a small jar filled with peppermints, a pocket-sized Kleenex pack, and a stack of postcards wrapped with a blue rubber band.

He looked over his shoulder. Margaret continued to hum and rock. He removed the band and thumbed through the cards. There were eleven in all. Pictures of Paris, a mountain chalet, the Italian Riviera. On the other side, in slanted handwriting, Thane read: *Dear Mother, This morning Hassan and I . . .*

They were signed: *Love, Damita.*

Thane shuffled through the rest of the cards. The Matterhorn. Piccadilly. And then, two postcards with the same picture: a waterfall. The caption: CHIG-GER FALLS/ISLAND POND, VERMONT.

Thane turned both cards over and began to read: *Dear Mother, Hassan and I are spending the weekend at our very own cabin. I'm having a wonderful time enjoying the hikes and wildlife—quite a change of pace for me. When you feel better you'll have to visit.*

The other card read: *Thought I'd write. I've got plenty of time on my hands. Hassan's land deals keep him busy when we're here, so I'm enjoying the cabin by myself most of the time.*

Island Pond, Vermont.

Feeling a surge of adrenaline, Thane rewrapped the postcards with the rubber band and tucked them back in the drawer.

He hobbled over to Margaret, knelt down once more, and gave her a soft kiss on the cheek. "Thanks Maggie," he said. "You're wonderful. I'll find your babies for you."

54

DANIELLE SAT IN AN OVERSTUFFED peach-colored chair, staring at Hassan. Without warning, she had been dragged from her cell and ushered to his private quarters without Damita.

Now Cali waited outside the door, and Hassan, dressed in a satin robe and black slacks, reclined on one elbow on the slate-gray bedspread of his round bed.

"Accept my hospitality," he said, more a command than an offer. He tapped the ashes from his cigar into a bronze ashtray and pointed again to the white marble tub in his bathroom. "You may as well enjoy."

Danielle's anger prevented her from responding. He had offered the use of his Jacuzzi, implying that he would stay and enjoy the view.

"You are now a part of my household. Think of yourself as my companion."

Danielle studied the room, seeking an escape. Hassan's extravagant surroundings were furnished with wall mirrors and massive blue draperies. Bulky pieces of Byzantine furniture lined the walls, including an ornately carved mahogany armoire.

"Come." Hassan sat up, stubbing out the cigar. "I'll show you how to operate the tub, and if you insist I will wait outside." He rose and approached with arms extended. "I'm sure you want to be clean again." He was about to take her hand.

"I prefer my dirt to your kind of filth."

"Your insults are meaningless." Hassan grabbed her wrist so hard that it hurt. "I could take you as my own this moment if I wanted to, you know that."

Danielle fought his grip. "Sure, you could force me. But you want me to *desire* it, don't you?"

Hassan maintained his hold, but gently eased the pressure. "You're an intriguing woman. Even more beautiful than your sister, and delightfully complex."

"You *married* my sister." She punctuated the statement by yanking her hand free. "And I never want you to touch me."

Hassan let his hand fall to his side. He shook his head. "You don't really understand, do you? I'm all you have left. Your world is about to end." He reflected a moment. "Let me show you something." Stepping to the armoire, he opened the doors, and turned. "Behold the dove."

He held a device shaped like a large vitamin pill, oblong and smooth, with an unearthly sheen, the surface a creamy copper color.

"That's your death machine?"

"Yes. Isn't it fantastic?" Hassan's eyes gleamed as he caressed the shiny object. "If I wanted to . . ." He pointed to a red button. "I could simply push this panic alarm, and everyone within range would be dead in sixty seconds." The dove measured approximately fourteen inches long and ten inches in diameter. Twin digital timers and a trigger housing were recessed in the top, and a red button bulged slightly at its apex.

Hassan pointed to the LED that remained frozen at 12:00, while the other rolled vertically with its current minutes and seconds on display. "I keep this one by my side, because this particular device will end two centuries of tyranny by lighting up Pennsylvania Avenue. Can you imagine? On Monday at noon, the White House will be bleached even whiter with its glow." He placed the dove on the bed. "I've become your future. You may as well accept that."

"I don't accept you or your mindless brutality."

"Oh, hardly mindless. And don't be concerned. You'll be adequately insulated from the unpleasantness. Tomorrow evening, we will give you a sedative. During a gentle sleep, you will be transported by helicopter to New Brunswick. There, transferred to a private jet in St. Johns. And when you awake, I will be with you in the air over the Atlantic on our way to Iran."

"And if I refuse?"

"You want to stay here, amid the chaos in the streets? Women like you will be considered booty when the gangs rule. Why be around when that scum rape and pillage?"

Danielle stood. "Oh, so you assume I'd rather be raped by your scum."

Hassan smiled and retreated to the doorway. "I don't blame you for your anger, but believe me, I can be a most cordial host. And since you'll be out of here in less than thirty-six hours . . ." He opened the door and summoned Cali, who walked into the room dressed in a black turtle-neck and jeans. "To insure your comfort, I invite you and Damita to give a wish list to Cali. As you may know, we do not cater to most Western needs in Iran. And I'm sure there are things you will want, certain cosmetics, hair spray . . ."

"Fuck your hair spray," Danielle said, no longer able to tolerate the condescension.

Hassan snapped a command in Iranian to Cali, who stepped forward and slapped her across the face. Stunned by the blow, Danielle stumbled back into the chair. With a hand massaging her sore cheek, she looked up in time to see Hassan perform a mock half bow. "You asked that I shouldn't touch you," he said, smiling. "As you see, I have not."

55

SAMIR HOBBLED INTO THE LARGE cement chamber near the elevator. As he passed under the large orange girders, the scent of hydraulic grease from the lift hung in the air.

Off to the left, two Jeeps, a troop truck, and the Chevy Suburban waited in the motor pool. To the right, the munitions dump bristled with conventional weapons: rifles, handguns, and explosives.

In the center of the chamber, under the glow of fluorescent lights, Armitradj had assembled the men to give them last-minute instructions. This gathering of warriors, ages twenty-eight to forty-one, was comprised of members of the Islamic Revolutionary Front, some Iraqi, some Lebanese, and some Iranian, planted in the United States prior to September 11, 2001. Hardened, reliable operatives, many had trained in the Middle East and the United States, and had been recruited from Hamas, the Red Hand, and other terrorist organizations that had their own agendas until they learned of Salaar's master plan.

The assault group, dressed identically in black Levi's and brown shirts, was lined up in two rows, seventeen in one, sixteen in the other, kneeling on the cement floor next to their olive-drab duffel bags.

Armitradj squatted at one end. On the floor at his feet sat five other duffels, void of equipment but each containing a bomb. He pulled his own bag toward him and whistled for the men's attention. "Each of you open your bags."

The men obeyed and the room echoed with zippers.

Armitradj opened his duffel. "The top layer of civilian gym clothes conceals your weapons. You should check your dove to see that the digital timer is operative and that the right-hand LED reads two days from now—12:00 P.M., Monday."

The men opened their flaps.

Satisfied, Armitradj continued. "Check survival-gear items." He picked up a foil-wrapped packet. "The first is tomorrow's food ration. You are forbidden to eat at public establishments." He reached into the bag and grabbed a gun. "You each have a silenced Intertec TEC-DC9 assault pistol, with two spare magazines containing ninety-six rounds. Use it to defend yourselves." He held up an envelope. "Check your maps. Each of you has a specific target location. Be sure it is the right one as I call the roll." He jerked his head toward the first man. "Achmed?"

Achmed held his envelope in the air. "The White House, Washington, DC."

Habib was next. "The Pentagon, Washington, DC."

Oman followed. "The New World Trade Center, New York." Each man named his target in succession.

"O'Hare Airport, Chicago."

"Air Force Headquarters, Nebraska."

"Wall Street, New York."

"The Federal Triangle, Washington, DC."

"Tactical Air Command, Virginia."

"The Hanford Nuclear Plant, Washington."

"Dobbins Air Force Base, Atlanta."

"Kennedy Space Center, Florida."

The list went on: thirty-three locations; airports, defense command centers, transportation sites, public communications centers.

As the roll call ended, Armitradj pointed to the five remaining bags. "Remember, with these remaining doves, Samir and I will be ready to back up the prime targets in Washington, DC, if the phone calls from those sites do not verify." He picked up the next item from his bag, a small plastic case. "All of you have a cellular phone that will allow you one call once your doves are in place. Remember your code. Also . . ." He held up a leather sheath. "We've provided you with a dual-edged combat knife. Avoid contact with other individuals, but if *you must* overcome resistance, use the silence of the knife first and make sure the body is removed far from the dove site." He held up a packet. "You each have a wallet, complete with fake identification— driver's license, voter's registration, and Social Security card."

Armitradj gave Samir a stern glance. "Would you like to address the final issue?"

"No, proceed," Samir whispered.

Armitradj reached into the duffel and retrieved a first-aid kit, a small blue-and-white plastic case marked with a red cross. "You must avoid capture at all costs. The American agencies are currently using sodium amathol, a truth agent, to extract information from suspects. You must not allow this to happen to you. In here, among the Band-Aids and antiseptic cream, you will also find"—he opened the small box and pulled out a tiny silver plastic pouch—"what Americans call a disinfectant wipe."

One of the men smirked at the expression.

Armitradj focused on the man. "That may sound feeble, but the moisture inside carries death. Remove them from the first-aid kit now." The men complied and held the small silver polyethylene packets in the air. "We suggest you carry this on your person, here." Armitradj demonstrated, patting his front right pants pocket. "If you are in danger of capture"—he pointed to the packet's small red tab—"simply open this seal, hold the napkin to your nose and inhale. You will die painlessly in five seconds."

Armitradj looked back at Samir. "That is all I have to say."

Whispering as loud as he could, Samir addressed the gathering. "You men have pledged your life to Allah, and your service to the leadership of Hassan Salaar."

On cue, Hassan surprised them all by emerging from the shadows of an adjacent doorway. The men came to their feet, acknowledging his presence with a chorus of cheers.

Hassan stepped forward and joined Armitradj. The yells subsided as their leader addressed the men. "Sons of Mohammed, if you are detected and must sacrifice yourself to assure this victory, let that moment be your final act of consecration."

He placed a hand on Armitradj's shoulder and cast a glance in Samir's direction. "You have been well trained, and Allah is with you." He pointed to the large freight elevator that sat ready beneath the orange girders. "Let me embrace each of you as you depart." Hassan walked to the large black steel doors, where he pushed a red button and the doors parted. Then he turned and began to hug each man as they passed, stepping into the elevator, lining up in even rows.

Samir limped over and joined Hassan, raising a right fist over his head, giving the men a salute. The men, each with a duffel in his left hand, returned the salute with his right.

Hassan raised both his hands in the air, palms out. "Recently, one of our Islamic brothers in Egypt defiantly told the Western press, 'We of the jihad will choose our *time* and *place* for a great battle.' We have fulfilled his prophecy. Today is the time. The place is within the walls of the great Satan's own heart. May Allah bless this day and his soldiers in this holy war. I will see you in Tehran in one week's time. If not . . . remember that those who fall abide with us eternally in the garden of holy souls."

56

AS HE WAITED FOR THE clerk's attention, Thane looked through the dust-smeared window of the Island Pond Feed Store.

Outside, the late sunlight shimmered on the asphalt as a few citizens wandered the main street.

With a population of only a few hundred, Island Pond was a village that looked as if it had been lost in a crease of the map. And since the residents all seemed to know one another, finding someone who looked as different as Hassan and as striking as Damita should have been easy. But Thane had made the rounds, including the bait shop, the grocery store, and the drug-store across the street with no luck. No one knew of a man by Hassan's name or even remembered having seen someone fitting his description three months before, the time when Damita's postcard had been written.

Thane's focus returned to the activities at the sales counter.

The clock on the barn-wood wall over the cash register read 4:47—nearly closing time. The female clerk, a chunky friendly-faced woman in her early fifties in a Pendleton shirt, had just stuffed some pansy seeds, snail bait, and a new hose nozzle into a brown paper bag.

Her elderly customer grabbed his booty with a clawed hand as he spit the last of his sunflower-seed shells into an oak bucket that served as a waste bin. "Thanks, Wendy," the man said, pushing money into her hand. "See ya next weekend."

As the old guy headed for the door, the buxom woman turned to Thane. "And for you?"

"Mmmm, well, I'm looking for someone."

She measured him with a twinkle in her eyes. "Are you? A date for the dance, or the fella that mushed your face?"

Thane smiled. "No. I took care of him. This is a man about six-two, dark looks. Visited here last spring with his beautiful redheaded wife. Last name is Salaar. Ring a bell?"

"We get a few tourists," Wendy said. "But I think I'd remember folks with a name like that." Her gaze traveled the width of his shoulders, up one arm and down the other, and came to rest at his waist.

"The manager over at PJ's Market told me you're the only real-estate agent in town."

"Got my license, if that's what you mean. Property doesn't move up here. Though a real-estate company bought up a slew of land some years ago. Can't remember their names. Started building houses, but nothing came of it. Not like the 1980s, when this place was booming."

"Booming? Hard to imagine." Thane didn't intend to belittle the community. "Sorry. I like small towns, without the boom."

"Well, we had one all right. Silver. Would you believe it? A mother lode up in the mountains, about forty miles east. 'Course when the vein ran out, so did the people. Most folks don't even remember."

"I'm glad you do. You remember anything about a place called Chigger Falls?"

"Sure. Up the highway towards Norton. The falls spill off Norton Pond."

"This Salaar couple owns a cabin somewhere nearby, or at least that's my guess from a postcard they sent."

"Postcards?" She opened the drawer and pulled out a handful, shuffling through until she found one. "Like these?"

She held three blank cards identical to the one Thane had seen at the Tarrington Nursing Home.

"That's it. The redheaded woman, Damita, must have been here."

Wendy cocked her head. "She mean something to you?"

"That's why I'm trying to find her."

"What's your name?"

The question seemed to be a qualifier. "Adams."

"You've got the look of tanned leather about you. Are you a hunter or something?"

"No. Photographer."

"Ah. Well, Mr. Adams, the mountains around here are chock-full of cabins. Lots of cross-country skiing up here, some hunting. But I haven't sold a cabin in a couple of years. Sold two homes and five lots. Things stay much like they are, you know."

"Well, thanks anyway." He was about to leave. "If you think of anything, I've checked in at the Lake Front Motel."

His disappointed expression seemed to have an effect. She smiled at him sympathetically. "Have you tried the post office?" she asked, leaning forward.

"Closed until Monday."

"Oh, that's right." She pointed east. "Well, try the gas station, everybody lights there at one time or another."

Thane smiled. "Thanks."

"But if you strike out . . . well . . . give me a call, I'm in the book." She winked. "Wendy Dinsmore."

"I'll keep it in mind. Thanks again." Sensing her inquisitive glances at his back, he eased toward the door. A final wave from Wendy and he launched himself back into the heat of the day.

There was little traffic, and since he'd parked his car at the motel, Thane decided to ignore his limp and walk the short distance to the gas station.

He passed several small houses, a closed five-and-dime, and then came to an overhead sign advertising a fast-food place. The loud music inside distracted him and he decided to get a cold drink.

As he entered the restaurant, three giggling teens dressed in shorts and sandals exited. A small radio on a rear shelf spewed a staccato heavy-metal refrain and the walls were adorned with rock-concert posters. An overhead fan kept the air circulating. Thane rested on a stool while a young woman in a T-shirt and stiff-spiked bleached-blond hair poured him a root beer.

He downed the liquid a few gulps at a time, staring into the street. A man in overalls helped his wife out of a pickup truck across the way. They entered a small white building with a sign that read CHIROPRACTOR. Just then, a Chevy Suburban approached.

Thane tilted the paper cup again as the four-wheel-drive vehicle passed. Then he almost choked. He suddenly realized he'd seen the driver's face before.

In a flash, he recalled the words Cali, tie him. He'd never forget those homely features—it was one of Danielle's kidnappers.

Thane set the cup down and dashed to the window, trying to memorize the Connecticut license plate. He stepped outside but immediately jumped back into the doorway.

The Suburban had parked only feet away along the sidewalk. The man named Cali emerged and disappeared inside the drugstore.

Thane turned to the young woman. "Do you have a phone I can use?"

She wiped the counter with a rag, shook her head, and pointed out the door. "We've got a land line. But there's a pay phone down the street."

"No. This is very important." He lowered his voice. "Please. It'll just take a minute."

The young woman appeared confused by his intensity, but she nodded to a wall phone by the freezer.

"Thanks a lot." Thane rushed to the phone. "This is . . . I'll make it up to you." Thane dug in his wallet for a slip of paper and found the number. Without mentioning that he was calling long distance, he direct-dialed the number in Boston.

The phone rang five times and was picked up. "Agent Gere."

"Gere. Is Carver there?"

"He's out on a case. Who's this?" Gere asked.

"Thane Adams."

"Adams. Did you know he's been looking for you? Where—"

"Listen. It's vital you get word to him. I'm in Island Pond, Vermont, and I've spotted one of Hassan's men, driving a Chevy Suburban, Connecticut license BQH 232. I'm about to follow. Tell Carver that Hassan's got a place up here . . . Wait." Thane cupped the receiver with his hand and spun around to the young woman.

"Could you see if the Chevy van is still parked in front of Darby's?"

The blonde looked more confused.

"The blue one," he said as she timidly made her way to the window. She looked back and nodded.

"Gere. Tell Carver to get his ass up here. And remember this. Chigger Falls. I'm driving a Dodge Charger rental, staying at the Lake Front Motel. Okay? I'll call again if I can."

"Adams. Stay put. Don't try—"

"I've gotta go."

Thane hung up and headed for the door. "This is our little secret for now, okay?"

She nodded awkwardly as she backed away.

Thane gave her a quick smile, eased out of the eatery, and crept down the street.

The Suburban hadn't moved.

As Thane approached the Chevy, he hung to the rear of the vehicle, peering from around the back.

In the drugstore, the small Arabic-looking man had grabbed a shopping basket, working his way down the aisles. How odd it was in this environment to see Cali—this weasel who had tried to kill him—engaged in an act of domesticity.

Thane shielded his eyes from the sun and looked inside the Suburban. From what he could tell through the blackened windows, the nine-seater was empty. He knew he wouldn't have time to get to his own car. But could this be his chance? He grabbed the back-door handle of the Chevy and cranked. It opened easily. The street was almost vacant except for a car that had just passed in the other direction.

Two elderly men in fishing caps had exited the grocery store fifty yards away, and were busy with their bags.

Keeping an eye out, Thane opened one of the two rear doors, hoisted himself into the aft compartment of the wagon and closed the door from the inside.

Moving to the middle seat, he crouched low and waited. Minutes passed as he planned his strategy. When Cali returned, he would probably use the driver's-side door, perhaps the passenger-side cargo door to load. Or even the rear doors, if he were laden with purchases.

The blackened windows were a blessing. Thane would be able to move around once he knew Cali's chosen entry.

His scheming was interrupted as Cali emerged from the store carrying two cardboard boxes, one of which he put on the hood. As Cali reached for the passenger-side door handle, Thane crept quickly and carefully around the seat into the rear of the Suburban. Making himself as small as possible, Thane felt the Chevy's shocks give as Cali's weight hit the running board. This was followed by the sound of two boxes being slid onto the middle seat, where Thane had knelt only seconds before.

The side door slammed.

Thane lifted his head up over the seat, watching Cali walk around the front of the car toward the driver's side.

Catching a quick peek into the boxes, Thane ducked just in time. Cali swung into the driver's seat and started the car, backing it into the street.

As the Suburban accelerated in the direction from which it had come, Thane again huddled on the floor. He couldn't imagine where he was going, but realized that it really didn't matter.

At least he was headed in the same direction as the hair spray, curlers, and styling gel . . . to a place where Danielle and Damita surely must be.

57

WITH THE FUTURE LOOKING AS dark as their concrete prison, Danielle and Damita were left to lie on their cots and wait for the terrorists to execute their timetable.

From what Damita had been told an hour ago on her last visit to Hassan's chamber, the assault force had left the stronghold. The doves were on their way to their targets. Cali had run his errands, and besides Samir, Armitradj, and Hassan, Damita had only seen three other men in the compound. One of those stood guard outside their room.

During the previous hour, while Damita dozed, Danielle had paced the floor, racking her brain for some plan of action. Though nothing had yet come to mind, the rhythm of Danielle's repetitive walk within the confined space reminded her of Thane's pacing, his catlike gait when he'd been irritated at Carver's office.

Now, with the lantern on its lowest setting and Damita still asleep, Danielle lay on the cot telling herself to cling to hope. The more she stared into the gloom of the concrete ceiling, the more that hope took the shape of Thane's face.

She had never met anyone like him. Thane lived in a world far removed from the artificial values of her own career experience. He was a multidimensional human being with his own standards. What a contrast to those empty impotent shells she'd worked with, men like Dennison, paper-thin reproductions of a GQ lifestyle editorial.

Even in the brief time she had known him, Thane had become more than just a fascinating man, or an attractive challenge. He was a friend.

That revelation spurred a strange longing that felt more like a sexual need. Could friendship stir this impulse? Could personal synergy provoke desire?

She brushed aside the notion that her own jeopardy had spawned these yearnings. In fact, she believed that if she had the time to know Thane under less harried circumstances, she would still feel the same.

She hadn't prayed a great deal since childhood, but now her muddled thoughts coalesced into an appeal to God. Somehow, if Thane was out there, she had to see him again.

Even if she had to fly to Iran, somehow, in some way, she and Thane would find each other. And if there were only the slightest chance of escape . . . As Damita awakened, the determination to find that chance burned within Danielle.

"What time do you think it is?" Damita asked, sleepy-eyed.

Danielle rolled over and faced her sister. "Well, from the aroma in the hall, I know it's nearly dinnertime. And it's Saturday."

"Our last day," Damita said with resignation.

A hush followed. Due to Damita's despondency Danielle had not yet told her about Hassan's attempted seduction, explaining instead that she had simply been questioned by him. Even more than before, Damita seemed immersed in her own sadness. "Danny, I feel like all this is my fault. I'm so sorry."

Danielle understood her sister's remorse but wished to focus on action, not regrets. "Don't think about the past."

"What else is there? The future? I hate the idea of it."

Danielle sat up and swung around. "Look, I understand. But we have to get out of this dung hole. I don't want to hear talk like that. Hate your future? That's bullshit. I'll give you something to hate. Hate Hassan and that whispering geek." Danielle leaned forward and glared at Damita. "If I could get my hands on a gun, I'd blow the shit out of both of them. If you and I have to die, we'll take a few of these idiots with us."

Still lying on her side, Damita seemed shocked at Danielle's sudden anger.

"God." Danielle slapped her hands together. "I don't know if I can stand another minute of this." Damita swallowed hard, her eyes widening as Danielle continued. "We're not going to lie here and you're not going to lay for him, either. No more. Let him threaten to kill me, Dee, but don't let him touch you.

He won't kill me and I'll tell you why." She pointed to her forearms. "These razor marks are clean. He'd like to lay me, too. One of us isn't good enough. You understand that, don't you?"

Damita was speechless, but Danielle felt suddenly empowered. "Promise me something," she said, clutching Damita's hand. "Promise me we won't ever stop trying to escape. Even if we get to Iran. Promise."

"But how?"

"I don't give a shit how. The how will come from wanting it badly enough. The minute we stop willing something better than this, we become the mistresses Hassan wants us to be." Danielle tugged on her wrist. "Now let's review what we know about this pit. Okay?"

Damita sat up, absorbing some of Danielle's determination. "Well, as you know, we're on the lower level of two floors," she said, wiping her face. "On my way up to Hassan's bedroom, I've noticed a conference room right next door to us; he called it their 'war room.' Then there's a kitchen and some storage. But when I see Hassan I climb a flight of stairs around the corner from the men's bathroom. His room is directly above ours."

"All right," Danielle said. "But that long corridor beyond his bedroom leads out, I'm sure of it. I felt the movement of air in that hallway. Do you know what's beyond his room?"

"I know there are sleeping rooms down that hall, and I hear that chunking noise from the other end, and sometimes another sound with it, a kind of whine."

"So what do you think it is?"

"Something big, moving." Damita seemed charged up.

"Like a truck? A conveyor? Whatever it is, the assault team used it. And that's our way out. We'll try to find it tonight."

"But how?"

Danielle leaned forward. "That guard outside wears a gun."

"Yes. I remember."

"Late tonight, perhaps we can lure him in here, pretend one of us—say it's me—is knocked out from the sedative, but you've gotten very sick. One of us will distract him somehow, maybe with some partial nudity, whatever, to allow the other one to club him. Think about it. They'll unlock this door, give us our dinner and probably our pills, so we'll sleep." Danielle lowered her voice. "We'll tuck the pills under our tongues and spit them back out. If that doesn't work, when they leave, I'll make you gag so you vomit. You do the same for me. Anything to not be knocked out. Do you agree?"

Damita nodded, but still looked slightly confused.

"Good. That's a plan," Danielle said, wanting to reassure her. "Now stay strong, lie back and relax until they come. We'll see how this thing plays."

The two sisters settled back on their cots, again lost in their individual thoughts.

After a good half hour, the latch on the heavy wooden door finally clicked.

Their guard, a bulky unshaven Iranian in his mid-thirties, entered with two trays of food. As he set them on the ends of the cots, Danielle noticed the gun in his holster.

"You will eat now," he said, pointing.

Damita lay still and Danielle sat up casually, faking a yawn. She looked at the plates. Soup, rice, and focaccia bread. No sedatives. "When do we take our pills?" she asked, looking at the floor.

The guard stepped back and the heavy door swung open, revealing Samir's gaunt face. "Pills? Are you looking forward to your pills?" he whispered.

Though his voice sent a shiver up her back, Danielle tried not to react.

"If we're going to take a nap, let's get on with it. I'm bored to tears."

"Oh, you'll sleep. But by injection."

"I told Hassan I wanted no more of that," Damita protested.

"His regrets. I convinced him a shot would be more effective."

"Where is he? I want to see him," Damita demanded.

"Don't be concerned. The injections are painless. You won't feel a thing. I'll be back later tonight to give them to you personally." Samir smiled. "You know how gentle I can be."

58

FROM THE INCLINE OF THE car and the way he was being tossed around, Thane knew the Suburban was off the main road and they were climbing. He stayed low, not daring to raise his head, not wanting to be spotted in the rearview mirror.

Well outside Island Pond, trees had filled in behind the 4X4 and filtered the late-afternoon light. Judging from the sun's position, they were heading north.

During the ride, Cali listened to a disc of Middle Eastern music. He howled and hummed along to the twang of a sitar, enthusiastically pounding on the dash. But after forty-five minutes, he turned down the audio and the Suburban slowed.

From the sound of the tires, they had crossed from dirt onto thick gravel. The Chevy stopped, then started again.

Chain-link fencing became visible on either side of the vehicle. Then, through the rear window, a wire gate closed automatically behind.

Rolling slowly, the tires crossed from gravel to smooth pavement. The last rays of the sun were inexplicably shielded and Thane could no longer see out of the car, which came to a full stop.

Cali opened the door and exited. He spoke to someone else in a foreign language.

Thane ventured a look over the rear seat. The Suburban had parked in front of large black metal gates between two huge concrete retaining walls built into the side of a mountain. Above the gates, thick steel girders supported a vented, covered hood, and within, a system of cables and pulleys appeared to suspend something below. The cables spooled up onto large steel wheels, lifting what Thane now presumed was some kind of elevator.

Near the hood of the Suburban, Cali stood with another man, who had stepped out of a guard shack. He pushed a button on a panel and the gates, some eight feet in height, parted and receded into the mountain on either side, as the cage of a black-and-orange freight elevator rose to ground level.

Thane ducked as Cali returned to the driver's seat and put the truck into gear. Metal clanked under all four tires as the Chevy drove over the threshold into the elevator.

A slight rocking and the gate closed with a rumble. Then, with a hiss and a whine, the descent began.

Thane was suddenly struck by his circumstances. Since they were headed underground, Carver would never find this place. The Chevy Suburban and its license plates had disappeared from the face of the earth and Thane had become Dante descending into the inferno alone.

The total darkness reinforced the hellish image as they dropped into the shaft, although the gloom was intermittently interrupted by the passing of an occasional red bulb on the shaft wall that illuminated the inside of the Suburban with an eerie crimson glow. Thane began to count the bulbs, gauging the interval between them. It was roughly twenty feet. After the ninth bulb, the darkness of the shaft opened and yellow light flooded the interior of the vehicle.

The elevator settled with a clunk, and a nearby rumble indicated that another gate had opened in front of the truck.

With tires squealing, the Suburban drove onto what sounded like a smooth surface and, as yellow lights reeled by on a concrete wall, took a right turn and stopped almost immediately.

Cali hopped out of the vehicle again. The side cargo doors opened with an echo. Thane scrunched himself into a ball on the floor, squeezing as far as he could into the corner of the rear compartment.

Cardboard scraped against the seat ahead as Cali recovered the boxes. Then the cargo door closed. If Danielle and Damita were the recipients of the hygiene products, Thane would somehow have to follow Cali. He faced the rear of the truck while Cali's footsteps faded off to his right. All was deadly quiet. Thane crouched and moved forward to open the side cargo door. The keys of the Chevy were still in the ignition. As Thane took them, another set of footsteps passed behind the Suburban, causing him to collapse onto the floor. He lay on his side listening, but after several minutes with no further sound, he got to his knees and peeked out the rear windows.

He was amazed at what he saw.

The Suburban was parked in an alcove alongside two Jeeps and what looked to be a military troop-transport truck, complete with canvas cover and a white American star on the door. The alcove evidently served as a garage, outfitted with a workbench, a tool rack, and several fifty-gallon drums of gasoline.

From the garage, Thane looked across a main underground chamber some eighty feet wide; the elevator was forty feet to his left. A tunnel, the route Cali must have taken, disappeared to the right. Large double doors stood directly across the way, a no-smoking insignia stenciled on each one.

That insignia fascinated Thane. Something flammable inside.

What had Damita's postcard read? Real estate deals. Somehow, Hassan had created this underground fortress of cement and steel. From what Wendy had said, it might have been an abandoned silver mine. In this underground strong-hold, the Iranian had hidden his arsenal, the doves and undoubtedly Danielle and Damita.

Thane checked his watch: 6:50 P.M.

It was time to explore.

He was about to open the Suburban's side door when he heard more foot-steps. As he crouched again, he watched three identically dressed dark-skinned men enter the large chamber. Two approached the double doors. The third peeled off and headed in his direction.

Thane ducked, wondering where to hide, but then realized he was out of danger when the troop-truck door slammed and its ignition turned over. He watched as the olive-drab truck backed across the main chamber and came to rest in front of the double doors, which the other two men had opened. Then all three men began to load guns. Scores of them. Automatic rifles and shotguns were being stacked into the canvas-covered bed of the truck. The men seemed to be in no hurry, pausing occasionally to toy with the firearms.

Why were they loading weapons? Were they leaving for an assault? Regard-less of their plans, Thane was pinned down until they were finished, and their work seemed to take forever.

As he watched, Thane tried to keep a running inventory of the cargo. It might be useful and yet, as time dragged on, it became difficult to keep track.

The men switched to loading boxes of what appeared to be ammunition, and, yes, a rocket launcher. Christ. Enough firepower there to hold off an impressive force . . . was *that* the plan? To protect this bunker from an attack from above?

After another five minutes the men finished and drove the truck back across the main chamber into the garage. As it moved, Thane caught a glimpse into the munitions room before the doors were closed again. At least ten cases of explosives remained stacked against the walls. Difficult to tell from this distance, but they appeared to be dynamite.

The men bolted and padlocked the double doors and, much to Thane's frustration, gathered together at the garage entrance, where they remained for several minutes talking and laughing.

Finally, they walked off in the same direction Cali had gone.

Thane checked his watch. Three wasted hours. At least he had benefited from their delay. He knew where he could find a weapon.

Easing the side door open, he stepped onto the garage floor. He kept his eyes open as he tried to limber up his wounded leg. Stiffness had set in from sitting in a cramped position. The thigh began to loosen up as he slowly began to walk, creeping between the vehicles toward the far wall. At the workbench he found an elbow-shaped tire iron with a flattened end that he suspected he would need. Then he hoisted himself into the dimly lit back of the troop truck.

Hundreds of weapons had been stacked in wire bins along both sides of the bed. As quietly as he could, he sifted through the AK-47s, Uzis, and twelve-gauge shotguns. Every single weapon was empty. All the guns, even the automatic rifles, were brand-new, but all without clips. He needed ammunition. In the darkness he felt along toward the cab of the truck and located more crates. At the risk of being noticed, he opened the back flap of the troop truck's canvas cover a crack to create enough light to read the labels. What he'd assumed might be crates of ammunition were actually crates of hand grenades. At least they'd be ready to use. Using the tire iron, he jimmied one of the wooden lids.

Feeling inside among the styrofoam padding, he located a couple of grenades and tucked them in the front pockets of his jeans. Now he was armed, but unfortunately with something very loud that would alert the entire complex. Considering that problem and anticipating his potential needs, Thane suddenly realized that he'd feel better with a gun in his hands—even without the shells. Not knowing exactly why, he grabbed a Remington twelve-gauge shotgun and tucked it under his arm. He paused to run through his battle plan, and

Kuintala's grin invaded his thoughts. If he were here, Kuintala would recognize the irony of the inane choice of weapons—Thane, the great hunter, outmanned and armed with a shotgun that could serve only as a club.

With a hope that he might see Kuintala's bright smile again, Thane climbed down from the truck bed and worked himself along the far garage wall. He reached the edge of the alcove. From there he peered around the back of the troop carrier. Cali's concrete tunnel stretched off to the right some seventy yards. The bare cement walls were lit every ten feet by a fluorescent light. Several shadowed doorways some thirty feet apart created dark hollows along both sides.

Thane limped down the tunnel, choosing to hug the right side, coming to rest in the darkness of the first doorway.

He listened, then tried the door handle. It was locked.

On to the next doorway. Locked again.

He was a few feet from the third door when suddenly the second one opened, casting a bright light. Voices echoed in the tunnel as two men stepped into the hall. Thane scurried to the next doorway and hoped for—yes, the latch clicked and gave way.

He pushed inside as the men headed in his direction. Easing the door closed, he looked around. The room was thankfully unoccupied and very dark, though it was noisy; there was a low-pitched hum resonating from the back, where a large gray generator sat against the far wall. Red-and-green lights blinked on its panel. Thane had located the power plant. He waited, breathing hard, estimating the time it would take for the men to pass. Then he cracked the door and heard voices trailing off to his right. One voice was immediately recognizable. No one could mistake that eerie whisper.

Thane thrust his head outside and barely caught a glimpse of Samir's back as he limped along, carrying something flat and shiny in his right hand, a tray of some kind. The gimpy Iranian was accompanied by another husky man, apparently a guard, wearing a holstered handgun on his belt. The two reached the end of the hall and turned right, moving down concrete stairs.

Thane cautiously stepped into the corridor and followed at a safe distance, constantly looking over his shoulder.

As he reached the top of the stairs, he could see that Samir had descended to the bottom, where he and the guard took a left turn into another corridor.

The size of the complex was astonishing.

He sneaked down the stairs and, reaching the base of the stairwell, peered around the corner. Samir and his companion were halfway down the hall, standing before yet another door, the third of five. The guard unlocked it, pushed it open, and both he and Samir stepped inside.

Holding the shotgun across his chest, Thane ventured forward. The door to the room was still ajar as he approached.

He knew instinctively that Samir would lead him to the heart of the action.

As he edged closer he could hardly believe the conversation inside. Listening carefully, he was overwhelmed to recognize Danielle's voice.

59

ON TIPTOE, THANE APPROACHED THE doorway, craning his neck to see inside, wondering how to deal with the situation.

Samir's companion, the burly guard, stood closest in the foreground. Thane could just see his torso through the crack in the door. Samir's shadow wavered on the wall beyond, thrown by what appeared to be a kerosene lantern.

Another cautious step and Thane was only a few feet away now, trying to formulate his game plan.

From inside the room, he heard the unmistakable whisperer, though he couldn't discern specific words. Then he understood Danielle quite distinctly as she said, "She doesn't want a shot, and if she wants to see her husband, goddammit, she should be allowed."

Another whisper. As the guard stepped further inside, Thane caught a flash of Danielle's red hair, and of the black sweatshirt she was wearing. Damita was seated next to her on some kind of cot. The guard and Samir were leaning over, trying to remove Damita's warm-ups.

Damita was resisting, and Danielle cried out, "Don't touch her, you sadistic bastard."

This was Thane's cue. Without another thought, he heaved the door with his shoulder, crashing into the room, shotgun held chin-high in both hands.

Samir and the guard looked up in amazement. With a leveraged thrust of the shotgun's wooden butt, Thane caught the guard square in the face. The guard went down with a groan, out cold in a heap between the beds.

Samir stepped back, dropping the tray and needles and, in a twisting move, grabbed his own right leg. To Thane's surprise, Samir suddenly held a wicked-looking pearl-handled blade and like a cobra began thrusting at Thane, who fended him off with the stock of the shotgun.

Preoccupied with Samir's threatening jabs, Thane yelled over his shoulder to Danielle. "Get the gun."

While Damita threw her body on the guard's chest, Danielle successfully yanked the nine-millimeter handgun from the guard's holster and rose to her feet, pointing the weapon straight at Samir. "I'm going to kill this asshole."

Thane retreated a step, astounded by the look in Danielle's eyes. "Danielle, wait."

"Yes," Samir smiled. "Why don't you shoot and alert the others."

"I don't give a fuck about the others," Danielle said, breathing hard. "I want to see you bleed for a change."

Thane reached for the gun. "What—?"

"This pig sliced me." Danielle pointed to the Band-Aids on her forearm.

"He tortured her," Damita said, still on her knees.

"Drop the knife," Thane said, gripping the shotgun's barrel, brandishing the weapon like a baseball bat.

Samir shook his head, glaring at Danielle. "You drop the gun and you won't be hurt," he rasped. "You can't get out of here and you know it."

"I'm going to take a piece of you with me," Danielle said, aiming the weapon at Samir's face.

Thane was about to implore her to hand him the gun, when Damita was suddenly thrown back. The guard had regained consciousness and after shoving Damita, kicked sideways from his prone position, striking Danielle in the wrist. The nine-millimeter was knocked out of her hand, and clattered across the cement floor, coming to rest under the far cot.

Seeing Danielle disarmed, Samir made his move, thrusting at Thane.

Out of the corner of his eye, Thane saw an enraged Damita throw herself on the guard, joining Danielle, who had already jumped on him. Though he wanted to help, Thane was forced to defend himself against Samir, who was jabbing at his mid-section. Instinctively, Thane went for the weak spot, and with all his strength swung the shotgun low and hard, catching Samir in the right thigh. The force of the blow caused a tearing noise as Samir's upper leg was detached from his hip and he was knocked backward, collapsing awkwardly on the floor.

Thane was amazed to see the leather straps shredded and the inner wiring sprung loose, as the artificial limb protruded at right angles from Samir's body through the torn jeans.

A broken man, Samir had dropped the knife. Struggling with his leg, trying to bring it back into position, he scrambled like a crab toward the far wall, trying to evade Thane.

With Samir momentarily disabled, Thane looked back. The skirmish behind him still raged. The guard's legs kicked the cement floor while Danielle and Damita were both piled on his upper body.

Thane stepped over quickly and raised the gun butt, prepared to drive it into the guard's forehead. "I've got him," he said, but hesitated as Danielle and Damita sat up, revealing the guard's face. With his eyes rolled back in his head he went limp on the ground. Two hypodermic needles with plungers depressed stuck out of his neck near the carotid artery.

"Whoa." Thane glanced at Danielle. "Nice work."

But Danielle was distracted by Samir, who had just recovered his knife and was crawling toward them, dragging the artificial limb behind. "You're all going to die," he whispered.

"Like hell," Danielle growled, scrambling over to the cot. She reached underneath for the handgun and jumped to her feet and took aim. "I'm taking you out."

Thane took three steps across the floor and smacked Samir across the top of the head with the shotgun. Samir's head snapped to one side and he slumped to the ground, unconscious.

Thane stepped between the body and an angry, gun-wielding Danielle. "Don't," he said. "He's toast." He pointed up toward the ceiling. "Life's up there. Let's worry about that, what do you say?"

"He deserves this." With fire in her eyes, Danielle took a step forward. Thane headed her off, but not wanting to disarm her, caught her in an embrace instead. They struggled for a moment.

He held her tight. "We'll forget," he said, whispering in her ear. "I promise you. I'll help you forget."

After a moment of indecision, her body relaxed. She dropped the gun to the floor and buried her face in Thane's chest. He felt her heave, breathing hard; then, apparently resigning herself, she reared back and wiped a tear away. "All right. Let's go."

"That's the idea." He turned. "Damita, shut the door a minute."

As Damita complied, Danielle stepped over and took her hand.

Thane was struck by the sight of both sisters. Incredible to see them standing there together like this, even in a crisis. He couldn't help smiling as he leaned down and picked up the handgun. "Okay, you two. Talk to me."

Damita spoke up. "I just want to get out of here."

"We will. I've got the keys to a car and an elevator. Do you know of any other way out?"

"No," Danielle said. "Haven't seen one."

"The halls were pretty quiet when I came down. How many men upstairs?"

"We don't know. Damita heard that their assault team left."

Thane's stomach pitched. "Holy shit."

Danielle nodded. "The doves."

"Where? How?"

"We're not sure, but we've got to warn the government." Danielle started for the door.

"Wait." He pointed to Samir. "Do you have anything to tie him up?"

"How about this?" Danielle leaned down, loosening Samir's leather belt.

"Good."

Danielle strapped Samir's wrists.

With the shotgun in the crook of his arm, Thane leaned down and smacked Samir on the face barehanded to see if he was still out cold. He didn't stir. "He's gone." Then he picked up the curved knife and tucked it into his pants.

Danielle gestured to the guard. "And he's not going anywhere with that sedative in his neck."

Thane handed the nine-millimeter to Danielle. "Take this. And you, Damita . . ." He took a grenade out of his pants pocket. "You hold on to one of these."

She appeared confused.

"Just pull this pin. When you let go of this lever and throw it, it blows in five seconds." He handed her the grenade and she stuffed it in her warm-up pocket. "Danielle, you lead. I'll pick up the rear." He gave them both a reassuring wink. "Whatever happens, stay together. We'll get there. Okay?"

Both women nodded. Danielle opened the door and they ventured into the dimly lit corridor. Thane paused to lock the door from the outside, then turned to follow the women.

Along the length of the hallway, all was remarkably quiet.

Hugging the wall, Danielle led the way until they came to the next door on the right. She tried the handle and pushed. It opened, and with Thane looking back to make sure no one had seen them, they walked in.

"This is their war room," Damita whispered, as she found a light switch. A grouping of folding tables sat around the perimeter with a single red telephone in the corner. A series of black-and-white photographs hung on the walls.

Thane quickly grasped the meaning of what he saw. "Look at that. Those must be the dove sites. Shall we—?"

"Yes, grab them."

Thane stood by the door as Damita and Danielle pulled the thirty-three prints out of their clips. As the women rejoined him, Thane looked at the photos. "Do you recognize any of these?"

"This one, I do," Danielle said. "That's Wall Street."

Thane gathered the pictures and handed them to Damita. "Zip them in your warm-up." As she secured them in her jacket, Thane's attention was drawn to a cloth pile in the corner.

"What's this?" He walked over. "Duffels," he said, picking one up, unzipping it. "Oh God."

The women scurried over.

"Look. These must be . . ."

"They're doves," Danielle said bitterly. "Hassan showed one to me when he bragged about it." The bright coppery egg gleamed in the light. A digital clock scrolled numbers—the current time of day read 11:27 P.M. She pointed to the other timer. "That's the detonation time—Monday at noon."

"And this?" Thane pointed to the red button.

"I think that's the trigger housing," Danielle said. "Hassan indicated that if you push that, you've automatically got an explosion in sixty seconds.

"Let's each take one," she suggested. "Here." She handed Thane the nine-millimeter.

"Good," Thane said, zipping the bag. "Let's go." He laid the useless shotgun against a table and moved toward the door.

Back out in the hall, with a duffel in one hand and the nine-millimeter in the other, Thane hung to the rear. The stairs were the next stage of their escape. As quietly as they could, they climbed, the women ahead, each carrying a bag.

At the top, Damita pointed to a room across the hall. "Hassan's bedroom," she whispered.

Thane knew that of the three doors on the left, two were locked. But he was wary of the ones on his right. He pointed. "Do you know . . . ?"

"The other men sleep in those."

Thane nodded and waved them on.

The long hallway stretched ahead. They tiptoed past the sleeping quarters, creeping along the opposite wall from the one Thane had taken during his approach.

After forty yards of gloom, the smell of oil and brightness loomed ahead. They were only sixty feet from the main chamber.

Suddenly, a door opened behind them. A man in skivvies stepped out of the sleeping quarters and spotted them. He burst into shouts of panic, babbling in Iranian.

"Run," Thane said, pushing the women ahead.

Danielle and Damita took off in a sprint with Thane hobbling behind.

The man in the hall was joined by another, and this one had a gun. The hallway blossomed with light as bullets ricocheted off the walls over Thane's head.

"Keep going," Thane shouted, kneeling to return fire, letting three rounds go from the nine-millimeter. The two men retreated into the doorway.

Hobbling backward, Thane fired again. The women were some twenty feet ahead. The Iranian fired another round from the doorway.

Damita cried out and fell to the ground, clutching her ankle, as her duffel bag scooted away.

Danielle dropped to her side, and Thane fired twice more, hopping backward until he reached them.

"She's hit," Danielle screamed.

"Damita, get up. You've got to keep going," Thane yelled. Turning, he fired again.

"I can't," Damita whimpered, clutching her leg as blood gushed onto the floor.

"Drag her!" Thane shouted.

Another door had opened and two men were firing shots.

Danielle dropped her own duffel, grabbed Damita by the arm, and began pulling her up the hall.

Squatting, Thane fired again. One of the men fell backward, struck in the shoulder, while the other darted back into the sleeping quarters. Thane dropped his duffel momentarily, pulled the grenade from his pocket, yanked the pin, and threw it as hard as he could. The grenade clattered along the cement and came to rest some seventy feet away.

"Go, go, go!" Thane shouted, picking up the bag and firing one last shot. Then he tucked the gun in his belt and clutched Damita's hand, helping Danielle.

They had just reached the threshold of the main chamber when the grenade blew. The concussion was deafening, echoing in the tunnel hallway. A strong blast of air rushed up their backs, knocking them forward. Thane stumbled momentarily with his ears ringing, but he helped Danielle regain her footing. Together, they heaved Damita along as her blood trailed behind them.

Praying that he'd bought them precious seconds of time, Thane pointed at the blue Suburban. "Get her in there." Danielle appeared nonplussed. Thane realized that she was suffering temporary hearing loss from the grenade. Rather than explain, he thrust the duffel into her hands and picked up Damita in a fireman's carry, leading Danielle to the car.

He pushed Danielle toward the driver's seat and carried Damita to the passenger side, dropping her into the passenger bucket seat.

Danielle got in and placed the duffel on the middle bench.

Leaning through the passenger door, Thane ripped off his shirt and quickly wrapped Damita's ankle, using the ends of both sleeves to tie the cloth as tight as he could.

Danielle noticed his scar. "Thane, what happened?"

"Never mind. Start the car." He handed her the keys. "I'll get the gate."

Danielle understood and cranked the ignition.

Hobbling as fast as he could, Thane hustled to the control panel by the elevator and hit the black button. The gates parted.

Just as Danielle backed the Suburban out onto the painted cement floor, Thane turned, and beyond the moving car saw Hassan Salaar entering the main chamber firing an Uzi, flanked by Cali and another man. As the automatic weapon spit bullets, pelting the girders and the wall near Thane, he had no choice but to dive for cover into the elevator itself, rolling across the grid floor toward the near wall. On his stomach, he pulled the nine-millimeter from his belt, aimed at Hassan, and fired. The gun clicked empty.

Danielle seemed to sense Thane's predicament and gunned the Chevy's engine. From floor level, Thane watched as she maneuvered the vehicle in reverse.

Intent on firing at Thane, Hassan failed to notice the angle of the approaching vehicle. Cali shouted as he and the second man scattered. Suddenly aware, his eyes wide with panic, Hassan now fired the Uzi at the Suburban as he stumbled toward the tunnel.

Shots pounded into the rear cargo door, but Danielle had accelerated and was on him in an instant. As if he understood the inevitability of his death, Hassan dropped the Uzi and screamed Danielle's name as he fell under the speeding wheels.

Thane jumped to his feet as Danielle reversed direction and screeched the Suburban forward. The vehicle leapt into the elevator and nearly pinned Thane against the passenger-side door. Thane would have run around the back of the car to reach the panel, but didn't get the chance.

Flanked by his companion, Cali had briefly knelt at Hassan's side, but now picked up the Uzi and came forward shouting and firing steadily.

"Get down!" Thane screamed. Danielle and Damita both ducked as bullets shattered the rear windows of the truck and riddled the elevator, throwing sparks off the lift's rear wall. In the hail of ricochets, Thane dropped to the elevator floor. Looking out under the Suburban's chassis, he was amazed to see Samir appear at the tunnel entrance, his artificial leg dragging along the ground, his weight supported by yet another man.

Cali screamed back at them, "Armitradj! Help me kill them." Enraged by the sight of Hassan's crumpled body, Armitradj dropped Samir to the ground and ran forward, firing his handgun.

Thane knew he and the women would die immediately unless he reached the elevator's interior control panel by the driver's-side window. And there was only one way to get there. Bare-chested, he rolled under the Suburban and crawled on his belly over the rough grated metal flooring toward the driver's door.

As he clambered out from under the Chevy by the steering wheel, shots smashed into the truck's body, and Thane was forced to huddle at the side of the truck while Armitradj approached head-on and Cali moved to his left, attempting to get a better firing angle.

Thane knew he had no more than a few seconds. Amid the flying bullets, he strained to reach up and touch the black button on the panel.

Inside the vehicle Danielle called his name as bullets sprayed the Chevy's roofline. The tempered glass windshield had blossomed with multiple pockmarks, charring with each new slug. A bullet smashed the sideview mirror, splattering its glass and cutting Thane's wrist. Still crouching, he thrust his hand toward the panel, his fingers searching blindly.

Finally he found the button and pushed.

The elevator lurched just as Cali gained the advantage, looking straight down the side of the truck. Thane was directly in his line of sight, and as the Uzi sprayed, Thane dropped to the floor and rolled back under the vehicle. He immediately feared that the tires might be pierced, but the rear metal mud flaps had apparently deflected several stray bullets.

As Thane hugged the metal floor, the elevator rose slowly and shots continued to patter within. Mercifully, twenty feet up, the cement shaft closed around them, even as firing continued below.

Thane rolled back out from under the chassis, stood up, and looked into the driver's-side window. On the floor in the front seat, Damita lay curled in a ball. Danielle was sprawled on the center seat floor. "Are you guys all right?" he asked. Both women barely stirred, still shell-shocked from the attack. "Are you hit, dammit?"

"No," Damita groaned.

Danielle sat up on an elbow. "I'm okay."

One of the red construction lights passed by. "Hand me that dove." Thane leaned in the truck window.

"What are you doing?"

"I'm dropping the son of a bitch," Thane said.

"It's the only one we have left. The analysis—"

"Danielle, there's still a guard up there. They've got two Jeeps and a truck full of firepower down below. When we reach the top, they'll recall the elevator and before we get down this mountain, they'll be on our ass. I don't want to try dodging their rocket launcher." Thane reached out. "I'm ending it. Here. Now."

Danielle handed him the duffel. "But how will—"

"Sixty seconds, right?" Thane took the dove out of the bag. He looked up. Moving cables stretched upward into the blackness. It was difficult to see the top of the shaft, particularly since the motor housing above blocked any view of the sky. "I'm counting the lights."

As Danielle watched from the window, Thane took the smooth, egg-shaped bomb out of the bag and stepped to the side of the open-air elevator. Thane estimated roughly a foot and a half of space between the elevator rail and the cement shaft wall. Another red construction light drifted by. Had Thane wanted, he could have reached out and touched it. A stiff breeze blew up from below, thick with the smell of gunpowder.

Thane held the dove just beyond the elevator's rail. One more light to go until the top. A hundred and sixty feet would be a hell of a drop. He prayed the dove would stay in one piece, and then he prayed for enough time to escape the concussion.

As the final light passed, Thane punched the red button and let the dove fall down the shaft.

He opened the car door and jumped into the driver's seat. The engine was still running.

"You guys stay down." Thane looked back at Danielle, then leaned over and recovered the remaining grenade from Damita's warm-up. The elevator jerked to a stop, the black gates slid open, and Thane pulled the pin on the grenade.

From the security of his shack some forty feet away, the gate guard, alerted by communication from below, waved a flashlight toward the Suburban and began firing.

Bullets punctured the car's hood as Thane tossed the grenade out the driver's-side window toward the shack. Then he huddled below the dash as the grenade detonated.

Thane didn't wait for the smoke to clear—he gunned the engine. The Suburban lurched forward, and the gate guard, stunned by the explosion and firing aimlessly through the smoke, wandered into the path of the Chevy and was thrown to one side.

Thane accelerated and the Suburban shot across the asphalt, breaking through the chain-link fenced gate. Seconds later, just as the Chevy's tires hit the gravel roadway, a beam of orange light illuminated the top of the shaft.

Immediately on the heels of that glow, a tremendous explosion shook the earth.

Thane looked back over his shoulder as steel girders, the motor housing of the elevator, and some sixty square feet of ground, including the guard shack and the retaining walls, disappeared in a vibrant cloud of smoke, caving into the tunnel below.

DAY TWO

60

THE ILLUMINATION OF THE EXPLOSION seemed to have acted as a homing beacon. Suddenly the side of the mountain flared with lights.

As Thane guided the Suburban down the winding wilderness road, headlights from what appeared to be four-wheel-drive trucks began moving through the trees in their direction. Two helicopters lit the sky with floods, panning the forest.

Danielle and Damita sat up in their seats, disturbed by the display.

Damita looked back with an agonized expression. "God, you don't think . . ."

"It's a damned army," Danielle said. "You think they're his?"

"If they are, we're screwed," Thane said, craning his neck. "We've got nothing left to fight with."

The choppers had reacted to their headlights and soon hovered over them as they drove.

"Stop the vehicle," a voice ordered on a loudspeaker.

A full-sized delivery van with halogen lights mounted on the roof rapidly headed in their direction.

"I repeat," the helicopter voice said, "stop the vehicle or you will be fired upon."

The Suburban dropped down into a hollow on the hillside, and as the olive-drab van closed the distance with all its lights trained on them, Thane slowed and brought the Chevy to a halt.

Two Jeeps came bouncing over the rough terrain on both flanks, their lights trained on the Suburban. The flood from a large helicopter bathed the area as the chopper landed in a meadow some eighty feet away. The delivery van jerked to a stop, blocking the roadway as a dozen men emerged with rifles, taking positions in the ditch nearby. Six men came running from the chopper.

Still shirtless, Thane stepped out of the driver's-side door, hands over his head. "We're not armed," he shouted over the roar of the chopper's engine.

Danielle climbed out the side door and stood by Damita, who remained in the passenger seat as they were approached by men dressed in dark blue windbreakers. The second helicopter came in and settled nearby.

The first man to reach Thane stuck the muzzle of an MK5 rifle in his face while another blasted him with light.

"Are you Adams?" the man asked.

"I am. Who the hell are you?"

The man turned and yelled toward the meadow. "It's him, sir."

While Danielle was led over to Thane and Damita was held at gunpoint, the party from the choppers hustled forward, and silhouettes became recognizable faces. Thane was astounded to see Carver, complete with pockmarks and glasses, leading the team, three of whom wore the same SWAT jackets as the men from the van.

"That was a hell of a blast," Carver said. "I thought you were dead, and it might be Hassan escaping."

"No. He's the one who's dead." Thane dropped his hands. "But we don't have much time."

"Back off, guys," Carver said, waving the men away from Damita.

"My sister needs medical attention," Danielle said desperately. "She's been shot."

Carver turned to a man in a flight jacket. "Jackson! Get a medic over here. One wounded to fly out."

Carver shouted more orders to the other team members, settling things down as Thane's patience grew thin. It was great that Damita would be cared for, but the country was still in danger.

He grabbed the agent by the jacket. "Carver, dammit, listen. The doves. Hassan's men are planting them all over the US. You've got to stop them."

"What? You mean they really—?"

"Yes," Thane said. "They've got a damned heat weapon."

"Where?" Carver gestured to one of the other agents. "Miller, get this." The younger man pulled a cell phone from his jacket.

"Over thirty sites from what we can tell," Thane said. "Wall Street, The White House—"

Danielle interrupted. "Thane. What if Hassan had time to get word to his men and moved up the deadline? They might blow any time."

Carver barked at Miller. "Call Washington, have the White House evacuated immediately. Notify the State Department and the Pentagon. Thank God Wall Street's closed tomorrow." Miller turned away and began the call. Obviously disturbed, Carver continued, "How large an area can these bombs destroy?"

"I'd count on ten or twelve square miles," Thane replied. "That's a hell of a lot of ground to cover."

"Just a minute." Danielle scurried over to Damita, who was about to be carried away. She bent down and gave Damita a quick kiss on the cheek. Then she helped Damita undo her sweat jacket and pulled out the stack of photos. Returning to the men, she held them up. "Here. These are pictures of the sites. See, here's Pennsylvania Avenue . . . Wall Street."

Carver looked them over in the uneven light. "But these others. It's a jumble of chain-link fences, park benches, trees."

Danielle grabbed the pictures. "Can't we figure them out? This looks like an air base."

"Okay, it's an air base, but which one?" Carver asked pointing. "And on which perimeter? Look at this. It's a fence and some bushes." Carver brought a hand to his forehead. "God. We have to mobilize hundreds—thousands of people to search for these specific locations." Carver grabbed the rest of the photographs from Danielle. "Miller!"

"I've contacted Washington."

"Good." Carver thrust the pictures at the young agent. "Take Andrews and Bates with you. Fly Chopper One to the nearest airport, commandeer a jet to DC. Have our main computer cross-reference any and all aerial photographs of the locations on these pictures. Government installations, bases, you know the routine. Our satellite-imaging people have been bragging about their pinpoint infrared work, let's see how they do. Go!"

As Miller and the other two men took off, Carver shouted to Damita. "You're in Chopper Two along with the rest of us." He turned to Thane and Danielle, pointing to the helicopter. "You can help our people with the photos after we get cursory satellite analysis. Meantime, you two are going to be glue on me until you tell me everything. I want to know every detail you can remember about Hassan's plans, the doves, his men, everything. Start talking."

61

"HERE'S ANOTHER UPDATE," AGENT JAMIE Gere said, staring at the computer screen. Inspector Hughes stood by with a clipboard. All morning the salt-and-pepper-haired agent had acted as liaison between Gere, Thane, Danielle, and other personnel in the outer offices.

Clad in a dark blue shirt he'd been supplied by the FBI, Thane had taken a break and was watching the fall drizzle through the conference room window. Gere's comment shook him out of his thoughts. "Is it Hanford?" he asked as he looked up at the white-faced wall clock. He threw Danielle a glance as he stepped to the desk.

"Yes, it's all here," Gere said, tapping the keys.

"Stay on the line, Dee," Danielle said. "I'm putting you on hold." Wearing a clean pair of jeans and a white blouse, Danielle had been seated at the other end of the large glass table in one of twelve tan leather chairs, but she put the receiver down, joining Thane and Hughes behind Gere.

"It's not good." Gere slid back so the others could see the information scrolling up the screen in ten-point type. It was hard to make out, so she read it aloud. "'The suspect fired several rounds at the officers, retraced his steps around a warehouse, recovering the dove he had placed in a dumpster. He then attempted to escape by running across the plant grounds.'" She gave them a quick look. "We're damned lucky he didn't just let it go then." She turned back to the screen. "'After having traveled some three hundred yards with officers in pursuit, the suspect entered a lunchroom, which apparently contained well over a hundred nuclear plant employees. Now he's threatening to detonate the dove unless he's given safe passage out of there. He's holed up pretty good.'"

"Dammit, why would it have to be Hanford?" Thane gripped the back of Gere's chair. "That's the worst possible place."

"What are you saying?" Danielle asked nervously. "Does anyone know what a neutron bomb explosion does to other fissionable material? Suppose there's some nearby? From what I understood, a bombardment of particles could have some kind of chain reaction. I mean major fallout. Gere?"

Looking exasperated, Agent Gere turned in her chair. "I'm no expert, Mr. Adams. What was the name of the professor, the one you talked to at Yale?"

"Colfax. Ronald Colfax."

"Would he know?" Hughes asked anxiously.

"If anyone would. He's the leading authority," Thane said. "You can find him at Bradley Hall. You want me to call him?"

"No," Hughes said. "It's best if I handle this. Please remember, we have certain procedures." Hughes glanced at the wall clock, then down at Gere. "If I don't reach him, I'll put some people on it. We've got to find him." Hughes yanked on the knot of his tie as he made his way across the room. "And I'll make sure Carver knows." He exited through the large wood-paneled double doors.

"What else?" Danielle asked, squinting at the PC as she leaned down.

"The man identifies himself as Qadim," Gere said, scrolling up the screen. "He's been wounded in the shoulder. It's a dead standoff. Our SWAT people won't risk picking him off with his hand on the red button."

Thane shook his head. The wall clock read 11:47. "But the timer. What if this Qadim doesn't switch it off?" Danielle chimed in. "It will go off at twelve."

Thane smacked a fist into his left palm. "And we were doing great."

"Now hold on, we still might be okay." Gere's hands flicked across the keyboard and the screen paged back to the spread-sheet containing data from the field—rescue-mission stats on each and every projected bombsite.

It had been a desperate race against time, particularly the last six hours, as the clock ticked down to the final deadline—noon, eastern time—the moment at which the remaining doves would detonate.

Working with the FBI during the night, Danielle and Thane had barely slept, trying to help pinpoint the photo locations, giving detailed descriptions of Hassan's men and their common dress code. The duffel Thane had shown Carver gave the authorities something to go on, plus the computer analysis of the photographs, all of which were scanned and sent to the target locations so that police could initiate an immediate reconnaissance.

Then they waited as the hours passed and reports from around the nation documented skirmishes at various dove sites. Thane had visualized the action: Hassan's men confronted in the darkness, doves being seized, the terrorists attempting escape as floodlights cut through the smoke of gunfire. Several law enforcement officers had been killed and many terrorists had died from a bullet or by their own hands. Each arrest made for tense drama, each with its own unique twist as one by one the doves were recovered and the battle for the security of the United States unfolded.

Agent Gere scrolled to the bottom of the graph and pointed. "Look. Vandenberg Air Base just reporting in. All secure. Another terrorist dead. Small-arms fire."

"What's that make it?" Danielle asked as police descriptions of the terrorist and other casualties appeared on the screen.

"Twenty-seven now. Six to go, counting Hanford." Gere tapped the keys.

Heaving a sigh, Danielle nodded to Thane. "I can't just stand here." She headed back to the phone. Danielle had been in touch with Damita several times, trying to keep her spirits up while she recuperated at the hospital. The emotional injuries Damita had suffered from her husband's abuse were clearly more damaging than the bullet in her ankle. She faced the isolation of recovery and a sense of guilt. The marriage, the millionaire, the lush life she had expected had disintegrated into a nightmare that threatened millions of people, something Damita felt she might have helped to prevent.

Not wanting to hover over Gere, Thane walked back to the window. As he watched the rain gather in small droplets on the pane, he caught part of Danielle's conversation.

"Sure, Dee, more casualties," she was saying, "but all this would have happened regardless."

Part of the healing, Thane thought. They were all still reeling from the crisis. Thane's call to another hospital in Congo had brought encouraging news that Kuintala's leg would mend well, and that he was recovering from his other wounds.

His thoughts were interrupted by Agent Gere. "Here's two more." She spoke with her back to them. "The refinery at Galveston and O'Hare Airport. They got 'em."

"Four to go," Thane said softly to himself. Besides Hanford, the Kennedy Space Center in Florida, Dobbins Air Force Base in Atlanta, and Nellis Field in

Nevada were still unaccounted for.

Thane glanced up at the clock. 11:50. He checked Danielle, who was still giving Damita the play-by-play as it unfolded. Thane felt proud of her. Tired and somewhat battered by the ordeal, Danielle had maintained her vibrancy. She had been admirably strong during the firefight and remained supportive to her sister in the aftermath, wanting to share the progress and keep her involved.

Lucky, Gere had said. They were all lucky to be alive, to have been found so quickly on the mountain.

During the debriefing, Carver had told them that Thane's call to the Boston FBI office had prompted a computer search for Island Pond property in Salaar's name. Finding nothing, Carver's hunch directed him to several hundred acres purchased under the name Reynolds. The rogue cop had been involved from the beginning.

Immediately after taking Thane and Danielle's affidavits, Carver had left on a whirlwind tour of the east to track the entire recovery operation. Thane wished Carver were with them now. He was due back any minute.

"Nevada," Gere sang out. "Nellis is secured, plus one live captive."

Thane looked up at the clock. It was now 11:52. "Nothing more on Hanford?"

"Not yet."

Danielle made eye contact with Thane. Her brow furrowed anxiously, though her voice remained calm and optimistic as she gave Damita the news.

Thane shot her a reassuring smile. All in all, things had still gone amazingly well. Not one dove had exploded and it was fortunate that in the confusion of Saturday night, Hassan had not had the opportunity to communicate with his task force.

Because of the dove's sixty-second trigger, Carver had issued instructions that under no circumstances should members of the assault teams be confronted before the doves were placed into position. They were to be taken by force after they had dropped the doves and left the area. That meant waiting for exactly the right moment to move in.

Hundreds of FBI field agents, government troops, military police, and even local authorities had been seconded to the search for the doves and the men who were to plant them.

"Now here's Kennedy," Gere said, scrolling down the screen. "Looks like the bomber is alive, though badly hurt. A NASA official was shot as well. Oh, and here's Dobbins. That's the last." She turned in her chair. "That means except for Hanford, we—"

A knock at the door interrupted her; Hughes leaned in.

"Gere. Carver just got in. He wants to see you ASAP."

Sensing concern in the man's voice, Danielle cautioned Damita that she would call her right back and hung up. She got to her feet and faced Agent Hughes. "Can we see Carver?"

"He . . . uh . . . said to wait."

Thane didn't like Hughes's tone. "Is there a problem? Did we get Hanford or didn't we?"

The agent ignored the question, gesturing out the door. "Gere, now. Please."

Gere apologized with a look. "I'll be right back." Hughes closed the door behind her as they both disappeared.

Danielle circled the large table and joined Thane at the window. "What do you think?"

"Why is Hughes so uptight?"

"He looks like he was born uptight. I think we'll be okay." Thane shrugged and squinted. The computer screen showed nothing new. He glanced up at the clock: 11:55. "We'll know anytime now." He looked outside. Danielle followed his gaze.

A lazy rain continued to fall as both of them stared out in silence. The drizzle had a calming effect as if to remind them that regardless of what happened, nature would continue its agenda.

The clock ticked on.

Danielle took Thane's arm. "My mother used to say that the sky was crying," she said, gazing at the mist.

"Your mother has a poetic sense about her." Thane gazed at the clouds above the Capitol building. "I noticed that when I was there."

"God. That's right. I keep forgetting. What did the two of you talk about?"

Thane turned to face her. "We communicated without words."

"I'm amazed they let you in."

"I am, too." Thane brushed the windowpane with his finger. "I looked pretty beat-up. But I lied to them and preyed on their sympathies."

"What did you say?"

He turned toward her, suddenly feeling a strong freedom. "I said I was Margaret's future son-in-law."

A gentle smile crept across Danielle's face. "An impostor?"

He searched her eyes. "If things . . . if everything's all right, how would you like to come to Africa with me for a few days?"

"You avoided my question."

"It's the heart of the question. What is Danielle Wilkes going to do with herself? Run an ad agency?"

"How does Africa fit into this?"

He gripped a chair back with both hands. "Fit? Maybe I've made some assumptions here. I know we were kind of thrown together under stressful circumstances—"

"You're saying we still don't know each other?"

Thane suddenly feared that she misunderstood. "Oh no. I'm not saying that. I saw into your soul back there. Crisis is a mirror. You can't fake it."

Danielle moved a step closer. "Then let's make it real." She toyed with his shirt collar. "Don't misunderstand me either. I look forward to seeing your world. Maybe head south, find out what's so fascinating—maybe meet Kuintala."

Thane caught a hint of her perfume. "I think Kuintala would love you." He leaned down. "I know I do." He kissed her and she responded, pressing herself to him.

She laid her head on his chest and he held her.

"Africa," she said. "If I get to the agency tomorrow, sell off my stock, bargain with Hampton to let my people keep their jobs, I can be ready in three days."

He took her by the shoulders and smiled, nodding. He was about to kiss her again, but they had to separate when the conference room door opened and Carver burst in, still wearing a wet raincoat. His face damp with perspiration, he looked totally unnerved.

Thane clutched Danielle's hand. "What is it? Hanford?" The clock now read twelve o'clock.

"No." Carver approached the table and gripped its edge. "We just got that guy. He gave himself up a few minutes ago. Every single one of Hassan's doves has been secured. They'll be flown here to Andrews Air Force Base."

But Carver's news and his body language didn't match. "Well, that's great," Thane said. "So why—"

"I just talked to the White House," Carver said bitterly. "The president insisted on speaking with me personally to express his gratitude for recovering the doves. He says we may need them."

"What?" Thane pushed a chair out of the way. "What are you saying?"

Carver seemed reluctant to respond. "It seems that the White House just received an urgent message from England. Interpol agents in Eastern Europe picked up a Russian military courier last night carrying a strange explosive device. After a long interrogation he admitted that there are twenty-two other devices like his already placed in Europe and Japan. They were meant to explode after the US attack and could go off at any time."

"Not doves."

"Yes. But that's not the half of it. The White House also heard from Moscow that both the Duma and the Russian president have been given an ultimatum to abdicate in favor of the communist front-runner named Guyenov, or else they would witness the nuclear destruction of what they're calling the tools of capitalism in their own country."

"In other words . . . ?"

"There are doves nesting in Russia."

"Dear God," Thane said, staring at Carver. "What do you think it means?"

"Very effective blackmail from all indications, and a coup of the first order. And what follows, at the very least, will be the beginning of a nuclear confrontation with brand new rules—or no rules at all. A cold war with a hot temper." Carver's eyes darted around the room. "You'll excuse me."

As Carver hustled out the door, Danielle squeezed Thane's hand so hard it hurt.

Thane looked out the window in shock. In an age when the world's only superpower had lost its hold on dominance due to technological threats from rogue revolutionaries, there was now, and likely would never again be security in power. What had begun with 9-11 was about to peak, as America's newest enemies—the radical Islamists—and America's traditional enemies—a Communist regime—had succeeded in trumping the United States with a new brand of nuclear chaos.

As Thane instinctively took Danielle in his arms, his gaze fell on the Capitol dome, which stood out on the horizon—a dark silhouette against the gray clouds over Washington.

The day had grown much darker.

And Danielle's mother, Margaret Wilkes, was right.

It looked very much like the sky was crying.